Cultural diversity in music education

Directions and challenges for the 21st century

First published in 2005 by Australian Academic Press Pty Ltd in collaboration with Queensland Conservatorium Research Centre (QCRC), Griffith University, on the occasion of the VIIth International Symposium on Cultural Diversity in Music Education (CDIME), held in Brisbane, Australia, from 10–13 November, 2005.

The contributions to this publication were blind peer-reviewed by a panel consisting of Brydie-Leigh Bartleet, Patricia Shehan Campbell, Scott Harrison, Keith Howard, Elizabeth Mackinlay and Trevor Wiggins.

Editors:
Patricia Shehan Campbell
John Drummond
Peter Dunbar-Hall
Keith Howard
Huib Schippers
Trevor Wiggins

Subeditors:
Jocelyn Wolfe
Brydie-Leigh Bartleet

Publication coordination:
Brydie-Leigh Bartleet and Huib Schippers for QCRC
www.griffith.edu.au/centre/qcrc

ISBN 1 875378 59 6

Designed and typeset by Australian Academic Press
www.australianacademicpress.com.au

Contents

CONTINUED OVER

Contents CONTINUED

Section Three

Voices From the Classroom

Section Four

Case Studies From Asia, Africa and Australia

Introduction

Local Musics, Global Issues

Ten years ago, the landmark publication *Teaching Musics of the World* (Philipp Verlag, 1995) celebrated the explosion of initiatives across the world to do justice to a musical diversity that has now become the norm for most cultures. It documented a lively interaction between musicians, educators and scholars, and helped to launch a new platform for interdisciplinary discourse addressing the transmission and learning of musical cultures in formal and non-formal settings. With a decade of additional experience, *Cultural Diversity in Music Education: Directions and Challenges for the 21st Century* documents recent achievements and issues in this exciting and dynamic field.

In terms of content and approach, we can see that the field has come of age. Many practices of cultural diversity in music education have shed dogmatic approaches from 19th century music education and 1960s ethnomusicology. At least in some areas, we can witness a receding emphasis on notation and analytical teaching methods in the way material is being presented to learners of all backgrounds and levels. Issues such as context and authenticity are increasingly approached from their delightfully confusing contemporary realities. The challenges posed by music travelling through time, place and contexts are being addressed for what they are: fascinating studies in the dynamic life of music, education and culture.

Although a number of promising projects have sizzled out over the years, underlining the vulnerability of young initiatives to institutional constraints and their dependency on passionate and visionary individuals, other projects and initiatives signalled 10 years ago have come to further fruition. The total immersion programs piloted by the Malmö Academy (University of Lund) have set the standard for programs to introduce future music educators to learning and teaching world music by making them live a different musical culture. Dutch initiatives of world music schools and the world music department of the Rotterdam Conservatoire (CODArts) are merging into a 12 million euro, custom-built World Music and Dance Centre in Rotterdam. A number of tertiary-level programs worldwide now prepare performers, teachers and composers for their professional work through a core of academic and applied courses that offer considerable depth of experience in some of the world's musical cultures. And introductory courses on 'world music' are gaining popularity with a generation of students for whom cultural diversity in music is almost as common as cultural diversity in food for the previous generation.

At the same time, there have been worrying developments. The movements against tolerance that we have witnessed in the United States from the late 1990s have now found resonance in many European countries. Xenophobia has struck in even the most tolerant environments, and the fear-driven desire to return to an idyllicised monocultural past is a force to be reckoned with in maintaining established projects and developing new initiatives. Yet as the doors and windows of many nations were newly opened to the world only a generation ago, the masses of newly arrived peoples have required solutions to the hard-pressed questions of accommodating differences in societies that recognise the beauty and logic of intercultural communities of this age.

We have time on our side. Even with borders closing, societies are getting increasingly diverse, and the tastes of music lovers across the world are getting more eclectic. A young African may listen to Ghanaian *highlife*, reggae and Bach; a Turkish teenager to traditional *saz*, *arabesk* and hiphop; and an Australian of Greek descent to gamelan, jazz and klezmer. The direct links between ethnicity and musical tastes are weakening, but the interest in diversity in music is increasing. At the same time, musical identities are holding in the ways that a Navajo retains the monophonic melody of traditional vocables above the full texture of his country band, and an Irish *sean nos* singer continues her melodic embellishment for international audiences despite the fact that they may understand neither the Gaelic language nor the complexities of the improvisational style. All of this makes for a complex and demanding, but at the same time rewardingly fertile field of activity.

The richness of the past 10 years of harvesting is evident in this volume. While the emphasis in the 1990s was much on handing down 'pure' traditions from (mostly Asian) *Hochkulturen*, and on collecting and reworking material for use in schools and theoretical courses, we are now witnessing the rise of community music activities and African music as major sources of learning and inspiration. Indigenous music of a nation, and national heritage musical styles, have emerged as important curricular and programmatic inclusions in primary and secondary schools, and in university programs in music education. Where there was once an over-emphasis on performing 'authentic' music 'authentically', there is a growing understanding that no music is frozen in time. Individual differences do occur from performer to performer, and from one performance to the next. A hesitation to perform or even participate in music 'outside one's own culture' has given way to a more sensible and sensitive approach to performing world music, taking into account the origin of the tradition and its new circumstances in each musical event. This is leading to a deeper awareness that many types of music transform in new times and places.

With that, appropriate strategies for learning and teaching are being reconsidered as well. This was initially brought on by the very obvious challenges of teaching forms of world music outside their cultures of origin. However, at the forefront of the debate, this now does not only concern music traditions from non-western cultures transplanted into western settings, but also western music. Successful strategies from other cultures have made us question preconceptions we have about learning and teaching music in western mainstream traditions and institutions. In that way, our musical culture has almost come full circle: from exotism to tolerance to acceptance to inclusion. It is safe to say that the world of music education is now intrinsically culturally diverse, and so are its challenges and potential.

This book is divided into four sections. In Section One, four essays outline key issues in cultural diversity in music education. Drummond investigates claims made for multicultural music education over the past 40 years, Wiggins examines institutional challenges in teaching cultures other than one's own, Folkestad explores the significance of community music activities for world music, and Schippers presents a new model to understand learning and teaching practices from a 'global' perspective.

In Section Two, Marsh speaks of fieldwork to change preconceptions in tertiary students, and Laycock pleads for a greater use of musical vernaculars in composition. Omolo-Ongati provides an African perspective on learning and teaching, while Smith takes Irish music in workshop format as a starting point. Finally, Louhivuori, Salminen and Lebaka take an intercontinental choral perspective from Africa to Europe.

In Section Three, the classroom is the focus. Cain looks at the challenges of world music at elementary school level, while Barton links Indian and Australian practices to more general considerations. In the final essay of this section, Harrison searches for a national identity in music education.

Culture specific approaches are highlighted in Section Four. Dunbar-Hall, Howard and Hamill present Asian perspectives based on practices from Bali, Korea and India respectively. Joseph, Klopper and Robinson represent African approaches. To conclude, Hartwig and Dillon and Chapman add views and experiences from Australia.

In that way, this volume traces local traditions that have become global in their dissemination, not only through concerts and recorded sound, but embedded in practices of learning and teaching across the world. Conversely, it documents global issues and concerns in music education feeding back into a rich diversity of local practices.

This diversity leads to a great variety of perspectives, depending on working environments, cultures, countries and levels of experience. Some contributors are overtly searching for directions; others have clearly taken positions. Contradictory viewpoints are put forward in this volume. No effort has been made to homogenise these, as they accurately represent a field in constant movement. In fact, in this fluidity and constant questioning may well lie the key strength of cultural diversity in music education for the 21st century.

Patricia Shehan Campbell
Huib Schippers

PATRICIA SHEHAN CAMPBELL is Professor of Music at the University of Washington, and widely considered as a leading authority and advocate for cultural diversity in music education. She is a teacher and an active musician, and authored numerous books on music for children. She has lectured on world music education and children's musical involvement throughout the United States; in much of Europe and Asia; and in Australia, New Zealand and South Africa.

HUIB SCHIPPERS is Director of the Queensland Conservatorium Research Centre at Griffith University, Brisbane. He was trained as a sitar player, and has headed numerous projects bringing world music to new audiences for over 20 years, publishing and lecturing on the subject across the globe. In 1992, he established the international Cultural Diversity in Music Education (CDIME) network, which has become a lively platform for exchange of practices and ideas between performing musicians, educators and scholars.

Challenges and Issues

Cultural Diversity in Music Education: Why Bother?

John Drummond

The idea of including in a music education program more than the music of the dominant culture or social group is comparatively new in western nations and in those countries colonised by Europeans. Traditionally, the function of universal education had been, to use Durkheim's language, to be 'the socialisation of the individual into the collective mores of society' (May, 1994, p. 12). In colonised countries, this meant socialisation into the settler culture. Changing political, social and demographic patterns during the 1960s, together with processes of decolonisation, brought a new awareness of cultural plurality. Within the discipline of music itself, the gradual mainstreaming of ethnomusicology and the shift within it from comparative musicology towards ethnography began to create a wider understanding of the plurality of musical cultures on planet Earth.

During the 1970s, these considerations began to influence educational thinking and planning, and the prevailing liberal democratic view — that education was a means to provide all young people with the same cultural attitudes and skills, and the same opportunity for social and economic success — came under fire. The new sociologists pointed out that educating all children in the dominant culture privileged those who came from that culture; children from a different class or ethnicity tended to perform poorly. Following Bourdieu, they argued that schools are locales in which the dominant culture engages in symbolic violence against social groups disadvantaged by the monocultural curriculum. The answer, it was suggested, was to introduce more multicultural elements.

By the end of the 1980s, however, it was beginning to be argued that 'the multicultural curriculum' was insufficient on its own to redress disadvantage among pupils from minority cultural backgrounds. Programs supporting cultural pluralism were being added to existing curricula but were having little impact upon the continuing transmission of the dominant culture within schooling. The 1990s therefore saw the beginnings of a demand for 'structural pluralism, that is, structural or institutional change within the school' (May, 1994, p. 41). It was at this time that schemes to create new kinds of educational settings for the learning of a range of musical cultures developed in music education.

Although this historical framework reveals a sequence of changing attitudes towards multicultural education, in 2005 it is quite common to find schools and tertiary institutions providing education only in western classical music, or allowing multicultural elements but privileging the European tradition. Still others include multicultural materials in the music curriculum but discuss them from an entirely European perspective. Elliott's (1989) presentation of six models of 'multicultural' music education and Schippers's (2004) offering of four (monocultural, multicultural, intercultural and transcultural) display the range.

The discourse surrounding culturally plural music education contains more than definitions and descriptions, however. It makes claims for the benefits of such educational activity. These claims tend to follow more generic claims for multicultural education, which may be seen to take three forms, themselves emerging from the historical context (see, for example, Becker, 1979; Bullivant, 1981; Dunlop, 1983; Fisher & Hicks, 1986; Crozier, 1989; Banks, 1994).

The First Justification: We Live in a Culturally Plural World

Societies/nations/communities/the world have become/are becoming more culturally plural, and education can enable this change to be managed well. Cultural plurality is seen as a new situation, one that needs to be addressed on a personal and social level. It can, of course, be pointed out that plurality is not in fact new, and that 18th century Britain (to cite but one example) contained a wide range of different cultures and social practices. But, what made people in 1960s Europe more aware of cultural plurality was the fact that it was now evident in different skin colour, language, and an overseas birthplace or heritage. The traditional *e pluribus unum* approach did not seem capable of assimilating such wide-ranging diversity, any more than it had assimilated involuntary African immigrants or indigenous peoples into the United States (and, of course, some people did not want assimilation to occur). It was the Enlightenment that introduced the idea that behaviour and attitudes can be modified through the formal acquisition of knowledge and understanding. As Crozier put it in 1989, multicultural education will 'break down the ignorance of white children and through this put an end to "racism" which is (sometimes) fostered by ignorance' (see May, 1994, p. 37). In other cultures, and in Europe at other times in history, the 'problem' of cultural diversity has often been 'solved' through pogrom. It was easier to deal with cultural plurality through a program of ethnic cleansing than by developing an education program and structure.

The Second Justification: Removal of Disadvantage

In a culturally plural society, minority groups and their individual members are disadvantaged unless education includes their cultures too. This justification takes a more active position, and uses less neutral language. Education is seen in 19th century terms as a way for the underclass to gain social influence, economic success and political power. Acknowledgment of subcultural identity, then, is part of the struggle for a place in the sun. There is good evidence, from the inclusion during the period 1850 to 1920 of working-class music in British culture, and of minority African music in American culture, to suggest the price was commodification by the dominant culture and a loss of identity, and it may be that the price continues to be paid in more recent cultural inclusions.

The Third Justification: The Majority Can Learn From the Minority

Lynch (1989) speaks of '*the urgent imperative to learn from the policies and practices of other nations and regions, and to find new sources of inspiration for flagging western*

2

values, which are based increasingly on material exploitation and rampant consumerism' (p. xi). This argument introduces the concept of cultural transformation and renewal on individual and community levels. Although there are certainly individuals who claim a personal renewal from intercultural and transcultural experiences, the lessons of the last 50 years are that it is the exploitation and consumerism of the West that has transformed the world's other cultures more than vice versa. Indeed, one difficulty with this justification is that it suggests cultural transformation is a good thing, but only if it happens in one direction.

In addition to particular flaws, there may be incompatibilities lurking within these three justifications. The first justification argues that wellbeing in society depends upon understanding a range of cultural traditions that reflect diversity — moving beyond one's roots; the second argues that it depends upon an understanding of one's own cultural heritage — strengthening one's roots. The third moves towards the position that cultural traditions are processes not products, and that growth is more important than the roots of tradition.

Cultural Plurality in Music Education

Many music education documents claim the general benefits identified for multicultural education as a whole. The US National Standards for Music, for example, argue that 'to participate fully in a diverse, global society, students must understand their own historical and cultural heritage and those of others within their communities and beyond' (CNAEA, 1994, p. 26). It may be argued that the full participation of American armed forces in Iraq and Afghanistan did not require any understanding by the individuals involved of the historical and cultural heritage of those countries,[1] but perhaps this discrepancy merely reveals that the values lying behind such a claim are not universally agreed within the culture whose educational authorities make the claim.

Other documents claim that music education is an effective pathway to achieving general benefits. Patricia Shehan Campbell (1996) offers a familiar list:

> Is it 'teaching the culturally different' in order to assimilate students of colour into the cultural mainstream …? Is it a human relations approach intended to 'help students of different background to get along'? Is it single group 'ethnic studies' programs designed to foster cultural pluralism …? Is it a 'social and educational equity' program, based upon a reformed curriculum that is reflective of the cultural diversity of the school, community or nation? (p. 7).

With rhetorical flourishes, the International Society for Music Education (1994) takes the same line:

> The International Society for Music Education believes in the validity of all the musics of the world, and respects the value given to each particular music by the community that owns it. The Society believes that the richness and diversity of the musics of the world is a cause for celebration, and an opportunity for intercultural learning for the improvement of international understanding, cooperation and peace (p. 49).

Elliott (1989) cautiously suggests that 'if the process of music education reflects, distils and abstracts musical values — if music education functions as culture — then music education may also have the potential to change prejudicial attitudes and behaviours' (p. 14). The view of the new sociologists is expressed by Mansfield (2002):

> Music education, underpinned and informed by an aesthetics of difference, would involve a recognition, an exploration through musical practice, procedure and composition, of the musical knowledges of traditional non-Western cultures, of when cultural appropriation

3

and commodification of cultural property has occurred and in whose interests it has occurred (p. 260).

Music education should be able to help students understand appropriation and commodification, but whether it can actually change prejudicial attitudes is another matter. Schroeder (1998) argues that Haydn composed his later symphonic first movements to educate concert audiences in the validity of the process of negotiation and reconciliation in situations of potential instability and conflict, but whether Haydn's London listeners, let alone modern audiences, actually learned that lesson from the experience of hearing symphonies remains questionable.

Nonetheless, an International Music Council Congress held in Denmark in 1998 on Music Education in a Multicultural Society noted that cultural diversity in music education helps to break down existing cultural boundaries, adds social respect and understanding across borders, reduces ethnic tension in schools, builds new social structures of cultural identity, satisfies our human curiosity, and brings joy to the participants (Traasdahl, 1998, p. 104). The last two claims are sadly missing from more general justifications, but suggest that cultural plurality in music education may have some special benefits. 'Music education can help foster an awareness and appreciation of various cultural traditions. A culturally diverse society, such as ours, provides a rich resource for the exploration and enjoyment of a wide range of musical experiences' (NSW Department of Education, 1984, p. 8). This curriculum document suggests that in addition to extrinsic ones there are purely musical benefits to be gained.

Music Education's Special Benefits

The first musical benefits are practical ones. Schippers and Kors (2002) note, among other driving forces for world music, that it can 'prepare young musicians better for professional musical activity in the coming decades', presumably because listeners are becoming more aware of the diverse range of musics available for consumption. Boele (2001, p. 26) suggests that:

> we should teach our students to act in a musical world of choice. We should make them aware of the manifold of musics in society [sic] and, in order to enable them to survive in this world of choice, to relate their activities to many kinds of music and to an audience that is constantly making choices.

Preparing people for a culturally plural world here becomes preparing musicians for a musically plural world.

Schmidt (2004) echoes Elliott's idea of music *as* culture when he argues that:

> to insist that our music students develop the ability to navigate and discern different perceptions of reality, vis-à-vis its social, cultural and political implications and constructions, is to empower them to become real musicians, able to see a world of sounds as their own, and in the process interpret and re-conceptualise situations and possibilities.

Here, the implication is that learning the music and its cultural context is a unified experience that empowers the individual both politically and musically. Volk (1998) puts it more practically:

> Studying the music of other cultures can broaden the students' sound base, enabling them to be more open and tolerant of new musical sounds. Learning the concepts of music as they are applied worldwide also give students a wider palette of compositional and improvisational devices. It can also help them place the Western classical (art) music tradition in perspective as part of the world of musics (p. 6).

A second kind of intrinsic musical value for culturally plural music education is identified by Campbell, who writes:

> beyond a demographic rationale ... more than a few music educators are teaching the music the Vietnamese call *cai luong* (theatre), the Indian *bharata natyam* (dance), or the Ewe (Ghana) percussion ensemble sheerly for the beauty and intrigue of the music — music they have selected as worthy of their students' listening attention, participation and thought (Campbell 1996b).

The purpose and benefit identified here is an aesthetic one, and elsewhere Campbell writes:

> for reasons that range from the sheer wonder and beauty of musical cultures of our world, to a sense that 'they are us' ... we are now choosing music from a grand variety of cultures to bring to our students (Campbell, 2001, p. 59).

Here an aesthetic value is placed before the social one. Terese Volk puts it this way:

> Listening to, performing, or composing music from any culture can lead to aesthetic experiences for the students. The intrinsic value of music from any culture may be appreciated to some extent by anyone, regardless of background. Bennett Reimer and Abraham Schwadron say these aesthetic responses derive primarily and inherently from the music itself, while for Lucy Green ... both the intrinsic and the delineational (cultural-contextual) elements of music contribute to this response (1998, p. 6).

Is aesthetic appreciation a function of biology or a function of culture? Some argue that music is in some way a universal language, that the relationships between musical sounds operate according to fundamental laws of balance and proportion that also govern our own physical, physiological and psychological structures, and that we can recognise and appreciate their presence in any music. This thought may lie behind Nyome's remark that 'it goes without saying that while political barriers, economic barriers and language barriers continue to separate people, music and the performing arts continue to build bridges all over the world' (2001, p. 64). Others argue that our response to musical sound is determined not by nature but by nurture: it is a function of acculturation. When we hear the music of another culture, we judge it according to criteria we have established from our experience, and our judgment may therefore not be true to the music's context. Those whose musical perceptions are founded in a single culture tend to favour the notion that aesthetic judgments are universal, and this belief may lead them to give less value to contextual study, which in turn will make it unlikely for them to argue that such study can achieve social goals. On the other hand, those whose musical perceptions have been moulded as a result of exposure to a range of different musics tend to favour the notion that aesthetic judgments are relative, and favour the study of the music in context, accepting the social impact of such study.

The Fly in the Ointment

The claims made for the benefits of cultural plurality in education and in music education are credible and powerful, although they are not without flaws. However, there is a larger fly in the ointment, for all the claims are predicated upon the idea that people are capable of changing their attitudes towards their own cultures and the cultures of others, and this may not be simple.

The attitudes we hold in relation to others develop as part of the processes of identity formation during childhood and adolescence. The processes are complex; a large number of factors are influential including family, school, peers and social context. It is clear that those who argue for cultural plurality in education expect to see

5

identity formation affected by experiences gained during multicultural schooling. Lynch proposes that 'both teachers and pupils must come to see cultural diversity as a creative momentum to their own development throughout their lives, influencing the relationships they forge, the professional and personal judgments they make and the social transactions they negotiate' (1989, p. vii). Is this a reasonable hope?

The initial step in the formation of identity is taken when an infant becomes aware of the difference between Self and Other, and this distinction remains crucial in the later development of more complex understandings of identity (see Haig, 2004, p. 21). The pre-school child develops not only its sense of individual Self/Other distinction, but also a sense of group Self/Other difference. The group is likely to be a family or extended family group, but neighbour groups and friend groups also begin to be recognised. The groups are classified by the child according to identified behaviour and values, and thus a sense of cultural identity begins to be formed. Already, the influence of the media is beginning to be felt.[2] These processes are extended when the child attends school, and forms a clearer sense of personal identity in relation to peers. Here the first serious conflicts may occur between the cultural identity of the child's own family and those of others in the classroom, as well as the culture of the school itself. Processes of identity formation now become more complex: media influences grow more powerful, often via peer pressure, and identity confusion can grow. As the child develops towards and into adolescence, four identity statuses can be identified (Kroger, 2003; Marcia, 1993, 1996):[3]

1. The individual with 'identity-foreclosed' status has accepted the culture, values and beliefs of significant others, usually parents, and has no desire to change. S/he has not explored alternatives, and makes decisions without thinking much about them. Otherness tends to be judged by the Self culture, and is usually rejected.

2. The individual with 'identity-diffuse' status has formed no clear sense of personal or cultural identity, perhaps because no consistent modelling has been provided by parents or significant others. S/he tends to be lacking in confidence (or compensates by irrational over-assertion), to be isolated and to have low levels of intimacy in personal relationships.

3. The individual with 'identity-moratorium' status is in the process of exploring options. Cultural values adopted from significant others are being examined and accepted or rejected. S/he may be rebellious but also actively seek guidance.

4. The individual with 'identity-achieved' status has been through a process of exploration; s/he has weathered the pressure of significant others (family, peers) and has developed an identity based on self-selected values.

This fourth phase is regarded as the desirable goal of identity development. However, 'there may simply be large percentages of individuals at the end of late adolescence who do not change their earlier, less complex forms of identity resolutions' (Kroger, 2003, p. 205) and, according to Kegan, 'one-half to two-thirds of the adult population appear not to have fully reached the fourth order of consciousness' (as cited in Kroger, 2003, p. 205). Researchers have also found 'the conventional level of moral reasoning to be associated primarily with the foreclosed ego identity status' (Kroger, 2003, p. 206). This suggests that values used by most people in judging the culture of others will be based on a closed rather than open mind.

These matters have important implications for the desire of educators to see cultural otherness accepted by individuals. The introduction of elements from other cultures into education programs will have differential impact according to two factors: the level of immersion in the other culture, and the identity status of the individuals in the classroom. For those in identity-foreclosed status, low levels of immersion (such as occur when a number of different cultures are included) will have minimal impact, for the Others will be denied and resisted. A level of total immersion may lead to a major identity change and commitment: this is the condition described in earlier western literature as 'going native'. But the memory of the earlier commitment may linger, in the form of a longing for 'older, better days' (Kroger, 2003, p. 213).

For those in an identity-diffuse status, a low-level introduction of elements from other cultures may well add more confusion. Since there is no real Self identity there is no real comprehension of Otherness. A high immersion in one culture may be a first encounter with cultural authority, and may lead to a wholehearted commitment to it, and the adoption of identity-foreclosed status. For those in an identity-moratorium status, encounters with other cultures may be positive or negative. Individuals in this status have a problem with authority. A teacher taking Lynch's view that pupils must interact with cultural alternatives is likely to receive rejection; such a student encountering such alternatives on his or her own is likely to have a more positive response.

For those in an identity-achieved status, Other cultures are likely to be treated with respect and evaluated as 'cool'. Individuals in this category have already been through a process of exploring and evaluating cultural options; introducing them to new cultures is not a challenge. This group may well benefit the most, and the most quickly, from low or high immersion in Other cultures, but it is likely to be the smallest group. Pupils in a classroom are at different points on the continuum of identity formation, and this inevitably makes the task of teaching more complex.

The Influence of Media

Another important factor should be included in my discussion. As already suggested, the formation of cultural identity by young people is significantly influenced by the media, in particular by the global media, and this creates new challenges:

> In this situation, the individual searches to secure stable meanings under changing conditions which include an increasing consciousness of global others, an increase in the number and demands of roles, and changing social organisation under pressure from economic realignments, deterritorialisation, cultural relativisation and the 'hegemony of choice' (Butcher, 2003, p. 88).

Access to cultural plurality through the media — and this includes crossover pluralities — creates a wide array of options for young people. The distinction between Self and Other becomes one between Selves and Others. In a world of multiple identities the individual faces two particular difficulties:

> Firstly, a problem of legitimation: who has authority to legitimise decisions if there is no overarching model with which to compare action, particularly if the self has less sense of coherence and its judgments therefore cannot be relied upon. Second, a greater sense of

> cultural disorder has resulted, at the social and individual level, as ultimately a 'culture of distraction' … is presented, mediated with increasing volatility and velocity, from which meaning, including identity affiliation, is difficult to derive. Identities are now described as increasingly 'fragmented', 'disjointed' and discontinuous' (Butcher, 2003, p. 90).

For many young people, connection with the media is a high-immersion process. The cultural values it communicates, whether they be the preponderance of violence in personal relationships suggested by cop shows, the equation of music with hedonism portrayed in music videos, the demonisation of Moslems displayed in news programs or the worship of material possessions shown in commercials, are powerful influences upon those engaged in the processes of identity formation, probably far more powerful than the more traditional authorities of home and school. At the same time, young people are evidently more expert at controlling and manipulating their own access and response to cultural phenomena: they assert authority, for example, in their Internet and mobile phone transactions, and this weakens the impact of external traditional and contemporary authorities.

Indeed, it may be that traditional perceptions of identity formation, and of the effect of multicultural education, are both out of date. Many young people may well now form their cultural identity through their own manipulation of technology, and the identities formed are pluralistic both in terms of cultural content and personal shifting individualities. For them, the notion of learning another culture to form culturally open attitudes may be as strange as the idea that they themselves can be categorised in only one cultural group or status or identity. Leaving aside those whose status as identity-foreclosed individuals has been determined by parents with answers to life's problems, it seems that many are now achieving a sense of identity that allows for multiple interactions with different cultures and subcultures. Individual identity may be a collection of subcultural relationships with porous boundaries, a much more flexible sense of identity than is recognised by those who have devised the claims for multicultural education. In a world of interactive technology and multiple virtual realities, young people absorb cultural contents easily and take them or leave them at will, acknowledging them as just parts of the world they live in. They may well regard as quaint and irrelevant the proposals put forward by educators and psychologists brought up in an earlier monocultural generation.

Multicultural Music Education in the Contemporary World

The claims made for cultural plurality in education and music education now appear rather naive. In making them there seems little acknowledgment of the actual processes of identity formation, and we must question whether culturally plural education is able to have any direct effect upon young people whose access to cultural elements and forms through the media is already far wider than can be achieved in a formal educational context. When Lynch suggests that 'both teachers and pupils must come to see cultural diversity as a creative momentum to their own development', perhaps it is only the teachers who have a problem.

As we have seen, however, the learning of the music of other cultures has a musical impact, in that it can increase musical vocabularies, stimulate creativity and enlarge music-making choices. The validity of this is not undermined either by the processes of identity formation or by the impact of media technology. Indeed, it may be reinforced by them. Here we may consider musical identity, in the context of the four statuses of identity-formation defined by Marcia and

8

Kroger. Some young people have been brought up in a monocultural musical context (frequently western art music). Their musical identity is often foreclosed at an early stage, in accordance with parental culture, and their introduction in adolescence to the music of other cultures, or their own discovery of popular musics, may well cause an identity crisis. Denial and rejection of the Other may well be followed by a switch of musical identification: an equally firm commitment may be made to the new music, and the old Self-music may be rejected. In this process identity-foreclosure is maintained, but merely changes allegiances. In practical terms, however, the generic musical talents and skills already possessed can be transferred to the new, and they may well continue to grow as practising musicians.

Young people in identity-diffuse status may well encounter a music that speaks to their particular condition, since the texts of many popular songs address general experiences of adolescence. Music may therefore become part of identity formation, and its practice may become part of an assertion of identity. Through it, these people may move into the status of identity-moratorium. Here contact with significant practitioners in a range of musics may help the development of individual identity and lead to a range of musical vocabularies and practices. In time, a musical identity-achieved status may be arrived at.

The impact of cultural diversity in music education, then, may be one in which the main benefit is to musicians and music itself. This is, of course, as good a reason as any for having it, and better than most. It may not seem to be as helpful a form of advocacy as the apparently more compelling argument that those with culturally plural musical experiences and understandings are better equipped to participate in a culturally plural world, but it has the advantage of being more truthful. And while the claim for the aesthetic impact of culturally different musics is unpersuasive, Christopher Small (2002) argues that:

> when we take part in that human encounter which is a musical performance, we collectively bring into existence within the performance a set of relationships, and those relationships model those of the cosmos as we believe they are and as we believe they ought to be (p. 23).

The emergence over recent decades of intercultural and transcultural musical practices certainly reflects a growing respect for cultural plurality, and much of the intercultural music-making that takes place models relationships that the participants certainly believe 'ought to be'. If these practices and the results are transmitted through media technology into the hot-wired, identity-seeking brains of young people, and leads them to accept plurality as a fact of their contemporary lives, then maybe the goals of multicultural education and music education are being achieved, albeit in a roundabout way not envisaged by those who devised them.

Endnotes

1 Members of the American military forces in Iraq are issued with a small card providing an instant guide to Iraqi culture. It can be found at http://cryptome.org/iraq-culture.htm

2 This analysis of the process of identity development is based on the widely accepted theories of Erik Erikson, although his *Eight Stages of Man* (1950) was written before the media had become so influential in identity formation.

3 The following is based on Kroger's analysis and discussion of Marcia's work and the extensions of it provided by others (Kroger, 2003, pp. 201–213).

References

Banks, J. A. (1994). *Multiethnic education*. Boston: Allyn and Bacon.

Becker, J. (1979). The world and the school: A case for world-centred education. In J. Becker (Ed.), *Schooling for a global age*. New York: McGraw Hill.

Boele, E. B. (2001). Contemporary music and the conservatoire. In *Music education in a multicultural European society* (pp. 32–36). Utrecht: Association of European Conservatoires.

Bullivant, B. M. (1981). *The pluralist dilemma in education*. Sydney: Allen and Unwin.

Butcher, M. (2003). *Transnational television, cultural identity and change: When STAR came to India*. New Delhi and London: Sage.

Campbell, P. S. (1996a). Music, education and community in a multicultural society. In M. McCarthy (Ed.), *Cross currents: Setting an agenda for music education in community culture* (pp. 4–33). Maryland: University of Maryland.

Campbell, P. S. (Ed.). (1996b). *Music in cultural context: Eight views on world music education*. Reston: Music Educators National Conference.

Campbell, P. S. (2001). Heritage: The survival of cultural traditions in a changing world. *International Journal of Music Education, 37,* 59–63.

Consortium of National Arts Education Associations (CNAEA). (1994). *National standards for arts education: What every young American should know and be able to do in the arts*. Reston: MENC.

Crozier, G. (1989). Multi-cultural education: Some unintended consequences. In S. Walker & L. Barton (Eds.), *Politics and the processes of schooling* (pp. 59–81). Milton Keynes: Open University Press.

Dunlop, J. P. (1983). *International and multicultural education programme, working papers*. Glasgow: Jordanhill College of Education.

Elliott, D.J. (1989). Key concepts in multicultural music education. *International Journal of Music Education, 13,* 11–18.

Elliott, D. J. (1995). *Music matters: A new philosophy of music education*. New York/Oxford: OUP.

Fisher, S., & Hicks, D. (1986). *World studies 8-13: A teacher's handbook*. Edinburgh and New York: Oliver and Boyde.

Haig, C. (2004). *Our music, their music: Identifying meaning in musical experiences*. Unpublished doctoral dissertation, University of Otago.

International Society for Music Education. (1994). Declaration of beliefs for worldwide promotion of music education. *International Journal of Music Education, 24,* 49.

Kroger, J. (2003). What transits in an identity status transition? *Identity, 3*(3), 197–220.

Mansfield, J. (2002). Differencing music education. In J. Drummond & D. Sell (Eds.), *Taonga of the Asia Pacific Rim* (pp. 259–263). Auckland: NZSME.

May, S. (1994). *Making multicultural education work*. Toronto: Ontario Institute for Studies in Education.

New South Wales Department of Education. (1984). *Music K-6 syllabus and support statements*. Sydney, New South Wales, Australia: D.West, Government Printer.

Nyome, S. (2001). Heritage: The viewpoint of an African committed to intercultural exchanges. *International Journal of Music Education, 37,* 64–66.

Pring, R. (1992). Educating for a pluralist society. In M. Leicester & M. J. Taylor (Eds.), *Ethics, ethnicity and education* (pp. 19–30). London: Kogan Page.

Schippers, H. (2004). *Practicing what you preach – exploring the discovery and integration of world music in formal music education: 1983-2003*. Paper presented at the ISME International Conference, Tenerife.

Schippers, H., & Kors, N. (2002). Playing together in the global village? History, promises and realities of cultural diversity in higher music education. In *Proceedings of the Samspel – ISME 2002 Conference* [CD-ROM]. Bergen.

Schmidt, P. (2004). *A world of sounds to teach: Music education through social lenses*. Paper presented at the ISME International Conference, Tenerife.

Schroeder, D. P. (1998). *Haydn and the Enlightenment*. Oxford: Oxford University Press.

Small, C. (2002). Acts of musicking. In J. Drummond & D. Sell (Eds.), *Taonga of the Asia Pacific Rim* (pp. 21–31). Auckland: NZSME.

Traasdahl, J. O. (1998). Music education in a multicultural society. In H. Lundstrom (Ed.), *The musician in new and changing contexts* (pp. 97–105). Malmö: Malmö Academy of Music.

Volk, T. M. (1998.) *Music, education, and multiculturalism: Foundations and principles.* New York and Oxford: Oxford University Press.

JOHN DRUMMOND, BA, MUSB, PHD, is Blair Professor of Music and Dean of the School of Language, Literature and Performing Arts at the University of Otago in New Zealand. A past president of the International Society for Music Education, he has presented at several CDIME conferences as well as at ISME seminars dealing with cultural diversity, and chairs the Cultural Transformations Research Network at Otago. He is a professional composer of opera, and sometime Mozart musicologist. This article investigates the general claims made over the past 40 years for multicultural music education. It reports the first stage of a research project investigating music programs and projects in different parts of the world for which success is claimed in the way they include a diverse range of musics. The project's aim is to analyse the claims, the criteria used to measure success, and the extent to which there are common features between the programs.

11

12

Cultivating Shadows in the Field?: Challenges for Traditions in Institutional Contexts

Trevor Wiggins

Kwabena Nketia wrote about the differences between traditional instruction and an institutional approach nearly 50 years ago (Nketia, 1961). We could expect that there would have been further research into the different outcomes and that we would be more aware of the issues in the transmission of traditional music in different contexts, but this hardly seems to be the case. Ethnomusicology has developed a greater understanding of the multiple meanings embodied in a piece of music, and recent research in learning methods and styles in popular music has revealed the extent to which learning, rather than teaching, is a significant area for enquiry. Can these be brought together to address the question: Does the close relationship between a musical tradition and the way it is handed down form the basis of maintaining traditional formats of instruction?

Ethnomusicology has identified many modes of learning that bring understanding of a music. Recently it has begun to include the understanding derived from participation in musical performance as well as the observation of it (Titon, 1997). But learning to play another music, especially outside its indigenous setting, still raises many questions about what is learned and how it is understood. Cooley (1997) suggests that 'Ethnomusicologists often feel as if they are chasing shadows in the field when striving to perceive and understand musical meaning, [which] is often ambiguous or liminal' (p. 3). When students (including ourselves) are learning another music we are engaging with the physical manifestation of sound, the actions needed to create it and the question of what this sound means — something that has many answers located in context and culture. Even if the learner seeks to disregard the cultural context as far as possible (something I have encountered when people just want to learn 'the music'), questions of meaning and significance are almost inevitably raised by the inherent differences in the sonic and performative aspects. So the teacher is effectively collaborating with the learner in the creation of another 'shadow', a personal one located with respect to the learner's experience mediated through the teacher. It can be argued (see for example, Clifford, 1986) that the understanding of the learner from outside the culture will only ever be partial and personal with respect to the cultural location of the music, what Clifford refers to ethnographically as 'true fictions' (p. 6). Taken to its logical conclusion, this becomes a nihilist approach where there are no common understandings. Students studying music as practice from another culture do so for a

13

variety of reasons, often starting with something that captures their musical imagination. What do they believe they have learned and understood about this music, and to what extent are they aware of what they do not know? How important is the learning approach in conveying 'meaning' as well as action?

Approaches to Enculturation

Within the last 10 years, more emphasis has been given to exploring the nature of the learning activities that contribute to the development of skills, knowledge and the self-validation as a 'musician'. Lucy Green (2002) in her research into learning in popular music styles, recognises the cultural component of learning: 'The concept of musical enculturation refers to the acquisition of musical skills and knowledge by immersion in the everyday music and musical practices of one's social context' (p. 22) and draws on established ethnomusicological approaches, citing Merriam (1964) and Nettl (1983). Merriam, drawing in turn on Herskovits (1948), sets out a clear concept for the various aspects of enculturation, which include socialisation, education — defined as a formal and informal process of directed learning, and schooling — being a more restricted aspect of cultural learning 'carried on at specific times, in particular places outside the home, for definite periods, by persons especially prepared or trained for the task' (Herskovits, 1948, p. 310). Merriam goes on to illustrate processes of enculturation in several traditional locations, effectively supporting the understanding of the learning process as non-formal, mostly by observation and imitation in a manner that Nketia recognised. Nettl's contribution is in describing the creation, mostly but not exclusively within western classical music, of a whole repertoire of music for didactic purposes. The development of music notation has enabled the separation of the creator from the performer, and hence the identification of specific skills often referred to as 'technique' that are seen as a prerequisite to making a meaningful music statement through the recreation of a piece of music. Both Merriam and Nettl offer some provocation to our thinking — if learning is a subset of enculturation, you can only learn within your own culture, so is your 'culture' extended when you learn music from another place? Nettl's observations might imply that the creation of a didactic repertoire is a good indication that the musical style in question has lost its original cultural meaning, being represented as a skill to be acquired, so has already entered a preserved and fully institutionalised state.

Green (2002) presents a detailed examination of the learning processes for popular music for a number of musicians mostly outside institutions. The musicians all describe initial phases of exploration and experimentation, perhaps trying out received ideas but also finding out the possibilities of the instrument and selecting some ideas for further repetition and variation. Their sources for developmental material that would in the past have been direct contact with other musicians are now mostly recorded music. This has the advantage that the material can be repeated many times until it is internalised but loses out on the additional visual material provided by a live performer. The parallels with Nketia's model of 'slow absorption through exposure to musical situations and active participation' (1961) are clear. This process is not one found only in 'traditional' musics, societies or instruction but is integral to the nature of the musical genre. It is about a process of learning rather than one of instruction, and a key part of this is the control of direction, development and pace given to the learner rather than the teacher — *not* an institutional approach. An institution generally wants to see teaching as an active didactic process rather than the provision of an environment for learning. It needs to see weekly progress monitored and evaluated rather than a process that follows the interests and struggles of the learner. Education is *not* a linear process (although schooling may be). The other key element for both Green and Nketia is that the process of 'absorption', arguably a synonym for 'enculturation', requires a frequent location within situations where the musical material is composed, created, developed, transformed and performed within its culture. This has to be key in understanding what can be said and why, rather than how to say it — in other words, understanding the function and meaning of the music rather than simply its realisation.

Green further explores the musical activities of the learner in popular music who throughout their musical life is involved in something variously described as embellishment, improvisation, jamming and composing. Even within cover or tribute bands where the emphasis is on fidelity to an original, there is a sense that 'during the solos ... you can put your own stamp on it' (Green, 2002, p. 52). It is this aspect of creativity that is deeply embedded within the culture, far more so than recreative performance. An experienced rock performer described how on one occasion he performed with a new group and singer with no rehearsal. This was possible because he knew the work of the group well, listened carefully, and was able, in performance, to make a creative contribution that brought together both his idiolect and the known stylistic features of the group. This is only possible if you are completely tuned in to all the cultural and social as well as the musical aspects of that style.

One implication of these observations is that the ability of the cultural outsider to learn and understand a different music will relate to where a particular music is located along an imaginary line between entirely pre-composed and created completely spontaneously (there are no musical styles occupying the extremes to my knowledge). With abilities in analysis and reductionist approaches to problems learned through a western-style education, students from America and Europe and some Asian countries have often become expert learners in the performance of the music of another culture. This is most marked in students coming from or to a classical music background who have developed a series of concepts embedded within a technical language that are then applied to the learning of any new music. The approach often makes for apparent rapid progress in many of the performative aspects and may even support a passable attempt at pastiche composition. What is missing is the understanding of the cultural context that an 'outsider' can never fully understand.

Learning in Africa

Returning to Nketia, what is the situation for African music in its traditional setting and in institutions in Africa? An example from my own experience is the xylophone of the Dagara and Lobi people of northern Ghana (*gyil/dzil*). Traditionally people do not 'teach' the *gyil* in the north of Ghana. Players develop their own style through the observation of other performers, remembering new ideas and trying them out later when they have access to an instrument. The only pedagogic support for this process when the learner is young may be the presence of another person who plays a timekeeping rhythm (*kpagru*) on an unresonated bar at the end of the instrument. A musical idea borrowed from another player

15

will often be transformed to some extent. The transformation may be inadvertent through an imperfect memory, although the learner may be aware of a difference and add material of their own so that the relationship with the *kpagru* is maintained. Alternatively, a more experienced performer may consciously adapt the ideas for several reasons: first that your music should not sound like that of another person or place — you need to be proud of your own style and not simply copy others. As Ephraim Amu advised the young Nketia, 'Young man, I gather you are interested in composition. Don't copy my music!' (Akrofi, 2002, p. 9). Second, the musical material is almost invariably associated with words, either directly as a song, through implied meaning drawn from the convocation of rhythm and pitch, or at least through mnemonics used by performers to remember phrases — again often with an associated meaning. Languages and dialects can change within short distances so the words usually need to change to suit the new location and the musical material will be varied to suit these changes. Thus a new song will often consist of words created with local meaning and interest, fitted to an altered version of an admired song from elsewhere. So the processes of learning and those of creation of a new personal repertoire are inextricably linked. Learning in the traditional way comes closest, of course, to an understanding of the meaning of the music for its original creators (although this is far from static), but will only be available to people who learn in that environment and live within the culture for long enough.

From the 1980s, *gyil* performance began to be taught at the University of Ghana — the instrument had previously been briefly studied from an ethnomusicological perspective by Atta Annan Mensah (1967) and Mitchell Strumpf (1975). What was taught at the university was dependent on the repertoire of the specific instructor — for most of the 1980s this was Joseph Chogri Kobom Taale. The material he passed on was mostly recreational music, sometimes described as 'neo-traditional'. Kobom did not teach words to any of the songs and also included simplified funeral music and music borrowed and adapted from elsewhere in Ghana and Africa — in summary, a typical postmodern repertoire. The method of instruction was by example and imitation, with Kobom often playing music at a slower speed, but not breaking techniques down, using technical exercises or music notation. In many senses, although some of it clearly derived from the traditions of his home town of Nandom, it was a specifically pedagogic repertoire arranged to suit the needs of learners. So, even in the home country (if not the cultural location) of this music, it has defaulted to a preserved institutionalised form that misses out a major part of the meaning, significance and creation of the music. Given that I have argued earlier that access to the cultural aspects of the music that make for a complete transmission is only possible within the indigenous location and learning method for the music, any learner outside that situation will have only a partial understanding. This does not invalidate the value of learning the music in other contexts or through other methods, provided that it brings benefits for the students and that they have a developing understanding of what they have, and have not, learned.

UK Experiences

To see what might be the understanding of learners outside the indigenous culture, I set out to research the experience of students who have passed through my institution, Dartington College of Arts. I was interested in what they felt they had learned, how they had learned it, what they had understood and their comparison with other learning environments. The responses to my limited survey come from a range of students: some who learned more than 10 years ago and have now integrated this material into their professional practice, some who went on from Dartington to study in the indigenous location of the music and/or at higher degree level, and some who have been learning for only a few weeks. Mostly they had studied Ghanaian drumming, Balinese Gamelan or Samba, with one student who had also studied Indian music in the United Kingdom.[2] I asked them a number of questions covering their expectations and perceptions of the teaching, their preferred learning methods and their understanding of what they had learned. Their initial motivations had a common thread around being engaged by the music and wanting to learn to play some of it, usually in relation to their perceived portfolio of abilities:

> to expand my knowledge of rhythm (JD).
>
> to improve my personal skill as a drummer (DC).
>
> to learn how to be a drummer (GW).
>
> there is no clear reason why I want to learn these musics but the rhythms keep me awake at night. [Later] to gain musical and technical skills that I can apply to any other musical context (KB).

As students gained more experience, other elements were generally added to this. The change is probably quite predictable; the initial excitement with the musical material led to a wish to understand more of the musical construction and aesthetic precepts, then a concern for the people who made this music, for their lives and the place of music in them:

> knowledge of whole pieces and their appropriate ensembles is important (DC).
>
> to play the music confidently and develop an understanding of the way in which pieces are constructed (JL).
>
> I aim to learn to play a music and to understand its original contexts enough to know why it is the way it is and which of its elements are important to those who originally create, perform, and listen to it. By implication, I wish to know where I, as simultaneously a relative musical insider and a relative cultural outsider, stand in relation to these considerations — i.e., what *my* performance means to a western and a 'native' audience (KB).

There seems to be an early recognition by students that they learn as an extension of their existing musical practice, usually based in western music, but they welcome the challenge of learning a different music that may (and perhaps should) require them to question their learning techniques and adopt new ones. This is not the same for all students — some may have a highly structured background in classical music, whereas others have learned popular or folk music more through aural approaches. A sense of the internal debate can be seen in these responses:

> I pull on a number of resources from my western training while at the same time trying to unlearn some of the ways I have learnt. It is a trial and error issue, but the unlearning aspect is gradually replaced by being able to have both views with the ability to change between them when I need to (GW).
>
> I think it is an extension of my skills as a western musician. Learning about various 'world musics' has broadened my musical perspective enormously but my learning has been from a western perspective. This is fine when dealing with the technical demands of the music but when it comes to the 'feel' it is necessary to be able to move beyond western musical ideas (JL).

17

> I am interested in the musics for both their qualities as sources of challenges for me as a percussionist and for their own sake. Perhaps I assume different perspectives when I actually *perform* the music, depending on the audience and situation (KB).

There is considerable thought given by the students to the appropriate learning style for themselves, for the musical style and for the teacher. Teachers whose background was within western education were more concerned about learning styles and the impact on the understanding of the music than indigenous teachers. Indigenous teachers and many students favoured practice far more than explanation as the best way to establish and consolidate learning, but other issues of cultural expectation and perception are also common:

> My preferred method [of learning] is intensive repetitive traditional learning, playing with a goal or aim in mind — something to work towards, like a performance (JD).

> I find when I concentrate on watching someone play music I need to learn, I listen a lot less. Using my eyes too much I worry about fingerings, notes, frets etc. Just sit back and listen until you familiarise yourself with melodies, techniques, styles, scales etc. (SM).

> I have also been taught by Afro-Cubans and by a Ghanaian drummer. In both these situations I felt a certain amount of frustration coming from the teachers because the students were struggling to get the right 'feel'. ... I think the learning has to be controlled by the teacher but it is important for the teacher to be sensitive to the needs of the student. In my experience this isn't always the case with non-European teachers who tend to have a more authoritarian approach to teaching. The lessons tend to be run to their agenda rather than that of the student (JL).

> I went to Ghana and studied music and I developed further techniques for learning. It was more pushed upon me — 'watch and do' was the catchphrase in the drumming and the dancing ... I would have to repeat and repeat until a part was in my head and in my hands. ... We soon learnt that you would learn the way that it was taught. A case of 'get with the programme or get off the programme (GW).

> In general, the approach of learning by doing (i.e. listening and playing) is in my opinion superior to the approach of theoretical analysis and verbal instruction favoured in the west — at least for [African and Balinese] musics. ... Within a West African drumming ensemble, musical 'information' is transmitted between each of the players in an immediate fashion, on a musical level. The best strategy to learn this music is therefore to 'simulate' this structure as closely as possible (depending on the skill of the learner) rather than explain it verbally (KB).

Related to the method of transmission is also the allocation of time. Students recognised the value of different configurations for different sorts of learning and development:

> Generally speaking, the intensive blocks of study were most fruitful. I came away each time having got to grips with several pieces of music (JL).

> The temporal 'density' of the learning experience corresponded strongly with the intensity of the learning experience. In Ghana, I was in direct contact with the culture *all the time* and with the music up to eight hours a day. The density of the learning experience was such that I soon hit the limits of my mental capacities. Completely immersing myself in Ghanaian culture constituted the ideal learning environment for me (KB).

> The more intensive periods of study can really push you and get things absorbed on a deep level, while the regularity of a weekly session helps to develop ability in a more sustained and gradual way ... In ones own practice, short but regular bursts can be more effective than less frequent but lengthy workouts (DC).

I also asked about the element of cultural information provided with the teaching. Was it provided at the 'right' time, was there not enough, too much? How much did they want?

18

Enough but not enough — but I'm just greedy when it comes to cultural information (LW).

Enough to understand what I was doing and not make it seem too abstract (JD).

With most formal tuition, the cultural information given was just the right amount in relation to the practical activity. Too much talking/explanation leads to frustration amongst musicians who always want to get on with playing (JL).

Both at Dartington and in Ghana, there was a lot of cultural information given about the music and the lifestyle, but this is important to understanding the music and developing more of a feeling of how the music should go. If I know that a particular pattern can be played/clapped as if pounding fufu, there is a particular movement and feeling from my personal experience of doing the activity that takes me to the right place to put this into the music (GW).

I think the cultural context of a music is an element of the learning process that should never be underestimated. The more a student knows about this context, the better s/he will understand the music. In the light of this the-more-the-better logic, I could say that in certain circumstances *even more* comprehensive explanation of cultural background information would have been *even more* helpful (KB).

All of these students are pretty clear that there needs to be substantial cultural information (begging the question of exactly what that might define) provided, with the proviso that the format needs to be more that only talk and not interrupt a flow of practical work until an appropriate moment for both teacher and students.

When asked what they had learned, there was a great variety of responses:

that Africa has a very different sense of rhythm to us (the Bell?!)[1] (LW, after only a few hours' experience),

how to play the rhythms, techniques, scales. Learnt to work with other people (SM).

insight into music of a different culture — different ways of thinking about music/of putting musical ideas together (JL).

I have learnt new ways to learn. I have learnt that I don't always have to learn in the same way as the person sitting next to me. I don't have to learn in the same way that my teacher learnt. I've learnt about other cultures and the impact on my own culture (GW).

how culture shows you a lot about its native music, how the two are connected (JD).

The students were also clear about the limits of what they had learned and could potentially learn. Their learning had increased their respect for another culture and music. Their approach to learning was open and honest, they knew they had learned a limited amount and did not overestimate their knowledge, although there was a concern that teachers and learners should be motivated by a love of the music, not doing it because it was part of a prescribed curriculum:

I might [aspire to] play a style well with good and recognisable understanding/sympathy. Any learning expands my ability and opens more doors through musical experience (JD).

I very much enjoy playing traditional arrangements and there are aspects of the traditional form I am quite strict about wanting to maintain, mainly because in my experience they simply 'work'. I think as music migrates it will surely also evolve. I think this is a good thing and in no way insulting to another musical culture. Involvement in a different musical style can surely only help to enhance our understanding (DC).

I set out to learn what is played but understand that the context I will be playing and performing these pieces in will never be 'authentic' and I will never come from another culture (GW).

I think that any level of skill and experience can be acceptable, even though an insufficient understanding of music may result in an insult [to the culture]. This depends much more on

19

> the contextual factors than the skills of the musician (for example, the way a performance is presented and 'justified') (KB).

> I do object to 'bitesize' chunks of African drumming or Balinese gamelan being given to schoolchildren, often without practical experience or any idea of context, by teachers who have no interest in or knowledge of the music, but are just fulfilling the needs of the curriculum. I don't think even a small amount of learning is an insult to the culture as long as the teaching is done with enthusiasm and love for the music concerned (JL).

Returning to the question, Does the close relationship between a musical tradition and the way it is handed down form the basis of maintaining traditional formats of instruction?, my research would support Nketia's observation and conclude that it is virtually impossible for an institutional context to provide an appropriate method of handing down a tradition in respect of most musics. An institution located close to the origin of the music may come close, but even that will often have acquired various pedagogical requirements and approaches that may militate against the tradition. In an institutional context, I believe that the best we can aim for is a negotiation between and understanding of different methods of learning, and cultural knowledge about the music (not of the music) appropriate to the level of the learner. As one of my students observed:

> I suppose in some ways I don't aim to play like an African drummer, but to absorb as much of the form as I can, then do it my way (DC).

This is certainly an approach that the Dagaba people and many other Africans in my experience would recognise and support. The students understand that they are not copying shadows as a one-dimensional obstruction of light, but cultivating an autonomous, knowing shadow, perhaps more akin to a ghost. They can recreate and imitate reality but cannot create originality except in their own culture, exchanging ideas with other musicians.

Endnote

1   The perception of 'difference' in African rhythm is a topic of some debate — see for example, Agawu (2003, pp. 151–171), but unsurprisingly, the difference from western rhythmic approaches is the most common initial reaction from western learners.

2   Responses from the following students have been quoted. I would like to express my thanks to them for the time they took to think about and complete a long set of questions.

  LW. Female, recently joined Dartington College studying Arts Management. (Drumming)

  KB. Male, ex-student who studied in Ghana and has since completed a masters degree and is now planning to go to Bali. (Drumming/Gamelan)

  DC. Male, a local resident, not a student but has studied in several African countries for more than 10 years. (Drumming)

  JD. Male, recently joined Dartington College studying Music. (Drumming/Gamelan)

  JL. Female, ex-student who left the college more than 10 years ago but has continued to attend various classes. Now teaches at a local music school. (Drumming/Gamelan)

  SM. Female, second year student, with some experience of Indian and Chinese music prior to Dartington. (Gamelan/Samba)

  GW. Female, ex-student who studied in Ghana and has continued to attend classes. Is now planning to train as a teacher. (Drumming/Gamelan)

References

Agawu, K. (2003). *Representing African music: Postcolonial notes, queries, positions.* New York and London: Routledge.

Akrofi, E. A. (2002). *Sharing knowledge and experience: A profile of Kwabena Nketia*. Accra: Afram Publications.

Clifford, J. (1986). Introduction: Partial truths. In J. Clifford & G. Marcus (Eds.), *Writing culture: The poetics and politics of ethnography*. Berkeley and Los Angeles: University of California Press.

Cooley, T. J. (1997). Casting shadows in the field: An introduction. In G. Barz & T. Cooley (Eds.), *Shadows in the field: New perspectives for fieldwork in ethnomusicology* (pp. 3–19). Oxford: Oxford University Press.

Green, L. (2002). *How popular musicians learn: A way ahead for music education*. Aldershot: Ashgate.

Herskovits, M. J. (1948). *Man and his works*. New York: Alfred A. Knopf.

Merriam, A. P. (1964). *The anthropology of music*. Evanston: Northwestern University Press.

Mensah. A. A. (1967). The polyphony of Gyil-gu, Kudzo and Awutu Sakumo. *Journal of the International Folk Music Council, XIX*, 75–79.

Nettl, B. (1983). *The study of ethnomusicology: Twenty-nine issues and concepts*. Urbana and Chicago: University of Illinois Press.

Nketia, J.H. Kwabena (1961). Continuity of traditional instruction. In K. William Archer (Ed.), *The preservation of traditional forms of the learned and popular music of the Orient and the Occident* (pp. 203–213). Urbana: Centre for Comparative Psycholinguistics, Institute of Communications, University of Illinois.

Strumpf. M. (1975). Ghanaian xylophone studies. In *Notes on education and research in African music No. 2* (pp. 32–39). Legon: University of Ghana.

Titon, J. T. (1997). Knowing fieldwork. In G. Barz & T. Cooley (Eds.), *Shadows in the field: New perspectives for fieldwork in ethnomusicology* (pp. 87–100). Oxford: Oxford University Press.

TREVOR WIGGINS is Director of Music at Dartington College of Arts in the United Kingdom. His work reflects on music and issues of education, pedagogy and change, explored through recording and writing. He is currently working on a book about the recreational music of the Dagaba people of north-west Ghana.

21

The Local and the Global in Musical Learning: Considering the Interaction Between Formal and Informal Settings

Göran Folkestad

W hat does the fact that one can hear a didjeridoo at a Swedish wedding in a Medieval-period stone church tell us about today's and tomorrow's society? What does it tell us about the relationship between the local and the global, and about the tension between globalisation and localisation, that rap music has found its way back to Africa, after being developed in American exile (Lundberg et al., 2000)? One thing it tells us is that issues regarding world music and the cultural diversity in music are likely to be increasingly important in music education at all levels. Accordingly, research in this field will become increasingly important, as it has the potential to contribute valuable knowledge for educators who implement and develop multicultural musical activities in and out of school (Folkestad, 2002).

The inclusion of world musics in music education has a lot in common with the way in which other forms of popular music, such as rock and jazz, have found their way into the classrooms. Like popular music, world music is a broad concept, constantly undergoing change. Like popular music, world music is (a) based on playing by ear rather than by notation, (b) created and performed to a large extent on collective processes, and (c) learned by employing traditions that mostly include informal learning situations outside of formal educational school settings (Folkestad, 2000). What consequences and implications do these factors have for the development of teaching methods, which harmonise with the origin of these musics?

Popular music has only entered the formal institutional settings in terms of content (Olsson, 1993). However, there are interesting projects with promising results, implementing different approaches to musical learning, both in teacher education and in municipal music schools for young people (Lundström, 1993; Saether, 1993, 2004). This article's aim is to examine research studies that focus on *formal and informal learning situations and practices* or *formal and informal ways of learning*. First, *the field of research in music education* is defined, followed by discussion of the relationship between music education as a *field of praxis* (music pedagogy) and as a *field of research*, and the relationship between these two facets of music education and the *surrounding society*.

Music Education in Research and Praxis

Most research in music education has so far dealt with music training in institutional settings, such as schools, and is accordingly based on the assumption, either implicitly or explicitly, that musical learning results from a sequenced, methodical exposure to music teaching within a formal setting. However, during the last decade there has been an awakening interest in the issue of taking into consideration not only the formalised learning situations within institutional settings, such as schools, but also all various forms of learning that goes on in informal musical learning practices outside schools. Folkestad (1998) summarised this change in perspective as a general shift in focus; *from teaching to learning*, and consequently *from teacher to learner* (pupil). Thus, it also implies a shift of focus, from *how to teach* (teaching methods) and the outcome of teaching in terms of results as seen from the teacher's perspective, to *what to learn*, the content of learning, and *how to learn*, the way of learning. A point of departure of this perspective on music education research is the notion that the great majority of *all* musical learning takes place outside schools, in situations where there is no teacher, and in which the intention of the activity is not to learn about music, but to play music, listen to music, dance to music or be together with music. Each of these examples typifies situations in which music is experienced and learned, one way or another. Today, this is further accentuated as a result of computers and new technology and all the musical activities on the Internet in which the global and the local interact in a dialectic way, what Giddens (1991) calls *glocal*.

Applying a sociocultural perspective on music education, the question of whether or not to have, for example, popular music in school is irrelevant: popular music is already present in school, brought there by the students, and in many cases also by the teachers, as part of their musical experience and knowledge. The issue is rather: How do we deal with it? Do we deny the fact that popular music and world music is an essential factor of the context of music teaching in school, or do we acknowledge the students' musical experiences and knowledge as a starting point for further musical education? This shift of focus from teacher to learner, and this widened definition of the field of research in music education has the following implication: while music education as a *field of praxis* (music pedagogy) is defined as all kinds of formal musical teaching and institutionalised learning settings, music education as a *field of research* must deal with *all* kinds of musical learning, regardless of where it takes place (is situated), and of how and by whom it is organised or initiated.

This also defines the relationship between the field of praxis, music teachers, and the field of research, music education researchers, in that the role of the latter is not to 'produce' teaching methods, but to deliver research results to the praxis field, results by means of which the professional teachers may plan, conduct and evaluate their music teaching. An important strand in this relationship between researchers and practitioners, and with the rest of the surrounding society, is the mutually shared need of a continuous dialogue, and also that research questions induced in the reflections of the praxis field become the object of attraction to research.

Formal and Informal Learning Situations

24

The study of informal musical learning outside institutional settings such as schools, has proved to contribute to important knowledge and aspects of music education. Different ways of formal and informal learning are presented in Folkestad (in press). In *New Youth: On Uncommon Learning Processes*, Ziehe (1986) defines two types of learning: (a) common and (b) uncommon learning processes. Notable is that the main distinction between these two categories is not *where*, but *how* the learning occurs. In their 1988 study of three young rock bands, published in English in 1995 as *In Garageland*, Fornäs, Lindberg, and Sernhede found that typical of this kind of informal learning is that it involves more than just the core subject of learning, in this case the music; it has more the character of an integrated learning on a more holistic level. These aspects are also illustrated in the intimate and longitudinal ethnographic study of Berkaak and Ruud, published in 1994, which gives an in-depth insight into the context of informal learning within rock bands.

One of the results of a research by Folkestad (1998) was that studying *how to compose* also is to study *how to learn how to compose*. In a *situated practice*, like composing, the division between the artistic performance and how it is learned becomes dissolved in the correlation of these aspects of the process; one cannot exist without the other. In Folkestad (1998), the theoretical conclusion of the 1996 study is further elaborated, resulting in seeing *musical learning as cultural practice*. This involves that by *participating* in a practice, one also *learns* the practice. From this, a distinction between formal and informal ways of learning with respect to intentionality is presented: in the formal learning situation the minds of both the teacher and the students are directed towards *learning how to play music (learning how to make music)*, whereas in the informal learning practice the mind is directed towards *playing music (making music)*. This difference in intentionality is described by Saar (1999) as a distinction between a *pedagogical framing* (i.e., *learning how to play music*) and an *artistic/musical framing* (i.e., *playing music*), respectively.

Estelle Jorgensen presents a model in which she differentiates the concept of education, which as stated earlier, involves *all* kinds of learning, by defining five categories, or sub-concepts: schooling, training, eduction, socialisation and enculturation (1997). In my view, the two first categories might be seen as descriptions of formal learning situations. Similarly, the two last categories might be seen as descriptions of informal learning. The middle category, *eduction*, might be viewed the meeting place for formal and informal learning. Formal in the sense that it is organised and led by a teacher, but informal in the sense that the kind of learning that is obtained and the ways in which this is achieved has much in common with the characteristics of everyday learning in practices outside school.

In her interview study of professional and non-professional rock musicians, aged between 15 and 50, Green (2001) describes their musical learning strategies to become rock musicians as an example of informal musical learning. Interestingly enough, and what might seem as a paradox, is that when these rock musicians teach others they rather teach in very formal and traditional ways, in spite of their own personal informal musical training. Accordingly, when starting to teach, the *construction of teaching* and the conception of what it means to be a teacher are so strong that even with totally different personal experiences of learning music, these experiences give way to, the generally known construction of teaching.

Two main discourses are identified in Ericsson's (2002) study of how adolescents experience (i.e., talk about) musical learning: the discourse of *music* and the discourse of *the school subject, music*. The discourse of *music* is wide and embraces music in leisure time as well as in school. The discourse of *the school subject music* is narrow and legitimised only through its position as a school subject. Ericsson found that what many of the students wanted *in* school was more of the kind of musical activities and learning that takes place *outside* school, that is, the discourse of *the school subject music* to be replaced in school by the discourse of *music*. In summary, the discourse of *music* (Ericsson, 2002) has bearing on what Folkestad (1996) called *playing music, musical framing* in Saar's (1999) terminology, whereas the focus of the

25

discourse of *the school subject music* corresponds with *learning how to play music* and *pedagogical framing*, respectively.

So far, the studies presented have dealt with musical learning, in and out of school, within western societies and cultures. However, in order to acknowledge the importance of attaining a cultural diversity in music education by integrating world music and indigenous music in the curriculum music, studies of musical learning in non-western settings is indispensable. In this respect, Saether's (2003) study of the attitudes to music teaching and learning among *jalis* in the Gambia has interesting findings: that which on a surface level, and from the perspective and prejudice of western music education, might seem as an informal practice, was in fact found to be a very formalised and 'institutionalised' way of knowledge formation and knowledge mediation. The title of her thesis, *The Oral University*, refers not only to this main result, but also to the notion that there is no causal relationship between orality and informality.

In the descriptions in the literature presented above, four different ways of using and defining formal and informal learning are identified, respectively, either explicitly or implicitly, each one focusing on different aspects of learning:

1. The situation: Where does learning take place? That is, formal and informal is used as a way of pointing out the physical context in which learning takes place: inside or outside institutional settings, such as schools.
2. Learning style: As a way of describing the character, the nature and quality of the learning process.
3. Ownership: Who 'owns' the decisions of the activity; what to do as well as how, where and when?
4. Intentionality: Towards what is the mind directed — towards learning how to play or towards playing (Folkestad, 1998)? Within a pedagogical or a musical framework (Saar, 1999)?

One conclusion of the research on formal and informal musical learning is that it is far too simplified, and actually false, to say that formal learning only occurs in institutional settings and that informal learning only occurs outside school. On the contrary, this static view has to be replaced with a dynamic view in which what is described as formal and informal learning styles are aspects of the phenomenon of learning, regardless of where it takes place. Used as an analytic tool, what characterise most learning situations is the instant switch between these learning styles and the dialectic interaction between them. It is also a misconception to claim that the content of formal musical learning is synonymous with western classical music learned from sheets of music, and that the content of informal musical learning is restricted to popular music transmitted by ear. Since what is learned and how it is learned are interconnected, it is not only the choice of content, such as rock music, that becomes an important part in the shaping of an identity (and therefore an important part of music teaching as well), but also, and to a larger extent, the ways in which the music is approached. In other words, the most important issue might not be the content as such, but the approach to music that the content mediates.

Conclusion

Why are the issues presented in this article important in music education research? It is appropriate to return to Ziehe's (1982) description of 'common' and 'uncommon' ways of learning. Children's learning occurs in common ways outside school, adopted from an early age by their interaction with music, movies, video and computer games, the Internet. On the other hand, the ways that children learn in school appear to be uncommon ways. In order to contribute to the development of a cultural diversity in music education, in its true and full meaning, music education researchers need to be not only in schools doing all kinds of various research in the classrooms, but also to be where children and students encounter musical learning in all its various forms. Moreover, as a result of the globalised world in which the local and the global interact, particularly in the musical learning of young people, music education researchers need to focus not only on the formal and informal musical learning in western societies and cultures, but to include the full global range of popular, world and indigenous musics in their studies.

References

Berkaak, O. A., & Ruud, E. (1994). *Sunwheels. Fortellinger om et rockeband* [Sunwheels. The story of a rock band]. Oslo: Universitetsforlaget.

Ericsson, C. (2002). *Från guidad visning till shopping och förströdd tillägnelse. Moderniserade villkor för ungdomars musikaliska lärande* [From guided exhibition to shopping and preoccupied assimilation. Modernised conditions for adolescents' musical learning]. Malmö: Malmö Academy of Music.

Folkestad, G. (1996). *Computer based creative music making: Young people's music in the digital age.* Göteborg: Acta Universitatis Gothoburgensis.

Folkestad, G. (1998). Musical learning as cultural practice. As exemplified in computer-based creative music making. In B. Sundin, G. McPherson, & G. Folkestad (Eds.), *Children composing.* Malmö: Lund University, Malmö Academy of Music.

Folkestad, G. (2000). Editorial. *International Journal of Music Education, 36,* 1–3.

Folkestad, G. (2002). National identity and music. In R. A. R. MacDonald, D. J. Hargreaves, & D. Miell (Eds.), *Musical identities* (pp. 151–162). Oxford: Oxford University Press.

Folkestad, G. (in press). Formal and informal learning situations or practices vs formal and informal ways of learning. *British Journal of Music Education.*

Fornäs, J., Lindberg, U., & Sernhede, O. (1995). *In garageland* [Youth and culture in late modernity]. London: Routledge.

Giddens, A. (1991). *Modernity and self-identity: Self and society in late modern age.* Cambridge: Polity Press.

Green, L. (2001). *How popular musicians learn. A way ahead for music education.* Aldershot: Ashgate.

Jorgensen, E. (1997). *In search of music education.* Urbana and Chicago: University of Illinois Press.

Lundberg, D., Malm, K., & Ronström, O. (2000). *Musik, medier, mångkultur. Förändringar i svenska musiklandskap.* [Music, media, multiculture. Changes in Swedish music landscape]. Hedemora: Gidlunds Förlag.

Lundström, H. (1993). Världsmusik eller mångkulturalism, eller … [World music or multi culturism, or …]. In E. Saether (Ed.), *På jakt efter en mångkulturell musiklärarutbildning* [In search of a multi cultural music teacher education] (pp. 29–37). Malmö: Malmö Academy of Music.

Olsson, B. (1993). *Sämus-en musikutbildning i kulturpolitikens tjänst? En studie om en musikutbildning på 70-talet.* [Sämus-music education in the service of a cultural policy? A study of a teacher training program during the 1970s]. Göteborg: Musikhögskolan i Göteborg.

Saar, T. (1999). *Musikens dimensioner. En studie av unga musikers lärande* [The dimensions of music. A study of young musicians' learning]. Göteborg: Acta Universitatis Gothoburgensis.

Saether, E. . (1993). "Gambian maybe time" – About studies in the music of a foreign culture. In E. Seather (Ed.), *På jakt efter en mångkulturell musiklärarutbildning* [In search of a multicultural music teacher education]. Malmö: Malmö Academy of Music.

Saether, E. (2003). *The oral university. Attitudes to music teaching and learning in the Gambia.* Malmö: Malmö Academy of Music.

27

Saether, E. (2004). Den gränsöverskridande musikläraren. Kulturmöten som metod i musiklärarut-bildningen [The border crossing music teacher. The meating of cultures as a method in music teacher training]. In O. Pripp (Ed.), *Mångfald i kulturlivet* [Plurality in the cultural life] (pp. 153–157). Botkyrka, Sweden: Mångkulturellt centrum.

Ziehe, T. (1986). *Ny ungdom. Om ovanliga läroprocesser* [New youth. On uncommon learning processes]. Stockholm: Norstedts.

GÖRAN FOLKESTAD is Professor and Chair in Research in Music Education at the Malmo Academy of Music, Lund University. He has published and lectured widely on composition and music for children. The article above is based on a contribution submitted to the *British Journal of Music Education*.

Taking Distance and Getting Up Close: The Seven-Continuum Transmission Model (SCTM)

Huib Schippers

From the early 1980s, many institutes for formal music education across the world have formally abandoned the view that western classical music from the common practice period should be the only reference for music education. Terms like 'doing justice to the multicultural environment' abound in policies and statements of principle. This has led to a journey of discovery for many music educators and institutes into understanding new sound worlds and sharing these in teaching. A significant number of initiatives have been realised; some of these have proven quite successful, others less so. But after 25 years of practice, the question arises: to what extent have we been successful in incorporating the new musics we have discovered and do we really present them on a basis of equality? Answering this question truthfully obliges us to dig deep into the values underlying our beliefs, approaches and organisation of music education.

Approaching Cultural Diversity

In discussions and research on the subject of cultural diversity in music education over the past two decades, referring to both cultural diversity of content and ethnic diversity of learners, a number of concepts and ideas have featured prominently, but often uncritically; terms such as multicultural, ethnic, traditional, authentic, contextual, oral and holistic are used frequently, but often ill-defined. A thorough study of these terms and the meanings attributed to each reveals that at the basis of any situation of musical transmission and learning lie plethora of explicit and implicit choices, which have a direct bearing on the musical transmission process. Understanding and applying these creates new perspective for both practice and understanding of world music in formal music education.

For cultural diversity as a whole, a useful framework is provided by distinguishing between *monocultural* approaches, in which the dominant culture is the only reference; *multicultural* approaches, where plurality is acknowledged but no contact or exchange is stimulated; *intercultural* approaches, which are characterised by loose contact between cultures and some effort towards mutual understanding; and *transcultural* approaches, which represent an in-depth exchange of ideas and values.

Tradition, Authenticity and Context

In music education, the implication of the words *tradition*, *authenticity* and *context* often appears to be that these are valuable aims to strive for per se. However, closer examination reveals that tradition, authenticity and context are not static concepts. In fact, they allow for a broad range of interpretations, to the point of being almost contradictory. Tradition, for instance, can be defined as a canon, a performance practice, a set of rules, a mechanism for handing down music, or by its place in culture. Consequently, a *tradition* can be defined by its static nature, or by its very capacity to change: the concept of living traditions is crucial to understanding many forms of world music.

Similarly, *authenticity* can refer to attempts to copy or *reconstruct* an original as closely as possible, or to the need to *be* original, and thus true to one's individual expression. Authenticity in music is rarely a comprehensive reconstruction of an original; it is marked by subjective choices and conjecture. Striving for authenticity can be defined by following ancient sources, choice of instruments, composition of ensembles, recreating original settings or contexts, following established rules, or striving for vitality of expression, as in rock music. This can lead to conflicting interpretations of authenticity, ranging from academic reconstruction of a work or genre to liberal interpretation of only its spirit.

Finally, *context* is a crucial factor in all music making. Music takes place in context: in time, in space, in society, in ideology. Sheer formalistic and aesthetic approaches to music transmission are not likely to be successful, as they do not take into account the full reality of each distinct musical practice. However, having established that context is an undeniable presence, contemporary performance and teaching practices demonstrate that traditions can be successfully *recontextualised*. The 're-rooting' of numerous traditions in new cultural settings challenges the idea that (particularly world) music should always be experienced in its original context. Many musics travel remarkably well from one context to another, and this should be taken into account when creating situations in which music is taught and learned.

Holistic and Analytical Approaches

As earlier research has demonstrated (Van den Bos, 1995, pp. 170–179), the learning process can be viewed in a similar way, with approaches ranging from *oral* to *notation-based*, from *holistic* to *analytical*. We can also distinguish approaches with emphasis on *tangible* aspects (such as technique and repertoire) to *intangible* aspects (such as creativity and expression). Each of these represents choices that are a matter of degree rather than of extremes. A thorough deconstruction of the phenomena discussed above makes it possible to identify seven 'core' continua, which cover broad ranges of choices, each with specific indicators. These continua can be divided over three categories: learning process, issues of authenticity and approach to cultural diversity. This leads to a descriptive model that enables us to consider music teaching and learning in depth from a crosscultural perspective: the seven-continuum transmission model (SCTM; see Figure 1).

The SCTM maps out a range of choices and decisions applicable to almost any situation of music teaching and learning. These become particularly evident when music is moved from one context to another, as underlying values are highlighted

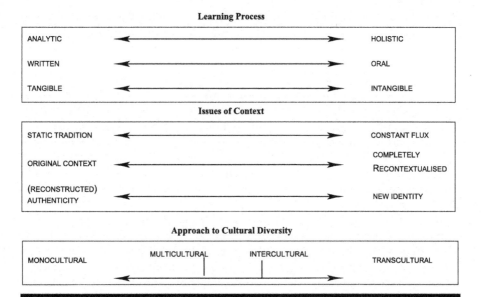

FIGURE 1

The seven-continuum transmission model (SCTM).

by a change of context. The model can be considered from three 'inside' *perspectives*: that of the learner, that of the teacher and that of the teaching environment (e.g., the institution). All three are forces of some significance in determining the process of music transmission and learning. Finally, it can be looked at through the eyes of an outside observer, who abstracts from the process the result of the interplay between the three actors.

Although the clusters and indicators are relatively independent, some degree of *coherence between the clusters* can be inferred: a tendency towards the left of the continua suggests a more institutionalised/formal organisation of music transmission of learning, with emphasis on analytic, notation-based and tangible aspects in the learning process; relatively static interpretations of tradition, authenticity and context; and a generally monocultural outlook. A tendency towards the right of each continuum points towards more informal, community music settings, with holistic, oral and intangible accents in learning; open attitudes towards living traditions, recontextualisation and new identities; and more often an intercultural approach to society.

In essence, the model does not entail any value judgments: there are no predetermined right or wrong positions on the continua. Of course, any given situation will invite certain approaches, and the music teacher who is aware of the scope of approaches and able to vary and utilise them may be more likely to be successful as a music educator, in harmony with contemporary constructivist views on education.

Applying the Seven-Continuum Transmission Model

The most obvious application of the SCTM is to describe any given teaching situation, whether it is a moment in a lesson, or an entire acculturation process.

Description of musical transmission can be based on a full analysis of an observed teaching process, and extensive interviews with the facilitator/teacher and learner/student, but it may also be based on video registrations, ethnomusicological accounts of musical transmission, or oral reports by observers and participants.

In order to provide insight into a specific situation of music transmission or learning, the graphic representation alone is not sufficient. Not only the position, but also the reasoning behind choosing the position on each continuum is crucial. This enables the researcher to establish the difference between lacks of clear arguments for either extreme position on the continuum, or two forces pulling with equal force, which could both result in a middle position. Consequently, the precise position on the continuum is of limited meaning. The model emphatically remains a *qualitative tool*; quantitative use of the model is not likely to lead to dependable results.

Research results indicate that a fairly uniform picture emerges when the model is applied to a *single moment* in education. A broader range of variation (and consequently less unambiguous position on the continua) appears when applied to *longer processes*. This corresponds with the reality of practices of teaching and learning, which tend to alternate between choices over various stages of development. In all cases, subjectivity plays a role, steered by the background of the user, understanding of and preconceptions about the tradition, and their role in the transmission process. Although more difficult to define precisely, the description of longer trajectories do of course provide us with the most valuable information on how musical skills and knowing are acquired within a specific tradition over time.

Implication for Organisations

Not only music transmission processes, but also the organisation is conducive to particular ways of teaching and learning, and less so to others. These structures can in fact be considered as a crystallisation of the educational philosophies of the present or the future, but more often of past decades or even centuries. As such, it can be a progressive or conservative mechanism of considerable importance.

This particularly holds true for formalised forms of instruction: 'Curriculum is grounded on philosophical assumptions about the purposes and methods of education', Jorgensen writes, 'as a practical entity, it expresses the philosophical assumptions of its maker(s) much as an art work expresses the ideas and feelings of its creator(s) and performer(s) ... embodying the assumptions that comprise it, practically speaking, one cannot separate the curriculum from the assumptions that ground it ...' (Jorgensen, 2002, p. 49). Speaking of curriculum as 'the practical application of reason,' Jorgensen states: 'As such, curriculum is simply the outworking in practice of thoughts, desires, and beliefs about what ought to take place in education' (2002, p. 55).

32

Considering approaches to music teaching and learning from a crosscultural perspective only makes sense when we take into account how it is organised. The effectiveness of particular choices will differ vastly between, say, a weekly one-hour lesson in a public music school, or 20 years spent living with an Indian guru. Factors we have discussed before, such as methods of teaching, tradition, context, authenticity and the position of the music in society are greatly influenced by the institutional environment.

Teacher Strategies

Turning to the actual practice, we can basically distinguish between three answers to challenges to the system of musical transmission when musicians find themselves teaching in new contexts:

- The teacher maintains the way of teaching that he has experienced in the culture of origin. This is an attitude that can be fed by conviction, arrogance, ignorance or an intelligent appraisal of the market. The first three are obvious. An excellent example of the latter is the emphasis Indian music teachers in the late 1960s placed on their position as gurus. This answered to the expectations a generation of searching westerners had of all things Indian. In general we can say about this approach that it is not likely to produce great results. While key qualities in the music may be retained, the frustration level among students from another culture causes a significant drop-out rate.

- The teacher completely assumes the style of teaching of the host environment. This generally occurs when a musician strives to be accepted into an established institution, seeking validation for himself and his music. It is sometimes difficult for musicians that feel truly foreign in these institutions to resist being intimidated and adapting to the dominant culture.

- The teacher adopts a mix of the two traditions of teaching, and possibly adds new elements. In practice this is the most common approach, sometimes by necessity, mostly by choice. The intelligent music teacher sees the profile of his students, weighs the alternatives in relation to the musical ambitions and possibilities of his students, and proceeds accordingly. When done consciously, this can be a very effective way of adapting the method, even at a superficial level. However, a well-considered approach takes a great deal of thinking through what needs to be taught and what is the best way to teach it. When done unconsciously, this can be a half-hearted attempt to marry the irreconcilable.

In fact, this again creates a continuum: from extreme adherence to traditional styles of musical transmission to complete adaptation to the dominant styles of teaching and learning in a new environment. The practices of private teachers (non-formal) and in community settings (informal) are less heavily influenced by institutional pressures, and may serve as points of reference and inspiration for devising new course structures in formal music education.

Conclusion

When we consider the issues that have emerged in the formal discourse on music and education over the past 20 years (e.g., Colwell & Anderson, 2002), it is striking to remark that most have direct relevance to the considerations on world music teaching and learning above: teacher-centred versus student-centred learning, broadness versus specialisation, the order of learning and teaching styles, definitions of outcomes and competency-based learning; talent, motivation, authentic learning and the creation of a stimulating learning environment. But as those in the forefront of all new developments experience, the formal structures do not change as quickly as the insights do. Until such time, in spite of much rhetoric in policy plans, we may claim to have discovered, but not to have truly accepted and accommodated, world music in formal music education.

33

In order to achieve that, we must constantly monitor not only the sounds, but also the underlying systems of belief of the forms of music with which we engage.

This requires research, open-mindedness and a constant critical dialogue on the basis of equality with traditional culture bearers, young representatives of specific traditions and learners of diverse backgrounds. That is no easy task; but the first experiences from examining complex practices indicate that SCTM may facilitate the discourse in years to come.

References

Bos, P. Van den (1995). Differences between western and non-western teaching methods in music education — How can both methods supplement each other? In *Teaching musics of the world* (pp. 169–179). Affalterbach: Philipp Verlag.

Colwell, R., & Richardson, C. (Eds.). (2002). *The new handbook of research on music teaching and learning.* New York: Oxford University Press.

Jorgensen, E.R. (2002). Philosophical issues in curriculum. In R. Colwell & C. Richardson (Eds.), *The new handbook of research on music teaching and learning* (pp. 48–62). New York: Oxford University Press.

Melchers, M. (1996). *Muziek, een Wereldtaal.* Amsterdam: Amsterdamse Hogeschool voor de Kunsten.

Volk, T. M. (1998). *Music, education and multiculturalism: Foundations and principles.* New York: Oxford University Press.

HUIB SCHIPPERS is Associate Professor of Music Studies and Research at Queensland Conservatorium, Griffith University. He has a long and varied history of experience in music and arts education in Europe. He has worked as a performing musician, a teacher, a concert promoter and a music critic, and in the record trade. Over the past 10 years, he has run major projects in arts and arts education; lectured and published across the world; and served in a variety of capacities on numerous forums, boards and commissions, including the Netherlands National Arts Council and the International Society for Music Education. This article is based on a presentation at the XXVIth World Conference of the International Society for Music Education in Tenerife, Spain, and has been published on CD-ROM in the peer-reviewed proceedings of that conference.

Approaches to Learning and Teaching

Going Behind the Doors:
The Role of Fieldwork in Changing
Tertiary Students' Attitudes
to World Music Education

Kathryn Marsh

The international concern with teachers' approaches to cultural diversity in the delivery of music programs has been well documented in recent years (Anderson & Campbell, 1996; Biernoff & Blom, 2000; Campbell, 1991, 2004; Dunbar-Hall, 1997, 2000; Edwards, 1996; Hookey, 1994; Klinger, 1994; Lundquist, 2002; Lundquist & Szego, 1998; Reimer, 1994, 2002; Schippers, 1996; Standley, 2000; Solis, 2004; Teicher, 1997; Walker, 1996; York & Choksy, 1994). Such challenges for music educators are particularly evident in a culturally diverse nation such as Australia, where the population is drawn from more than 100 ethnic groups, including Anglo-Australians, immigrants and their descendants, and indigenous Australians (Aborigines and Torres Strait Islanders). This article discusses issues associated with teaching multicultural music education to music teacher education students in Sydney and outlines approaches that are seen to have affected student attitudes to the teaching of multicultural music in schools. In particular, the effectiveness of a fieldwork project in changing pre-service teacher education students' attitudes is discussed.

During the last decades of the 20th century, there have been major changes in government and educational policies relating to cultural and linguistic diversity in Australia, with concepts of assimilation being superseded by ideologies of multiculturalism, cultural pluralism and the need for equal educational opportunity and self-determination for members of Australia's immigrant and indigenous peoples (Allan & Hill, 1995; Jamrozik, Boland, & Urquhart, 1995). In the state of New South Wales (NSW) such ideological shifts have been reflected in policies that have been developed to meet the needs of its multi-ethnic population.

The NSW Multicultural Education Policy, formulated in 1983, includes among its goals the need to help all children develop:

> an awareness of the contribution which people of many different backgrounds have made and are making to Australia, ... intercultural understanding through the consideration of attitudes, beliefs and values related to multiculturalism, ... [and] an enhanced sense of personal worth through an acceptance and appreciation not only of their Australian national identity but also of their specific Australian ethnic identity in the context of a multicultural society (NSW Department of Education, 1983, p. 2).

This policy stipulates that '[a]ll curriculum areas should reflect multicultural per-spectives and all students should be exposed to these perspectives' (NSW Department of Education, 1983, p. 3).

In responding to this policy, NSW curriculum documents relating to music have affirmed the importance of representing music from a variety of cultural sources in school music programs. For example, the NSW Creative Arts K-6 syllabus, manda-tory for primary schools from 2000, states in its rationale that music, visual arts, drama and dance:

> provide students and other people with opportunities to explore social and cultural values about spiritual and worldly beliefs in Australia and in other regions and cultures, and to celebrate, share and negotiate these values and beliefs. Through the arts, the diverse and pluralistic values of Australian cultures, including those of Aboriginal and Torres Strait Islander peoples, reflect the interests and aspirations of groups, and their identities (Board of Studies NSW, 2000, p. 6).

Similar statements appear in other syllabus documents relating to various levels of schooling. The rationale for music in the Stage 6 (senior high school) curriculum, for example, notes that:

> Music occupies a significant place in world cultures and the recorded history of all civilisa-tions. ... Music has the capacity to cross cultural and societal boundaries. It plays a variety of important roles in the cultural and spiritual lives of people. ... The study of music ... allows for the expression of the intellect, imagination and emotion, the exploration of values, and fosters an understanding of continuity and change, as well as connections between different times and cultures (Board of Studies NSW, 1999a, p. 6, 1999b, p. 6).

The NSW junior secondary music syllabus stipulates content inclusive of:

> music of other cultures, folk music and world music as well as the diversity of music within Australia. Content should allow students to develop an understanding of the importance of the arts for maintaining culture and as a means of cultural expression (Board of Studies NSW, 2003, p. 22).

However, despite the acknowledgment of cultural diversity in current NSW music curriculum documents, guidelines in these curricula regarding the inclusion of a multicultural perspective in music programs have been limited. Consequently, in NSW, there has been little emphasis on the principles of multicultural education policies in the implementation of music programs within schools. In music pro-grams, involvement of members of ethnic or indigenous communities as owners of musical and cultural knowledge and co-participants in the teaching and learning process has also been limited, mainly occurring in schools which have a high popu-lation of immigrant or indigenous students (Dunbar-Hall, 1997). In incorporating a 'multicultural perspective' in their music programs, teachers have frequently used inappropriate examples of music taken out of context, examples derived from publi-cations which bear very little relationship to the manifestations of music within the Australian community, in direct contravention of the multicultural education policy that 'seeks to focus more specifically on the Australian multicultural experi-ence' (NSW Department of Education, 1983, p. 2).

38

Given that both human and published resources are available, it seems that insufficient resources or musicological understanding do not account entirely for teachers' lack of confidence to implement multicultural music programs. Rather, it would appear that this lack of confidence reflects the fact that, in their pre-service training, many teachers have not acquired an understanding of the necessity of such programs (Lundquist, 2002). In attributing this to the 'Eurocentric approach in which they were trained' (p. 416), Teicher (1997) also indicates that teachers perceive that the inclusion of multicultural materials is too difficult to manage within an already 'full' curriculum.

Another problem appears to be the inability of many teachers to view music or behaviour related to a particular culture from an 'insider's' perspective, relevant to their own lives and those of their students. In some ways, published music education materials relating to world musics have contributed to the distancing of the teacher and cultural 'other' by emphasising the differences between musical cultures and by placing music firmly in a geographical context that is removed from the lives of teachers. Some more recent publications have endeavoured to overcome this difficulty by foregrounding the role of music in the lives of real people who have bicultural experiences as members of a multicultural society (see for example, Campbell, McCullough-Brabson, & Tucker, 1994).

To encourage pre-service students to take a more active and personal approach to understanding and teaching the music of an unfamiliar culture represented within a pluralist Australian society, I have explored the potential of fieldwork research. The ethnomusicological model discussed by Titon (1997), in which there is 'an emphasis on understanding ... the lived experience of people making music' (pp. 91–92) seemed particularly appropriate. In this approach, fieldwork is 'defined as "knowing people making music", an experiential, dialogic, participatory way of knowing and "being in the world"' (Cooley, 1997, p. 15). The importance of interpersonal fieldwork relationships in developing musical understandings is further explained by Titon (1997):

> When I see that I and others are making the music that I hear, I want to know these others. ... If you were an object I might come to know you as other objects. But you are a person making music and I come to know you as a person. ... We seek to know each other through lived experience (p. 94).

This article discusses the efficacy of a fieldwork project in creating forms of 'lived experience' of music making in which students could engage with 'knowing people making music' as a way of effecting attitudinal change in relation to the teaching of musics representative of the Australian multi-ethnic population. The project operates through a form of cultural immersion that takes place within the relatively invisible context of music making of diverse ethnic groups in a large Australian city and entry into the immersion process is the responsibility of individual students.

The Project Context

The fieldwork project has been undertaken on an annual basis by students majoring in music education at the Sydney Conservatorium of Music, University of Sydney, in the years from 1998 to the present. The project constitutes a key component of Multicultural Studies in Music Education, a core fourth year subject of the Bachelor of Music (Music Education) program. Students within this program have had many years of formal music training but the majority of these students indicate that training has been almost entirely within the western music tradition, despite a considerable level of diversity in their personal cultural backgrounds. The few instances of music education relating to world music that students have experienced in a school context, either in their own previous schooling or during teaching practicum sessions, are reported as being reliant on information derived from books, decontextualised, and therefore relatively meaningless. There has been a similar lack of exposure to music from outside the western tradition in their previous university training and, with few exceptions, previous assignments have

39

exclusively involved library and internet research. However, since 1999, students' experiences of music beyond the western tradition have been expanded by participation in an additional core subject involving the learning of Balinese or Javanese gamelan. This subject is undertaken during the same semester as Multicultural Studies in Music Education to encourage the transfer of understandings gained through both of these subjects.

The project involves students in the recording and transcription of a number of musical items, including a song, performed by a non-Anglo-Australian member of the community. From its inception, students have contacted and recorded a wide variety of performers, ranging from professional musicians to community-based amateur groups, relatives and friends performing at backyard gatherings. The diversity of recorded performers can be seen in the following sample: Vietnamese zither teacher, Lebanese dance group, Macedonian community band, former member of a Czech pop group, Montenegrin guslar, Turkish community music school, Croatian dance troupe, performers in a Thai music festival, Welsh grandmother recalling her childhood, Taiwanese parent singing Taiwanese folk and popular songs, Chinese relatives singing with karaoke recordings, Italian family gathering and Italian women's choir, Greek neighbour singing Byzantine chant, Latin jazz group, north and south Indian performers, Korean singers and percussion ensemble, Fijian singers, Tongan school-based dance group, Ukrainian bandura performer, Sudanese refugees at a community party, and a number of popular fusion bands that combined varying aspects of world music contributed by members of different ethnicities.

By interviewing their informant/s and through further research, students have developed not only an understanding of musical characteristics but also background information on the recorded music in relation to cultural and performance context, and individual and social meanings. These understandings have then been used to formulate a school music program, aspects of which are used to enliven student presentations on their projects to other participants in the university class. Students are asked to reflect on the process of their learning in their written assignments and a number of students have been interviewed following the completion of the subject in order to further explore these reflections and the implications that the project has for students' attitudes towards incorporating such forms of learning in their future music programs.

Because notions of multicultural education were almost entirely new to the majority of these students, the outcomes of this project have been variable. Generally, however, there was a shift in disposition of many of the students towards the implementation of a more pluralistic approach to music programs, particularly those directly involving members of local ethnic communities. Over a number of years the outcomes of the project differed in relation to the backgrounds of the students and can best be discussed by examining changes in understanding and attitudes of several groups of students whose differing patterns of change are outlined in the following sections.

40

Anglo-Australian Students' Broadened Perceptions

For some Anglo-Australian students, the fieldwork project created an awareness of the previous narrowness of their musical and social experience: 'It makes you realise how you live your life in this very narrow corridor' (Sally, personal communication, October 23, 1998). For many of these students, the potential benefits of utilising the skills of community-based performers were evident for the first time in their years of training, the existence of these musical subcultures within Sydney having been beyond the scope of the students' previous social and educational experience. One of the major benefits of the project was perceived to be:

> just actually mixing with a part of society I had never had anything to do with before, because ... when I was growing up, "ethnic" music was their own thing and I never really saw a lot of it in concerts or public performances or anything. It was always behind the doors (Brooke, personal communication, October 15, 1998).

Students outlined their previous feelings of personal distance from music of cultural 'others':

> I sort of distanced — the first time I taught it on prac last year. I sort of just said, oh, this is music from other cultures. But when I did [the field project with a Papua New Guinean fusion band] I actually realised how much it does relate to us (Jenny, personal communication, October 8, 1998).

This was contrasted with the personal association created by their interactions with musicians within the community. Brooke, a clarinet player who had discovered that the father of one of her clarinet students was an accomplished Turkish musician who ran a private Turkish and Arabic music school, expressed this eloquently:

> [N]ow I was behind the doors in this group practising their music. ... opening my eyes up and making me think, yeah, there are all these different sorts of music and they're here and they're alive and they're accessible and I can use them (Brooke, personal communication, October 15, 1998).

The change in knowledge and attitudes developed through contact with a lived music experience in cultural context was so intense that it was described by one student as akin to 'a hit on the head' (Phil, personal communication, 1998). Students had a high level of personal engagement in the experience, leading to a greater understanding of music and culture:

> When you're there, you feel like you are from the culture and you're really experiencing it . ... I could write about what the culture was like when I was there but someone else wouldn't have the same feeling as when I was there. Listening to these Croatian voices, like, ringing in the room was just an incredible sound (Joanna, personal communication, October 6, 1998).

> You're going out, really — I guess you'd say living the culture ... Because I was there and was experiencing it, it was a personal experience. It was first hand and I was researching first hand what actually goes on and I think that was a lot more fascinating ... (Brooke, personal communication, October 15, 1998).

For a number of students, the immersion in the lives of informants also led to a much greater understanding of the personal, economic and political issues facing people within the Australian community, from recent immigrants to those of mixed descent. Perhaps most poignant were developing understandings about the lives of refugees, for whom music was a link to lost homelands and a means of maintaining identity and social cohesion amidst the sense of dispossession, economic hardship and loss.

The fieldwork project, for many students, promoted a greater commitment to a more pluralist approach to music programming in their future teaching:

41

> ... everyone is always talking about Australia is such a multicultural nation or whatever, and imagine not including that in your teaching. ... you've got to ... And this is a pretty new perspective for me (Anne Marie, personal communication, October 30, 1998).

Students also saw the necessity of continuing to utilise the field approach in order to increase their own knowledge and to create opportunities for school students that were similar to their own:

> I think the teacher really has to have a thorough understanding and a really great appreciation for that culture and be motivated to make the kids feel the same way. I don't think it's worth doing if you're going to get into it half-heartedly, so I would say if you're going to teach any music of another culture you would need some way to experience it first before you taught it (Joanna, personal communication, October 6, 1998).

> I think there is an assumption that the teacher knows everything, that the music teacher will know all there is to teach, but I certainly don't and I think that it would be a great resource to use those people within the school community to come in and teach about those things or even if I learn from them and can use them as a resource within the classroom. And also the students ... [can teach] each other, if they've got different cultures (Fiona, personal communication, October 27, 1998).

> I found that it's the one way I could really, I guess, live the topic. ... So I would definitely, definitely use that with a school group for my own purpose for finding out information for me and also having the kids maybe try something like that ... I think that's such a great way for them to find out for themselves (Brooke, personal communication, October 15, 1998).

For the latter student, the experience of going 'behind the doors' was an incentive to continue to engage with that culture:

> [T]here is that sort of connection that makes me keep thinking that, yeah, I would like to be involved in that: be a part of somebody's culture that I've never had an experience with and they are willing to have me as part of their culture (Brooke, personal communication, October 15, 1998).

Her engagement with the musical culture that had been the focus of her initial fieldwork project was continued by travelling to Turkey, her correspondence from Turkey indicating that her knowledge of the music (even in limited form) had acted as an entry point for cultural interchange in that country.

In recent years other Anglo-Australian students have demonstrated their ongoing commitment to the principles established during the project, either by successfully incorporating performers in residence from local communities into their school practicum programs or by supporting inclusion of community-based ensembles after gaining permanent teaching positions in schools. One student attested to the continuing value of her experiences within the course:

> I thought I'd email and let you know that I've just survived my first week as the music teacher at W Girls HS ... it's overwhelming. The school as you might know, ... is 97% NESB with over 60% Arabic. ... Out of the 250 new names, perhaps 15 are Anglo ... But I'm getting there — have a lot of help as you can imagine. Glad I did Multicultural Studies? ... you bet! The music department has no ensembles established though it does have a large Pacific Islander population in the school that organise their own singing and dancing. The staff are incredibly supportive and positive. I'm liking it very much (Katie, personal communication, February 6, 2003).

Bicultural Students' Rediscovery of Culture

In 1999, Chinese Australians formed a significant proportion of the students undertaking the course. The majority of these students, having been born in Australia, had a bicultural home life but many aspects of their parents' culture had been subsumed as they grew older, as a way of reducing the 'difference' between themselves and their peers. Most of these students did not speak their parents' first language and had studied music entirely within the western tradition, though they had been exposed to various forms of Chinese music at home.

For these students, the fieldwork project, often conducted with their parents or ethnic Chinese friends or relatives, opened a different set of doors towards a rediscovery of their partially obscured cultural heritage. The reflections of one such student, Hsu-Ming, expressed some of the changes in knowledge and attitudes brought about by the fieldwork experience with her mother, an ethnic Chinese woman born in the Philippines who had migrated to Australia as an adult:

> I am the first to admit that I do not know enough about my own cultural heritage. I knew enough beforehand to say that I was of a strange cultural mix (my mother's influences combined with my father's childhood in Shanghai, Hong Kong and later years travelling the world). This fieldwork collection immersed me into my mother's adolescent culture and allowed me to see what things shaped her in her youth. It also gave me an opportunity to find out about Taiwan and China in a broader historical context (extract from Hsu-Ming's assignment, 1999).

Hsu-Ming discussed the way in which she had come to appreciate music that had previously seemed 'a hilarious blend of trashy western harmonies and mushy Chinese singing', through researching the Taiwanese popular music and Cantopop that her mother enjoyed. In so doing, she discovered the value of such personal links in creating access to knowledge:

> I never dreamed of obtaining materials for teaching from such as source as my own mother. I can now say that is rather a confining view. The verbal and personal reactions and experiences of a person of the culture are just as valid as academic and formal reactions (extract from Hsu-Ming's assignment, 1999).

The experience also resulted in a greater understanding of her own personal and cultural identity:

> This ... has personally allowed me to place my own family's history into the broader framework of social and political events. I have a greater understanding of why my Taiwanese relatives decided to live there, and why my family has so much cultural diversity which has been passed on to my brother and myself. Stories that I have been told about Uncles, Aunts, my grandparents fit into a larger picture of the countries' histories and I feel richer for knowing these contexts ... (extract from Hsu-Ming's assignment, 1999).

Empowerment of Culture Bearers

Bicultural students in previous years had shared knowledge of their cultures anecdotally (for example, by helping with pronunciation and translation of songs in their first languages). However, it was not until 2000 that a number of bicultural students drew attention to their own active participation in music from their parents' birth cultures. For these students, the fieldwork project provided a forum in which to display an expertise that was not always evident in other academic areas, due in part to difficulties with English as a second language.

A Vietnamese Australian student, Tin, had learned the piano from an early age because there was no-one available at that time to teach her a Vietnamese instrument. In 1997 she had begun to study the Vietnamese 16 string zither, Dàn Tranh, at a Vietnamese community music school, although she had stopped learning the instrument in 1999 because of pressures of university study. Although there was strong bicultural maintenance at home, Tin saw her whole schooling process as assimilationist, in direct contrast to the tenets of the multicultural education policies previously discussed:

> ... from the education system you're just supposed to assimilate and learn what the other people are learning (Tin, personal communication, June 26, 2000).

She had not had any previous opportunities in a school or university context either to display or explore her Vietnamese cultural identity or to research

43

Vietnamese music. By contrast, she saw the fieldwork project as a vehicle through which she could highlight 'her music'. Tin's success in sharing her musical and cultural expertise was evident in the enthusiastic response to her presentation by her classmates. As she demonstrated performance characteristics and encouraged other students to discover playing techniques for themselves, the students were clearly engrossed in the learning process. Her confidence in answering questions from peers was supported by the research into her music that she had undertaken with the assistance of her zither teacher.

She commented that the project had given her the opportunity to explore the background to her music and culture in more detail. It had also provided her with the incentive to start learning the Dàn Tranh again:

> ... when I got the chance to do multicultural music I ... start[ed] playing, start[ed] learning again ... When I was researching I learned more about the music and the reason why we're actually playing the music. Before that [the teacher] used to tell us stories about the music but I never took it into consideration. I never thought it was that important. ... but when I did the research ... that got me thinking ... I thought that every piece of music ... plays a special part in Vietnamese musical culture (Tin, personal communication, June 26, 2000).

It was also clear that the form of the project had empowered Tin to succeed in an academic field where her difficulties with written English had often prevented her from doing well. In this case the doors had not only been opened to intercultural exchange but also to alternative ways of establishing and acknowledging different kinds of expertise in what was a largely monocultural institution. It was interesting to note that her increased confidence was reflected later in the year in a greatly improved performance in her teaching practicum, conducted with aplomb in a school with a highly diverse population.

Tin was able to generalise from her own experience as a culture bearer and to consider the implications for school students who were also culture bearers. In discussing her previous teaching practicum in a school with a large Vietnamese Australian student population, she clearly saw, in retrospect, the opportunities for empowerment of students that could be provided by inclusion of a music program utilising music of their own culture:

> It would have been good because then those students themselves could have told me a bit about their music and what they know about the music and maybe I could get them to understand about the music that their parents listen to ... I think they would have enjoyed it a bit more. Some children have English problems and they speak Vietnamese more fluently and maybe that would have helped them to actually enjoy music classes a bit more — something that they're familiar with and that they can teach others instead of teaching something that they don't quite understand ... they're happy to share their views [because they understand this] (Tin, personal communication, June 26, 2000).

More recently, a greater proportion of the students undertaking the course have been empowered to draw on their own cultural backgrounds, musical skills and expertise for their projects. Greek Australian students have demonstrated songs and dances learned in community schools, community events and Orthodox church gatherings that form part of their lives. Malay, Indonesian, Korean, Ukrainian and Maori students have acted as informants for other students' projects, confidently recording and performing songs learned as children or (in the case of the Ukrainian student) through a lengthy training process as a professional performer.

44

Conclusion

For the students engaged in the fieldwork projects these modes of learning have provided avenues to 'understanding ... the lived experience of people making music' (Titon, 1997, pp. 91–92) which completely changed their approach to the teaching of music from one of monoculturalism to pluralism. These experiences are transformational, particularly in regard to removing the boundaries between 'insider' and 'outsider' knowledge and power, in a manner described by Rice (1997) where the researcher and researched are 'potentially interchangeable' and 'capable of change through time, during the dialogues that typify the fieldwork experience' (p. 106).

However, in facilitating such projects, difficulties still arise and some questions remain unanswered. For example, the relative 'invisibility' of musicians working outside the cultural mainstream is problematic. The Turkish musician studied by one student in 1998 (and in subsequent years by other students) has run a number of Turkish music schools in different parts of Sydney since the late 1970s; has given sessions as a guest teacher in several schools; has performed in a variety of Turkish and fusion groups in Sydney schools, concerts and festivals; and has worked as a guest lecturer at the University of Sydney and University of Western Sydney for a number of years and yet he is still relatively unknown in the Sydney musical mainstream. In pondering such anomalies, it is tempting to assign the blame for this invisibility to the level of diversity of the Australian population as no one group is large enough to constitute an alternative, visible majority. Although the relative success of multiculturalism in Australia is attributed in part to this diversity (Collins, 1991), some of the criticisms levelled at multiculturalism, for example, lack of equal distribution of power and non-permeation of the social, cultural and political mainstream by ethnic groups (Jamrozik, Boland, & Urquhart, 1995) may be reflected in the microcosm of musical life in Australia.

It is to be hoped, therefore, that projects such as this may, in some small way, create avenues for decreasing invisibility and enabling musicians from the broad spectrum of ethnic groups represented within the Austalian community to emerge at least into the educational mainstream. Students have been able to open pathways through cultural barriers that were previously seen as impenetrable and to explore the cultural and musical identities of both themselves and others, in so doing, discovering that diverse groups 'do not merely co-exist but interact' (Reyes Schramm, 1982). Through making personal connections with members of hitherto unknown or unexplored musical cultures, students have been able to broaden possibilities for future musical exchange and growth of musical knowledge and to directly establish the importance of enabling culture-bearers to take a collaborative role in implementing music education in schools.

References

Allan, R., & Hill, B. (1995). Multicultural education in Australia: Historical development and current status. In J. A. Banks & C. A. M. Banks (Eds.), *Handbook of research on multicultural education* (pp. 763–777). New York: Macmillan.

Anderson, W., & Campbell, P. S. (Eds.). (1996). *Multicultural perspectives in music education* (2nd ed.). Reston, VA: MENC.

Biernoff, L., & Blom, D. (2000, July). *Crossing boundaries: Musical and educational aspects of cultural exchange within two non-Western ensembles in a university music performance program.* Paper presented at the ISME Commission on the Education of the Professional Musician Seminar, Cape Breton.

Board of Studies NSW. (1999a). *Stage 6 syllabus music 1: Preliminary and HSC courses.* Sydney: Author.

Board of Studies NSW. (1999b). *Stage 6 syllabus music 2: Preliminary and HSC courses.* Sydney: Author.

Board of Studies NSW. (2000). *Creative arts K-6 syllabus.* Sydney: Author.

Board of Studies NSW. (2003). *Music mandatory and elective courses: Years 7-10 syllabus.* Sydney: Author.

Campbell, P. S. (1991). *Lessons from the world: A cross-cultural guide to music teaching and learning.* New York: Schirmer.

Campbell, P. S. (2004). *Teaching music globally: Experiencing music, expressing culture.* New York: Oxford University Press.

Campbell, P. S., McCullough-Brabson, E., & Tucker, J. C. (1994). *Roots and branches: A legacy of multicultural music for children.* Danbury, CT: World Music Press.

Collins, J. (1991). *Migrant hands in a distant land* (2nd ed.). Leichhardt, NSW: Pluto Press.

Cooley, T. F. (1997). Casting shadows in the field: An introduction. In G. F. Barz & T. J. Cooley (Eds.), *Shadows in the field: New perspectives for fieldwork in ethnomusicology* (pp. 3–19). New York: Oxford University Press.

Dunbar-Hall, P. (1997). Problems and solutions in the teaching of Aboriginal and Torres Strait Islander music. In E. Gifford, A. Brown, & A. Thomas (Eds.), *New sounds for a new century. Proceedings of the 30th National Conference of the Australian Society for Music Education* (pp. 81–87). Brisbane: ASME.

Dunbar-Hall. (2000). Concept or context? Teaching and learning Balinese gamelan and the universalist-pluralist debate. *Music Education Research, 2*(2), 127–139.

Edwards, K. L. (1996, March). *Cultural perceptions of fourth-grade students toward American Indians and their music.* Paper presented at the MENC Social Sciences SRIG Session, Music Educators National Conference, Kansas City.

Hookey, M. (1994). Culturally responsive music education: Implications for curriculum development and implementation. In H. Lees (Ed.), *Musical connections: Tradition and change. Proceedings of the 21st World Conference of the International Society for Music Education* (pp. 84–91). Auckland: ISME.

Jamrozik, A., Boland, C., & Urquhart, R. (1995). *Social change and cultural transformation in Australia.* Cambridge: Cambridge University Press.

Klinger, R. (1994). Multiculturalism in music education: Authenticity versus practicality. In H. Lees (Ed.), *Musical connections: Tradition and change. Proceedings of the 21st World Conference of the International Society for Music Education* (pp. 91–104). Auckland: ISME.

Lundquist, B. R. (2002). Music, culture, curriculum and instruction. In R. Colwell & C. Richardson (Eds.), *The new handbook of research in music teaching and learning* (pp. 626–647). New York: Oxford University Press.

Lundquist, B., & Szego, C. K. (Eds.). (1998). *Musics of the world's cultures: A source book for music educators.* Reading, UK: ISME/ CIRCME.

NSW Department of Education. (1983). *Multicultural education policy statement.* Sydney: Author.

Reimer, B. (1994). Can we understand music of foreign cultures? In H. Lees (Ed.), *Musical connections: Tradition and change. Proceedings of the 21st World Conference of the International Society for Music Education* (pp. 227–245). Auckland: ISME.

Reimer, B. (Ed.). (2002). *World musics and music education: Facing the issues.* Reston, VA: MENC.

Reyes Schramm, A. (1982). Explorations in urban ethnomusicology: Hard lessons from the spectacularly ordinary. *Yearbook for Traditional Music, 14,* 1–13.

Rice, T. (1997). Toward a mediation of field methods and field experience in ethnomusicology. In G. F. Barz & T. J. Cooley (Eds.), *Shadows in the field: New perspectives for fieldwork in ethnomusicology* (pp. 87–100). New York: Oxford University Press.

Schippers, H. (1996). Teaching world music in the Netherlands: Towards a model for cultural diversity in music education. *International Journal of Music Education, 27*, 16–23.

Solis, T. (2004). *Performing ethnomusicology: Teaching and representation in world music ensembles.* Berkely and Los Angeles: University of California Press.

Standley, J. M. (2000). Increasing prospective music educators' tolerance for student diversity. *Update: Applications of Research in Music Education, 19*, 27–32.

Teicher, J. M. (1997). Effect of multicultural music experience on preservice elementary teachers' attitudes. *Journal of Research in Music Education, 45*(3), 415–427.

Titon, J. T. (1997). Knowing fieldwork. In G. F. Barz & T. J. Cooley (Eds.), *Shadows in the field: New perspectives for fieldwork in ethnomusicology* (pp. 101–120). New York: Oxford University Press.

Walker, R. (1996). Music education freed from colonialism: A new praxis. *International Journal of Music Education, 27*, 2–15.

York, F. A., & Choksy, L. (1994). Developing a culturally appropriate music curriculum for Torres Strait Island schools. In H. Lees (Ed.), *Musical connections: Tradition and change. Proceedings of the 21st World Conference of the International Society for Music Education* (pp. 111–119). Auckland: ISME.

DR KATHRYN MARSH is Chair of Music Education at the Sydney Conservatorium of Music, University of Sydney, where she teaches subjects relating to primary and early childhood music education, multicultural music education and music education research methods. Her research interests include children's musical play, children's creativity, and multicultural and Aboriginal music education. She has written a variety of scholarly and professional publications and has been actively involved in curriculum development and teacher training for many years. She has been the recipient of major national research grants which have involved large scale international crosscultural collaborative research into children's musical play in Australia, Europe, the United Kingdom, the United States and Korea.

47

48

Musical Vernaculars as a Starting Point: Inspiration for Creative Composition in Formal and Informal Educational Environments

Jolyon Laycock

Many composers and musical animateurs have discussed the potency of traditional musical forms as a starting point for creative work in music. A hundred years ago, Zoltan Kodály emphasised the importance of Magyar traditional songs and dances in his educational work in Hungary. More recently Keith Swanwick, John Paynter and George Odam in Britain have discussed the importance of beginning music education from a known tradition of music. The work of Professor Nigel Osbourne with young people in Sarajevo suffering from war trauma relies fundamentally on music drawn from a rich indigenous tradition of Balkan folk music.

But the world is divided into the 'haves' and the 'have nots'. Paradoxically, many of those nations, which are richest in financial capital, have lost or squandered the less tangible cultural capital of their living and vital indigenous musical traditions. Is it too late for affluent western nations to rediscover their native musical traditions and to benefit again from the resulting cultural and historical continuity, the sense of belonging and identity, and the ability to unite communities across generations? Can commercial popular musical cultures and idioms fill the vacuum, as George Odam (1995) argued that they could? Are all native musical traditions in danger of being corrupted, dumbed down and finally overwhelmed by the forces of globalisation?

There are many composers, particularly in Britain, who, taking up the challenge of pioneers like Kodály (1974), have chosen to 'render their art accessible to as many people as possible' (p. 185) by working in schools, community centres, hospitals, old people's homes and many other contexts. Working from a variety of philosophical or political standpoints these composers have departed from the 19th century romantic view of the 'heroic' composer, creating music as an expression of his own inner emotional life, and moved towards a more socially conscious and less self-obsessed idea of the composer as inspirational catalyst whose role is to stimulate musical creativity in other people (Tippett, 1974, p. 184).

This implies a thorough rethinking of pedagogical strategy. In this context, it is interesting to recall that the educationalist Basil Bernstein (1971) used 'weak' and 'strong' as terms in what has come to be known as the Bernstein diagram.

49

This is an orthogonal matrix of which the two axes are labelled 'classification' and 'framing' (see Figure 1).

Classification is concerned with the subject matter to be taught. Framing with the approach to teaching. Strong framing can be defined as 'instruction'; weak framing as 'encounter'. The teacher either instructs us in rules and facts (strong framing), or provides us with examples and leaves us to find out for ourselves (weak framing). It could be argued that the difference between strong and weak framing is the same as the difference between formal and informal educational contexts. The formal classroom is the proper place for an instructional strong framing approach; weak framing encounter situations are appropriate to the more relaxed atmosphere of informal after-school clubs and societies. In the case of music strong classification means that the choice of musical style or idiom is determined by the teacher, in other words the teaching is 'repertoire-based'. Weak classification means that the choice of musical idiom is left to the pupil, in other words the teaching is 'child-centred'.

Many leading figures in classical music, including Peter Maxwell Davies (in his Royal Philharmonic Society Lecture, 2005), have commented on the challenges this produces for western classical music in schools, as well as influential authors such as Christopher Small (1977). Music educationalists such as John Paynter or George Odam wanted to find a way of bringing a meaningful experience of music education to the majority of pupils by looking for an alternative starting point. Odam is perhaps one of the chief proponents of the child-centred approach to music education. As Odam (1995) commented:

> The matter of musical styles is largely immaterial except in the sense that pupils need to have a wide experience of styles. ... Teaching should always progress from the known to the unknown. ... Children's creative work must stem from the musical languages with which they feel comfortable: style in musical composition should normally be the choice of the child (p. 56).

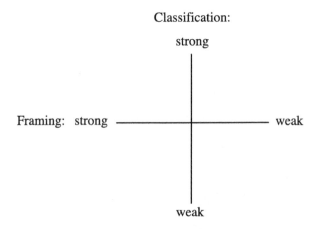

FIGURE 1
Bernstein diagram.

For Odam (1995) the use of musical vernaculars like rhythm-and-blues, reggae, soul and ballad was therefore of utmost importance as a point of departure: 'There should be a focus on the music of today's society, not defined exclusively as the music of today's youth culture, which is too particular, and largely ephemeral, but emphasising the foundations of music that is popular generally' (p. 56).

It is interesting to examine the historical processes by which we have arrived at the standpoint adopted by Odam. Let us return for a moment to Kodály. Early in the 20th century, he advocated the use of musical material from the indigenous folk tradition as the single most important starting point for the musical training of Hungarian children. He wanted to 'make the masterpieces of world (musical) literature public property, to convey them to people of every kind and rank' but he set folk music at the centre of his approach to musical education (Járdányi, 1966, pp. 11–24).

> Anyone for whom the treasury of folk songs is not a dead museum but a living culture, which has only been checked in its development, will peruse even such unassuming tunes as these with the excitement of constant discovery. They are full of bustling life; a child's imagination and ingenuity clothing some simple basic forms into a thousand guises (Kodály, 1974, p. 53).

According to Kodály 'the first musical language a child must learn is his own', but what was his own language? Even in those early days, the task was not a straightforward one, for most town children brought 'another kind of music from home'. Already forms of popular and commercial music were driving out indigenous Hungarian folk music from its previously held central position in national cultural life. Even then children had to relearn their musical mother language, forgotten by their parents. The champions of the Kodály method have made great claims on its behalf, supported no doubt by its success in Hungary and other east European countries. Cecilia Vajda's book *The Kodály Way to Music* was launched in Britain in 1974 with a foreword by Yehudi Menuhin.

It is difficult now to take this book seriously as a teaching aid. British school children will not find any useful point of contact. Kodály's method was based on taking, as a starting point, tunes and musical games the children already knew, or which were at least part of a musical tradition they or their parents had only recently lost touch with. Throughout most of England and, I venture to suggest, most of western Europe as well, we have lost touch with almost all of our indigenous folk tradition, and, regrettably, the only sources of musical material now familiar to most people come from popular culture available in the mass media. It seems we can only make something like the Kodály method work if we substitute material taken from those kinds of sources. Even in 1961 Kodály was aware of the threat to his beloved folk tradition: 'Little by little, all over the world, folk music will be destroyed by technical and social development and the expansion of civilisation. Mechanical music penetrates the life of even the most hidden villages'.

51

Globalisation

Since then, the globalisation of musical culture has continued unabated. It is perhaps as much if not more to blame for the eclipsing of the European classical tradition lamented by Maxwell Davies, at least in the United Kingdom, than faults in the education system. I suspect it may not matter what educational methodology we use. We are battling against a tide of history.

In fact, globalisation presents a complicated picture: some 'local' musics have become 'global'. Pop music of primarily Anglo-American and Afro-Caribbean origin now dominate the global music market. It has become the greatest threat to the regional diversity of all musical styles, and not just to the European classical tradition, which was perhaps its greatest rival for global domination. I do not wish to criticise the music itself because of any intrinsic qualities, nor necessarily to question the skill and integrity of those who make it, but rather to draw attention to the exploitative nature of the commercial forces that control its dissemination. It certainly risks destroying many other ethnic traditions. But some of these have themselves become briefly global: nine-day wonders on a tide of fashion that represented the downside of a process that has been dubbed 'glocalisation' (Robertson, 1994).

One such example is Bulgarian music, as exemplified by Mystère des Voix Bulgares, which is a striking example of a regional music transformed to be marketed in the West. My visits to Bulgaria during a creative music project as part of the Rainbow Across Europe program showed me how effectively the country has until recently managed to ward off the global threat to its folk culture at a local level. Recently set free from the puritanical constraints of former Communist governments, the signs of a people enjoying social liberation are all about you. In most large towns, clubs and discotheques pound out English and American rap music till the small hours, and the shopping streets are becoming depressingly full of branches of McDonalds and The Body Shop. But the hedonistic pursuit of these manifestations of 'global culture' coexists with traditional culture.

My visits to the southern city of Plovdiv in 1999 revealed folk music that was still very much alive, rubbing shoulders with mass-oriented, commercialised popular music. The same youngsters who were bopping to four-in-a-bar rap music till the small hours were enthusiastically giving up several nights a week or large parts of their weekends to play or sing traditional music to the highest standards. It was taught in the schools to enthusiastic children who would just as soon spend a couple of hours singing and playing together on traditional folk instruments as kicking a ball round the playground. They encountered traditional modes, melodic forms and the mind-bending rhythmic complexity of additive time signatures.

What lies behind the enviable success of nations like Bulgaria in preserving their folk traditions, and how long can this last? Today, the former Communist regimes of the countries of the Soviet block are reviled by many of those who lived under them. One of the few positive legacies was the state's support of folk culture, especially music. There is an ever-present danger that, with the rejection of Communism and the rush to embrace the western consumerist way of life, all values that were associated with the old regime, including the state patronage of folk culture, will be thrown out. I have not been back since 1999. If I return will I still find the same commitment, the same enthusiasm? I hope so. A cultural form that has such a firm hold on a nation's psyche should be hard to dislodge. This devotion to folk music is an aspect of Balkan life from which we, as apparently 'culturally dominant' western Europeans, can learn an important lesson.

In Bulgaria, at least, folk music and dance are still supported by state patronage at various schools and conservatoires such as the National Academy of Folk Music and Dance Art in Plovdiv. Professor Nikolay Stoykov, former Head of the Department of Folk Music, is a composer who forged a personal style steeped in the

52

melodies and rhythms of Bulgarian folk music, successfully integrating them into the context of a dissonant contemporary idiom using proportional notation and indeterminate scoring. He applied it equally to works for professional ensembles and orchestras, and to a vast repertoire of music for young people. Typical is his *Ala bala nica*, a divertimento for children's choir, piano and percussion based on a Bulgarian folktale. This sparse score makes effective use of silence between fractured gestures, and dramatic climaxes built out of accumulations of simple diatonic ostinati.

Musical Meetings

In Bulgaria, the Kodály philosophy can still work. In Plovdiv, we could and did use the folk tradition as the starting point for a creative project since it was, in a real sense, the pupils' own music. Thus 180 young people of ages varying from 8 to 20 worked together for 10 days in a creative project led by British composer Barry Russell and five members of the Cornelius Cardew Ensemble. It was managed and coordinated jointly by the White, Green and Red Jazz Formation and my own organisation, Rainbow Over Bath. Taking part were two youth choirs, two folk orchestras, an accordion band, a boys choir and youngsters from an institution for abandoned street children. The project took place within a framework devised by Russell based on the myth of Orpheus whose traditional birthplace, Thrace, is the modern day province of Trakia of which Plovdiv is the capital.

Barry Russell called on his own large repertoire of well-tried compositional devices designed to generate impressive and effective-sounding musical textures with simple means, while still allowing maximum flexibility for the display of individual skill and virtuosity on the part of the participants. The Cardew Ensemble is a team of musicians who are well used to working together on creative projects of this kind, and although we were working with young people who spoke a completely unfamiliar foreign language, the truth of the assertion that music is a universal language, able to transcend cultural and international boundaries, was abundantly demonstrated. All members of our team made some attempt to learn Bulgarian, a gesture which was appreciated by our hosts, and helped further to cement the 'entente cordiale'.

Thus the sounds and colours of Bulgarian folk instruments and the open-throated Bulgarian singing style enriched and coloured the improvisational techniques and aleatoric compositional devices of Russell's music to create sonic textures into which Bulgarian and British folk melodies were woven.

We were impressed by the level of instrumental and vocal skill of the Bulgarian children and students, most of whom were fluent in the folk-idioms of their country. At one school, whenever members of the school's folk band had a break in their rehearsal timetable, they filled it, not by running out in the playground to kick a ball but by organising impromptu jam sessions on traditional gadulkas, rebecs, kavals and timbura in any convenient corner of the school they could find.

Rituals for Orpheus was covered by Bulgarian National Television and later broadcast as a 45-minute documentary. I am sure that the presence of the television cameras at the final performance was a further encouragement to the participants to give it their best shot, but even if the cameras had not been there, the presence of an audience of over 2000 people in the wonderful setting of the ancient ruins of the open-air Roman amphitheatre would have assured the same level of commitment.

53

White, Green and Red Jazz Formation were at the time collaborating with the women's vocal quartet Vai Doudoulay in a very unusual fusion of jazz-rock idiom with Bulgarian folk-singing. The different perceptions which Bulgarian and British audiences had of these cultural fusions was instructive. When White, Green and Red played in their own country, audiences wanted to hear an imitation of funky jazz-rock in 4/4 time in a British/American style familiar to western audiences. But when the band visited Britain, audiences here wanted to hear those Bulgarian modes and additive time-values, something at which the Bulgarians were experts, but which stretched the capabilities of British musicians. *Samba in 7/8*, a track from the group's CD, is just one of many compelling examples (Vai Doudoulei & White, Green and Red, 1998).

Purists might object vehemently to this hybridisation of musical forms. Do such fusion experiments in themselves risk polluting the purity of the original folk idiom, thus bringing about its destruction just as surely as the globalised commercial forces I have just been denouncing? White, Green and Red have indeed been criticised for doing just that. But I take the view that music, like all the other arts, must grow and develop in order to remain vital and alive.

What possible starting point for creative music-making can we substitute in most other countries of western Europe? The Irish, the Scots, the Spanish and the Fins are especially privileged. They still have their unique cultural capital to spend. The rest of us squandered it years ago. The following incident serves to exemplify this point. The score of *Rituals for Orpheus* incorporated the British folk song melody *The Lark in the Clean Air*. I choose this example because it exemplifies what strikes me as a basic truth of human nature. We all have a fascination for the exotic. The Bulgarians were beguiled by this sinuous tune from another country, and thought it just as exotic as we might regard a Bulgarian melody. For them this strange and haunting melody from a distant misty island was charged with all the same kind of romance with which we invest *Mystère des Voix Bulgares*. Yet a straw poll among British students at a seminar in Bath revealed that none of them knew the melody or had even heard of it although its sinuous beauty might hopefully at least briefly affect them. The true irony of the situation is that *The Lark in the Clean Air* is an Irish melody. Russell did not choose to incorporate a folk song from his own country of England, let alone one from his native Yorkshire.

Popular Music Forms as Starting Points for Creative Music-Making

Do the various manifestations of globalised mass popular musical forms really represent the only available material from which we can begin our voyage of discovery into the musical unknown? Rainbow Over Bath projects like Igor's Boogie tackled the issue head on by inviting youngsters to choose a favourite pop song as a starting point. Devised in collaboration with the Composers Ensemble, and led by composers Deirdre Gribbin and Philip Cashian in March 1999, it was designed as a holistic project with educational workshops, concerts of children's compositions and a final professional concert with first performances of commissioned works. The project was related to a concert by the Composers Ensemble in which the program consisted of musical treatments of popular music by established contemporary composers. During the education project, school pupils took a favourite pop song as the starting point for their own compositions.

54

The inspiration for Igor's Boogie came from the music of Frank Zappa. The educational workshops were weak as to classification in that they used vernacular musical idioms as a starting point. The aim was to progress towards a strong outcome in the sense of encouraging children to compose music in a contemporary style. The opportunity to encounter several excellent models of such a process being used by professional composers was given in the final concert (Stage D in the Paynter model).

The project took its methodology from John Paynter and Peter Aston's (1970) book *Sound and Silence* with its four-phase model designed to encourage children first to create their own music by following a particular process. At the end of the creative process they encounter music written by one or more professional contemporary composers (perhaps including the work of the composer leading the project) that has been created following a similar process, the presumption being that the children are more likely to understand the 'difficult' new music they are hearing if they have had some hands-on experience of the processes behind its creation.

Great claims have been made for this approach, but does it really work? In the case of Igor's Boogie many of the results were in fact strongly influenced by the personality and creative imagination of the class teacher. No bad thing that! The problem with this project was that few of the pupils who took part in the creative part of the project actually turned up at the professional concert in which they were intended to encounter this 'new music'. Were the composers themselves really committed to the 'popular' music they were using as their own starting point?

Was the project based on a valid conception? In the hands of professional composers such as John Woolrich or Deirdre Gribbin, the outcome of a musical process based on treatment of a favourite piece of popular music was unmistakably their work, recognisable by hallmarks of style. However, to the children taking part in the project, the work of these composers was unknown, and their style unfamiliar. Would the fact that these pieces grew out of treatments of popular material in itself make the end result any more accessible to the young people, even if they had attended the final concert? Or were the Composers Ensemble guilty of the same lack of coherent rationale discussed by Julia Winterson (1998, p. 200) who suggests that the whole procedure may be some kind of cynical ploy to beguile young people into the concert hall merely to boost the audience ratings? On the other hand, if the end-product of a creative process based on treatments of familiar popular material sounds like another piece of pop music, then there has been no progression and the process has been of little value, unless the aim actually was to reinforce the desire of the boys to become a mini James Blunt and the girls to be just like Kelly Clarke in a kind of glorified karaoke machine masquerading as education and legitimised by a travesty of modern educational theory.

55

Finding Balanced Approaches

For some composer/animateurs, the exploitative nature of the world of popular music may rule it out as a legitimate starting point for creative music-making on moral grounds. Some project leaders may decide to adopt a pragmatic attitude, as Paynter (1982) advocated, allowing teenagers to play and sing in a style which they know and understand to begin with: 'They will tend to have pronounced likes and dislikes and their first need will be to be able to play and sing what they like, in a style as near as possible to the model they admire' (p. 116). Only later will they draw the pupils away from familiar ground, opening their ears to a wider experience of music in all its multiplicity of forms.

For others, the commercialism of popular music may present an insurmountable ideological barrier. They must look for other living traditions of music present in our society which are still close to their 'grass roots', or spring 'from the soil' in some way, and possess something that can be defined as genuine 'soul'. Such thinking has led to the widespread adoption of African drumming rhythms and chants, rhythms borrowed from Bhangra disco, salsa, samba, reggae and many other popular forms, as well as Indonesian Gamelan, not only as the starting point but sometimes as the central raison-d'être for creative music projects.

But perhaps the most important phrase among the quotations from Odam (1995) is 'proceed from the known to the unknown' (p. 56). If we do not 'proceed' we have not 'progressed'. Education is all about 'progression': progression from a state of ignorance to a state of knowledge and understanding. As Murray Schafer (1975) said in one of his famous maxims: 'a class should be an hour of a thousand discoveries' (pp. 132–133). If our finishing point is the same as our starting point, then there has been no progression. Nothing new has been learned. There has been no education. Perhaps it does not really matter where we start from, as long as we start from somewhere.

When it comes down to it, then, good teaching, and by inference, good leadership of community music groups, is bound to be fundamentally instructional and repertoire-based in motivation, even if it uses encounter and child- or person-centred approaches along the way. In the end we need, as musical animateurs and teachers, to find a balanced approach. I characterise this in terms of a modification of the Bernstein diagram that, by thickening the axes, becomes three-dimensional. Strong has not one opposite but two: weak or 'closed', where closed is the negative aspect of strong. Likewise weak has not one opposite but two: strong or 'open', where open is the positive aspect of weak.

The dichotomy now emerges as more complex. Maxwell Davies may be right when he accuses British orchestras of 'feebleness' in their education outreach. But what is required is not a return to the bad old days of closed and doctrinaire rule-based teaching. Instead we need to seek out that 'openness' of approach that is summed up in Murray-Schafer's (1975) exhortation: 'A class should be an hour of a thousand discoveries' (pp. 132–133).

This, I believe, to be our mission as composers. It is to inspire musical creativity in other people, both by example, and by working directly as animateurs. We may be encouraged by the inspirational example of Kodály, but the task is not an easy one. It requires great skill and knowledge, and above all qualities of inspirational leadership. As Gillian Perkins (1990–1998) once wrote in one of her evaluation reports on the PRS Composer in Education scheme 'Composers have to be rather special people'.

56

References

Bernstein, B. (1971). *Class, codes & control* (Vol. 1). London: Routledge & Kegan Paul.

Járdányi, P. (1961). Folk music in musical education. In S. Frigyes (Ed.), *Musical education in Hungary* (pp. 11–24). London: Barry & Rockcliffe.

Kodály, Z. (1974). *Selected writings*. London: Boosey & Hawkes.

Laycock, J. (2005). *A changing role for the composer in society.* Bern: Peter Lang A.G.

Odam, G. (1995). *The sounding symbol.* London: Nelson Thornes.

Paynter, J., & Aston, P. (1970). *Sound and silence.* Cambridge: University Press.

Paynter, J. (1982). *Music in the secondary school curriculum.* Cambridge: Cambridge University Press.

Perkins, G. (1990–1998). *Composer in education evaluation reports.* London: Performing Right Society.

Robertson, R. (1994). *Globalization: Social theory and global culture.* London: Sage.

Schafer, R. M. (1975). *The rhinoceros in the classroom.* Wien: Universal Edition.

Small, C. (1977). *Music society education.* Hanover: Wesleyan University Press.

Swanwick, K. (1988). *Music mind and education.* London: Routledge.

Tippett, M. (1974). *Moving into Aquarius.* St Albans: Granada.

Vájdá, C. (1974). *The Kodály way to music.* London: Boosey & Hawkes.

Winterson, J. (1998). *The community education work of orchestras and opera companies – Principles, practice and problems.* York: University of York.

JOLYON LAYCOCK was born in Bath in 1946 and studied music at the University of Nottingham. During the 70s he pursued a freelance career as an experimental artist working with sound based at Birmingham Arts Laboratory and Spectro Arts Workshop in Newcastle on Tyne. From 1979 to 1989 he was Music and Dance Co-ordinator at Arnolfini, Bristol. As a concert promoter, his programs for the Arnolfini, and for Rainbow Over Bath at the University of Bath and Bath Spa University College from 1989 to 2000, were regarded as among the most innovative outside London. Rainbow Over Bath twice won the PRS Award for Enterprise. In 1996 Laycock initiated Rainbow Across Europe, a network of concert organisations in France, the Netherlands, Austria, Bulgaria and Hungary funded by the European Union Kaleidoscope Fund. He left the University of Bath in 2000 to complete his doctoral thesis at York, *A Changing Role for the Composer in Society,* now published as a book by Peter Lang A.G., Switzerland. He was appointed Lecturer in Arts Management and Administration in the School of Arts and Humanities at Oxford Brookes University in December 2004.

This article is based on the findings of a series of practice-based creative music projects with children and young people, conducted since 1996 in collaboration with educational and music promoting institutions in France, the Netherlands, Austria, Hungary and Bulgaria, and most recently with Chinese musicians in the United Kingdom. The projects were led by a number of composer/animateurs including Sean Gregory, Peter Wiegold, Deirdre Gribbin, Nikolay Stoykov, Tunde Jegede and Jolyon Laycock. The program was undertaken under the auspices of Rainbow Over Bath, based at Bath University and Bath Spa University College, and by its successor organisation The Rainbow Foundation, with funds from the EU Kaleidosope Fund, the British Council, Arts Council England, and Youth Music. The research continues at Oxford Brookes, but the findings up to 2002 are discussed in Laycock's (2005) book *A Changing Role for the Composer in Society.*

Prospects and Challenges of Teaching and Learning Musics of the World's Cultures: An African Perspective

Rose Omolo-Ongati

Teaching and learning of musics of the world's cultures has been at the core of debate by music educationalists, music artists and scholars in other fields (anthropology), the world over. The issues of concept, content and context, methodology, resources, human expertise, facilities, style/idiom, and curriculum development have engaged the minds of many scholars, yielding diversified perspectives and beliefs on the viability of teaching and learning world musics. These issues have been problematic to the extent that some scholars have passed a death sentence on the subject as an over-ambitious endeavour that cannot be achieved, contending that the world cannot be referred to as a global village (Kofie, 2004). Some have claimed that musics of cultures foreign to us cannot be understood easily, if at all. Others believe that because of the diversity and uniqueness that exists within cultures where these musics come from, there can never be a universal approach to the teaching of musics of the world's cultures, not even developing some respect and admiration, an attitude referred to by Elliott (1990) as 'cultural democracy'. They wonder whether world music does more to promote or erase musical diversity. Others complicate matters even more by bringing in the cultural nuances of context and association, claiming that teaching a piece of music to a non-native audience without reference to the social situation and context in which the music was born is a complete mockery of that connection. They see 'indigenisation' as a response to globalisation; a resistance to cultural imperialism and essentialising tropes of homogeneity. These people also hold an emic view that music is bound to culture and that no-one outside that culture can penetrate it. According to them, music should not be a commodity but should be in its very essence communal, spiritual and a totally shared experience. Keil (1994) supports this view when he proclaims that there should not be a music industry. He insists that music should not be written or mechanically reproduced and mass mediated. It should exist live, for the moment, in present time and the makers should be rewarded with happiness and barter-like reciprocation.

There are, however, others who see great potential and prospects in the teaching and learning of world musics. Current developments in the social, political and economic life of peoples around the globe have created fresh awareness of the considerable diversity and diffusion of cultures. The confrontation and convergence of cultures has become inevitable due to the tremendous speed of modern technologies that continually reduce the globe in size. Consequently, the musics of the world have combined with each other — with elements of melody, rhythm, harmony, performance practice, instruments combining to produce new kinds of music appealing to a large multicultural audience (Nettl, 1998, p. 23). As a result, the ever-growing clarity of ethnic boundaries and cultural distinctions have fertilised aspirations for sociopolitical autonomies — a condition that has also created the need to build channels of communication, not from a hegemonic perspective, but on principles of equality, respect and understanding (Santos, 1994, p. 25).

People travel across and beyond national boundaries. In the same way, music travels and is continually being created, recreated, modified/refashioned, adapted and reinterpreted, transcending the limits of local culture and the personal self. This has made the musics of world cultures more readily available to most people through the mass media, so we come to learn about the culture of other people mediated through television, which act as a cultural stage.

Whether the motivation is searching for a supplement to add to one's culture, expanding the notion of music, providing a platform for minorities and majorities to interact through musical activities, or encouraging a form of exchange in order to create a new expression, world music as a global phenomenon is a reality with which we have to contend. Our increasing awareness of cultural variation in musical practices and the rate of global musical interaction force us to reconsider how to respond to these developments. Therefore, denying the existence of world music is refusing to see the reality.

This article discusses the prospects and challenges of teaching and learning music of the world's cultures by attempting to answer the following questions:

- How can music be understood and appreciated outside its cultural context?
- How do we make a case for studying and teaching a specific musical culture?
- When music travels and is used for teaching in a decontextualised context, how should the music be transmitted or handed down to the learners? Should traditional formats of instruction be maintained?

An African Perspective on Music-Making

African music arises naturally and spontaneously from the functions of everyday life. There are functional roles that connect music to the daily lives of those composing, performing or listening to it, giving it cultural integrity. Consequently African music represents an extremely 'high context culture' closely tied to the particularities of place and time. The contexts of performance dictate the content, venue and participants of a particular musical genre. Music is seen in terms of its role and meaning in society.

The aim of African music has always been to translate the experience of life and of the spiritual world into sound, enhancing and celebrating life through cradle songs, songs of reflection, historical songs, fertility songs, songs about death and mourning, and other song varieties (Bebey, 1969). Musical practice is therefore linked to musical beliefs and musical beliefs are specific to and determined by the culture in which they arise. Music is closely bound up with the details of daily living and is interwoven with every part of an African life. Elliott (1994) observes that music is something that people do and make in relation to standards of informed musical and cultural practice — it is a diverse human practice. African music is considered good when it achieves its utilitarian objectives, that is, the purpose for which it was meant.

Music is culturally cultivated. In African communities, the selection and use of any component of musical vocabulary, like rhythm, is bounded by ethnicity. Music-making is essentially a matter of knowing how to construct musical sound patterns in relation to the traditions and standards of particular musical practices (Elliott, 1994, p. 12). Individuals whose musical experiences are rooted in a particular society naturally develop standard musical responses based on the collective experience of that society. These collective experiences are in most cases circumscribed by tradition and history. Consequently the boundaries of musical culture are defined and preserved by their contextual association and mode of application within that cultural matrix (Anku, 1998, p. 75).

African musical forms are formed out of a spiritual impulse. Spirituality is its core and power. The essence of a particular musical form outlines the style/idiom. So, one can tamper with the forms in order to maintain the spirit. Okumu (2005) maintains that it is more important to preserve the spirituality in African music than the tunes, because that is what forms the basis of the discipline. Recognition of the main pulse and timeline in African music is therefore an important aspect to consider when teaching this music to non-native learners. The rhythmic aspect of African music is so intricate that various scholars (Chernoff, 1979; Tracey, 1986) have described the rhythm as 'crossing' and 'conflicting' respectively. Looked at critically, African rhythms do not conflict and they do not cross. Nzewi (1997) says that the term 'cross rhythm' is misinforming and inappropriate. He asserts that the idea of crossing implicates movements in contrary or opposing directions, and adds that a community/family/team does not work together at cross-purposes. The rhythm is a musical structure, which has depth essence and derives from the African philosophy of inter-independence in human relationships. The rhythms do not go against the main pulse, but fall within it. They are therefore complementary and not conflicting together as Tracey (1986) proclaims. One thing that needs to be clear is that in African music, simple times have their interfaces in compound times. Within a performance in 4/4, one is able to play rhythmic patterns or dance in 12/8. The 12/8 is therefore an interface of 4/4 since the 4/4 metre has the same pulse feeling as 12/8 in performance. The structural combination of a pattern in common metre 4/4 with a pattern in compound metre 12/8 is rationalised and performed in the African thought perspective as two with three, an inter-rhythm that normatively implicates tonal depth (Nzewi, 1997, p. 40). This is why an identification of the pulse is paramount in African music. An African is used to timbres that contrast rather than blend. Doubling of parts in instrumental performance is not an African practice.

Blacking (1977) maintains that music-making is a symbolic expression of socio-cultural organisation, which reflects the value and the past and present ways of life of the human being who creates it. Omondi (1992) supports Blacking when he observes that African musics and dances arise directly from the life of an African society, and are performed to express shared values. This means that the genres nearly always carry some information, which for the most part is intended to elicit some response from the listeners to whom it is performed. African music is therefore a performer–participant kind of music not performer–audience. This implies that, to function properly, African music requires a unique kind of culturally inside, participatory sharing/loving knowledge that according to Lees (1994) is perhaps less a mode of understanding and more a mode of feeling.

African music is learned in a form of practical knowledge, that is, knowing in action. Africans believe that true knowing comes from actual experiencing, through interactive music-making. Africa also perfected the philosophy and practice of holistic music education, which enables the competent composer to be equally a competent performer and critical audience (Nzewi, 2001). The moment one starts singing, movements automatically come in. Music connects with participation, without which there is little or no meaning to music-making. Aural instruction, with students participating actively in music-making through imitation, should be the teaching–learning process. The virtual musical experience, which lays emphasis on abstract literary and non-participatory auditory encounters with music, is not an African concept. It leads to partial music-knowing.

African music has been ringed with functions and contextual associations confining the music to a meaning and place in the society. But gone are the days when African music was either reduced to a functional status or endowed with a magical or metaphysical essence that put it beyond analysis, especially when the social or extra-musical context was ignored. After all, what music does not serve functional ends? The musics that were protected by contextual associations are now performed out of their cultural contexts for aesthetic listening and appreciation. This has transformed most African music into a contemplative art form. Nercessian (2002) is therefore right when he concludes that time and space are increasingly compressed in such a way that cultures cease to enjoy the 'purity' that might validate the emic–etic dichotomy. When dealing with the musics of the world's cultures therefore, a polysemic approach to meaning in music should be embraced.

Appropriability of Music in Decontextualised Settings

Appropriation of music is everywhere — the existence of world music is a result of appropriation. A great deal of music is appropriable by cultures foreign to it, while some is not. This is due to a certain independence or autonomy of meaning which, as Nercessian (2002) states, is not only an attribute, but also a necessity of musical production. The central question is, why appropriate particular musics, and which musical elements are appropriable by a particular culture? The *Macmillan English Dictionary for Advanced Learners* defines appropriation as 'the action of taking something, especially when you have no right to take it'. In our case, it is the action of taking music from a culture where you do not belong. This is almost similar to Keil (1994), who defines appropriation as the use of some elements of music by some person or culture with whom it is not historically connected. He reiterates that the nature of appropriation is such that while the act is neutral, some might even say inevitable and desirable, context confers various possibly contested judgments in each case. Feld (Keil, 1994) eloquently describes the cultural paradox in the act of appropriation. He says, 'Musical appropriation sings a double line with one voice. It is a melody of admiration, even homage and respect. ... Yet this voice is harmonised by a countermelody of power, even control and domination'. He concludes that the issue is either unimportant or dormant when the stakes are low, but when the financial differences between the appropriator and 'culture-owners' is so great, greater attention is generated. Judging from these statements, appropriation itself is not the issue. The concern is with the loss of rights of those from whom the music is borrowed especially when power, prestige and large sums of money become involved.

The process of appropriation is seemingly unstoppable and vital. It involves reinventing and reinterpreting foreign music/musical elements to make them work for you and become part of your system. When this happens, we say the music has adapted to a different environment and can now be accommodated by that musical culture. We therefore create or construct our own identity of/in the music, to establish a different meaning from its meaning in the country of origin. But the whole of this process is not possible without the act of borrowing.

Why do we borrow music foreign to us, and when we borrow these musics how should we treat them? To answer these questions I will recount my conversations with African delegates in the ISME 2004 conference in Tenerife, Spain. Bosco, a delegate from Zambia supported the idea of borrowing music foreign to our cultures reasoning that it gives one more reasons to seek contact and become acquainted with new people including people with national, ethnic or cultural backgrounds different from ours. He reiterated that achieving an understanding of, and identification with other people's diverse forms of expression, particularly how they express themselves musically, helps to open new channels of communication. Onyeji, a delegate from Nigeria insisted that one should treat the borrowed music 'with respect' — what does that entail? Treating the music in a way that if he encounters it in a different environment, is able to recognise it, that is, maintaining the spirituality of the music. He suggests that before borrowing music, one must identify the most important features or elements that should be maintained in order not to distort the music. This would keep the musical experience real. This is what I refer to as the negotiation process, which makes it possible to treat a song with the respect it deserves.

Most of the time we borrow something because there is need. Borrowing always serves the need of the borrower. It is this need that should make clear our intentions in borrowing musics from foreign cultures. Are we borrowing to understand what the musical sounds express, or maybe to know the lifestyle, behaviour and the values certain people hold? Whichever is the case, it is important to establish which aspect of music one is preoccupied with. In the African culture, music has three components, that is, sonic (or the music itself), behaviour (brought about by human activities) and concept (the idea and beliefs about music). If you are concerned with the last two aspects of music then you must learn the techniques, understand the theories and survey the cultural context to which the music belongs. Consequently the view that music cannot be properly understood and appreciated without the knowledge of its social and cultural context is applicable or not dependent on which component of music one is preoccupied with. The necessary prerequisite for one to have a meaningful experience when borrowing music will be quite different, depending upon which aspect of music one is dealing with at the moment, whether sonic, behaviour or concept/context. The aspect of music one is concerned with and the intentions of borrowing will eventually determine the teaching method to use, that is, do we want to master an entirely new instrument, or analyse the melodic structures and intervals in a particular musical tradition? Whatever our intentions are, we need to analyse our perspectives on music first. This will determine what we teach and how we teach it.

As we appropriate musics of foreign cultures, we need to realise that there is a nucleus to a musical system that holds it together giving it shape and value, outlining the idiom. This is sometimes referred to as the deep structure by Nzewi (2003). Then there are the surface structures, which may be altered, eliminated or

63

introduced and reinterpreted in the face of confrontation or change (Hampton, 1979). I refer to these as variables or the appropriable components. To elucidate this point I want to give an example of a well-known tune brought to Kenyans by the missionaries, and popularly used to teach the concept of a round, *Row Your Boat*. Different ethnic communities in Kenya have appropriated the song to fit their own needs. One ethnic group, the *Luo*, is worth mentioning since, unlike the other communities, they have not translated the text but have looked for *Dho-Luo* words with rhyming sounds, but with a totally different meaning to the original. Their version is *Rao Rabet* (the hippo is huge). Here are the two examples:

Row |Row| Row| your |boat

Rao |Rao | Rao| ra | bet (The hippo, the hippo, the hippo is big)

Gentle | on| the| stream|

Gino | nyono| piny | (If that thing steps down)

Merrily| merrily| merrily | Merrily|

Wololo| wololo | Wololo| Wololo|

Gino | nyono| piny (That thing steps down).

The nucleus in this case (the tune) is constant and the variable (the text) has been changed to fit the needs of the *Luo*. They have therefore accommodated the appropriated version of the borrowed music to be able to gain a culturally relevant musical experience and meaning. The music has now adapted to the changing situations. Should we still insist on a culturally situated sonic interpretation after the music has travelled and gone through these processes? The music has now acquired a new identity and has regenerated a new cultural heritage different from its origins. Applying the cultural nuances of rule and procedure or context and association becomes not only imperceptible but also irrelevant, for at this level, music appropriation and use serves the purpose of aesthetic experience, making music an object for contemplation.

Another case of appropriation can be explained with the aid of one of the widely travelled Kenyan popular musics *Malaika*. The song is a lamentation of a young man to a beautiful girl whom he refers to as his angel. In African tradition a man has to pay a dowry to the parents of the girl he intends to marry. The young man laments that, although he loves the girl and wants to get married to her, he cannot because he is poor and cannot get the dowry to pay towards their marriage. The mood of the song is a sad one. This record has been performed by about nine artists apart from the original composer Fathili William:

Malaika nakupenda Malaika (Angel, I love you angel)

Nami nifanyeje, Kijana mwenziyo (What should I do? A young person like you?)

Nashindwa na mali sina we (I have no wealth at all)

Ningekuoa Malaika (Otherwise I should have married you my angel.).

The original version was in Rumba with lyrics in *Swahili*, and moderate tempo. Miriam Makeba, a South African, maintained the *Swahili* lyrics but changed the style to slow samba, probably to fit her audience at that particular time since she was in exile in America. Boney M also maintained *Swahili* text, but changed the style to rock and roll with a fairly fast tempo to fit the needs of his audience and extend their musical experience. In the process he compromised the lament mood. A Kenyan analysis of Makeba's *Malaika* would probably render it a wrong choice since a woman cannot refer to her fellow woman as her angel whom she would want to marry. At the same time I do not believe Makeba was ignorant of what the music meant.

Probably she just liked the tune and wanted to give it some creative dynamics and perform it in another environment. Suppose people in Europe found Makeba's version and decided to use it for teaching, would we expect them to trace the developments of that music from Kenya so they could apply culturally appropriate/congruent methods in teaching it? They may not even know that the music is from Kenya, because even Makeba wrongly introduces it as music from Tanzania, possibly because of the *Swahili* language used. Maintaining traditional formats of instruction may not be possible in this case because that would mean first tracing the origin of the music to the time of the recording.

Challenges of Teaching and Learning Musics of the World's Cultures

Santos (1994) maintains that to understand any of the world's cultures, one should understand something of its music, because of the importance of music to the self-esteem and cultural integration of each society, a view with which I strongly agree. He reiterates that, in more recent experiences where intercultural conflicts have long threatened the coexistence of people around the world, the knowledge and appreciation of artistic traditions other than one's own, have not only attenuated prejudices but also enhanced the trust and opportunities for social interactions between cultures long divided by race, religion and cultural heritage, as well as political, economic and social heritage. Music arts therefore bridges and mediates between cultures.

In today's geo-political scene, the process of forging international ties is often preceded by an exchange of cultural information and artistic products. This can be achieved through studying musics of the world's cultures. When we teach a variety of musical practices as music cultures, such teaching amounts to an important form of intercultural or multicultural education. Elliott (1994) says that entering into unfamiliar musical cultures activates self-examination and the personal reconstruction of one's relationships, assumptions and preferences. Students come to realise that there is clearly not one, but many positions from which a musical culture can be understood and each position has much to offer. Consequently students are obliged to confront their prejudices (musical and personal) and face the possibility that what they may believe to be universal is not. Consequently, they learn to have a polysemic interpretation of musical meaning. In the process of introducing learners to unfamiliar music practices, music educators link music education to the broader goals of humanistic education (Elliott, 1994, p. 13). Elliott seems to suggest that meaningful teaching of musics from other cultures implies the teaching of new ways of life, conduct, behaviour, moral values and musical thought. With all these aspects in place, the challenges in teaching musics of the world's cultures are still overwhelming. Questions like, how do we make a case for studying a specific musical culture? How much and to what extent can/should a musical tradition and its cultural setting be taught? Which teaching methods should we use? How do we address the phenomenon of change in the world's musical cultures if we still insist that music cannot be understood intelligibly outside its culture? These and other questions have been problematic to scholars of world music.

The first thing we need to clarify is that we are teaching music *within* diverse cultures not teaching *about* them. We should therefore concentrate on the musical cultures as a component of the culture of the people we are teaching. Second, however hard we may try, we cannot replicate an external cultural tradition in the

65

classroom. For example, the African concept of time in a performance is decided by participation. The more active the participation, the longer the time a performance takes. A formal class is controlled by chronological time; so the content has to be organised to fit the allocation. Third, we need to bear in mind that we are now treating the classroom as the music-making community and therefore we can only bring to class what that environment permits. This has been a problem because African music has a lot of extra-musical activities, and these are what bring out the meaning in a performance.

In making a case for teaching a specific musical culture, various approaches have been used. Lundquist (1998) advises us to choose musical culture that reflects a global perspective. The term 'global' is relative and the scope needs to be defined, because anything that is beyond my worldview in relation to my cultural orientation and exposure, is global. Sometimes we tend to choose a certain musical culture because we like or know something about it and hope the students would like it too. In connection with this approach, I would like to recount an incident that occurred when I was a masters student in a university in Kenya. The topic was music in African cultures, taught by a visiting professor from Nigeria. He chose to teach us the *Ibo* musical culture and the students' task was to apply/relate the information to what appertains in their cultures. I assume he chose the *Ibo* culture of Nigeria because he is an insider and therefore had resources (expertise) and facilities to teach the subject. We were a multi-ethnic class consisting of nine students from four Kenyan ethnic communities — *Luhya* (5), *Luo* (2), *Meru* (1), *Abagusii* (1). The experience prompted these thoughts:

- Prospect: It was interesting and very captivating for us to learn new musical culture and expand our worldview.
- Challenge: Some students had nothing to apply to their cultures from the *Ibo* musical culture because they are divergent, apart from the Luos whose culture is similar to the *Ibo* in some respects.
- Problem: The lecture did not establish the cultural backgrounds of the learners in order to find out which aspects of musical heritage from the *Ibo* could be shared universally by the Kenya students from diverse ethnic communities. Second, he never evaluated the lesson to find out what was applicable or not to different people so he could bridge the gap to be able to address all the students.

In the two Kenyan public universities that offer music, we teach music of India and Pakistan. The choice is due to the fact that Indian residents have become Kenyan citizens and we have to learn to coexist with them, respecting and appreciating their culture, that is, good neighbourliness. Second, resources for these musics are available in both print media and expertise. We are therefore able to use culturally congruent methods to teach the subject because we have a trusted source. The teacher should guide the resource person and channel the discussion to cover his/her objectives. An ethnomusicological perspective, which allows us to value each musical tradition for what it tells us about human musical expression, would be useful in this case because we have the insiders from the Indian culture.

Conclusion

The proposal that African music cannot be properly understood and appreciated without knowledge of its social and cultural context is appropriate, depending on the type and component of music studied. Musicians decorate, improve, improvise, borrow and adapt — they rarely simply reproduce music. For this reason, it is insensitive to say that we cannot understand music without understanding the culture from which it comes, especially when music has travelled. It all depends on the kind of meaning one draws from the music, since as Elliott (1994) explains, musical works are multidimensional 'thought generators'. The human cognition of musical works (even purely instrumental works) always involves several dimensions of musical meaning or information that listeners actively generate in consciousness. It is for this reason that Kenyans sing *Lingala* music from Zaire with a lot of passion and feelings, yet the language is unfamiliar to them. There are, according to Trainor and Trehub (1992), three types of meanings in music: emotional (the representation of emotional state), attributional (whereby music evokes particular qualities independent of specific objects or events) and concrete meaning (referring to specific events in the world).

We have to accept that it is not easy for music educators to help students comprehend all kinds of world musics. Collaborative action research with scholars in different parts of the world, through sharing of experiences and works in settings such as music education conferences, would expose us to diverse musical cultures of the world. Teaching of world music should not be a mere expansion of an intellectual horizon, but rather a social necessity that helps engender an equilibrium in intercultural understanding, with direct effect on the future lives of world communities.

References

Anku, W. (1998) Teaching creative dynamics of African drumming: A cross-cultural teaching approach. In L. Barbara & C. K. Szego (Eds.), *Music of the world's cultures: A source book for music education* (pp. 75–84). United Kingdom: Callaway International Resource Centre For Music Education (CIRCME).

Bebey, F. (1969). *Musique de L'Afrique*. Paris: Horizons de France Press.

Blacking, J. (1977). Some problems of theory and method in the study of musical change. *Year book of International Music Council, IX*, 1–26.

Chernoff, J. M. (1979). *African rhythm and African sensibility: Aesthetics and social action in African musical idiom*. Chicago: University of Chicago Press.

Elliott, D. J. (1994). Music, education, and musical values. In H. Lees (Ed), *Musical connections: Tradition and change* (pp. 8–24). Tampa, United States: The University of Auckland.

Floyd, S. A. (1995). *The power of black music: Interpreting its history from Africa to the United States*. New York: Oxford University Press.

Hampton, B. L. (1979). A revised approach to musical processes. *The Journal of Urban Studies, 6*, 1–16.

Keil, P., & Feld, S. (1994). *Music grooves*. Chicago and London: The University of Chicago Press.

Lundquist, B. (1998). A music education perspective. In L. Barbara & C. K. Szego (Eds.), *Music of the world's cultures: A source book for music education* (pp. 38–44). United Kingdom: Callaway International Resource Centre For Music Education (CIRCME).

Lees, H. (Ed.). (1994). 'Something rich and strange': Musical fundamentals and the tradition of change. In *Musical connections: Tradition and change* (pp. 8–24). Tampa, United States: The University of Auckland.

Nercessian, A. (2002). *Postmodernism and globalisation in ethnomusicology: An epistemological problem*. United States: Scarecrow Press.

Nettl, B. (1998). An ethnomusicological perspective. In L. Barbara & C. K. Szego (Eds.), *Music of the world's cultures: A source book for music education* (pp. 23–28). United Kingdom: Callaway International Resource Centre For Music Education (CIRCME).

67

Nzewi, M. (1997). *African music: Theoretical content and creative continuum. The culture-exponent's definitions*. Olderhausen, Germany: Institut für populärer Musik.

Nzewi, M. (2001). Music education in Africa – Mediating the imposition of western music education with the imperatives of the indigenous African practice. In C. van Niekerk (Ed), *Selected conference proceedings from PASMAE conference* (pp. 18–37). Lusaka.

Nzewi, M. (2003). Acquiring knowledge of the musical arts in traditional society. In A. Herbts, M. Nzewi, & K. Agawu (Eds.), *Musical arts in Africa: Theory practice and education*. Pretoria: University of South Africa.

Omondi, W. (1992). *African music as an art of communication*. Paper presented for the UNESCO-UNFPE Population Communication Project, Nairobi, Kenya.

Santos, R. P. (1994). Authenticity and change in intercultural music teaching. In H. Lees (Ed.), *Musical connections: Tradition and change* (pp. 8–24). Tampa, United States: The University of Auckland.

Roberts, J. S. (1972). *Black music of two worlds*. Tivoli, NY: Original Music.

Tracey, A. (1986). Key words in African music. In C. Lucia (Ed.), *Proceedings of the First National Music Educators' Conference* (pp. 29–45). Durban: University of Natal.

Trainor, L. J., & Trehub S. E. (1992). The development of referential meaning in music. *Music Perception*, 9(4), 455–470.

ROSE A. OMOLO-ONGATI is a lecturer in music at Mesono University, Kenya. She holds a BA (Music and Education) degree from the University of Pretoria, South Africa, and a M Mus (Composition) from Kenyatta University, Kenya. She is currently pursuing a PhD degree (Composition) at Kenyatta University and has presented research papers locally and internationally. Published papers include:

(2005). The concept of aesthetics as applied to and in the musical experiences of the Luo. *Maseno Journal of Education Arts and Science,* 5(1).

(2005). Songs of games and folk tale songs as teaching resources in musical arts education of a Luo child. PASMAE.

Performance practice of traditional musical genres in contemporary Kenya: The case of Orutu. *East African Journal of Music, Issue 1.*

Trusting the Tradition: The Meaning of the Irish Session Workshop

Christopher Smith

The historical context for Irish traditional music and dance is in an informal, often cross-generational gathering, whose members may participate by playing, singing and dancing, or by telling jokes, stories or riddles. These sessions, rooted in a sense of cultural identity, participation and sharing, have followed the Irish throughout the diaspora. Through them, Irish musicians have found ways to recreate traditional contexts and behaviours even in alien physical or economic settings. Such environments are not the standard paradigm of classroom education, but I believe that learning to play Irish music in the traditional way builds community, develops musicianship and crosscultural insight, and teaches collaborative skills. Learning and playing tunes in the traditional way, avoiding the intrusion of alien teaching models, techniques or resources, provides individuals with essential skills and musical/social insights that cannot be passed on via notation or in the classroom.

This essay provides a historical and theoretical basis for a pedagogy based within the tradition of Irish music but with adaptations for teaching those raised outside the Irish context. Such an approach avoids alien tools (particularly western musical notation and terminology), instead drawing its inspiration, philosophy and teaching techniques from those developed within the tradition itself. It is thus intended not as a substitute for or improvement upon methods that have been developed over several centuries, but rather as a complement for traditional methods, one uniquely suited to those entering the tradition from outside. It is my conviction that such methods, based in respect for the tradition's own pedagogical expertise, are both more practically effective and more culturally sensitive than conventional or literate approaches to teaching music skills.

As with other vernacular cultures, the pedagogy of traditional Irish music has always included a strong commitment to aural means and to demonstration–imitation teaching paradigms. Over the 200-plus years of its development, the tradition has developed efficient and irreplaceable means of musical pedagogy. Such methods are precisely evolved to accurately and reliably convey what that particular tradition itself finds significant. Those crucial skills and stylistic insights differ from one tradition to another — for example, in Irish music they tend to emphasise melodic recognition and musical memory; in west African music ensembles concepts and polyrhythmic acuity — but in each tradition they are apt, effective and, most importantly, time tested.

69

Attempts to import alien tools are prone to ignore essential factors and to emphasise irrelevant ones. Moreover, when pedagogical or analytical tools distort musical priorities, they not only impede transmission but also erode stylistic specificity. Thus, teaching with the wrong tools does not aid but in fact damages musical insight and crosscultural appreciation.

The best resource for models, methods and philosophies in this music is the tradition itself. In this article, drawing on anecdote, qualitative fieldwork, scholarly literature, and three decades of practical experience in both literate and aural traditions, I will argue for the validity — indeed, the irreplaceable advantages — of traditional teaching methods.

An Introduction to the Tradition

The term 'tradition' has been a slippery one when applied to various musical vernaculars, but for our purposes it may be defined as a set of transmission processes, not a specific repertoire of pieces or of style characteristics.[1] A song, tune or story is traditional because, regardless of its origin, it has come to be learned, taught and passed on aurally and in the memory. 'Traditional Irish music', then, is a body of repertoire and of performance practices that are learned, taught and passed on in like fashion.

The original contexts from which traditional Irish (or 'trad music', in the universal parlance of its players) emerged, with the small Gaelic speaking farming and fishing communities of the south and west of Ireland, have, in the age of the Celtic Tiger, largely disappeared. Trad music has become a very different sound, phenomenon and commodity: one no longer shaped so much by local vernacular culture as by global economies' mass media and communications.

Yet the processes of the tradition have proved surprisingly resilient. Even in very different physical, linguistic or economic contexts, tunes are retained or rotated in and out of the repertoire, new instrumental approaches are accepted or rejected, and new techniques are explored. Such processes are still managed through person-to-person contact, often in the heavily social context of the trad music session, and in remarkably traditional ways. Trad players with a basic understanding of repertoire, technique and behaviour can walk into unfamiliar sessions around the globe and, rather like jazz musicians, make music together because they share a body of material and procedures in common.

Learning to play the music in a traditional fashion teaches not only skills but also appropriate perspectives and social behaviours. In this sense, the tradition — the repertoire of tunes, instrumental techniques, ensemble procedures, and expectations of decorum and conduct — itself recreates the contexts it requires, not only for performance, but also for pedagogy. Thus, even in the 21st century, even dealing with vastly more cosmopolitan (if less patient), more verbal and literate (if less thoughtful, subtle or insightful) students, the traditional pedagogical practices are remarkably and demonstrably effective, as I have discovered in the years of my teaching. Traditional pedagogy is, in fact, far more effective for this music than are more complex, literate or supposedly sophisticated practices drawn from western art music models.

Trad music was historically a solo music, played in kitchens or at crossroads dances. Players supplying music for listening or dancing would alternate tunes, often passing the fiddle or flute from hand to hand, and their repertoires were intensely local.[2] The analogy here would be to local dialects; thus, in mountainous, densely forested, or isolated seaside communities, the musical vocabulary and local accent might differ drastically between communities separated by only a little more than a day's walk. Different musicians would shape local approaches; different tunes would be played; variant versions of common tunes would develop; nuances of phrasing, tone, tempo and articulation would all diverge.

The music travelled outward with the Irish Diaspora, and from the mid-18th century communities of trad musicians developed in Irish-emigrant neighbourhoods, particularly in Britain (London, Glasgow, Liverpool), Australia (Sydney, Melbourne) and the United States (Boston, New York, Chicago). These new communities in turn developed their own lineages of teachers, shared expectations and regional accents. However, the performance venues for the music changed as well: instead of being played as a solo music in kitchens or at crossroads, musicians living in rented digs (particularly in London) began to gather not at home but rather in local pubs. Hence, for example, the birth, by the mid-1950s, of a vibrant and more visible 'trad' scene in London's Camden Town or Liverpool's Merseyside, where groups of musicians would gather for after-Mass Sunday sessions:

> With the changed living conditions under which many migrants found themselves, the pub took over as a venue for social and community interaction, and music played a role. The first documented "pub sessions" by groups of musicians are thus thought to have taken place in London's Irish neighborhoods in the late 1940s, amongst the expatriate populations who sought the talk, drink, social interaction, and music of "back home" (Smith, 2005c, pp. 5–6).

In Ireland, in the post-Independence period as the de Valera government and the Catholic Church sought to mandate a pastoral national vision, outside influences such as modern literature, film and jazz (really any popular music broadcast on radio) were viewed negatively. In the south and west of the country, which was hardest hit by emigration and unemployment, house dances, perhaps with a raffle or contest, were one of the few ways in which rural people could cobble together a few shillings to pay rents (O'hAllmhurain, 2005). The church was suspicious of such domestic gatherings, and particularly wary of the opportunities they provided for contact between 'innocent country girls' and boys from outside the locale. Even the humble bicycle, to say nothing of the radio, the gramophone and the Ford (car), was seen as encroaching incitements to sin. Seeking church support for various nationalist initiatives, in 1935 the de Valera government was persuaded to pass the *Dance Halls Act*, which established a hefty tax and required licensing for establishments offering dancing, thus provided a means of social control. Sponsored dances were subsequently most often held in parish halls, which was doubly attractive to the church because it both facilitated moral scrutiny and swelled the coffers.[3] In North America on the other hand, at a greater distance from the Dublin bishops, there was a boom in public dancehalls where a mixture of modern and traditional musics were played (see Gedutis, 2004). But traditional music in the traditional context and its pedagogy was changing.

The shift of dancing from the intimacy and familiar faces of the country kitchen to the size, modernity, clamour and potential anonymity of the public dance hall fuelled a change in playing style. Instead of solo fiddlers or melodeon players passing an instrument from hand to hand, the 1920s and 1930s saw the

71

development of 'ceili bands', groups borrowing jazz-band instrumentation (piano, drums, occasionally banjo or guitar) to back a front line of multiple flutes, fiddles and accordions. Parishes and counties sponsored bands, and the ceili band competitions broadcast nationally brought the sound of ensemble playing to every part of Ireland.

Yet despite the fervent desire of successive Irish governments and bishops to contain 'foreign' influences, the post-1945 period brought inevitable social and musical change, both in Ireland and abroad. The phenomenon of the show band, essentially a pop band playing skiffle, rockabilly and show tunes with the occasional set of trad waltzes for older folks, largely supplanted the ceili bands by the late 1950s. And so trad music played in a traditional fashion became a largely underground phenomenon, kept alive in Irish emigrant communities, in occasional friendly pubs which did not mind the rural connotations of the music or were themselves in isolated regions, and (especially in America) sustained by several generations of émigré master musicians like James Morrison, Lad O' Beirne, Jack Coen, Andy McGann and Paddy Reynolds, who fostered schools, house parties and house dances. In these post–World War II diaspora, even more than in Ireland, it was possible for young people to enter the tradition in a relatively traditional way, by exposure to the music, study with a master musician and apprenticeship with others in similar situations.

However, the ballad boom of the 1960s, fuelled by the commercial success of groups like the Clancy Brothers and the Dubliners, and the Celtic revival of the 1970s, powered by urban bands like Planxty and the Bothy Band, spread the music to more distant and disparate communities. By the 1980s, trad-based groups like De Danann and Altan were able to tour regularly overseas and play to festival-size audiences, while their recordings could be heard widely, often on public radio. Such wide exposure meant that persons outside the Irish-American communities often heard and sought to learn to play the music, outside the traditional lineages of aural/oral learning. Traditional pedagogy was actually subverted by the logarhythmically enhanced access would-be players had to learning resources: books, CDs, videos and the Internet. So much music and so many models were so readily available that both local musical accent, and the formerly mandatory emphasis upon extended teacher-to-student personal contact, became optional. Individual style became a product not of geographical point-of-origin or of local models, but rather the selection and synthesis of multifarious influences.[4]

Traditional Pedagogical Approaches

This eroded, if it did not entirely transform, traditional pedagogical approaches. The historical model for learning to play was through direct contact with an older mentor: a relative, neighbour or travelling teacher. This was a relationship of mutual exchange, in which the student received instruction, repertoire and encouragement, while the teacher received deference, in-kind recompense (lodging, work, goods) or modest fees: the 'Sliabh Luachra Fiddle Master' Padraig O'Keefe, for example, one of the last travelling teachers in Cork/Kerry, charged sixpence per tune (Hickey, 1999, p. 91). Such exchange occurred in a rural culture of small communities in which individuals and families lived in close physical and social proximity to others, and with regular, repeated contact between teachers and (sometimes generations of) students. In such communities, modesty, subtlety, indirection and what Karol Polanyi calls 'reciprocity' — the presumption of exchange, not pur-chase-and-sale — were essential strategies that minimised conflict and made social business possible (Polanyi, 1957, p. 48; Smith, 2005b, p. 6). These played out in music pedagogy no less than other aspects of daily interaction.

Crucial information, conveyed person-to-person in an apprenticeship model, included but was not limited to technical musical insight (phrasing, tempo, tone, articulation, repertoire choices), performance practice (solo versus ensemble play-ing, sequencing, repertoire), interface with other traditional art forms (particu-larly playing for dancing) and, most subtly and most crucially, insight into the social dynamics of which the music is both locus and catalyst. These social and cultural insights were by-and-large unavailable to the many non-Irish (especially North Americans) who have sought to learn to play Celtic music since the 1990s.

In various articles I have explored the complex and conflicting dynamics that inform session conduct outside the ethnic communities, and have suggested that contrasting expectations of social conduct, public versus private and of interper-sonal obligation frequently lead to confusion or communicative dissonance (Smith, 2005c, pp. 7–8). Non-Irish players wishing to enter the tradition from outside often encounter what they perceive to be indifference, clique-ish behaviour or outright hostility. These misapprehensions arise from contrasts in North American versus Irish normative social behaviour. The problem is suffi-ciently significant that both serious and parodic delectations of session etiquette have been offered, discussed and sometimes absorbed (Carson, 1998; Foy, 1999; O'hAllmhurain, 2004).

To cite only a few examples from my own direct experience: among North Americans, the fact that a pub session occurs in a public place often carries the connotation that the gathering is therefore open to anyone who wishes to par-ticipate. North Americans who attempt to enter or crash such a session are sometimes offended when rebuffed. Similarly, North Americans sometimes pre-sume that a musical gathering without a specific labelled or titled leader must therefore be democratic, that since there is no leader anyone's contribution is of equal value and merit. This can fly in the face of the Irish tradition's preference for tact, subtlety and indirect feedback about conduct, and again can lead to communicative dissonance.[5]

The Teaching Context

In a teaching context, the typical profile of North Americans entering the tradition (Smith, 2005c, p. 9) is also very different — in age, income, prior experience, social expectations, and so on — from that of native Irish entering the tradition. Middle-class, college-educated, leisure-equipped Americans accustomed to a linear, verbal, textual, logical, sequential, fast-moving and mercantile educational model some-times find themselves at a loss with a teaching method that emphasises intuitive connections, non-verbal observation and imitation, repetition and patience. The uneasy relationship between idiomatic pedagogical demands and students' conflict-ing expectations has been beautifully described by Michael Frisch in his study wherein he alludes to 'an encounter on the uncertain border between traditional music and a mass-mediated, music-saturated, consumption-driven capitalist society from which come students drawn without always sensing why to very different sounds and the alternative cultural values they may carry' (1987, p. 87).

73

As has been the case throughout the history of trad music, in a pub session the playing itself is still only one part of a complex social and communal context. Anthropologists describe the process by which learned skills teach social behaviours as enculturation. As with many other such behaviours, learning trad music requires that players learn not only how to play, but when and, most importantly, why to play. The music becomes a tool for teaching behaviour as well as musicianship, in other words, a tool for enculturation. But, only if it is taught in the traditional, person-to-person, one-tune-at-a-time; enculturation cannot be transmitted in prose, audio or video. Absent apprenticeship, and there is no way for would-be players to understand.[6]

Musical *insight* — the why in addition to the what of the music — is driven by informed cultural perspectives. Those lacking such insights can have trouble playing the music right.[7] Thus, those wishing to enter a tradition of music and play it traditionally must be enculturated, whether they are toddlers born within or adults born without. The advantage of music as a tool of enculturation (like language, handicrafts, cooking and many other oral traditions) is that (a) explicit, formalised and organised mechanisms exist for helping the novice develop skills and thus cultural insight, and (b) within such oral traditions it is permissible within the culture for an individual, whether toddler or adult, to be a novice, provided he or she accepts that status.

However, some adult students wishing to enter the tradition from outside are unaccustomed to being novices and find such status uncomfortable. Moreover, when they discover that the pedagogy of trad music avoids familiar tools they can become deeply resistant, as Frisch comments:

> The nature of what we were studying probably magnified issues of power and stature that must be involved in any teaching of elementary skills to adults not used to feeling incompetent or being asked to submit to a radically new discipline, however much they have willingly elected the submissive position. This tension often became explicit, characteristically in informal moments that not coincidentally often involved the tape recorder, so apt an embodiment of the complexity involved in middle class visitors presuming to absorb traditional culture (1997, p. 96).

In my own observation, the greatest resistance to 'a radically new discipline' — though a very old one in the history of musical pedagogy — is in the realm of learning by ear. Because trad is a quintessentially melody oriented music with something like 12,000 tunes extant, developing a repertoire that permits playing with other musicians in a pub sessions requires aural facility and an adept musical memory. But the amount of time spent learning what is for many an intimidatingly unfamiliar skill — learning and playing by ear — leads some to fall back on more familiar but less appropriate crutches; the most obvious example being music notation.[8]

Among North American novices, the ability to read notation is relatively common. But in the tradition of Irish music notation plays an almost purely archival role, that is, as an aide-memoire outside the context of the playing session. Use of notation is ineffective in a session because the sequence of tunes selected on-the-fly is unpredictable, a sight-reading musician may lack notation for any given tune, attention to notation drastically reduces a player's ability to respond to others, and insistence upon notation implies a resistance to spending time studying and learning the tunes by ear.[9] Hence, an experienced Irish musician who walks into an unfamiliar session and sees music stands, tune books or a

74

disproportionately large incidence of guitars, keyboards or *bodhráns* versus melody instruments, will know immediately and with remarkable accuracy that this session has a high percentage of novices from outside the tradition. Ethnographic research confirms that presence or absence of contact with tradition-bearers also informs perspectives about its importance: those who have experienced such contact on a repeated basis are far more inclined to view it as essential, while those who have not tend to rank its importance much lower (Smith, 2005c, pp. 8–10).

The reality is that the tradition has always incorporated both more and less formal pedagogical methods, from occasional lessons with wandering fiddle or dance teachers to semi-regular visits with a relative or neighbour to quasi-formalised classes in community centres or summer schools to the avid and rigorous study of various recorded media. Padraig O'Keefe (1887–1963) travelled a regular circuit from student to student, 'Professor' James Morrison (1893–1947) ran a Bronx-based music school, recordings had been a key self-teaching method all the way back to the wax cylinders of Patsy Tuohey (1865–1923) and the 78s of Michael Coleman (1891–1946).

In the contemporary subculture of trad music fans and players, and particularly for those participants living away from direct contact with tradition bearers, the modern phenomenon of the summer school is important. These, for a weekend, week or longer, bring together a (typically small) staff of master musicians and a group of students, usually in a rural or campus environment with dormitories and dining commons, for an intensive period of all-day study, practice, sessions and concerts.[10] For students, these are invaluable opportunities for extended contact with tradition bearers; for staff, they can be a central part of annual income. Students are typically energised by the calibre of music, the contact with master musicians who they may have admired for years on recordings and the opportunity to think about music all day every day for a week or more.

However, I have come to believe that even these situations are problematic. A short but very intensive period of contact with master musicians attempts to remedy the absence of regular, week-by-week contact over a number of years; I do not think it is ultimately successful. By their temporary nature, by the degree to which the daily (and nightly) summer school experience is unlike the other 51 weeks of the student's calendar, by the smorgasbord element of the offerings and of student responses, and by the underlying and inevitable commercial expectations of (pedagogical) value for (student) dollar, the summer school distorts locally oriented lineage-based practices. I believe that pedagogy that moves closer to the original practices is ultimately more effective.

My insights are grounded in my own experience as both an entering student and a teacher of the tradition, as well as qualitative ethnographic fieldwork and statistical analysis (McEntire, 1999; Smith, 2005c). These sources also confirm the commonality of my own initial experience as a musician entering the tradition from outside. I was raised in a middle-class suburban environment in which live music-making was a rarity, and opportunities to hear or learn any traditional music person-to-person were essentially non-existent. My first contact with live music (in my case, traditional Irish music and Mississippi Delta blues) was electrifying: the immediacy, intensity, individuality, raw power and community of traditional music-making were profoundly attractive, and the desire to acquire skills that would permit entry was powerful. However, in the absence of

75

regular contact with tradition-bearers, my acquisition of performance skills, to say nothing of the social and interpersonal enculturation cited above, was a slow process. The process was immediately accelerated when I was able to maintain such regular contact.

I came back to playing and teaching trad music in the 1990s in a college community with a strong local population of master players. The sessions were very good but some learners had difficulty finding entry because their skills, repertoires or musical/social insight were not sufficient; my teaching evolved from a desire to serve them. The model was less that of the summer school or the conservatory than that of practical community service. In this respect, it was closer to the traditional models of reciprocal exchange and a shared 'commons' of knowledge (Smith, 2005b). The 'session workshop' was focused on repertoire and performance practice, based exclusively on learning by ear and developing melodic memory, emphasised the core tunes and most traditional approaches to the music, was open to all ages, and was offered without fee.

Virtually every aspect of this situation subverted North American expectations about learning: the emphasis on ear and memory rather than eye and notation, the preference for non-verbal demonstration versus articulated analytical approaches, the conglomeration of various skill levels in a single group, the modelling of extra-musical social or interpersonal behaviours, and the removal of the mercantile element.

Almost all students found these factors disorienting because they were alien. Most responded very favourably, coming to trust the aural/memory method; to develop patience with various ages, skills and learning paces; and to participate in social and enculturative experiences. Most also came to value the session more than they would had a fee been charged, as the removal of a financial impulse shifts the burden of responsibility. No longer is the teacher the servant of the student's financial investment. Instead, the student must assess the experience's value and share responsibility for its effective realisation. Most student responses suggested that this was recognised to be an unusual and precious opportunity (Smith, 2005c).

However, there were students for whom the absence of familiar crutches — a book of tunes, a linear verbal description of the method, a narrowly focused learning pace that served their individual needs most efficiently — was deeply disturbing, so much so that a few departed the session workshop, occasionally with great drama. But in the long term, and well after my departure, the session workshop endured. Those players who were regular participants truly did come to see the tradition both differently and more appropriately: as a network not only of repertoire and performance practices, but of social relationships and reciprocal obligations. Numerous members have gone on to participate in, lead or teach at other sessions, in other cities and countries, and have continued to further their own studies by apprenticeships with master musicians in the United States and abroad. In other words, some percentage of these students have been permanently enculturated into the multinational, grassroots society of the trad musician, a process begun, carried, grounded and solidified by pedagogy based in the tradition's own insights.

For the teacher, this approach does demand some expansion of skills, since one must have a command of a tradition's performance practice before one can teach it, but the most essential acquisition is a change of perspective on pedagogical

76

technique. One need not be an expert player of trad music, since the tradition has always made good use of individuals who were stronger teachers than they were players, but one must learn to trust the tradition's pedagogical expertise.[11] It is possible for a skilled musician and teacher to assimilate essential insights about appropriate musical and social behaviour, sufficient to start students off right, provided dedicated effort and a philosophical receptivity are in place.

Pedagogy grounded in traditional practices has far-reaching implications. As I asserted at the beginning of this essay, a given tradition develops its own best pedagogy to convey what that particular tradition itself finds significant. As educators seeking crosscultural diversity and sensitivity, this means we need to learn from the tradition's own teachers.[12] Their insights suggest that traditional pedagogical models can more effectively teach not only musical style and performance practice, but can also model social behaviour and provide a means of insight for students entering a culture from outside, particularly when those alien cultural behaviours conflict with our own. Music, like language, handicrafts, cooking and many other oral traditions, is thus an avenue for enculturation. If we want our students to encounter other traditions and practices with an enhanced level of not only musical but also cultural sensitivity, a pedagogical method that trusts the tradition's own insights and techniques is an important first step.

Endnotes

1   'Tradition: *noun* (1) the transmission of customs or beliefs from generation to generation. (2) a long-established custom or belief passed on in this way. (3) an artistic or literary method or style established by an artist, writer, or movement, and subsequently followed by others. ORIGIN Latin, from tradere "deliver, betray" (*Compact Oxford Dictionary* accessible at http://www.askoxford.com/concise_oed).

2   O'hAllmhurain argues that repertoires and style characteristics were directly shaped by patterns of foot travel and commerce in very specific topographies (2004).

3   In practice, the Dance Halls Act and the resulting social pressure to obey the law was the death of the traditional house dance context. Those who defied the Act and continued to host dances in their homes were liable for legal citation or ecclesiastical condemnation — indeed musicians and hosts were sometimes excoriated from the pulpit at Sunday mass.

4   For an erudite discussion of the problematic status of regional style see the archives of the Internet discussion group IRTRAD-L (https://listserv.heanet.ie/cgi-bin/wa?A2=ind0102&L=IRTRAD-L&D=0&I=-3&P=103984), retrieved May 16, 2005.

5   A useful parallel here can be to think of the pub session as analogous to the *Stammtisch* or 'special-interest table', in which friends sharing an interest (originally a foreign language) meet regularly to practice their skills. See http://de.wikipedia.org/wiki/Stammtisch, retrieved May 16, 2005.

6   Frisch describes Appalachian fiddle teacher Gerry Milnes's 'very strong sense of the difference between [his] tradition and the ingrained assumptions about music and learning music brought by beginning students from outside, however "into" old-time music they thought they wanted to be. This was most manifest in the patience in which he anticipated and managed the resistance his method inevitably created. ... in trying to introduce a diverse group of twelve or so beginners to something far more culturally and musically elusive than just the rudiments of a new instrument or the formal structure of a style' (1987, p. 89).

7   Frisch refers to the traditional fiddler Gerry Milnes's teaching as 'something far more culturally and musically elusive than just the rudiments of a new instrument or the formal structure of a style' (1987, p. 87).

8   'The plow of Gerry's method repeatedly ran into unseen rocks buried in the soil of the class's very different musical culture. At one point or another, every member came to resist one

aspect or another of Gerry's approach. ... In the long run ... the widening gulf in abilities traced more to such unconscious decisions than to innate abilities or level of prior experience' (1987, p. 94).

9   Trad musicians tend to be very wary of novice players of the Irish bodhrán (frame drum), and to a lesser extent chordal accompanists, for the same reason: because too often these novices have picked up what seems to be an 'easier' instrument in order to avoid the substantial investment of time required in learning to play and remember the melodies in a stylistically appropriate fashion.

10 The most notable Irish example is the Willie Clancy Summer School, held every July in West Clare. United States examples include the Swannanoa Gathering, the Augusta Heritage Festival, the (defunct) Gaelic Roots Festival, and many others. It is no coincidence that the United States school that most closely and effectively mimics the Irish model — the Catskills Irish Arts Week in East Durham, New York, which is carefully scheduled for the week immediately following 'Willie Week' — is also the most effective at teaching in a traditional fashion.

11 Notable examples of individuals who became great teachers without exceptional performance skills include Frank Custy, principal of a Normal School in Clare, who began playing whistle as an adult in 1963 in order to teach his students, and retired in 1999 leaving a powerful and direct lineage of teachers to assume his duties.

12 Frisch cites the 'commonality [which] is powerfully underscored by the similar process employed by traditional teachers, and [his] hunch ... that the implicit assumptions and values of such music and teaching are profoundly at odds with those of the dominant musical culture' (1987, p. 100).

References

Carson, C. (1998). *Last night's fun: In and out of time with Irish music*. New York: Farrar Straus Giroux.

Foy, B. (1999). *A field guide to the Irish music session*. New York: Roberts Rinehart.

Frisch, M. (1987). Notes on the teaching and learning of old-time fiddle. *Ethnomusicology, 31*(1), 87–102.

Gedutis, S. (2004). *See you at the hall: Boston's golden era of Irish music and dance*. Boston: Northeastern University Press.

Hall, R. (1994). *Irish music and dance in London, 1890-1970: A socio-cultural history*. Unpublished doctoral dissertation, University of Sussex.

Hickey, D. (1999). *Stone mad for music: The Sliabh Luachra story*. Dublin: Marino.

McEntire, N.C. (1999). *Chris Smith's celtic slow session: Building a music community in Bloomington, Indiana*. Paper presented at the Society for Ethnomusicology national meetings, Bloomington, Indiana.

Mullins, P. (Producer & Director). (1993). *From shore to shore: Irish traditional music in New York city* [video]. (Available from Ossian USA, 118 Beck Road, Loudon, NH 03307).

O'hAllmhurain, G. (2005). *'Dancing on the hobs of hell': The response of musicians and dancers to the public dance halls Act 1935 (The ethnographic evidence from Clare)*. Paper presented at the American Council for Irish Studies meetings, Notre Dame, Indiana.

The O'Brien pocket history of Irish traditional music. (2004). Dublin: The O'Brien Press.

Compact Oxford Dictionary Online. Retrieved May 17, 2005, from http://www.askoxford.com/concise_oed/

Polanyi, K. (1957). *The great transformation: A survey of the industrial revolution and the change from the Commons to Enclosure*. Boston: Beacon Press.

Smith, C. (1998). *How to start and run an Irish music slow session: Irish traditional music as community outreach*. [Self-published folio].

Smith, C. (2005a). Irish session dynamics. Retrieved May 16, 2005, from http://members.cox.net/eskin/sessiondynamics.html

Smith, C. (2005b). *Reclaiming the Commons: Oral-tradition music-making as intellectual property and community activism*. Paper presented at the American Council for Irish Studies meetings, Notre Dame, Indiana.

Smith, C. (2005c). *Sessions as virtual village: Irish traditional music as cultural construct and social tool*. Paper presented at the Southern American Council for Irish Studies meetings, Houston, Texas.

Smith, C. (2005d). *Traditional Irish music and local community* [Ethnographic survey, completed February 20, 2005].

Smith, G. (1997). Modern-style Irish accordion playing: History, biography and class. *Ethnomusicology, 41*(3), 433–463.

Vallely, F. (1999). *The companion to Irish traditional music*. Cork: Cork University Press.

CHRISTOPHER J. SMITH is Assistant Professor of Musicology/Ethnomusicology and Director of the Vernacular Music Center at Texas Tech University in Lubbock, Texas, United States. His research interests are in American and African-American music, Irish traditional music and folk culture, improvisation, music and politics and historical performance. He has authored numerous articles and book chapters on topics in jazz, classical and world musics; tours internationally with Altramar medieval music ensemble; and is the authorised biographer of Irish folklorist and broadcaster Séamus Ennis. He is also a published poet.

79

'Singing Together': A Crosscultural Approach to the Meaning of Choirs as a Community

Jukka Louhivuori, Veli-Matti Salminen and Edward Lebaka

Various disciplines are exploring the connection between communal networks and the wellbeing of people, even when the context is a society of uncertainty and individualism that is going through critical changes. The study *Singing Together* takes into consideration community-oriented musical hobbies as a factor which increases social capital. Social capital is significantly the property of the community, rather than the private property of any individual exploiting it (as human capital is; Putnam, 1994). The musical communities at the centre of this research might present examples of normative communal cultures that are exceptional by character, given that their societies emphasise individuality. If this is so, we can move on to these questions: What kind of expressions characterise this culture? What kind of effects does this culture have on the wellbeing of the people surrounded by it?

According to Hyyppä (2002), the quality of life and thereby the wellbeing of individuals and society is influenced by not only 'traditional' health factors and socioeconomic position, but also by the number of close friends, the amount of trust or distrust, and participation in associations, for example. Participation in choirs is one example of such social activity (Hyyppä, 2001; Hyyppä, 2002, p. 123). Hence, it is no coincidence that in the centre of this research there are choirs in which making music together forms the basis for participation. Active participation in associations is not only of political importance. It also has indirect cultural effects. The participants adopt norms of reciprocity and learn to trust each other.

Similar to the postulations of Hargreaves and North (1997), Durrant and Himonides (1998) view music's social and emotional dimensions as the main reasons for people to sing in a choir. They conducted a single case study of a British choral society in 1998 and found that the majority of members of the choral society had experienced wellbeing from being introduced to other people and forming friendships as well increasing their musical skill and knowledge (Durrant, 1998, pp. 67–68).

Choral Traditions in Finland and South Africa

Finland

The choir singing tradition in Finland goes back to Medieval times, when the Catholic church educated choir singers for the needs of services in Turku. The curriculum of the first Finnish university in Turku, founded in 1640, included music and choir singing. The close connection of choir singing to the academic world is reflected in the fact that the oldest choirs in Finland still have close links to the universities. At the end of the 19th century, the first Finnish speaking teacher education seminar was established in Jyväskylä. Music had a crucial role from the beginning of the seminar, and the first Finnish-speaking choirs were founded by the music teacher of the seminar. The choir singing tradition spread out fast with the help of teachers across the country. The first song festival, which had a great influence on cultural identity of Finns, was organised in Jyväskylä in 1895. Choir festivals are believed to have an important role in the process of gaining independency from Russia at the beginning of the 20th century.

Choir singing is an active and integral part of Finnish society, particularly in public ceremonies. Children have their first choir singing experiences at primary schools, with the possibility to continue in secondary and high school levels.

South Africa

In South Africa, choral music has its practical value in society. In religion, choral music can often assist a point of view, even a doctrine. Accordingly, listeners and performers of choral music need particular standards of judgment. Since evaluation of choral music is affected by considerations that lie outside the narrower field of 'abstract' music, it would appear that this form of art is our ideal introduction to music in general. In a sense no-one is ignorant of the material from which choral music springs. For this material is, in large measure, the epitomised thoughts, feelings and aspirations of a community rather than an individual.

Singing and being part of a choir is a strong tradition in many South African schools and churches. Music teachers and church choirs' conductors strive to create opportunities for children and congregants to be part of a happy, harmonious way of singing and making music together. Undoubtedly, most choruses exist for one or more good reasons. The primary goal, however, is to develop their fullest singing potential. Choir singing therefore provides an excellent opportunity whereby good singing habits can be taught. Choir training entails a vast field of knowledge which includes *inter alia* repetition procedures, choir seating, stage deportment, breathing control, resonance techniques, the use of dynamics, style interpretation and many other vocal aspects. Choir masters strive to achieve broad goals like helping singers develop a means of aesthetic expression and appreciation, helping them to experience the joy and satisfaction of performing well for themselves and others, and helping to develop skills and attitudes that will encourage them to use their singing voices as lifelong instruments.

The multicultural character of South African society gives a special flavour to choir singing. The cultural differences between whites and blacks or between single tribes are reflected in choir singing practices. The choir singing styles are not as homogenous as they are in Finland, which is culturally a very homogenous nation.

Theoretical Framework

The concept of social capital is here approached from the Anglo-American frame of reference and mostly adapted from the writings of Putnam (2000). The aim is to find out how the social capital of the participants is related to musical group activities and trust between the members of the community.

The community-based view of Putnam divides social capital into three components: (a) values and norms, (b) communities (for instance non-governmental organisations), and (c) trust. Art is one essential reflection and form of cultural values (a), but it is also possible for art to influence the formation of values and norms through art. Choirs, orchestras and other groups that have music as a hobby are expressions of community (b). Through a hobby that has been started at an early age one can learn important ways of action that help later on in forming social networks. This article is going to deal with the concept of trust (c) especially through the crosscultural comparison.

In this research the comparative research strategy adopts both an intercultural (crosscultural) and intracultural approach. Broad quantitative data from different sources concerning choir activities will be analysed in the framework described in Figure 2.

Social capital is described in this study as a two-dimensional space: (a) individualism–collectivism (Triandis 1995), and (b) community oriented–music/target oriented activities. It is assumed that Finnish and South African musical communities differ in the individualism versus collectivism as well as community versus music oriented dimensions.

Materials and Methods

The operationalising of the models described in Figures 1 and 2 was done by formulating several themes for the survey. The questions related to Figure 1 pertain to values and attitudes, the amount of voluntary work, political and social activity, parents' role in joining a choir, social networks and the friendships of choir singers, the significance of choir singing in the society comparing to other activities, and trust in institutions and democracy. The questions related to Figure 2 deal with the main motivations (music or community based) to join the choir and continue the hobby.

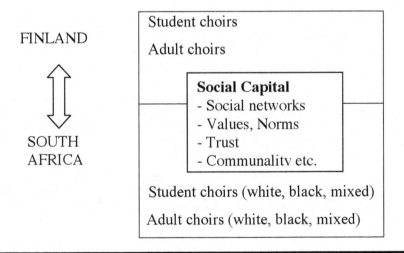

FIGURE 1

The central approach, key concepts and research subjects.

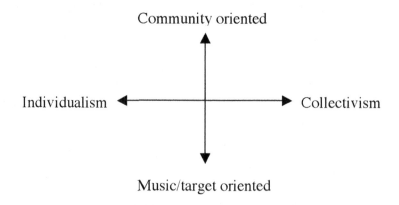

FIGURE 2

Two-dimensional model in the frame of which the musical activities will be analysed.

When approaching the choirs as communities, we raised questions pertinent to choir members' social interaction, local activity or attitude towards voluntary work. We were also interested in people's backgrounds in choir intercultural comparisons between Finnish and South African choirs. Comparisons between different types of choirs were also of great importance. When answers are needed from a wide range of people, and when set questions divide into several parts, it is reasonable to use survey methods in the research. Thus the data were collected with a structured questionnaire containing questions not only about background and musical hobbies but also the meaning of choir as a hobby, other communal hobbies, social activity, trust and distrust (the latter one is not dealt with in this article). In addition to quantitative methods, qualitative methods, such as interviews and observations, were also used. The interviews give examples on how choir singing is experienced on the personal level, and the findings support the conclusions that we have drawn from the quantitative data.

Parts of the questions in this research have been modified using the international surveys of World Values Survey, the World Bank and the Australian Bureau of Statistics that deal with trust and perceptions of community and social activity. Thus some of our results can be compared with similar questions of the international surveys, and it is possible to find out if choir singers differ from other citizens.

The quantitative data were gathered across 500 choir singers during autumn 2004 and spring 2005 in Finland and South Africa. They represent widely different age groups and educational degrees. All the usual types of choirs are represented: youth/male/female choirs, mixed choirs, church choirs and senior choirs. In this article, the meaning of choirs as a community is approached by describing the data in frequencies, and analysing the data with two methods: cross tabulation and comparison of means. This is done to assist in the comparison of Finnish and South African choirs. The statistical significance is shown based on the chi-squared values and p values. Through the comparative research approach (Finland vs. South Africa) and international cooperation, the understanding of the cultural dimensions of the concept of social capital is increased.

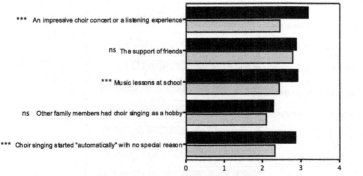

FIGURE 3

Important reasons for singing in choir (Question: How important have the following reasons been for you to start choir singing?).

Note: 0 = Do not know, 1= Not at all important, 2 = Not very important, 3 = Somewhat important, 4 = Very important.

Results

The question 'How important have the following reasons been for you to start choir singing?' gives an overview of the main motivations to join a choir (see Figure 3). The motivation to start choir singing activities can be influenced by many factors, including parents, friends, school and previous experiences in choir concerts. A good guess would be that the role of family members might be of great importance, but according to Figure 3, the influence of parents or other family members is minimal. The influence of friends is the greatest to start choir singing. This is in line with the fact that belonging to a group is of great importance for the choir members (Figure 5). Perhaps it is important for the person to know that at least one friend is presently singing in the choir before he or she makes a positive decision. Another significant reason to join a choir was the singers' own impressive choir experience. This was an especially important reason to join the choir for South Africans. Musical motivation for choir singing becomes clear from Figure 5 as well. The most important factor for singing in a choir, however, was the artistic experience itself. A great number of subjects agreed with the statement that the choir activity started 'automatically, without any special reason'. The influence of school seems to be great. In order to get new choir singers in the future it is important to continue active choir tradition at schools. The role of school was greater for South Africans than for Finns.

The question 'How important to you are the following factors in playing or singing?', was posed to give a possibility to compare choirs with other musical activities (see Figure 4).The most important factor in singing and playing is connected to the artistic nature of the experience. Another music-related factor is 'development of playing or singing skills' and the 'development of artistic expression'. These results give the impression that musical aims are more important than social. Social contacts and belonging to a group are not as significant

85

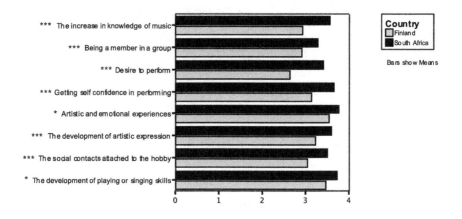

FIGURE 4

Important factors for singing or playing music (Question: How important to you are the following factors in playing or singing?).

Note: 1 = Not at all important, 2 = Not very important, 3 = Somewhat important, 4 = Very important.

factors as musical ones. In this respect, Finnish and South Africans differ from each other. For South Africans, the role of friends was less important to them than for Finns. The greatest difference between Finns and South Africans was the role of increasing musical knowledge: South Africans consider the increasing of musical knowledge as the fourth important factor in singing and playing.

The question 'How important to you are the following factors in choir singing?' was posed to clarify how strongly individual, social, emotional or musical factors are emphasised (see Figure 5). The previous question examined singing and playing in general, but this question was focused on choral singing. The two most important factors that draw individuals to choral singing are the improvement of singing skills and the artistic experiences. An interesting difference between singing and playing in general and choir singing, in particular, is related to the role of friends and belonging to a group: in choir singing, the social contacts attached to the hobby and the importance of being a member in a group are critical components.

In comparing Finnish and South African answers, it appears that for Finns the social relationships that develop within the choir, and the sense of belonging to a group, are relatively more important than for South Africans. For South Africans, the development of singing skills, the desire to perform and the increase in knowledge of music are the most important factors. The difference is not as significant when comparing the absolute means, but when comparing the relative ratings the difference is clear. An explanation of this perhaps surprising result might be related to the cultural differences between these two countries. Finns consider themselves as quite 'unsocial' and reserved. Perhaps choir singing gives the members a natural way to build up social networks and an extra

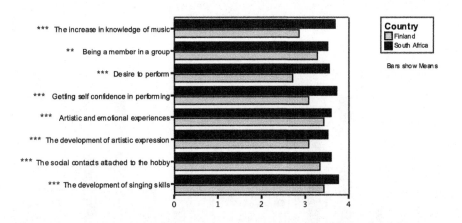

FIGURE 5

Factors in choral singing (Question: How important to you are the following factors in choir singing?).

Note: 1 = Not at all important, 2 = Not very important, 3 = Somewhat important, 4 = Very important.

dimension for their 'unsocial' life. To South Africans, active social networks are an integrated part of life and in this way 'nothing special'. To Finns, social life related to choir singing activities is something extra and special, that other activities or hobbies cannot give. The three most important factors to South Africans are the development of singing skills, gaining self-confidence in performing and the increase in knowledge of music. The first and third factors are technical and musical, not emotional or social.

A basic question about the role of choir singing for the social life of people is 'How important to you are the personal relationships among these groups?' (see Figure 6A and Figure 6B). The importance of relationships differs clearly between choirs and other hobbies: the personal relationships in choirs are more often mentioned to be very important than in other activities. The difference between countries is even more obvious: the most often chosen answer by the Finns was that relationships are somewhat (50%) or very (40%) significant, while in most South African answers the personal relationships in choirs was mentioned to be very significant (75%). The message is that for South Africans, although they do not mention personal relationships to be as important in choir singing as Finns, the significance of personal relationships is very important. In both countries the message is the same: personal relationships in choirs are much more important than relationships in other social groups.

In Figure 7, the question refers to how personal, even intimate, topics can be shared by choir members. The greatest differences can be seen between familial matters, matters of personal relations, spiritual matters and physical health. The last topic (physical health) is most often discussed among choir members, and corroborates other research on the relationship between health and choir singing (Hyyppä & Mäki, 2001). The topics that are more frequently discussed with choir members

87

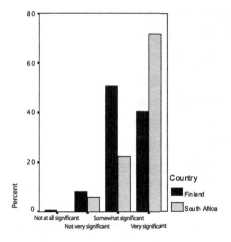

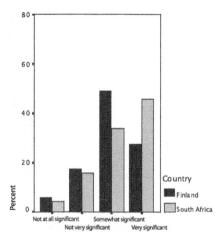

FIGURE 6A

Importance of personal relationships —
Choir (Question: How important to you are
the personal relationships among these
groups?).

Note: 1 = Not at all important,
    2 = Not very important, 3 = Quite important,
    4 = Very important.
    p = .000

FIGURE 6B

Importance of personal relationships —
Other group (Question: How important to
you are the personal relationships among
these groups?).

Note: 1 = Not at all important,
    2 = Not very important, 3 = Quite important,
    4 = Very important.
    p = .066

than with other groups include familial matters, religious and personal relations.
These indicate that there is an atmosphere of trust that is shared by members of the
choir, such that even therapeutic discussions are possible.

The question 'Compared to other hobbies and social activities, how significant is the choir for you as a community?' was a direct way for comparing the
significance of choir singing and other activities (see Figure 8). According to
the responses offered by choir members, the choir is more important or even the
most important community for the members. Responses in South Africa and
Finland are well in line with one another, although South Africans mention
more often than Finns that the choir is the most important community. In this
question, the important role of a choir as a community becomes very clear,
although the precise reason for this is less so. Questions in Figure 3 and Figure 5
refer to the main motivation for choir members' initiation of singing, and the
importance of different factors in choir singing. The social role of the choir does
not surface strongly; as musical factors were emphasised over social factors.

With the question 'How significant a role do you think choir singing has in
the formation of the following things?' we wanted to understand better the role
of different aspects of choir singing for the members (see Figure 9). Choir
singing seems to play a significant role in creating the feeling of togetherness
and helps the members to understand their role as members of a community. In

FIGURE 7

Sharing personal topics among choir members (Question: Which of the following personal matters can be shared and discussed with at least one member of these groups?)

Note: 0 = No, 1 = Yes. The bars show the mean values of the answers, thus describing the frequency of 'Yes' answers in per cents concerning each topic

addition to these social aspects, there is also the perception of oneself as a singer that some emphasise as important to them. No great differences between nations were found in examining these responses, although 'experiencing ethnic roots' seemed more important to South Africans than to Finns.

Discussion

Individual factors were mentioned most frequently as important motivations for singing in choirs, both by respondents from Finland and South Africa: the increase in knowledge of music (South Africa), gaining self-confidence in performing (South Africa), artistic and emotional experiences (Finland), and the development of singing skills (Finland and South Africa). Communal and social factors (being a member in a group and social contact attached to the hobby) were mentioned as important factors as well, but not to the same extent as individual factors. Comparing choir activities with other kinds of playing or singing (Figures 3 and 4), with choirs the social factors are emphasised more in both countries. The picture about the role of choir singing among different kinds of activities becomes clearer when looking results in Figure 6A and Figure 6B.

The message is straightforward: personal relationships between choir members are more important than relationships among other kinds of groups. Especially in South Africa, relationships among choir members are mentioned as particularly meaningful. This finding can be understood by looking at the answers in Figure 7 ('Which of the following personal matters can be shared and discussed with at least one member of these groups?'). Choir members are comfortable discussing more personal and intimate questions, including spiritual matters (South Africa), matters of personal relations (Finland), family matters (both) and physical health (both).

89

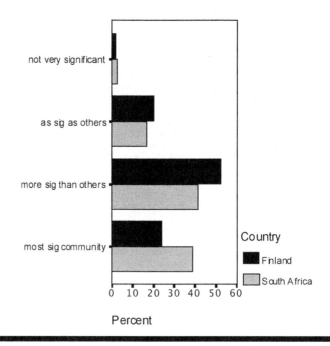

FIGURE 8

Choir in comparison to other hobbies and social activities (Question: Compared to other hobbies and social activities, how significant is the choir for you as a community?).

Note: *p* = .082

Methodologically, the use of a Likert scale is problematic in crosscultural approaches to research. Throughout the questionnaire, the style of answering seems to be different among Finns and South Africans. South Africans systematically tended to use higher ratings, with attention to the 'most significant' and 'very important' responses, while the Finns were more likely to offer moderate, midway responses. There may be cultural differences between the two respondent groups, in that Finns are often described as 'reserved and introverted' people while South Africans are more 'open and extroverted'. Thus, without further studies and clarifications, it is important not to offer over-simplified interpretations.

In general, the results offer an impression that singing in a choir supports both individual and communal needs of people. At the same time, strong artistic experiences can be felt and social needs are fulfilled. The ability of choir-singing to satisfy many and different needs of human beings might be one of the main explanations for the popularity of choir singing. Choirs offer an efficient way to build up social networks of trust that are elementary building boxes of the social capital, and give the members a natural platform to discuss the values and norms of their society. The results are aligned with those of Durrant and Himonides (1998), with the main reason for people to sing in a choir being music's social and emotional dimensions. No great differences were found in this respect between Finland and South Africa, although small emphases of performing orientation ('Desire to

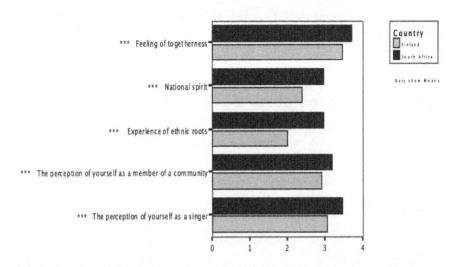

FIGURE 9

Choir singing for non-musical purposes (Question: How significant a role do you think choir singing has in the formation of the following things?).

Note: 0 = Do not know, 1 = Not at all important, 2 = Not very important,
   3 = Quite important, 4 = Very important.

perform', 'Getting self-confidence in performing') and learning experiences ('The increase in knowledge in music') were found in South Africa.

Culturally based differences were not as distinctive as expected. We initially considered that South Africans, widely viewed as more socially oriented people than the Finns, would emphasise the social aspects in choir singing to a greater extent than the Finns. This was not the case. The Finns mentioned more frequently that friendships and social aspects are very important aspects for them in choir singing. Our interpretation is that because active social life is in any case a common feature in South African societies; social relations pertinent to choir singing do not offer the extra value for them. On the other hand, the Finns typically do not have as many possibilities for fulfilling their social needs. For the Finns, choir singing is a special way to activate people's social life and to increase the number of friendships.

References

Durrant, C., & Himonides, E. (1998). What makes people sing together? Socio-psychological and Cross-cultural perspectives on the choral phenomenon. *International Journal of Music Education*, 32(1), 61–70.

Hargreaves, D. J., & North A. (1997). *The social psychology of music*. New York: Oxford University Press.

Hyyppä, M. T., & Mäki, J. (2001). Individual-level relationships between social capital and self-related health in a bilingual community. *Prevence Medicine*, 32, 148–155.

Hyyppä, M. T. (2002). *Elinvoimaa yhteisöstä. Sosiaalinen pääoma ja terveys* [Vitality from the community. Social captial and the health]. Jyväskylä: PS-kustannus.

Putnam, R. D. (1994). *Making democracy work: Civic traditions in modern Italy*. Princeton: Princeton University Press.

Putnam, R. D. (2000). *Bowling alone: The collapse and revival of American community*. New York: Simon & Schuster.

Triandis, H.C. (1995). *Individualism and collectivism*. Boulder: Westview Press.

JUKKA LOUHIVUORI, PHD, is professor of music at the University of Jyvaskyla, Finland, department of music. He is the president of the FiSME (Finnish Society for Music Education). His doctoral thesis is about Finnish spiritual folk hymns. His scientific interest has been focused on cognitive musicology, ethnomusicology and multicultural music education. The main topics of interest are cognitive processes in perceiving, memorising and production of music; improvisation and variation in folk music; and crosscultural music cognition.

VELI-MATTI SALMINEN, MSoSc, is research assistant at the University of Jyväskylä, Finland, department of music. He has studied sociology, computer sciences and physics. His current research topic is related to social capital in the context of music cultures. He is currently the sub-editor of the Finnish Journal of Sociology.

MORAKENG EDWARD KENNETH LEBAKA, MA, was previously an educator, a school director, an account executive at Buyers Network Unlimited (BNU) in Pretoria in South Africa, Regional Co-Coordinator (Arts and Culture) in Limpopo, Research Assistant at the University of Pretoria. He has many academic and professional publications to his credit. His research areas and interests include intercultural aspects of music education, the school music curriculum, African music in education, educational management, sourcing the ethnomusicological focus in musicology and musical tourism as a dimension of music education.

This research for this article was funded by the Academy of Finland.

Voices From
the Classroom

Creating a Balance: Investigating a New Model for Music Teaching and Learning in the Australian Context

Georgina Barton

The contemporary Australian music teaching and learning environment is rich and diverse. Students of music bring varied music learning experiences and knowledge into the classroom, yet the number of students studying music in schools is inordinately low. This article will explore current educational research that has focused strongly on how to address the diverse make-up of the Australian population via multicultural approaches to education. It will highlight that discussions tend to focus on 'west-centric' solutions to problems encountered in music education and will also explore the literature of prominent ethnomusicologists whose work has been influential in the education discussion. A common thread throughout has been the recognition of the need for a new model of music teaching and learning in context.

As an example, the article will then outline findings from a comparative study between two music cultures; Karnatic and Queensland instrumental music teaching contexts. It will propose that a balance between formal and informal modes of teaching should be explored in the contemporary Australian context, arguing that a model of teaching and learning that takes into account various modes of communication and instruction will be 'culturally responsive' to contexts such as those encountered in Australia.

The Multicultural Education Context

For a number of decades, the Australian student population in schools has been socially and culturally rich and diverse (Bullivant, 1981; Rizvi, 1986). Similarly, a large focus in education discourse has been on the notion of multiculturalism in Australia. Multicultural here is defined as a number of cultures present in one context. Culture is defined as the skills, arts of people in any given historic or geographic period (*Collins Australian Dictionary*) and further as according to Harris (1980) 'learned and shared behaviour'.

Integral to this discussion were the outcomes of the Galbally Report in 1978, which outlined four basic principles of multiculturalism:

1. the same opportunity for all to realise their potential
2. any person must be able to retain his or her culture without experiencing any prejudice
3. there should be special services and programs for migrants

4. these programs and services should be prepared and operated in consultation with the migrants themselves.

These precepts have continued to influence the ways in which policy, research and practice in the educational context are developed.

In a report about a collaborative project with the Australian Chamber Orchestra by Rebecca Baillie on ABC's *7.30 Report* dated March 31, 2005, it was noted that 97% of the student population at Cabramatta State High School were from non-English speaking backgrounds. In addition, the principal Beth Godwin stated that it was necessary to acknowledge the school's multicultural make-up for such projects to be successful:

> There is statistical evidence to prove that our students come from a socio-economically disadvantaged background. However, I believe that our students and our school is wealthy to the point of being rich in terms of its cultural background (March 31, 2005).

As educators, it is important to consider the fact that our classes are more than likely to be 'multicultural' for a number of reasons:

- every student has had personal experiences different to any other student
- students enter the classroom with varying cultural experiences
- each student's approach to learning may be very different.

The significance these aspects in developing programs and curricula has been a focus of much departmental policy generally.

The Music Education Context

Similar observations about culture have also been made within the music education context. Elliot (1995), for example, states that music listening and musical works always involve some degree of cultural–ideological information. He believes that:

- all forms of musicing are inherently artistic–social–cultural endeavours
- musical works are socialcultural constructions
- all musicers and listeners live in particular places and time periods.

Dunbar-Hall (1992) agrees and believes that musical works, as products of culture, are contextually specific and bounded by time and place. There are also other, more specific aspects that impact on the transmission of music within context. Blacking (1973) defines these as extra-musical features such as ritualistic actions and reactions, spiritual or religious meaning, other purposes or functions of the music, and the structure of processes used within the context. Also impacting on the transmission processes in music is whether or not the context is considered to be *formal* or *informal* (Merriam, 1964), *analytic* or *holistic* (Ellis, 1985), *group* or *individualised* (Lomax, 1976).

In regard to more formal institutionalised settings such as schools, Corpateux (2002) and Stowasser (1995) have observed that students bring extremely rich and diverse experiences in music into the classroom. They also comment that it is more than likely that students will feel detached from the practices of music teachers who base their approach on a west-centric model of education. Campbell (2004) agrees, outlining that the prevalent way of teaching is not necessarily the most appropriate:

> [T]his is but one model, and a colonial one at that, which fixes European music (and its staff notation) and its pedagogical processes highest in a hierarchy atop the musical expressions and instructional approaches of so many other rich traditions. Would such a

96

model be continued in the twenty-first century, in a time of postcolonial and democratic reconsiderations of cultures and their perspectives? (p. xvi).

As music education is itself seen to be multicultural, the students that comprise our classrooms are also diverse. Dunbar-Hall (1992, p. 188) and Elliott (1995, p. 291) attempt to define multicultural music education, concluding that as music itself is multicultural then so music education should be (Barton, 2003b).

Dillon (1997, 2001) states that students, more often than not, seek access to music making and meaning outside of the school's confines. This is evidenced by an inordinately low number of students studying music within the school context, particularly at the senior level, with many schools unable to offer music as a senior subject because of a lack of interest, resources and/or staffing and timetabling issues.

This situation has led government bodies to question the role that music education plays in Australian children's lives. In 2005, a national review of music education was undertaken with the support from the Department of Education, Science and Training (DEST). This review had a number of functions, including investigating the status and quality of music education, developing recommendations for further development of programs in Australian schools, and gathering information about examples of best practice.

In the opinion of Temmerman (2004), an address to Parliament on February 10, 2003 by Chris Pearce provided the catalyst for a national review, which should provide evidence of the quality of such programs and justify their continued financial support. She also comments on the fact that despite an increasing number of young people becoming involved in music as a leisure activity, school music participation is worsening. With reference to the state of school music experiences she states:

> Where dissatisfaction was expressed it was most associated with lesson content that was perceived to be useless; with activities that focused on passive rather than active music making; and with teachers whose attitudes appeared to demonstrate lesser tolerance towards students who lacked in knowledge and understanding of traditional/classical music forms (Temmerman, 2004, pp. 62–63).

The state of music education seems a far cry from the popularity of the music industry. Last year alone, according to the Australian Record Industry Association (2004) statistics, over A\$600 million was spent on music videos and sound recordings. The prevalent and increasing desire for young people to buy music suggests a passion for this art form. How can this difference be so great?

One may argue that there is a large difference between purchasing music recordings for listening pleasure and learning content-specific skills to perform and/or compose music. This may be true; however, the majority of students who enjoy listening to music say both that they could not live without it (*The Sunday Mail*, April 10, 2005, p. 22), and that they would like to learn to sing or perform/write songs themselves (Barton, 2005). With so many students investing time and money in music, why are numbers of school enrolments in music so minimal?

97

Many researchers and educators have consistently examined these problems of music education and offered ways to change current practices so that they are more 'contextually appropriate' (Anderson, 1991; Campbell, 1996; Leong, 1999; Smith, 1998; Stowasser, 1997), often focusing on how culture influences music teaching and learning (Barton, 2005).

Models of Teaching and Learning in the Music Education Context

Though the impact of culture on music and education is often cited in the literature, few robust reasons are offered for why it is important. Most of the research and literature addressing culture is focused on philosophical, theoretical and value assessments of the importance of culture rather than on practical application and the benefits of a contextual approach to the teaching of instrumental music. One clear exception rests in the experience and work of some ethnomusicologists who have written extensively on the nature of music cultures other than western art music (Blacking, 1973; Ellis, 1985; Merriam, 1964). Many texts authored by ethnomusicologists are seminal to understanding the role that culture plays in music teaching and learning.

Commenting on the value of an ethnomusicological approach to research in discovering what is important in a music education context, including the influence of culture, Stowasser (1992, p. 16) notes that:

> Ethnomusicology is primarily concerned with the objective study of music within cultures other than one's own; application of the same objectivity to the study of traditional secondary school music education in Western society reveals that, in general, the theory and the practice of a small, elite subculture has been imposed upon adolescent students regardless of their heterogeneous cultural backgrounds. Thus, ethnomusicological approaches may help us to identify the cause of the problem; but we need additional data in order to find a solution.

Without a clear understanding of the ways in which culture influences music, there is no consistent way of determining whether certain practices are more important than others in conveying music knowledge. As such, it may not be possible to respond to cultural aspects of music in a meaningful way within the tuition process, or to isolate which practices are more effective in reflecting culture, thereby limiting the capacity of teachers to respond to diversity and difference in their tuition practices. Ultimately it may also mean that teachers are not able effectively to engage with and utilise the resources that students bring from their cultures and communities of origin to the learning experience.

A number of models have been formulated in the process of investigating different approaches to the transmission of music knowledge. Many musicians reflect on this knowledge after experiencing cultures other than their own. These experiences have an impact in a number of ways:

- enabling researchers to understand their own culture more
- developing further skills in teaching their own music often specifically enhancing their own aural/oral skills
- increasing their understanding of various ways of knowing in a music teaching and learning context.

Most researchers found that many other cultures based their music transmission on aural/oral means, valuing and emphasising the skill of memorisation. It was also clear that the maintenance of the music tradition demanded a focus on memorisation rather than the extensive use of written scores. An emphasis on memory represents music as an aural art, critically located within a context (Blacking, 1973).

Many researchers (Boyce-Tillman, 1996; Brennan, 1992; Lundquist & Szego, 1998; Rose, 1995; Volk, 1998) have acknowledged that culture influences the processes and practices of music education today: 'How music is "lived" in education can, and does, reveal much about social and cultural ideals. Music education does not exist in isolation from the various expressions and institutions of culture and society' (Rose, 1995, p. 39). Rose continues this argument further with evidence from music educators stating that on the whole, it was clear that 'the diversity of musical and cultural backgrounds that exist in communities and music education classrooms needs to be addressed in curriculum development and teacher preparation' (p. 45). Despite extensive research in this area, no clear solutions have emerged and persuasive new models of contextual teaching and learning in music education are sought.

A Case Study

In 1993, I worked as an Australian Volunteer Abroad in Chennai, South India, and took up the opportunity to study the Karnatic classical music tradition. I had both vocal and violin lessons and was able, through this experience, to compare my learning in India with the familiar Australian context. This experience inspired me to embark on my doctoral journey — to investigate how, in fact, culture influenced the way that people taught music within a context.

Through a comparative study of Karnatic and Queensland music teachers it was found that culture specifically influenced a number of aspects within the music teaching and learning environments, including the teachers involved, teaching methods, modes of communication used and the context in which teaching took place. As a result, it was discovered that a balance between both an aural/oral and a text-based approach was desirable within the contemporary music education environment. Additionally, teachers in both the Karnatic and Queensland contexts were influenced by their past experiences of learning, with each teacher showing a strong connection with, or memory of, their own teacher. Similarly, the music chosen for teaching and the instruments used were selected according to cultural influences and the experiences teachers had when they were learning. Teachers tended to teach musical works that they had themselves studied (Barton, 2003a, 2004).

The research also showed that the influence of culture is evident in the teaching methods and modes of communication used by instrumental music teachers in a variety of ways (Barton, 2004). Despite the vast array of strategies chosen by teachers to convey music knowledge, there was considerable similarity in the teaching methods and modes of communication used in both the Karnatic music and Queensland instrumental music contexts. This could indicate that music knowledge is transmitted in similar ways across a number of cultural boundaries.

Many aspects in the instrumental music-teaching context were found to be influenced by the culture in which it was immersed — this extends to both musical and non-musical elements. While the teachers' own experiences and methods of teaching and modes of communication are important, culture also has an impact on the meaning of music making within these practices. In both the Karnatic and Queensland instrumental music contexts, it was evident that culture contributed to the way that music knowledge was transmitted as well as the purpose of music teaching and learning in these contexts.

Barton (2004) highlighted that the influence on these practices from the cultural and social surrounds is an integral aspect of the teaching process but is often understated. This is due in part to the subtlety of the cultural influences as discussed above, and to the teachers themselves not being fully aware of the impact that culture has on teaching practices. Understanding this effect, however, may assist

99

teachers in producing outcomes faster and more effectively in the music education context.

Investigating a New Model for Music Teaching and Learning in the Contemporary Australian Context

It is suggested that 'creating a balance' between both aural/oral and text-based methods of teaching and modes of communication in the music education context is desirable.

The potential impact of not addressing problems may result in ongoing limiting education practices in music teaching and learning (Stowasser, 1992; Walker, 2001). More specifically, the following aspects may be adversely affected:

- understanding of how culture, music and education interact
- capacity to gauge the extent to which culture is a determining factor in conveying music knowledge
- capacity on which to make decisions about the importance of culture and whether it should be a consideration in the delivery of instrumental music education content
- capacity to amend teaching practices to be more or less reflective of culture.

The benefits of building knowledge in this area include the potential to make informed decisions about what aspects of the interaction between culture, music and education are critical to conveying music knowledge in context. In addition, knowing the extent and nature of culture's influence may enable teachers to amend their approach to teaching where particular practices do not contribute markedly to transferring music knowledge. It may also increase the capacity for teachers to teach not only music from other cultures but also teach culturally thereby enriching the teaching experience and supporting greater opportunities for diversity.

Conclusion

It is now timely that we as educators consider a distinct change in the way that we approach the teaching of music within the contemporary context. Not only are researchers recognising the need for a change, but so are government bodies. An increasing interest in the quality of music education indicates that teachers should become more accountable and aware of not only *what* they are teaching but also *how* they are teaching. We can no longer expect our students who come from diverse personal, social and cultural backgrounds to accept learning from a west-centric perspective. Demands on teachers are ever-increasing; therefore, government bodies should also provide the necessary support for teachers to be able to extend their knowledge of not only content from music in other cultures but also the ways that this knowledge is traditionally taught. Only then will change be culturally responsive, resulting in higher quality outcomes.

100

References

Anderson, W. M., & Lawrence, J. E. (1991). *Integrating music into the classroom* (2nd ed.). California: Wadsworth.

Australian Record Industry Association. (2004). *Australian record sales – 2004 full year results*. Retrieved from www.aria.com.au/pages/australianrecordsales2004fullyearresults.htm

Baillie, R. (2005). *Orchestra tunes into mentor program* [Television broadcast]. Retrieved from www.abc.net.au/7.30/content/2005/s1335685.htm

Barton, G. M. (2003a). Student preference for learning: the notion of music literacy? In *Proceedings of the Australian Association For Research in Music Education Conference* (pp. 15–21). Brisbane: AARME Melbourne.

Barton, G. M. (2003b). *The influence of culture on instrumental music teaching: A participant-observation case study of Karnatic and Queensland instrumental music teachers in context.* Unpublished doctoral dissertation, Queensland University of Technology, Brisbane, Australia.

Barton, G. M. (2004). The influence of culture on music teaching and learning. In *Proceedings of the Australian Association of Research in Music Education Conference* (pp. 1–12).

Barton, G. M. (2005). The student voice: How children prefer to learn. In *Proceedings of the Australian Society of Music Education Conference.* Melbourne, Victoria, Australia: Melbourne University.

Blacking, J. (1973). *How musical is man?* Seattle and London: University of Washington Press.

Brennan, P. S. (1992). Design and implementation of curricula experiences in world music: A perspective. In H. Lees (Ed.), *Music education: Sharing musics of the world* (pp. 221–225). Seoul, Korea: International Society of Music Education, Conference Proceedings.

Boyce-Tillman, J. (1996). A framework for intercultural dialogue in music. In M. Floyd (Ed.), *World musics in education* (pp. 43–94). United Kingdom: Scholar Press.

Bullivant, B. (1981). *Race, ethnicity and curriculum.* Melbourne, Victoria, Australia: Macmillan.

Campbell, P. S. (1991). *Lessons from the world: A cross-cultural guide to music teaching and learning.* United States: Schirmer Books.

Campbell, P. S. (Ed.). (1996). *Music in cultural context: Eight views on world music education.* United States: Music Educators' National Conference.

Campbell, P. S. (2004). *Teaching music globally: Experiencing music, expressing culture* New York: Oxford University Press.

Corpataux, F. (2002). Children's songs around the world: An interview with Francis Corpataux. *Journal of the International Society for Music Education, 40*(1), 3–14.

Dillon, S. C. (1997). The student as maker: A narrative for a pragmatist aesthetic. In *New sounds for a new century* (pp. 75–80). Brisbane, Australia: Australian Society For Music Education, XIth Conference Proceedings.

Dillon, S. C. (2001). *The student as maker: An examination of the meaning of music to students in a school and the ways in which we give access to meaningful music education.* Unpublished doctoral dissertation, La Trobe University, Victoria, Australia.

Dunbar-Hall, P. (1992). Towards a definition of multiculturalism in music education. In H. Lees (Ed.), *Music education: Sharing musics of the world* (pp. 186–193). Seoul, Korea: International Society of Music Education, Conference Proceedings.

Dunbar-Hall, P. (1999). Ethnomusicology and music education: Issues of cross-fertilisation. In *Opening the umbrella: An encompassing view of music education* (pp. 48–53). Sydney, New South Wales, Australia: Australian Society For Music Education, XIIth Conference Proceedings.

Elliott, D. J. (1995). *Music matters: A new philosophy of music education.* Oxford and New York: Oxford University Press.

Ellis C. J. (1985). *Aboriginal music education for living: cross-cultural experiences from South Australia.* Brisbane, Queensland, Australia: University of Queensland Press.

Galbally Report. (1978). *Review of post-arrival programs and services for migrants.* Canberra, Australia: Government Printing.

Leong, S. (1999). Opening the musicianship umbrella: An inclusive aural education for planetary musicians. In *Opening the umbrella: An encompassing view of music education* (pp. 124–129). Sydney, Australia: Australian Society For Music Education, XIIth Conference Proceedings.

Lomax, A. (1968). *Folk song, style and culture.* Washington, DC: American Association for the Advancement of Science.

101

Lundquist, B., & Szego, C. K. (with Nettl, B., Santos, R.P., & Solbu, E.). (Eds.). (1998). *Musics of the world's cultures: A source book for music educators*. Nedlands, Western Australia: CIRCME.

Merriam, A. P. (1964). *The anthropology of music*. United States: Northwestern University Press.

Rizvi, F. (1986). *Ethnicity, class and multicultural education*. Victoria, Australia: Deakin University.

Rose, A. M. (1995). A place for Indigenous music in formal music education. *International Journal of Music Education, 26*, 39–54.

Smith, R. G. (1998). *Evaluating the initiation, application and appropriateness of a series of customised teaching and learning strategies designed to communicate musical and related understandings interculturally*. Unpublished doctoral dissertation, Northern Territory University, Australia.

Stowasser, H. (1992). The development of the music curriculum in Queensland secondary schools: A microcosmic view. In W. Bebbington (Ed.), *Sound and reason: Music essays in honour of Gordon D. Spearitt*. Brisbane, Australia: Faculty of Music, University of Queensland.

Stowasser, H. (1995). Honing the craft of audiation: Music is an aural art. In M. Barratt & H. Lees (Eds.), *Honing the craft: Improving the quality of music education* (pp. 257–261). Hobart, Tasmania, Australia: Australian Society for Music Education, Xth Conference Proceedings.

Stowasser, H. (1997). New sounds for a new humanity. In *New sounds for a new century* (pp.1–8). Brisbane, Australia: Australian Society For Music Education, XIth Conference Proceedings.

Temmerman, N. (2004). School, community and context. *Proceedings of the Australian Association of Research in Music Education Conference* (pp. 1–12).

Volk, T. (1998). *Music, education and multiculturalism: Foundations and principles*. New York: Oxford University Press.

Walker, R. (2001). The rise and fall of philosophies of music education: Looking backwards in order to see ahead. *Research Studies in Music Education, 17*.

Dr Georgina Barton is a music educator who values the diversity that music brings into the teaching and learning context. Her area of expertise is inclusive pedagogy and the development of teachers' skills in addressing multi-modes of learning. She has had experience in a diverse range of music cultures. Dr Barton is currently on staff at Griffith University in music and also works with Education Queensland.

Dabbling or Deepening — Where to Begin?: Global Music in International School Elementary Education

Melissa Cain

M any music teachers are excited at the prospect of incorporating music from around the world into their programs, but often balk at the effort involved, and the significant obstacles they encounter along the way. A lack of adequate teacher training and collegial and administrative support, combined with the absence of factual information, culturally accurate musical recordings, genuine instruments and proficient performance skills, often forces teachers to forego their desires to include the music of a wider variety of cultures in their programs.

Perhaps the greatest stumbling block to providing an experience for students in world musics is the issue of authenticity. If teachers struggle with being able to produce culturally authentic music in their classrooms, then should the performance of world musics be attempted at all? While a superficial dabble does nothing to enhance a program, nor provide a comprehensive understanding of the musical culture presented, I would argue that every attempt should be made to incorporate music that is as *culturally accurate* as possible.

More than ever, our students represent an eclectic blend of ethnicities, religions and cultural identities. We are educating citizens of the world. Therefore, it is essential that we work hard to move beyond these difficulties, in order to provide our students with more than just an awareness of cultures other than their own. There are many exciting and innovative ways to incorporate musics of the world into the school program. It takes much investigation and ingenuity on the part of the music teacher, but the benefits are many and lasting.

The elementary music teachers at Singapore American School (SAS) work with students of over 40 different nationalities; many of whom have already lived in three or more countries during their lifetimes. Despite receiving no formal training in ethnomusicology, nor in the performance of non-western instruments in their undergraduate studies, several music teachers have become committed to furthering their education and practical experience, in order to tap into the rich cultural heritage of the student body, and to share a practical appreciation of the music of these representative cultures with all elementary students. Exploring the challenges that teachers with backgrounds in western music face when incorporating music from around the world into their programs at the elementary music department at SAS, their experiences can be used to illustrate these challenges, and resulting successes.

103

Teaching Music From a Global Perspective

Australia is a land of many different kinds of people, who differ by race, religion, ethnicity, socioeconomic status, age and gender. It stands to reason that music education in Australia should reflect the social make-up of the country, and the multiple and dynamic identities of individuals who represent a broad cross-section of cultural groups. For many music teachers, however, their educational goals and learning outcomes have been filtered as a result of life experiences, and thus unintentionally coloured by prejudices, stereotypes and sometimes misconceptions. Despite the multicultural make-up of Australia, the music education of many students has been, and currently is, predominantly Eurocentric in nature.

Why should music teachers put in the time and effort needed to change what and how they teach, to suit a more global model? Those teachers who incorporate music from a variety of cultural groups into their programs know the answer. They choose to teach music from a global perspective, because the study of musics of the world is a privilege; it is invigorating, exciting, challenging and immensely rewarding for students and teachers alike.

Steven Loza suggests 'experiencing people's musical expressions may be one of the most direct avenues to intercultural understanding' (1996, p. 59). Indeed, arguably one of the most important and long lasting benefits of exploring the arts of a variety of cultural groups is the resulting increase in intercultural understanding and empathy, and the reduction of prejudice. Teaching music as culture allows students to begin to know the inner workings of a cultural group, to gain an understanding of how others view themselves, and how they think in terms of sound (Volk, 2002, p. 22). Musical thought is culturally defined, so to develop in-depth knowledge of a type of music, we must learn about its place in its respective culture.

Despite music being universal, its meaning is not (Slobin & Titon, 1992, p. 1). Patricia Shehan Campbell suggests that music communicates fully 'only to those who know the unique treatment of its components' (Campbell, 1991, p. 110). While this is undoubtedly true, this is not to say that those of us from outside the culture cannot do our best to learn the inner workings of a particular music, and the social messages contained in its performance in order to achieve aesthetic satisfaction. I propose that our students can achieve an emic (inside) experience of global music styles if given the opportunity to experience the music practically and in context.

Where to Begin?

How difficult is it for a teacher to make a change in perspective and work towards a more globally focused music curriculum? If we are without experience or education in music of cultures other than our own, the effort needed to learn and teach songs in languages other than English, and to perform on instruments for which we do not possess the correct techniques, may seem overwhelming.

104

Certainly, while it is infinitely easier to rely on the familiar repertoire and teaching techniques with which we feel most competent, taking risks and learning new skills in order to explore global music in its cultural context is, from my experience, well worth the effort involved. Who is suited to this challenge? It takes an open-minded and creative teacher with commitment, perseverance and initiative to take on the work of sourcing culturally accurate materials, recordings, instruments and live performances. It takes a teacher with energy and passion for global music, to work towards achieving administrative support, to find room in a crowded curriculum, to prepare new lesson plans and to keep upgrading in order to acquire new knowledge.

What types of music should be introduced into the music program? Victor Fung encourages teachers who are introducing global music for the first time, to do so in the least invasive manner. He suggests that we aim to work with musics that are most similar to those of the western tradition, and those to which our students can therefore best relate (Fung, 2002, p. 200). I disagree, feeling strongly that our students are capable of appreciating a wide variety of musical styles, and are not reluctant to depart from a western-like sound if given adequate opportunity to experience the music thoroughly. A number of leading ethnomusicologists (including Bruno Nettl, Anthony Seeger and Patricia Shehan Campbell) advocate exposing children to a variety of sounds as young as possible, as every new style gives students a new perspective, making them familiar with sounds not found in the music of their own culture (Campbell, 1996, p. 35).

As it takes much time to come to know a musical culture, it is wise that teachers choose one type of music to work with initally, and begin by accessing some of the quality publications available. There exists much culturally accurate global music literature which has been produced for teachers to use in the classroom. These consist of a repertoire of songs, dances and instrumental pieces. The text usually instructs the teacher in effective performance techniques, and explains the cultural context of the material, such as background information on the music: who typically performs it, why, where and in what circumstances. These resources often have an accompanying compact disc so that the music as performed by members of that culture using the original language, vocal qualities and instrumental techniques, can be heard.

Some music is better adapted for the classroom than others, and it is these types of music (such as particular African, Irish, Indonesian and Chinese styles and genres) that the majority of the global music literature focuses on. It is of course equally exciting to delve into a type of music for which there are fewer resources. Playing the role of an ethnomusicologist is playing the role of a musical explorer, and is both worthwhile and gratifying. Taking on small fieldwork projects by sourcing culture bearers in the community (or in other states or countries) allows one to experience first-hand the music and its cultural context.

Suggestions for getting to know a genre of music for inclusion in the music curriculum include:

- researching cultural knowledge at the library, museum, embassy or cultural centre
- visiting the local university to talk with an ethnomusicologist
- developing partnerships between the school and culture bearers in the local community
- sourcing music, materials, instruments and recordings
- sourcing visiting artists, festivals, live performances and conferences
- canvassing support from administration, colleagues and parents
- coordinating with classroom, art and language teachers for integration projects
- travelling to a place where the music can be experienced in context
- working towards obtaining postgraduate qualifications in ethnomusicology

- encouraging universities to include global music courses as mandatory in music education degrees, so that the next generation of teachers is better prepared.

Problems of Authenticity and Change

As mentioned, one of the most frustrating stumbling blocks is the issue of producing authentic music at school. When we perform music from cultures other than our own in the classroom, we must inevitably acknowledge that the music has been taken out of its original context and is therefore inauthentic. Should we be attempting to learn and perform culturally diverse music if we know this to be the case?

Careful consideration of the following questions is important, if we are to arrive at some definition of what constitutes authenticity, and what are acceptable limits concerning change:

- How much variation from a performance in its original context is considered acceptable?
- If we change not only the context but the content of the music and its method of transmission, do we do the original music a disservice?
- Can music go through changes and still be considered traditional?
- Is a historical arrangement more authentic than a contemporary arrangement?
- If a musical style has definite origins in a particular ethnic community, can that community claim sole ownership of that music?
- Are syncretic hybrids less than 'pure', traditional music?

While our best intentions may be to keep our experience as close to the original as possible, it is important to remember that most (if not all) music has felt the effects of acculturation. Music traditions are not static. Acculturation of musical styles has been occurring for many centuries, from minor adjustments to the abandonment of whole genres and concepts. Few completely isolated cultures exist today, and it is more probable that most music represents a synthesis of more than one cultural influence. In some instances, borrowed or acquired music becomes so closely identified over time with the new culture that it is accepted as 'traditional' to that culture. For example, indigenous Hawaiian forms have been adapted to include the use of western harmonies and instruments, such as the ukulele and guitar. Polynesian string bands and mixed choirs that emerged in the late 1800s are now viewed by many as characteristic of this region of the world.

These instruments and musical concepts are most definitely considered traditional, but are they still authentic? Anthony Seeger makes the distinction between these terms clear.

He uses the term traditional to describe music that is 'historically identified with a community' and non-traditional 'music that has been introduced' and points out that both can still be considered authentic (Campbell, 1996, p. 68). It is interesting that many ethnomusicologists and educators who work in the field of global music (such as Rita Klinger, Bryan Burton and Victor Fung) feel that the term 'authentic' is no longer a valid concept, particularly as globally shared music is constantly re-contextualised. Perhaps it is a more achievable for us to aim to make global music education experiences as culturally accurate as possible.

Barton (2002, p. 165) lists a number of ways to establish the cultural accuracy of the music we are thinking of using in the classroom. Some questions he suggests music educators ask are:

- Are the materials prepared by a "culture bearer" (a recognized performer/creator/researcher of music within a culture)?
- Is the music and the performance of it representative of a particular segment of the culture, and is it set within its cultural context?
- Has the original language been used for the primary lyrics and is a translation provided?
- Are the recordings of musical materials accurate models for performance?

One of the most important factors in presenting music with cultural accuracy is to honour the traditional methods of transmission and notation. Music taught from a western perspective would typically include an ensemble adhering to prescriptive staff notation and following a teacher or conductor who directs from the front of the ensemble. In many parts of Asia and Africa, however (and in oral traditions in general), musicians experience their craft and associated cultural conventions through trial and error, and by observation and imitation of master musicians. From a young age they sit in on rehearsals to listen and observe, gradually taking their place in the ensemble by performing simple parts, and then assuming greater responsibilities as they mature as musicians.

Very often, music in oral societies is learned by rote and from memory, with mnemonic devises used to aid the learning process. Spoken syllables that imitate the drum strokes used in India, for example, are typically used for practice and learning, and not usually for performance. Music that is difficult to notate in the western manner (such as scales with equidistant intervals) is often written for our convenience using cipher notation, such as the music of the Javanese gamelan and the east African Akadinda. Cipher notation is used to learn or recall music, and is an outline of the basic musical structure and a guide from which musicians devise related parts.

Singapore American School

SAS is a co-educational international school with approximately 3,200 students from 45 different nationalities. SAS is committed to providing students with an education based on an international perspective, recognising that respect for individuals and their diversity is essential for society to flourish. Students in the elementary school (ages 5 to 11) receive general music classes for 45 minutes every three days, and there are currently four specialist music teachers covering the 62 classes in this division.

The development of the elementary music program at SAS has, in general, paralleled the development of music education in the United States. As a base, SAS uses a music series that teachers supplement with a variety of other materials. Until some years ago, the music series used represented the prevailing philosophy of music education in United States schools. As a rule, music was presented from a Eurocentric point of view, with an occasional 'ethnic' song included. Rarely were these multicultural examples culturally accurate. 'A song from Africa' typically did not identify which country the song was from, included little or no information about its cultural background, nor the music's place in the society. The song was most likely sung by someone from outside that culture, and European instruments provided a western style accompaniment.

As interest in the place of global music in the classroom grew in the United States, SAS's curriculum began to reflect a commitment to the inclusion of global

107

music, and a desire to approach this from a culturally accurate perspective. Teachers with a personal interest in world musics were employed, and a noticeable difference in ethos emerged. *Share the Music*, a music series based on world musics (MacMillan, McGraw, & Hill, 2000) was adopted. This series was deemed the most culturally accurate, as recordings are made by native singers, instrumental music is characteristic of the culture and played on authentic instruments, pronunciation guides by native speakers are provided, as is background information concerning the music in its cultural context. Through using this series, students experience the music from over 30 different cultures.

The inclusion of global musics in the SAS curriculum has since become a priority, and is strongly supported by administrators and parents. The school provides each teacher with an annual in-service stipend, and pays for teachers to attend courses and for clinicians to perform for the students. Teachers actively seek out conferences and festivals, and bring in a variety of guest artists from both Singapore and overseas.

SAS teachers try to ensure that the music experienced is not isolated from the culture concerned, but integrated with social studies, art, foreign languages and other specialised subjects. Each of the major festivals in Singapore provides a foundation for the integrated units that students experience each year, gaining knowledge and skills appropriate to their age level. Essential to these musical experiences is hands-on performance, as teachers strongly believe that 'nothing in a book comes close to the actual experience' (McCullough-Brabson, 2002, p. 136).

In addition to music from the western art tradition, SAS's elementary music education focuses primarily on musical genres from Indonesia and China, reflecting Singapore's position in Asia and cultural heritage. The pride of the department is the Javanese gamelan on which students from all grades perform for a quarter of the school year. Teachers at SAS have found the gamelan an excellent medium for music education, as it can accommodate a full class, and all students can succeed in performing whether or not they have had prior experience on these instruments. The students enjoy making music in this communal and cooperative manner, taking great pride in working together as a team to play with musical accuracy and sensitivity.

In addition to musical knowledge, teachers incorporate the use of language (*Bahasa Indonesia*) into the lessons, as well as cultural background information, Indonesian literature and even samples of traditional foods. In the past, art and music teachers have collaborated to produce an abridged *Wayang Kulit* presentation, with the puppets and set made by students. Students learn the gamelan using cipher notation, understanding it to be a teaching guide and mnemonic device to aid their aural perception of the music. They do not approach the music from a western linear perspective, but from a cyclic point of view, and are acquainted with how the Javanese view music, and its place in time. The children are given mature concepts and skills to master, such as dampening the notes, playing appropriate elaborating patterns on the bonang and recognising the drum rhythms for the various musical forms.

SAS students understand and apply cultural conventions such as not stepping over the instruments, keeping their heads lower than the gongs and taking their shoes off before coming into the gamelan room. When students 'perform' for their parents and peers, it is understood that they are playing out of cultural context, and thus the concept of performance has changed. Students also come to appreciate the difference between Javanese and Balinese styles. As a result of connections made with an SAS parent, the school has had a Balinese cultural group consisting of orphaned children aged 6 to 12 years visit the school to perform for the SAS community, as well as provide practical workshops for the elementary students and middle and high school dance students.

Although Chinese music is studied throughout the year, Chinese Lion Dance music is the focus of the weeks preceding the Chinese New Year period. All students study Chinese culture (food, dress and literature) in their regular classrooms and in their Mandarin lessons. In art, Chinese culture is the focus of projects such as ink brush painting and prints of zodiac characters. Students watch a professional Lion Dance troop perform, before replicating the music and dance steps to the best of their ability. All music rooms are equipped with drums, gongs, cymbals, lion heads and dragons for the children to perform with.

Students in third and fourth grades experience Malay kampong drumming, culminating in performances during the United Nations Day celebrations. Teachers have been taught by members of a local professional ensemble, and students have learned about the cultural background of this music; often experiencing it live and in context in the community. Second grade students complete a comprehensive unit on west Africa in their classroom. Music and art support this experience through integration experiences. All students sing songs from this region and play a variety of interlocking rhythms on djembes. Culturally accurate songs, videos and compact discs are used to supplement this education. Even these younger students realise that the music they are playing has been taken out of its cultural context, primarily as they most often experience it without the essential element of dance.

Music of Polynesia has been incorporated into classes at fourth grade level in recent years. Interest in Polynesian music and dance began with the growth of the school's *Halau Hula*. At one stage this group consisted of 80 dancers, boys and girls, from preschool to 12th grade, who regularly performed for their peers and the parent community. In the music classroom, students gain an appreciation for the history of the Polynesian people, the countries that make up this region and the places that Polynesians live today.

Students learn about the significance of the dances they perform, their link to ancient poetry (*mele*) and the appropriate use of accompanying instruments. Students experience the two broad categories of hula, which are differentiated by the period of composition, the accompaniment used, the variation in tonal range and rhythmic structure, and the costumes worn by the dancers. Students become aware of the distinction between *hula kahiko* ('ancient' hula) and *hula awana* ('stray' or modern hula) that developed as a result of the introduction of western culture, religion, scales, harmonies and instruments. Even these quite complex musical concepts can be understood by students of this age, if underlined by practical involvement.

Unfortunately as the students' *kumu hula* (hula teacher) was transferred out of Singapore, the group is no longer in existence. As a result, students do not have access to instruments such as the pahu drum and ipu gourd, but music teachers use other instruments that have similar sounds in order to continue teaching about this music. As the movements in hula awana are not fixed as with hula kahiko, it is easier for teachers without much training in hula to compose movements to modern music, using a set of movements which allude to nouns such as birds, stars or flowers.

109

Other examples of music experienced from Polynesia that have been introduced in a modest manner include Maori songs and *hakas*. It is hoped that in the near future, art teachers will assist with the making of *poi* for use in dancing, and will explore the significance of *moko* (carvings of the flesh of the face). Rhythms played on the *pate* drums of the Cook Islands have been played in the music classroom, despite the school not possessing these slit gongs. From Melanesia, students have performed stick dances as well as imitating some of the more basic *tam tam* (long drums) polyrhythms from the islands of Ambae and Banks in Vanuatu. Children gain an understanding of the geographic position of this island nation, the significance of the drums in transmitting messages, as well as the basic differences in appearance, customs and music of Polynesians and Melanesians.

Naturally, the inclusion of the variety of world musics incorporated into the program has not been without challenges. All the staff members have come from teacher training backgrounds that have not included musics other than western art music and jazz. Consequently, the way information and resources have been gathered over the years has been somewhat haphazard. SAS is a hectic environment, and despite best intentions, teachers sometimes do not meet personal and curricular goals set for the school year. They constantly have to check to make sure that enough time is allotted to the musical genres presented, in order to achieve adequate depth and not just a superficial dabble.

While the prevailing attitude at SAS is one of enthusiasm about having a curriculum focused on musics of the world, not all teachers are equally passionate about this. Some have interpreted the inclusion of non-western musics as a threat to adequate exposure to western art music, and that western and non-western music form two camps that are somehow opposed. The underlying assumption that 'western' music is more culturally advanced, and more important to our clientele still lingers. We have had teachers that (mostly due to their lack of experience with 'non-western' musical cultures) feel seriously threatened by the unknown. As a result, the cultural information provided and performance techniques taught, have not only been inaccurate, but a complete misrepresentation, as they were concocted without any thought to cultural accuracy.

Continuity continues to be a challenge. Teachers in the elementary school tend to stay an average of fours years, and thus with the turn-over of staff, challenges arise with sharing the ethos, knowledge and skills with new teachers. It is possible, that despite musics of the world currently being part of the SAS curriculum, with a significant change in staff, the education provided may revert to being Eurocentric once again. As long as future generations of teachers receive tertiary training that includes little or no non-western music, the teachers employed at SAS will inevitably continue to teach their music classes from a western perspective. Another stumbling block is that very little global music is incorporated into the musical electives in middle and high school at SAS, especially as almost all are performance groups based on western models (band, chorus and string ensemble).

110

However, as interest in global music has grown over the years, so has the desire to include world music experiences in the classroom. While there may be some difficulties associated with achieving culturally accuracy and receiving the necessary support, it is the opinion of many music educators that the advantages of pursuing the inclusion of global music in the curriculum far outweigh these difficulties. Since teachers at SAS have made global approaches to music a priority, they have seen much cultural and musical growth in their students, as they come to know the music they encounter from an *emic* perspective; learning about music in context and how it operates as a human phenomenon. By experiencing a wider variety of ways of making and transmitting music, it is hoped that students will also experience a greater understanding and empathy in their everyday lives.

References

Anderson, W. M. (1975). *Teaching Asian music in elementary and secondary schools: An introduction to the musics of India and Indonesia.* Dallas: Taylor.

Anderson, W. M., & Moore, M. C. (Eds.). (1998). *Making connections. Multicultural music and the National Standards.* United States: Music Educators National Conference.

Anderson, W. M., & Campbell, P. S. (1989). *Multicultural perspectives in music education.* United States: Music Educators National Conference.

Blacking, J. (1995). *Music, culture, and experience: Selected papers of John Blacking.* Chicago: Chicago Studies in Ethnomusicology.

Bohlman, P. V. (1998). Traditional music and cultural identity persistent paradigm in the history of ethnomusicology. *Yearbook for Traditional Music, 20,* 26–42.

Burton, B. (2002). Weaving the tapestry of world musics. In B. Reimer (Ed.), *World musics and music education. Facing the issues* (pp. 161–186). United States: Music Educators National Conference.

Campbell, P. S. (1991). *Lessons from the world. A cross-cultural guide to music teaching and learning.* New York: Schrimer Books.

Campbell, P. S. (1996). *Music in cultural context. Eight views on world music.* United States: Music Educators National Conference.

Campbell, P. S. (2004). *Teaching music globally. Experiencing music, expressing culture.* Oxford: Oxford University Press.

Dunbar-Hall, P., & Hodge, G. (1991). *A guide to music around the world.* Sydney: Science Press.

Fujie, L. (1992). East Asia/Japan. In J. T. Titon (Ed.), *Worlds of music. An introduction to the music of the world's peoples* (pp. 318–375). New York: Schirmer Books.

Fung, C. V. (2002). Experiencing world musics in schools: From fundamental positions to strategic guidelines. In B. Reimer (Ed.), *World musics and music education. Facing the issues* (pp. 187–204). United States: Music Educators National Conference.

Goldsworthy, D. J. (1992). Tuning the gamelan: Process or product. *Sounds Australian, 33,* 13–16.

Kartomi, M. J. (1981). The processes and results of musical culture contact: A discussion of terminology and concepts. *Ethnomusicology, 25*(2), 227–249.

Kartomi, M. J., & Blum, S. (Eds.). (1994). *Music-cultures in contact. Convergences and collisions.* Australia: Gordon and Beach.

Loza, S. (1996). Steven Loza on Latino music. In P. Shehan Campbell (Ed.), *Music in cultural context. Eight views on world music education* (pp. 58–65). United States: Music Educators National Conference.

May, E. (Ed.). (1980). *Music of many cultures: An introduction.* California: University of California Press.

MacMillan & McGraw-Hill. (2000). *Share the music.* Macmillan.

McCullough-Brabson, E. (1996). Passing the cultural baton of music. In P. Shehan Campbell (Ed.), *Music in cultural context. Eight views on world music education* (pp. 119–138). United States: Music Educators National Conference.

Merriam, A. P. (1964). *The anthropology of music.* United States: Northwestern University Press.

Monfort, M. (1985). *Ancient traditions-future possibilities. Rhythm training through the traditions of Africa, Bali and India.* United States: Panoramic Press.

Nettl, B. (1985). *The western impact on world music.* NY: Schirmer Books.

Reimer, B. (Ed.). (2002). *World musics and music education. Facing the issues.* United States: Music Educators National Conference.

111

Romet, C. (1981). *Musical cultures of Asia volume 2, Indonesia*. Canberra, Australia: Curriculum Development Centre.

Slobin, M., & Titon, J. T. (1992). The music-culture as a world of music. In J. T. Titon (Ed.), *Worlds of music. An introduction to the music of the world's peoples* (pp. 1–15). NY: Schirmer Books.

Stokes, M. (Ed.). (1994). *Ethnicity, identity and music: The musical construction of place*. Oxford: Berg.

Titon, J. T. (Ed.). (1992). *Worlds of music. An introduction to the music of the world's peoples*. New York: Schirmer Books.

Volk, T. (2002). Multiculturalism: Dynamic creativity for music education. In B. Reimer (Ed.), *World musics and music education. Facing the issues* (pp. 15–30). United States: Music Educators National Conference.

Wade, B. (2004). *Thinking musically. Experiencing music, experiencing culture*. Oxford: Oxford University Press.

MELISSA CAIN is an Australian who has worked at Singapore American School as Head of Elementary Music for 14 years. Melissa enjoys teaching and learning about music from around the world, in particular the music of South-East Asia and the Pacific. Melissa has written educational material for the Singapore Symphony Orchestra, including the story *Musical Maestrosaurus*.

112

Who'll Come a Waltzing Matilda?: The Search for Identity in Australian Music Education

Scott Harrison

Before commencing an investigation into the identity of music education in Australia, two fundamental questions need to be addressed: what is Australian identity and what is the identity of Australian music? While both topics have been covered in considerable detail in other research, the question of how this applies to identity in Australian music education is rarely considered. The background contributing to Australia's existing standpoint in relation to its own culture, along with an understanding of musical footprints in Australian music, form the basis for discussions on music education philosophy, content and delivery. In reality, the students in our classrooms represent culturally diverse Australia, yet our systems and heritage, along with the active promotion of hegemonic Australian identity, prevent our pedagogies from enacting policy, despite the best of intentions.

Searching for an Australian Identity

The first Australians, the indigenous population, pre-dated European settlement by 40,000 to 60,000 years. Any discussion on Australian identity needs to begin with an acknowledgment of indigenous Australians, their role as the first Australians and their impact on our identity. The first European settlers brought to Australia were men and women convicts transported from 1788. With regard to the type of identity these Australians had, Colling (1992) notes that the convict was abandoned, robbed of skills, family and friends and, even on board the transportation ship, began to realise that no-one else could be trusted. The convict also needed to repress and divert any softer emotions that might make him or her vulnerable to exploitation.

From the early 1790s the convicts were joined by free immigrants. Migrants arriving after the First Fleet included Italians, Greeks, Malays and other Europeans. The early settlers developed a 'survival frontier mentality' that united them against authority. Bushrangers became role models. In this respect, Australia differed from America, where the Pilgrim Fathers were motivated by deep religious convictions, and from South Africa, where the Dutch reformers were strict and hard working. Early European settlers in Australia who took over Aboriginal land had to suppress feelings of pity, fear and compassion and value loyalty, reliability, ingenuity, courage, toughness and humour.

From 1851 to 1880 the gold rushes attracted a large number of immigrants from Britain, Ireland, Germany and China. Afghan immigrants also arrived, bringing camels with them for inland exploration. Japanese settlers started the pearling industry in Australia at this time. The gold rush of the 1850s reinforced competitiveness and distrust of authority. The Catholic Irish migrants who arrived brought a culture of struggle against oppression. The Eureka Stockade, says Colling (1992), embodied egalitarianism, the idea that the worker is as good as his master.

Such was the importance of maintaining Australia as a 'white' country that the *Immigration Restriction Act* was the first Act to be passed after Federation in 1901. The White Australia policy embodied in this act was a result of conflict with non-European migrants and had a particular focus on ending the employment of Pacific Islanders working on sugar plantations in northern Australia. From 1901 to the early 1970s, policies towards newcomers were based on the concepts of assimilation and, later, integration. Government policy at this time implied a monoculture with everyone living the same way. Pluralism was not tolerated and assimilation as a policy was an attempt to assure Australians that their way of life would not be undermined. This required migrants to break with the 'old country', its language, traditions of dress, dance, cultural ceremonies and social relationships. The integration policy, in effect from the mid-1960s until 1972, recognised that large numbers of people whose first language was not English were suffering hardships in settling in Australia. Most were Europeans of non-British origin who had come to Australia after World War II. According to Collins (1991), integration was really a two-stage assimilation process. Cultural differences were seen as valid in the short term, with a recognition that it would take time for migrants to fully assimilate. The expectation was that they would eventually merge with the 'mainstream'.

The Immigration Restriction Act 1901 was repealed in 1972 by the Whitlam Labour government. By 1973, the word 'multiculturalism' had been introduced to policy. Distinctive cultural features were to be celebrated and encouraged, with cultural pluralism replacing, at least in policy, monoculturalism. 'Multiculturalism ... is a theory (albeit vague) about the foundations of a culture rather than a practice which subsumes cultural ideas' (Harrison, 1984, as cited in Bhaba, 1990, p. 124).

On the large scale, multicultural is often used to describe societies that exhibit a range of distinct cultural groups, usually as a result of immigration. While such a description can question the stability of national identity, it can also contribute to exchanges that benefit the different cultural groups. On the small scale, the term can also be used to refer to specific districts in cities where people of different cultures coexist.

Grassby (1984) states that there are three steps toward the realisation of a multicultural country: first, each group makes its presence visible and accepts each other's presence; second, each group should have a clear-cut pride in its cultural tradition; third, all the ethnic groups try to find the best way to coexist through continuous communication. Grassby actively promoted this view of Australia until his death in early 2005.

In education, multiculturalism challenges and rejects racism and other forms of discrimination in schools and society and accepts and affirms the pluralism (ethnic, racial, linguistic, religious, economic and gender, among others) that communities represent. In specific terms, Nieto (1996, pp. 307–308) describes seven characteristics of multicultural education:

1. Multicultural education is antiracist education.
2. Multicultural education is basic education.
3. Multicultural education is important for all students.
4. Multicultural education is pervasive.
5. Multicultural education is education for social justice.
6. Multicultural education is a process.
7. Multicultural education is critical pedagogy.

In a subtle yet significant shift in policy, the government's Charter of Principles for a Culturally Diverse Society was launched in 1993. As stated in the *Ethnic Affairs Commission Report* (1994–1995), it:

> recognises our cultural diversity as a valuable resource. It sets out the responsibilities public sector agencies have to respond to a culturally diverse community. It determines that everyone should have the greatest opportunity to contribute and participate in all levels of public life. It makes all individuals and public institutions responsible for respecting and taking account of cultural, linguistic and religious differences in a society where the primary language is English.

In policy, therefore, cultural diversity now appears to be a hallmark of Australian national identity. As such, Australia accepts and respects the right of all Australians to express and share their individual cultural heritage within an overriding commitment to Australia's democratic foundations. This commitment comprises the following principles:

- cultural respect, which gives all Australians (subject to the law) the right to express their own culture and beliefs and obliges them to accept the right of others to do the same
- social equity, which entitles all Australians to equality of treatment and opportunity so that they can contribute to the life of the nation free from discrimination, including on the grounds of race, culture, religion, language, location, gender or place of birth
- productive diversity, which maximises the significant cultural, social and economic dividends arising from its plurality.

Cultural diversity is therefore promoted as an inclusive and harmonious concept where differences are accepted and respected. In today's language, cultural diversity is used to replace multiculturalism. The use of the word multiculturalism reflects in some people's minds 'tribalism'. It is regarded by some as divisive and as defining Australia as having coexisting cultures that do not necessarily interact. Cultural diversity does not necessarily carry the same connotations.

In purely empirical terms Australia is one of the world's most culturally diverse nations, with 40% of Australians being post-war migrants or their Australian-born children, and less than 40% of the migrant population being British born. People from around 200 countries have migrated to Australia. Today, about 23% of the population was born overseas and more than 200 languages are spoken. The diverse composition of our population has the capacity to contribute greatly to the dynamic, innovative and inclusive nature of Australian society.

As a result of this empirical proof of diversity and its enshrinement in policy, it is argued by Bell and Kenny in Jureidini (1997, p. 63) that Australia 'has no culture at all, at least none of its own'. Conversely, Jamrozik et al. (1995, p. 27) argue

115

that despite the embracing of cultural diversity in Australian policy, the core institutions are still essentially monocultural, and derived from Britain. These institutions include government, universities, education, health, trade unions and the churches. Jamrozik et al. also suggest that the 'new middle class' (which includes teachers and government professionals) defines policy, determines the accepted view of reality and decides whose knowledge is accepted as valid. There is therefore a hegemonic Australia.

Hegemony in Australia has a historical basis that continues to be maintained through many avenues including the media and sporting institutions. In contemporary Australia the media continues to present two-dimensional roles, reinforcing the stereotypes of the white (albeit tanned) beer-drinking, sport-watching, beach bum. This representation, along with the wide brown land (the outback), the unusual wildlife and the 'throw a shrimp on the barby' image are promoted as our identity domestically and internationally. What is created is an imagined picture of what it is to be Australian, a sort of quasi-community (King & Rowse, 1990, p. 40). The images presented of bush, beach and country along with the myths of a 'lucky country' (people at leisure, assumed ownership of land and property) perpetuate a belief that 'this' (these images, people, activities) is Australian. In this narrative there are no representatives of a culturally diverse Australia: the hegemonic view that is depicted is that Australia is a big, wide-open country populated by fun-loving white Anglo-Celts.

Furthermore, across more than 200 years of European settlement, Australians have adopted unusual role models and celebrated unusual events such as the Eureka Stockade, Ned Kelly, Gallipoli and Waltzing Matilda. The last of these embodies the cultural hero, with its incumbent sense of fearlessness, contempt for authority and hardship. In relation to music, historical conditions have not always been conducive to displays of singing and dancing, as associates ('mates') do not allow creativity.

In summary, culturally diverse Australia exists in policy and in demographics. There is in some respects a lack of a sense of true identity because of this pluralism resulting, in part, in a dominance of Anglo-Celtic images and societal structures. For musicians and music educators, this situation represents challenges in relation to philosophical approaches, content and delivery.

Searching for an Identity in Australian Music

> Australians perform and listen to a plethora of musical styles. Participation is numerically greatest in styles promoted by the international popular music industry — e.g. rock music, hip hop, dance/electronica. Other styles include country music, including a stream identified with indigenous musicians; classical music in all its forms; jazz; Australian folk and bush music derived from Anglo-Celtic folk styles; ethnic styles, especially but not exclusively those associated with the cultures of immigrants, including "world music"; traditional indigenous musics; fusion musics that experiment with couplings of any of the above; experimental music/computer-generated music/multimedia (Letts, 2003, p. 3).

116

Such diversity is both a reflection of and contribution to Australian society. An attempt to link music with the cultural diversity of Australian society can be found in arts policy. Since the 1980s, the Australia Council has attempted to develop multicultural initiatives. Any discussion in this field needs to begin by addressing the deficiency in emphasis on indigenous music. The current policy *Arts for a Multicultural Australia* states:

> The Australia Council values the traditions and capacity for innovation that exists in Australian multicultural and Aboriginal and Torres Strait Islander society and encourages the creativity and artistic expression resulting from this diversity.

Within its goals, the policy includes encouraging the development and creation of multicultural work by artists of all backgrounds and supporting artists' choices about engagement with their cultural heritage. As with Australian culture in the broadest sense as outlined above, there are significant issues for Australian music stemming from the reality described by Letts (2003), from articulated policy and from hegemonic image.

Turner (1992) states it is a 'waste of time' searching for signifiers of Australian-ness in music texts when attempting to draw parallels between Australian music and Australian popular culture. Turner then concludes, Australian popular music is Australian simply on the basis of its geographic/cultural location: 'It is produced here, consumed here, performed here, forms and is formed in the national consciousness here' (p. 71). Hayes (1995), on the other hand, contests that there is a recognisably Australian music, because of the country's history, location, geography and other factors. She further maintains that the rise of Australian music is not wholly explainable in terms of European or American music history. As described above, our identity as Australians in terms of image has been associated with our historical (the land of the indigenous, the rise from a convict past and moves towards diversity) and geographical features — the land, the beach, the weather and the outback. However, as with defining what it is to be Australian, identifying exactly what is an Australian 'sound' presents difficulties. The 1986 report of the Australian Broadcasting Tribunal (ABT; p. 6) into Australian music on radio found that some forms of music might be easier to recognise as having an Australian sound because of particular lyrical content or style. The iconic songs from the popular music canon reflect this. For example, in the lyrics of *Sounds of Then (This is Australia)*:

> Out on the patio (we'd sit)
> And the humidity (we'd breathe)
> We'd watch the lightning (crack over cane fields)
> Laugh and think: this is Australia.

For an Australian who has lived through summer in the cane fields of northern Australia, there is a strong resonance with an Australian experience embedded in these lyrics. Many more examples where the lyrics are unmistakably Australian in content are available. Internationally, the most recognisable of these may well be *Down Under*:

> I come from a land down under
> Where beer does flow and men chunder
> Can't you hear, can't you hear the thunder?
> You better run, you better take cover!

117

This is not to imply that all Australian men drink to excess and vomit (chunder) or that this does not happen in other societies, but the strong association of this song with the America's Cup win of 1983 gives it added Australian-ness in that it connects with the fascination with sport, the concept of the underdog, toughness and humour. In perhaps the most iconic national song, *Waltzing Matilda*, the story focuses on the themes of fearlessness and contempt for authority along with the use of words swagman, billabong, and coolabah:

> Once a jolly swagman camped by a billabong,
> Under the shade of a coolabah tree,
> And he sang as he sat and waited by that billabong
> You'll come a waltzing Matilda with me.

In a sense, this work captures Australia in geography and in spirit. In a slightly different genre, but equally as blatant in its use of Australian language, is *True Blue*:

> True Blue, is it me and you?
> Is it Mum and Dad, is it a cockatoo?
> Is it standing by your mate
> When he's in a fight?
> Or will she be right?
> True Blue ... True Blue.

The lyricist provides this explanation of the term 'true blue': a steadfast loyal Australian who displays the Aussie ideals of a fair go for all, mateship, having a go and solving problems. Again, these qualities are perceived as being closely associated with Australian culture in the broadest sense. While these lyrics refer to the mateship, the geography, the history, the wildlife and the weather, there are similar themes to be found in the titles of art music: *Kakadu* (Sculthorpe), *Sun Music* (Sculthorpe), *Rainforest* (Koehne), *Bakery Hill Rising* (Plush), *Tibrogargan* (Anderson), *Bennelong* (Conyngham) and *Kangaroo Hunt* (Lumsdane), to name but a few. The extent to which these represent these places and events is contentious. It is known, for example, that Sculthorpe did not visit Kakadu until after the work was complete. The ABT report (1986) also found that it was difficult to define an Australian sound in all genres of music. In instrumental works, this is clearly more problematic. Australian composers suggest that there is an openness and sparseness in orchestration that represents geographical features. While works may reflect Australian-ness, the sound could be construed as being derived from any culture.

There are also works that represent a more culturally diverse Australia: *Requiem 2004* (Sculthorpe), *Ice Carvings* (Conyngham), *Dawn Mantras* (Edwards), *New Gold Mountain* (Dreyfus). These and other similar works integrate indigenous music ideas and themes in addition to music representing other cultures within Australia. In popular music, perhaps there is no more poignant example of this than *I am Australian*, which, after giving an historical account of settlement beginning with indigenous Australians, has a chorus with the lyrics:

> We are one, but we are many
> And from all the lands on earth we come
> We share a dream and sing with one voice:
> I am, you are, we are Australian
> I am, you are, we are Australian.

118

It should be noted that while this work refers to cultural diversity through its lyrical content, it still uses popular compositional conventions. By the 1995 Contemporary Music Summit in Canberra, the problem of defining an Australian sound still remained. Participants noted Guldberg's (1987) evaluation of the music industry and stated that the multicultural nature of Australian society contributed to the problem of having a homogenised musical identity (p. 11; Jonker, 1995, p. 8).

Douglas (2000), in examining the actions of transnational corporations adds the further complications of the Internet and the way governments appropriate regional or local identities in order to 'infiltrate' a society. Such groups, he says, are also concerned with misappropriation of 'the local' in order to acquire a particular hegemonic position.

In the world of virtual reality, boundaries between the regional, the national and the global have become blurred, contributing to the homogenisation of music. Through the processes of cultural appropriation or cultural indigenisation, musicians appropriate various qualities of musical forms from diverse cultures and societies, contributing to the difficulties in trying to determine national identity through music. It is also true that transnational corporations are able to adapt the local in order to create new images of the nation, and thus serve their profit-making imperatives.

In summary, there are some obvious examples of Australian music identity in lyric content, names of pieces and incorporation of historical and geographical references. Furthermore, there are references to defined 'Australian' qualities (mateship, fearlessness and the like) along with indigenous melody and instrumentation that give some works an Australian flavour. Beyond this, there is reason to doubt the existence (or definition) of a distinct sound. Global forces can both appropriate the hegemonic local imagery and/or disregard it according to their commercial needs.

Searching for an Identity in Australian Music Education

> In Australia, we can distinguish three main levels of intensity in this challenge. Firstly, there is cultural diversity in terms of immigrants from various European cultures ... The second level is formed by immigrants from the Asia-Pacific region: this is ... more of a challenge, as they represent (musical) cultures with very different values. Thirdly, there is the layer of the cultural background of Aboriginal people and Torres Strait Islanders. This is by far the most challenging area, as we are dealing with major cultural and musical differences here, as well as great political sensitivity (Schippers, 2004, p. 329).

The challenges facing Australian music education are succinctly articulated by Schippers (2004) in identifying the three levels of population composition. The complexity this brings, along with the issues discussed in relation to Australian identity and Australian music above present significant challenges for the music educator. Music education has been slow to address the issues of cultural diversity so clearly articulated in policy and evidenced (in part) in the works cited above. What is required is a clearly articulated approach that puts policy into practice and challenges the status quo. This means that every aspect of music education from philosophical underpinnings and structures to pedagogy, content and teacher education require scrutiny.

In relation to philosophy and constitution, our system is, as Jamrozik et al. (1995) point out, largely Anglophilic. The structures of education have, with minor cosmetic adjustment, remained constant throughout the increase in cultural diversity. In music education, there are strong European traditions of structure and modes of delivery perpetuated in music classrooms from pre-school to tertiary level. In Queensland, a place within Australia with a substantial investment in human resources in music education, the *Arts Years 1–10 Syllabus* has core content in the music strand clearly focused on Kodaly philosophy in the terms used and sequence. This focus on one-dimensional skill development denies the need for broad music education encompassing, but not restricted to, popular and culturally diverse approaches to music education. In addition, this approach directly influences university students' entry tests in relation to theoretical and historical knowledge of music, which have been found to be somewhat limited in terms of western art music and more culturally broad awareness.

There are examples of effective practice that circumvent the curriculum documents: some schools have a focus on country music, while others focus almost entirely on popular forms. This gives voice to some of the specific needs in music education, but the broader principles embedded in a culturally diverse approach remain untouched.

In relation to content, an examination of school syllabuses and tertiary course content reveals a lack of attention to iconic Australian music of almost any genre and a fixation on Eurocentric or American music. Australian music education should be founded in our indigenous music and incorporate the wealth of repertoire from hundreds of cultures in our society. There is merit in the use of repertoire that refers to our cultural identity, whatever the genre. Music education largely ignores the value of popular music, jazz, country and modern art music. Through its fascination with Germanic traditions and the more recent flavours of Kodaly, Orff and the like, a national identity in music is stymied. There is little value in our students learning *Land of the Silver Birch* and ignoring *Bakery Hill Rising* or *Great Southern Land*.

As far as delivery is concerned, tuition models that vary from one-to-one or 'chalk and talk' are rare. In the tertiary setting, Schippers (2004) again provides a framework, suggesting that inspiration can be found in embracing the ways in which world music is learned. Similarly, methods of teaching popular music and music technology that draw on less traditional practices could be investigated.

In relation to teacher education, Australians would benefit from employing strategies such as those used in the United States where the National Association for Multicultural Education (2003, n.p.) adopted a resolution that:

> Staff must be multiculturally literate and capable of including and embracing families and communities to create an environment that is supportive of multiple perspectives, experiences, and democracy.

As contemporary Australian students literally represent cultural diversity, the process could begin by embracing the existing diversity in classrooms and using this as the catalyst for growth, inspiration and development. By embracing Nieto's (1996) structure as outlined above, examples of how this can be enacted could include:

- actively challenging overt or implied racism in curriculum, delivery and daily interaction
- putting cultural diversity as a basic tenet of education systems and individualised planning, rather than as an afterthought on the back pages of curriculum documents
- emphasising the importance of music as an international language and its capacity to embrace students regardless of race, culture, religion, language, location, gender or place of birth
- adopting diversity in classrooms to encompass the existing musics of students
- focusing on social justice issues as described in the lyrical and/or programmatic content of music, with particular emphasis on indigenous music
- realising that there is no end-point in the process, and therefore

- continuing to engage in critical pedagogy to identify and enact current trends and solutions.

The notion of multicultural Australia in relation to music education is perhaps politically incorrect. However, this use of this term is deliberate in that in reality Australian music education is more multicultural than culturally diverse. In other words, it projects the idea of the existence of many cultures that do not necessarily interact. Cultural diversity as a term, as policy and as a way of acting gives the opportunity for change. So who will come Waltzing Matilda and begin to change our approaches to the structure, content and modes of delivery of music education? From the philosophical to the delivery, let us embrace the fearlessness of our forefathers and foremothers to change our musical landscape.

References

Australia Council. *Arts for a multicultural Australia policy*. Retrieved March 31, 2005, from http://www.ozco.gov.au/resources/ama/object.html

Australia Council. (2000). *Arts in a multicultural Australia: Australia Council policy on arts in a multicultural Australia*. Sydney: Author.

Australian Broadcasting Tribunal. (1986). *Australian music on radio*. Sydney.

Bell, R., & Kenny, S. (1997). Popular culture. In R. Jueidini, S. Kenny, & M. Poole (Eds.), Sociology: *Australian connections*. St Leonards: Allen & Unwin.

Colling, T. (1992). *Beyond mateship: Understanding Australian men*. Sydney: Simon and Schuster.

Collins, A. (1991). The role of computer technology in restructuring schools. *Phi Delta Kappan*, September, 28–36.

Douglas, J. (2000). Identity through sound and image: This is Australia? *Transformations*, Issue 1(September). Retrieved April 4, 2005, from http://www.cqu.edu.au/transformations

Ethnic Affairs Commission of NSW. (1996). *A directory of ethnic media in New South Wales*.

Fiske, J. (1987). *Pleasure and play. In Television culture*. London: Methuen.

Frith, S. (1988). *Music for pleasure: Essays on the sociology of pop*. London: Polity Press.

Grassby, A. (1984). *The tyranny of prejudice*. Melbourne: Australasian Education Press.

Guldberg, H. H. (1987). *The Australian music industry: An economic evaluation*. Sydney: Australia Council.

Gunew, S. Denaturalizing cultural nationalisms: Multicultural readings of Australia. In Homi K. Bhaba (Ed.), *Nation and narration*. New York: Routledge, Chapman and Hall.

Hayes, D. (1995, March). *Australian music and the contemporary world*. Paper presented at the 1995 ASANA Conference, Orlando, Florida.

Jamrozik, A., Boland, C., & Urquharet, J. (1995). *Social change and cultural transformation in Australia*. Cambridge: Cambridge University Press.

Jonker, E. (1995). Ausmusic briefing paper for the music industry summit. In P. Rix (Ed.), *Report on the contemporary music summit for the Minister for Communications and the Arts* (pp. 1–21). Kirribilli: PRM.

Jueidini, R., Kenny, S., & Poole, M. (1997). *Sociology: Australian connections*. St Leonards: Allen & Unwin.

King, N., & Rowse, T. (1990). Typical Aussies: Television and populism in Australia. In M. Alvarado & J. O. Thompson (Eds.), *The media reader* (pp. 36–49). London: BFI.

Letts, R. (2003). *The effects of globalization on music in five contrasting countries: Report of a research project for the Many Musics program of the International Music Council*. Music Council of Australia.

Mulvaney, J., & Kamminga, J. (1999). *Prehistory of Australia*. Sydney: Allen and Unwin.

National Association for Multicultural Education. (2003). *Multicultural education*. Retrieved July 11, 2005, from www.nameorg.org

Nieto, S. (1996). *Affirming diversity: The sociopolitical context of multicultural education* (2nd ed.). New York: Longman.

Schippers, H. (2004, August). *Blame it on the Germans! A cross-cultural invitation to revisit the foundations of training professional musicians*. Paper presented at the ISME Conference, Teneriffe.

Schippers, H. (2004). Global resonances: *Beyond exotic sounds*. In *Proceedings of the XXVth annual conference, Australian association for research in music education* (pp. 329–340).

Turner, G. (1992). Australian popular music and its contexts. In P. Hayward (Ed.), *From pop to punk to postmodernism: Popular music and Australian culture from the 1960's to 1990's*. Sydney: Allen & Unwin.

Turner, G. (1994). *Making it national*. St Leonards: Allen & Unwin.

Walker, C. (1996). *Stranded: The secret history of Australian independent music 1977-1991*. Sydney: Pan McMillan Australia.

Wark, M. (1997). *The virtual republic: Australia's culture wars of the 1990's*. Sydney: Allen & Unwin.

SCOTT D. HARRISON has taught classroom music in state and private schools and singing to students in primary, secondary and tertiary environments. Prior to taking up his present position, he was responsible for the leadership of several expressive arts departments in Queensland schools and colleges. Dr Harrison now lectures in music and music education at Griffith University while maintaining an active performance profile. Recent publications have focused on a range of music education issues including teacher identity, gender and vocal education.

Case Studies From Asia, Africa and Australia

Training, Community and Systemic Music Education: The Aesthetics of Balinese Music in Different Pedagogic Settings

Peter Dunbar-Hall

Globalisation is increasingly discussed as an influence on music and the ways music is taught and learned (Leong, 2004; McCarthy, 2004; Perlman, 2004). Although its advantages and disadvantages are still in many cases unclear, and its effects on the cultural margins of music transmission are something writers are still working to define and assess, its power to reshape music education and to influence definitions of music as an object of study is becoming more explicit. One of the most significant effects of musical globalisation is its ability to focus debate on musical meaning, especially meaning that results from the use of music in pedagogic settings. As musical repertoires are globalised and become available to international audiences, the meanings ascribed to music at its points of creation, its original cultural sources, are questioned and new meanings dependent on new locales and personnel are assigned. For music education expected to acknowledge the cultural contexts of music, this raises questions of musical meaning and how it changes with time and place. In this discussion, I investigate this issue by considering the range of meanings assigned to Balinese *gamelan* music in three teaching and learning settings to demonstrate how a globalised repertoire adopts a range of potential meanings and uses. First, I describe how the learning of *gamelan* music in Bali fulfils a number of cultural agendas. This is followed by explanation of how the members of an Australian, non-Balinese, adult community *gamelan* assess their readings of Balinese music as an object of study and performance. The third context is that of systemic music teaching and learning in America and Australia, two countries where Balinese music is used to achieve the aims and outcomes of music education. The conclusions to be drawn from these case studies demonstrate how globalisation, defined as a series of localisations, is creating a new pedagogic site for music educators — one in which meaning creation for music becomes the focus of consideration.

125

Learning *gamelan* in Bali

The learning of *gamelan* music by Balinese people occurs primarily as a village activity in Bali, although some schools include *gamelan* lessons as part of their curriculum. In villages, this takes a number of forms: informal learning, where, for example, a child might observe and imitate adults until s/he is invited to join and play with an ensemble; structured learning, in which a group of children is formed into a *gamelan* and a teacher is employed to teach them a repertoire; employment of specialists to work with adult groups that are either village *gamelans* or exist to perform for tourists; individual lessons given by a teacher to a student of one specific instrument. In most cases, learning is in a group, and this reinforces cultural frameworks underpinning Balinese life, especially the ideology and practice of *gotong royong*, a culturally embedded way in which Balinese people perceive their role in the world as to fulfil group collaboration and to contribute to complex social networks that act as frameworks for life. In this way, learning to play in a *gamelan* differs from typical western views of music learning by accomplishing more than acquisition of skill and repertoire. Rather, it reinforces culturally transmitted ways of living and interacting with other members of society. It also contributes to the provision of music for Balinese Hindu ceremonial activity, thus fulfilling a religious role. In fact, alongside the chanting of priests, singing by attendees, sounding of the *kulkul* (large wooden bells) to initiate religious observance and use of small bells at stages of ceremonies, the music provided by a *gamelan* is one of the five sacred sounds required to give Balinese religious observance validity. Learning to play an instrument confers status and proactively preserves repertoires and ways of thinking and living as a Balinese person. Encouraging the learning of a *gamelan* instrument also contributes to a vibrant creative atmosphere in which *kreasi baru* (new works constructed through reference to existing ones) and *komposisi baru* (newly composed original works) are highly valued. The learning of an instrument, and by extension the power associated with the teaching of Balinese *gamelan* music by Balinese people, therefore, can be shown to respond to a range of social, cultural and religious purposes and agendas.

Of specific interest to this discussion is a movement to encourage the teaching of music and dance to children as a means of strengthening and continuing aspects of Balinese culture. This can be observed in many villages and institutions. For example, in the central Balinese village of Ubud, a local arts support network, Tedung Agung, provides lessons in *gamelan* to children from very young ages. In nearby Peliatan, the Agung Rai Museum of Art (ARMA) runs a music and dance program for children, the aim of which is to provide 'opportunities, free of charge, for Balinese children to become actively involved in cultural programs of classical dance, *gamelan* and drawing' (ARMA, n.d., p. 1). This is explained in the following way:

> ARMA has developed links with local schools to encourage extra-curricular programs. It provides space and the teachers who train the children in classical forms of dance which might otherwise disappear. Peliatan has been famous for Balinese dance for decades, and the classes at ARMA are provided to sustain that internationally recognised excellence. Older dancers are frequently brought in to teach the teachers who then pass the skills on to the young children ... though tourism continues to increase, the arts of Bali will also continue thriving into the next century (ARMA, n.d., p. 2).

126

On another level, the teaching of Balinese music and dance to children is positioned by Balinese people, in response to the 12 October 2002 Bali bombings, as an indication to the gods that Balinese culture is 'back on track' after a period in which it had been allowed to deteriorate. In this context, the teaching of music and dance are intended to reinforce culture, to reclaim ownership of cultural artefact, and to please the gods by strengthening performance of events through which they are honoured and entertained.

Through these agendas and activities, the purposes of learning to play Balinese *gamelan* music for Balinese people can be shown to be socially influenced, to appeal to policies of cultural vitalisation, to respond to events in Balinese life and to address proactive enculturation of young Balinese into aspects of Balinese culture. The necessity of providing music for the numerous ceremonial observances of the Balinese Hindu religion is acknowledged by Balinese people as central to learning music.

Running alongside the learning of Balinese music as a means to cultural preservation, religious obligation and social cohesion, Balinese *gamelan* music is taught by Balinese musicians to non-Balinese people. This constitutes a regular part of Balinese musicians' lives and makes a substantial contribution to their financial wellbeing; through this, the teaching of Balinese music is partly commodified and is removed from its cultural connotations. The purposes of the learners in this are diverse. Since the 1930s, when the Canadian composer Colin McPhee learned *gamelan* music there (McPhee, 1966), a steady stream of ethnomusicologists have learned *gamelan* music in Bali as their primary means of understanding Balinese music and its cultural contexts, or of explicating the purposes of music as a social activity (Bakan, 1999; Herbst, 1997; Tenzer, 2000). Others learn Balinese music as a means of analysing music teaching and learning and of theorising music pedagogy (Dunbar-Hall, 2000). For some writers it is a source of repertoire for non-Balinese music education (Myers, 1976), or as an adjunct to studies of cultural tourism (Dunbar-Hall, 2001). Various writers use such study as only one component of wider Balinese research (Eiseman, 1990), or as a comparison to studies of *gamelan* repertoires in other parts of Indonesia (Spiller, 2004). All of these undertakings assist, and are part of the process of, the globalisation of Balinese music. In each case, the purposes of learning dictate the various role/s assigned to music at the site of instruction, and influence the ways music is aestheticised and disseminated.

Sydney Community Group

Balinese *gamelan* music is learned by many groups of non-Balinese players outside Bali. The purposes of this vary. In some cases it is as a component of university studies in music; in others it is as a community music activity. My second case study is an example of the latter, an adult community group in Sydney, New South Wales, Australia. The reasons the members of this group want to learn Balinese *gamelan* are diverse. Some people join this group for social reasons, others to experience a complex music different from that of their backgrounds. Some members espouse affinity with tenets of Balinese Hinduism, or Asian cultural and religious thinking in general. Musical alternativeness, musicological understanding at a deep level and the chance to perform in public are also given as reasons for learning; the meanings assigned to Balinese music, therefore, are external to those observed in Bali among Balinese people (see Watson & Dunbar-Hall, 2002).

127

Even though the teacher of the group is himself non-Balinese, in this group the repertoires learned and the teaching methods employed replicate those found in Bali. In this way, a level of authenticity in some aspects of this group's learning is achieved. Authenticity is also striven for in performance practice, the group's use of traditional Balinese costume, and in their cultural address to music and the instruments on which it is performed. Members of the group travel to Bali for lessons, guaranteeing a degree of infusion of culturally shaped attitudes to Balinese music. As the instruments used originated in Bali, problems of sonic authenticity and adaptation to non-Balinese instrumentation, as arise when Balinese music is transferred to non-Balinese instruments, is not an issue.

In the multicultural context of Sydney, where performance of Asian musics is a regular event, performances by this group are one part of the musical diversity of a large cosmopolitan city. This is especially evident when this group performs at public events that include other Asian or non-European based musics. In the performances, Balinese music that has religious implications for members of the Balinese Hindu religion is desacralised, and pieces of music that refer to Indonesian personalities or to programmatic events of Balinese life (such as storms, rice-pounding, the lives and actions of animals and birds) replace their immediate sources of meaning with either purely abstract ones or something redolent of Asian music in general. Another factor that gives local meaning to music performed by this group is the association of members with the membership of a Javanese *gamelan* — many members play in both groups, forming an Indonesian music nexus offering contrasting interpretations of the term '*gamelan*' through observable and audible differences between Balinese and Javanese repertoires.

Australian and American Schools and Universities

Different uses of music can be assigned to Balinese music when it is used as an object for teaching in the systematised music education of western countries. To demonstrate this, reference is made here to school music education in Australia and university music study in the United States.

In Australian music syllabi, there is expectation that all musics from all periods, styles, locations and genres are suitable for study in schools. This occurs in a number of ways, ranging between all musics becoming a general holistic repertoire from which examples of musical practices are isolated for study, to study of the music of a specified culture or as exemplification of a topic or repertoire. The approach to music teaching and learning adopted across Australia is that loosely defined as 'the concept approach', in which any piece of music can be used to demonstrate how music works as the manipulation of sounds and silences; the ultimate aim of this type of music education is therefore structuralist, in that it focuses on methods for manipulating sounds and silences with little regard for the qualitative implications of such manipulation. In this setting, a piece of Balinese music such as *Baris Tunggal*, for example, can exemplify repetitive patterns (what a teacher might label as ostinato), the roles of different instruments (performing media), sectionalisation (structure), varying complexity and combination of instrumental lines (texture), in addition to melodic material (pitch) and rhythmic devices (duration). In addition to its structuralist nature, this way of treating music is colonialist. It teaches all music from an analytical perspective that imposes Eurocentric ways of understanding music that can be shown to contradict the ways music's creators may have of conceptualising their music and its meanings.

Although Australian syllabi list acknowledgment of cultural contexts as an aspect of music pedagogy, there is no guarantee that teachers have backgrounds that embrace all musics, or that they include it in their work. In many instances, pieces of music in this setting develop identities as purely pedagogic examples with no purpose beyond teaching an awareness of music as structure. In this way,

128

the original purposes of music as social activity or cultural artefact are negated (and often ignored) and pieces are given new aesthetic positions that derive entirely from their roles as pedagogic examples. This is not surprising, as it is an unrealistic expectation that music teachers will have received in-depth training in the cultural contexts of all types of music they teach, or that they have back-grounds in anthropological study through which to comprehend and teach the significance of culture as a force shaping human existence. Added to this are the implications of adapting Balinese music to western percussion instruments (often Orff Schulwerk instruments, since they can replicate pentatonic scales similar to those used in Bali). Such adaptation emphasises an attitude of neglect towards teaching and learning music through cultural context, and reminds that music education and authenticity regularly have little in common.

Issues of authenticity and context prove problematic for music educators, as two surveys I conducted demonstrate. These, one in New South Wales, the other national, ascertained the levels and nature of the teaching of Aboriginal and Torres Strait Islander (ATSI) musics in Australian schools. Many teachers indi-cated that while they include ATSI musics in their work, they are unsure of how to properly cover the cultural implications. In many cases, teachers indicated that this had become a dilemma. They also indicated that for them, the chance to make music education comprehensive — through the inclusion of ATSI musics as one of many types of music — governs their use of these musics as teaching mate-rial, rather than the ability to instruct students in cultural, social or political dimensions, or to raise issues of ATSI marginalisation and mistreatment within the Australian polity (Dunbar-Hall, 1997; Dunbar-Hall, 2002; Dunbar-Hall & Beston, 2003). I suspect the same situation exists for other types of music. Even when trainee music educators have been specifically trained in *gamelan* perfor-mance and the cultural implications of Balinese *gamelan* music, there is no guar-antee that they will cover the cultural aspects of music as a component of teaching *gamelan* to students (Dunbar-Hall, 2002).

The use of Balinese *gamelan* as a teaching tool is a feature of the program set up at UCLA by Mantle Hood in the 1950s. To Hood, experience of non-western music was a desirable way to study music, and performance the most efficacious means for learning: 'Making music is the most direct mode of music discourse'. Hood saw the experience of non-western music through performance as a means for redressing the inadequacies of western musical training: 'The student trained in Western music has some strongly conditioned limitations to overcome. Conventional Western training in musicianship produces a stunted growth in the perception and execution of rhythm and melody' (Hood, 1971, p. 35).

Hood instigated learning in Balinese, Chinese, Filipino, Greek, Indian, Iranian, Japanese, Javanese, Mexican and Thai ensembles under the direction of native specialists (Hood, 1960, 1963, 1995) through what he called 'bimusicality' (Hood, 1960, 1995). Hood's learning objectives were fluency in improvisation, proficiency in technique, mastery of the rules governing improvisation, assimila-tion of the tradition at hand and understanding of the cultural contexts of the music being studied (Hood, 1960). He saw this training as specifically aimed towards the preparation of students as ethnomusicologists through the development of 'unprejudiced ears' (Hood, 1963, p. 243), that is, the ability to listen to music without the influence of western music. The intended outcome was realisation that music:

129

may or may not have extramusical associations for members of the society, that it operates within a certain range of musical predictability ... that it may produce varied emotional responses ... will evoke different or no extramusical associations in non-members of the society, (and) that perception by the non-member will vary according to the natural limitations and capacities of the individual (Hood, 1963, p. 289).

A recording of Hood's students performing a section of *Baris Tunggal* demonstrates his use of Balinese music as a teaching device and his belief in bimusicality as a desirable way of developing ethnomusicological skills. It represents students' experiences of learning a small repertoire taught to them by the Balinese composer and performer I Wayan Gandra during his stay in America from 1960 to 1962, and of the efficacy and perhaps the problems of crosscultural teaching. The role of Balinese music in this case is clearly identified in Hood's response to his perception of the disadvantages of western musical training. The presence of Gandra raises other issues. For him, as a Balinese with connections to the spiritual world of the Balinese cosmos and music's role in it, these pieces would have had strong religious implications or would have connected to specific cultural functions in Balinese village life. The pieces he taught to students were the same as those he taught to other non-Balinese students in Bali and elsewhere. This became obvious to me when I worked in a *gamelan* under his tutelage in Bali, as the piece he chose to teach was one I already knew from listening to the LP made by his students at UCLA in the 1960s. A 1980s recording of an Australian *gamelan* taught and led by him includes the same or similar pieces. His choice of pieces would seem to rely on their usefulness in teaching, on their ability to act as vehicles for learning Balinese music, rather than the necessity of performing them to mark an event in the Balinese religious calendar. This emphasises the multivalent meanings of music used in the spaces between globalised teaching and localised learning, and points to ways that musical meaning is constructed through agendas of music's location and purpose.

Globalisation, Localism and New Order Music Education

... high-speed data communication tools have created a potentially boundary-less global space without the basic rules to ensure its stability (Brown, 1997, p. 47).

Geertz (1983), in an analysis of Indonesian jurisprudence, made a case for analysing culture through the interpretation of locally understood concepts, terminologies and systems. His method, based on local knowledge, superseded earlier ways of studying culture that worked from outsiders' perspectives (usually western academic ones) and attempted to understand through the epistemological lenses of researchers. Two decades later, the paradigm for studying culture and cultural artefacts has shifted to one that includes local knowledge but extends to other local knowledges as culture and its artefacts move in and out of different contexts, and concentrates on trying to understand the processes through which music adopts and adapts meaning. Perlman (2004) provides a good example of this in his use of ethnotheory and cognitive anthropology to understand Javanese musical thinking. In Java, learning and performing *gamelan* has its own, indigenous perspectives of understanding and interpretation, and subsequently when musicians move to teaching and research positions in the United States, the outcomes of their pedagogic activities lead to very different ways of interpreting Javanese music.

The situation created by globalisation is unstable, as Brown's (1997) comment on communication systems indicates. This instability has relevance to the current state of music education in the space between global and local cultures. In many cases, there

130

is an implication that globalisation leads to a world in which values and meanings are unilateral. Certainly, globalisation through technology, trade, travel and migration has had wide-ranging effects on music, on access to music and its creators and producers, and on music education. At the same time, the dangers of cultural imperialism as a ramification of globalisation are often discussed (e.g., Said, 1994), as are the detrimental effects it has on cultural specificity (e.g., Watson, 2002). To counter these claims, we might remember that in some situations access to the technologies of globalisation in the form of recordings and web sites has been proactively manipulated by communities for their own wants and needs (the case of Australian Aboriginal communities and their uses of technologies to preserve and disseminate music is a good example of this; Dunbar-Hall, 2000).

As my case studies of Balinese music in different pedagogic settings indicate, while globalisation provides music education with an ever increasing body of music for teaching, local uses of these musics, the ways music is employed to fulfil curriculum expectations, interpretations of pieces of music within sociocultural contexts, and the purposes behind adaptation, teaching, learning and performance indicate that specific local contexts remain the sources of musical meaning. Despite music's putative original meanings, the meanings people ascribe to music are context specific.

This raises issues for music educators, destabilises received conceptual bases of music education, and pushes music teaching and learning into new territory. Under the effects of globalisation, music education can no longer be seen only as training in executive skills on instruments or voices, the development of theoretical and historical knowledge, or the teaching of aural analysis. These are all current expectations of music teaching and learning. Rather, the issues that develop between global and local sites lead music educators to confront questions of musical meaning — original, derived, adapted, blended, transported — not only what meanings might be, but how meanings arise, are assigned, interpreted and contradicted. At present, this is not a focus of music education, and is problematic for a music education that continues to reflect the 1970s concept approach. Under the influence of globalisation, alleviation of the tensions between musical meanings arising from its origins and those assigned when it becomes the object of study emerges as a necessary focus of music education. That neither sets of meanings is privileged is important, as is also acknowledgment that musical meaning and how it evolves are an object of investigation, teaching and learning.

References

ARMA. (n.d). *Agung Rai Museum of Art* [Museum prospectus].

Bakan, M. (1999). *Music of death and new creation: Experiences in the world of Balinese gamelan beleganjur*. Chicago: Chicago University Press.

Brown, D. (1997). *Cybertrends: Chaos, power and accountability in the information age*. London: Penguin.

Dunbar-Hall, P. (1997). Problems and solutions in the teaching of Aboriginal and Torres Strait Islander musics. In *Proceedings of the XIth National Conference of the Australian Society for Music Education* (pp. 81–87).

Dunbar-Hall, P. (2000). Concept or context? Teaching and learning Balinese gamelan and the universalist-pluralist debate. *Music Education Research, 2*(2), 127–140.

Dunbar-Hall, P. (2000). Technologising culture: Access, control and Aboriginal knowledge. In *Proceedings of the 24th World Conference of the International Society for Music Education* (pp. 98–105).

131

Dunbar-Hall, P. (2001). Culture, tourism, and cultural tourism: Boundaries and frontiers in performances of Balinese music and dance. *Journal of Intercultural Studies, 22*(2), 173–187.

Dunbar-Hall, P. (2002). Politics or music? Australian music educators' attitudes to the teaching of Aboriginal and Torres Strait Islander musics. *Australian Journal of Music Education, 1*, 6–15.

Dunbar-Hall, P., & Beston, P. (2003). Aboriginal and Torres Strait Islander musics in Australian music education: Findings of a national survey. In *Proceedings of the 14th National Conference of the Australian Society for Music Education* (pp. 50–54).

Eiseman, F. (1990). *Sekala and niskala: Essays in religion, art and ritual* (Vol. 1). Indonesia: Periplus Editions (HK).

Geertz, C. (1983). *Local knowledge: Further essays in interpretive anthropology*. New York: Basic Books.

Herbst, E. (1997). *Voices in Bali*. Hanover: Wesleyan University Press.

Hood, M. (1960). The challenge of "bi-musicality". *Ethnomusicology, IV*(2), 55–59.

Hood, M. (1963). In terms of itself. In F. Harrison, M. Hood, & C. Palisca (Eds.), *Musicology* (pp. 240–289). Westport: Greenwood Press.

Hood, M. (1971). *The ethnomusicologist*. New York: McGraw-Hill.

Hood M. (1995). The birth pangs of bimusicality. In M. Lieth-Philipp & A. Gutzwiller (Eds.), *Teaching musics of the world: The second international symposium, Basel, 14-17 October, 1993* (pp. 56–58). Affalterbach: Philipp Verlag.

Leong, S. (Ed.). (2003). *Musicianship in the 21st century: Issues, trends and possibilities*. Sydney: Australian Music Centre.

McCarthy, M. (Ed.). (2004). *Toward a global community: The International Society for Music Education 1953-2003*. Perth, Australia: International Society for Music Education.

McPhee, C. (1966). *Music in Bali: A study in form and instrumental organization in Balinese orchestral music*. New Haven: Yale University Press.

Myers, D. (1976). Balinese music for use in the classroom with Orff instruments. In *Challenges in music education: Proceedings of the XIth International Conference of the International Society for Music Education* (pp. 268–270).

Perlman, M. (2004). *Unplayed melodies: Javanese gamelan and the genesis of music theory*. Berkeley: University of Los Angeles Press.

Said, E. (1994). *Culture and imperialism*. London: Vintage Books.

Spiller, H. (2004). *Gamelan: The traditional sounds of Indonesia*. Santa Barbara: ABC-CLIO.

Tenzer, M. (2000). *Gamelan gong kebyar*. Chicago: Chicago University Press.

Watson, D. (2002). *Death sentence: The decay of public language*. Sydney: Knopf.

Watson, G., & Dunbar-Hall, P. (2002). Ethnicity, identity and gamelan music: A contrastive study of Balinese music practice in Sydney. *Asia Pacific Journal of Arts Education, 1*(1), 51–59.

PETER DUNBAR-HALL is Associate Dean (Graduate Studies) at Sydney Conservatorium of Music (University of Sydney). He is widely published on Australian cultural history, popular music studies, Aboriginal music, Balinese music and the philosophy of music education. He is the author of *Strella Wilson: The Career of an Australian Singer* (Redback Press, 1997) and *Deadly Sounds, Deadly Places: Contemporary Aboriginal Music in Australia* (University of New South Wales Press, 2004). He is a performing member of Sydney based Balinese gamelan gong kebyar, Seakaa Gong Tirta Sinar.

132

Teaching SamulNori: Challenges in the Transmission of Korean Percussion

Keith Howard

SamulNori, essentially a quartet of percussionists, although increasingly performed by larger groups, is today arguably Korea's most successful traditional music. The quartet is a recent evolution of something much older; the name was coined in April 1978 by the folklorist Shim Usŏng two months after the first performance. Its antecedents are the local percussion bands, known under the umbrella terms of *nongak* and *p'ungmul* and preserved as an icon from Korea's past as Intangible Cultural Property (*Muhyŏng munhwajae*) 11, and itinerant percussion troupes, notably Namsadang, preserved as Intangible Cultural Property 3. SamulNori means 'four things play', a reference to the *kkwaenggwari* and *ching* small and large hand-held gongs and two drums — the double-headed hourglass-shaped *changgo* and the squashed barrel drum, *puk*. For much of the SamulNori repertory, one of each instrument is played. In performance, the small gong gives rhythmic models and the large gong the underpinning foundations. The hourglass drum uses two sticks, a thin whip-like *yŏl chae* to imitate the small gong patterns and a mallet-shaped *kunggul ch'ae* to fill in the large gong foundations, while the barrel drum emphasises and expands on the large gong. A small hand-held drum, the *sogo* or *pŏpko*, may appear for dance.

SamulNori, then, is rhythm. It is immediate in its appeal, and ideal for teaching as a performance ensemble. However, it has not made much impact beyond the Korean diaspora within performance courses abroad, whether in schools or universities. My contention here is that the teaching system that has evolved within Korea, and which is promoted by Koreans for use abroad, is not suitable for the sort of world music ensemble training that now typifies foreign (western) universities and conservatoires (for which see Solís, 2004). In the case of other performance ensembles, including gamelan, mbira, djembe (and other African percussion) and samba (and other Latin ensembles), results are expected after short periods of study. Working within a European university, I must comply with a syllabus that requires performance courses, as with lecture courses, to be taught in a single weekly lesson, examined after either a single semester or a year. Again, because my students will be studying many different musics, in which Korean music struggles for a place, I need to teach in a way that will sustain interest while challenging the competing traditions that form the core performance studies we teach at SOAS (of gamelan, mbira, kora, tabla, Sizhu, Nōh, Thai mahori and more). Here, I will contrast the Korean

133

system(s) with my own interpretation and teaching of the SamulNori repertoire. A fuller consideration of SamulNori will appear in my forthcoming book, *Creating Korean Music* (in press).

Aesthetic Principles

SamulNori have developed an aesthetic that informs both performance and training. Merriam (1964, pp. 259–273) has argued that aesthetic concepts are uncommon in traditional music cultures, while Bohlman has commented that the reason for this is because music functions as part of a contextualised broader performance complex in which distinction in ideas about sound is redundant (1999, pp. 30–31). If this is so, then it is reasonable to expect an aesthetic sense to have evolved since the first SamulNori concert in 1978 that had never formerly been articulated by either local percussion bands or itinerant troupes. However, the issue that Merriam and Bohlman address is one of verbalising as opposed to appreciating: aesthetics do exist amongst performers and form an essential core for so-called 'emic' accounts of music (by, for example, Stephen Feld, Hugo Zemp, Tom Turino and Marina Roseman). In Korea, nonetheless, contemporary aesthetic reflections typically contrast the music of pre-modern times with music since 1960. With SamulNori, I am referring primarily to the founding group, or its subsequent incarnations, and an authentic repertory, based on local and itinerant bands of old but updated and adjusted for contemporary performance. The repertory has a prescribed canon with archetypes that is now transmitted with little variation because of a strong and uniform aesthetic.

Developing the Aesthetic: The 'Right' Way to Perform

SamulNori use a dance aesthetic to inform performance practice that would, arguably, not be completely recognised by the rural farmers of previous generations who played *nongak* or *p'ungmul*. In dance, motion creates an essential feeling of Koreanness through a peculiarly Korean concept, 'motion in stillness' (*chŏngjungdong*). Characteristic features of dance (cited after Van Zile, 2001) show the concept in action. Dance emphasises verticality, up and down actions that at slow tempi alternate bending and extending at the knees to lift and lower the body; in percussion bands the bend sometimes generates a push to a jump. Verticality is emphasised by shoulder movements, initiated in the chest with apparent breath inhalation that causes the spine to lengthen, forcing the shoulders to rise, then releasing as the shoulders and back relax. Breath is key, and is felt internally rather than being the result of a conscious mechanical action. The arms frequently extend outwards from the shoulders, turned inward so that the thumb surface of the hand is directed forward, keeping the wrist relaxed and the fingers curved gently down. This sets off the movement associated most commonly with *kutkŏri*, the favoured 6/8 + 6/8 rhythmic cycle for dance. The arm will rotate or be gently curved, the interpretation in music being a balance between unequal front and back portions of a pattern, the *chŏnbanbu* and *hubanbu* as the *sanjo* master Ham Tongjŏngwŏl (1917–1994) told me in 1987. There is also a feeling of suspension, where a dance movement begins and rises then stops abruptly, releasing gently after a slight additional upward push. And, finally, feet caress the floor with toes curled upwards, steps beginning on the heel rather than the toe or ball of the foot.

134

To SamulNori, motion in stillness becomes harmonised movement generated through a realisation of unity. They utilise the term '*hana-a*', a term that at its most basic level is derived from *han/hana* meaning 'one'. In dance, one bends the knees (*ha-*), rises (*-na-*), and rebounds or kicks gently outwards (*-a*); or, with the upper body, breathes in (*ha-*), raises the shoulders (*-na-*) and relaxes (*-a*). Kim Duk Soo, one of the founder members of SamulNori, states that this sequence was one of the first things a budding itinerant troupe musician had to learn before progressing to any experiment in playing an instrument (1992, p. 22). So, small children, including Kim Duk Soo and the additional SamulNori musician Ch'oe Chongshil, had to begin as dancers, gradually progressing through dancing and playing with the *sogo* small drum to the important drums and gongs. Add to this a Taoist tripartite division of upper, centre and lower body, and movement should be focused in the torso; it should not project ballet-like away from the centre. The more it is conceived in this way then the more dance can be performed seated; importantly so, since the majority of the SamulNori repertory is performed seated.

Dance gives the way to count *hana-a* precisely because so much Korean music is in compound metre, in which beat subdivisions are spoken in rehearsal as *ha-na-a*. Rhythmic counting controls breath, creating a foundation for what Kim claims is 'natural and fluid movement'. This is the beginning of a technique known as *hohŭp*. When a person dies, a Korean will say their breath 'has gone out', hence breath defines *hohŭp*. Students of SamulNori these days practice from a relaxed position with chin slightly downwards (*ha-*). They inhale while raising both the head and torso to an upright position (*-na-*), then keep raising the head up and back (*-a*), falling back to start again. The fall extends forward after the end of the count, moving the student straight to the next sequence. One *hana-a* joins to the next, creating a circular movement that can continue endlessly: 'while there is constant movement in the sphere of infinity, there is also balance' (Kim Duk Soo, 1992, p. 11). Students are taught to repeat the syllables, *hana-a*, first adding head movement, then shoulders and chest, and finally stomach and pelvis, this last movement characterised as swing, *ogŭmjil*. *Hohŭp* is the root of dance; in other words, dance extends from *hohŭp*. So, swing is best initially experienced through dance and *hohŭp* effectively creates the required seated dance by assimilating dance characteristics then recreating them within posture where movement is limited. The elements of *hohŭp* are taught in sequence: rhythmic counting, body movement, swing and dance (Kim Dong-Won, 1999, pp. 6–11).

Yin and Yang

Circularity emerges from a pair of interlocking commas. These are the central red and blue commas of the South Korean national flag, blue *yin* (Kor: *ŭm*) below and red *yang* above. Beyond the flag, *yin* is dark, blue or black, negative, the receptive female; *yang* is light, red, positive, the penetrating male. The commas complement each other, being joined by a shared curved line. Hence, the circle is the *t'aegŭk*, the great absolute or great ultimate of Chinese philosophy, the source of the *yin/yang* cosmic principle. At a primary level, SamulNori superimposes playing techniques, an open sound being interpreted as *yin* and a closed or damped sound as *yang*. An open sound on the small gong is where the stick rebounds and allows the metal to vibrate, while a closed sound uses the fingers of the left hand to brush the rear of the vibrating surface or keeps the stick in contact with the metal. An open sound on the hourglass drum is where the stick rebounds, while a closed sound requires the stick to remain

135

in contact with the drumhead; for the thin whip-like *yŏl ch'ae* stick these are represented within verbal notation as *tta* or *ttŏk* for open sounds and *ttak, tta, ta* or *ki* for closed sounds.

At a second level, the small gong couples to the large gong, one *yin* and one *yang*. The barrel drum can be struck both on the skin and the wooden frame, or the skin can either be left to resonate or can be damped, again creating the duality of *yin* and *yang*. Moving back to the hourglass drum, the two skins are pitched differently, one producing a higher pitch, *yang*, and the other a dull thud of only relative pitch, *yin*. Cast in a slightly different frame, the higher-pitched head is associated with the heavens and the lower-pitched head with the earth. The latter marks the beats, and is therefore tied within *hohŭp* to the inhaling phase, while the higher-pitched head marks the exhaling phase. Taken one stage further, the hourglass drum encapsulates the other three instruments in a manner that places it at the centre of the band. Hence, whereas in local percussion bands and itinerant troupes the small gong had always been the leader, in SamulNori the hourglass drum takes more glory. It is, then, the hourglass drum for which the first three SamulNori workbooks are written (Korean Conservatorium of Performing Arts, 1990, 1992, 1995).

The philosophy of Taoism increases this duality by adding a third component, at its most simple man seated between earth and heaven. Within this, the two commas must gain a third to create the *samt'aeguk*, seen throughout Korea in, for example, the doors to Buddhist temples and shaman ritual spaces, where the red heavenly *yang* and blue earthly *yin* are joined by a third comma, the yellow of man. Taken back to dance, the shoulders and head are associated with heaven, the knees with earth, but the torso remains the central core where the soul resides. SamulNori found a tripartite division of musical structure within what began as the 15th century notation system for court ritual music, *chŏngganbo*. This is a square box notation consisting of a set of vertical columns, read across the page from right to left. Each column comprises one length of a rhythmic cycle, *changdan*, and divides into units each comprising sets of boxes, the boxes each containing single beats. The division is from large to small, from column to unit to box.

To SamulNori, *wŏn, pang* and *kak* designate the tripartite division. One should 'think of *wŏn* as the largest encompassing entity, *pang* as the first pillar which divides the entity, and *kak* as a further smaller division' (Kim, 1992, p. 16). The concept of *wŏn* avoids labelling rhythmic patterns as metrical within the conventions of staff notation, preferring at all times to give the *pang* division as a constant, because it tends to equate to a dance step. This, though, can counteract large gong strikes, removing the concept of *ch'ae* within which local bands identified specific patterns and introducing a lower level of division. The effect is, simply put, to resist metrical division, because this would require divisions that do not match pacing, the level at which *hohŭp* primarily functions The *pang*, due to its relation to pacing, is thus associated with the body's knees and with the earth, and by extension, *wŏn* links to the shoulders and to heaven, and *kak* to the torso.

136

The problem with this is that rigid technique created music that is a cardboard cut out. How can emotion and feeling be added? A separate set of aesthetic concepts, *mŏt* and *mat*, defining taste, richness and deliciousness, comes to SamulNori's aid. These challenge precision. They have broader provenance, despite typical assertions to the contrary: 'The extreme difficulty of translating the word *mŏt* into foreign languages demonstrates the uniquely Korean nature of the concept. *Mŏt* is a composite value formulated by the combination and integration of ... beauty, elegance and refinement' (Kim Su-doc, 1998, p. 4). In Samulnori, *mŏt* and *mat* measure how drum or gong strikes fit within *pang* and *kak*, stretching, pulling and adding emphasis by distending regularity. European art music invokes terms such as *rubato* and *tenuto* for much the same thing. *Mŏt* and *mat* are in SamulNori and percussion bands more broadly also applied at a macro level, linear development away from rhythmic models in which individual variants, *karak*, break from model patterns; jazz improvisers will recognise this in terms of working with riffs. SamulNori identify the aesthetic in terms of creative dissonance, visualised in their second workbook (1992, pp. 15, 27) as a process of developing proficiency, moving from the mastery of body movement (*hana-a*), breathing (*hohŭp*) and instrumental technique, through the development of individual variations that match the identity of model patterns, to internalised flow. Flow brings us back to the linear motion in stillness, but now with the appreciation that *mŏt* and *mat* are needed to energise and balance the *yin/yang* complex.

Notating the Canon in Korea

The development of notation for the SamulNori canon secured ownership while at the same time creating a context for teaching and learning. How, though, should the canon be notated?

In 1989, Kim Duk Soo introduced me to Lim Dong Chang, a graduate of Chungang University. He lambasted my use of a modified staff notation in *Korean Musical Instruments*, my 1988 book, as a misrepresentation of Korean rhythm. The problem was one of perception. In my transcription of the first sections of SamulNori's *Samdo sŏl changgo* I marked how triplet quavers became duple quavers by switching from a 12/8 compound metre to a 4/4 duple metre as the pulse increased. He maintained there was no metric change, since the relative size of the rhythmic cycle, the *wŏn*, remained the same because the number of units, the *pang*, did not change. He argued that notation must show this. I had followed fairly standard conventions, and my use of staff notation was not unusual: it has, since its appearance in a notation of the folk song *Arirang* in an 1896 copy of *Korea Repository*, been extensively used by musicians, musicologists and composers in Korea. It was also previously employed by Robert Provine (1975, 1982, 1985). This is not to deny its limitations and deficiencies (Hughes, 1989, p. 9; Hesselink, 1998, pp. 206–207) and, indeed, criticism of its use for non-western music is frequent (e.g., Ellingson, 1992). It is, though, useful and compact. It 'renders material immediately comprehensible' (Agawu, 1995, p. 195) and has low levels of redundancy (Bent, 1980, p. 343). None of this is to deny that the notation of rhythm is contentious.

Metric inconsistency led SamulNori and Lim to turn to Korean tradition. Initially, and as with many of the student bands of the early 1980s, SamulNori incorporated onomatopoeic verbal notation of a kind common but infinitely varied amongst local percussion bands. For the hourglass drum, SamulNori ascribe the syllable '*kun*' to single strokes of the mallet-shaped stick, '*ku kung*' to double strokes and '*kurururu*' to a trill. '*Ttak*' or '*tak*' mark a stroke on the right head by the thin whip-like stick where reverberation is damped by leaving the stick in contact with the head, while '*tta*' marks a stroke where the stick rebounds. '*Ta*' or '*ki*' signifies a light stroke played with the tip of the stick with rebound, while *tŏk* verbalises where the tip damps the head. '*Kittak*' is a sequence of two sounds within a single stroke, the first a grace note with the tip of the stick and the second a full but damped

137

sound, and '*tarururu*' is a trill requiring repeated rebounds. '*Tong*' signifies a simultaneous strike by both sticks. Similar onomatopoeia signify strokes on the other instruments.

The complexity of drum patterns — one basic distinction between SamulNori and bands of old Korea — was such that onomatopoeia could only work at slow tempo. Hence, SamulNori looked elsewhere, and adapted *chŏngganbo*. The vertical columns of old were rotated through 90° to read left to right as horizontal rows, and vertical lines were added that both extend above the row of boxes to mark each unit (*pang*). SamulNori expanded the vocabulary of signs to signify different strikes, offering circles of different sizes, some partially or fully shaded. Within the SamulNori adaptation, three interlocking circles are printed on the left before the start of a stave to denote rhythmic structure: *wŏn* at the bottom — always a '1' — *pang* units at the top left, and *kak* beats at the top right. Thus, reading clockwise from the bottom, 1+4+12 indicates either a 12/8 or 12/4 pattern, but without the metric and stress implications of European time signatures: 1 *wŏn*, 4 *pang* and 12 *kak*. The assymetrical *ŏnmori* rhythmic cycle, for example, would be rendered as 1+6+10 (5/8 + 5/8).

The system in totality is expansive, and all three workbooks published between 1990 and 1995 are devoted to one drum piece, *Samdo sŏl changgo*. The first volume, 199 pages of text and notated exercises and a 10-page photographic appendix, sets out basic principles, incorporating movement, breathing and performance techniques. The second, 28 pages of text and 185 pages of notation, gives a synoptic reading of the piece using all three systems (adapted *chŏngganbo*, oral notation and modified single line staff notation). The third is a memory aid, 54 pages of adapted *chŏngganbo* and then 36 pages of single line staff notation. At the National Center for Korean Traditional Performing Arts (Kungnip kugagwŏn) and based on the rival team of which he was part, the Kungnip Kugagwŏn Samullori P'ae, Ch'oe Pyŏngsam joined with Ch'oe Hŏn to transcribe their related piece, *Sŏl changgu karak*, within volume 27 of the venerable series *Anthology of Korean Music/Han'guk ŭmak* (Ch'oe & Ch'oe, 1992). They use single line staff notation, but mark strokes of the mallet-shaped stick on the right drum head with 'x' below the line. They distinguish four separate drum parts and notate all improvisation in a descriptive score lasting 52 pages. In 2000, Ch'oe Pyŏngsam issued a second volume, specifically designed for his students. This latter volume does not include the drum piece, but in its other notations reveals the impact of SamulNori's workbooks by incorporating a modified *chŏngganbo*. One of the first SamulNori pieces, *Yŏngnam nongak* (here called *Yŏngnam karak*), demonstrates, again, how expansive this needs to be: it runs to 65 pages.

The investment of time required to go through any or all of these volumes has the advantage of allowing aesthetic principles to be fully absorbed by students. That, though, to my mind also makes the system unworkable in a western university.

Notating the Canon Abroad

Using conventions adopted from Provine, I designed prescriptive scores of pieces, as teaching scores, that can each be contained in just a few pages. I count repeats or exactness where these were part of the versions taught to me, although improvisation and variability will still apply in performance.

Hesselink has briefly characterised three different approaches taken to the analysis of SamulNori pieces: recomposition or reorganisation (*chaegusŏng*), drawing together band music played for different occasions, and drawing together representative rhythms from *p'an kut* (Hesselink, 2004, pp. 413–414). I, together with Hahn Myung-hee (1993) and Ku Hee-seo (1994), am said to adopt the second approach. To me, these are not discreet approaches but stages on a journey. In the case of the drum piece, the journey is not from routine local or itinerant band practice, but from a solo drum dance found in two contrasting forms. One was performed as part of local band events by brawny farmers, while the other, created by and for pretty girls on urban stages, is quite distinct. Neither was suitable for a dramatic seated piece such as SamulNori wanted, and so a new source of inspiration was found, namely *sanjo*, the instrumental melodic genre that comprises a set of movements each cast in a single rhythmic cycle. The melodic variation of *sanjo* becomes rhythmic variation to SamulNori. The inspiration came because three of the SamulNori quartet had received schooling at the Traditional Music Arts School, where the concentration was on staging folk music, particularly *sanjo*.

So, just as *sanjo* opens with an introductory tuning section, so does *Samdo sŏl changgo*, though the need in the SamulNori piece is not to tune but to allow the quartet to settle and balance with each other. It is because the drum piece was a new creation rather than something closely derived from earlier practice, that each different SamulNori/*samulori* team has developed a distinct version. The National Center version that I use fits the local drum dances of, among others, my first drum teacher, Kim Pyŏngsŏp, and his former colleague Yi Tongwŏn. A different introductory section moves to a slow movement using a compound-time version of *hwimori* (12/8). Then come truncated versions of *kutkŏri* (6/8+6/8) and *tŏngdŏkkung* (6/4) movements. *Yŏngsan tadŏregi* (12/8), preceded by its 'half' version, lifts small-drum dances once given by local and itinerant band members wearing hats with rotating plumes, but it, too, had been part of the drum dances of Kim and Yi. *Hwimori* then returns, now a fast duple rhythmic cycle (4/4), leading to a dramatic and extended cadence reminiscent of the non-metrical coda with which *sanjo* performances end. This piece is particularly favoured by my students, and I suspect the reason is the potential for vamping: within the *kutkŏri* and *tŏngdŏkkung* movements there are elements when individual drummers can improvise. This, as David Hughes (2004) has elsewhere reported, is what foreign students routinely want to do with ensemble performance, unfortunately, usually before they have mastered the structural components of the piece in its totality.

Over the last 20 years, a stream of students have learned SamulNori repertory with me. Two things have become clear to me. First, my students have performed in Seoul at three SamulNori contests, where they have won respectable prizes. But, my students do not perform in the Korean way; they do not move with full and consistent *hohŭp*, and will be appreciated more within Korea as they introduce musical elements that are clearly not Korean. Hence, the best prize we received came when we added *tabla* and *djembe* to the Korean quartet. Second, if I teach the SamulNori aesthetic, students feel short-changed, because it takes too long to get to the 'music'. The effect is that attendance drops off, and I am left with merely a couple of dedicated students — too few to demonstrate to my colleagues that SamulNori is a worthwhile performance ensemble within the curriculum.

Could it be any other way? Yes, but only if I want to restrict my teaching to those determined to study Korean music. But, to do so would mean that interest in

139

Korea and its musical traditions will never expand. The aim, I admit, is to allow encounter rather than mastery by my students; to provide entry and musical knowledge rather than cultural competence. I have to have shortcuts; I have to use methods that inspire rather than frustrate. From this, further encounters become possible, normally, as so many have recognise, through deep immersion in the culture itself. This, simply put, is why teaching SamulNori to Koreans in Korea can never be the same as teaching SamulNori to foreigners abroad.

References

Agawu, K. (1995). *African rhythm: A Northern Ewe perspective*. Cambridge: Cambridge University Press.

Art Space. (Eds.). (1988). *SamulNori 10-nyŏn*. Seoul: Art Space Publications.

Bent, I. (1980). Notation II/7. In S. Sadie (Ed.), *The new grove dictionary of music and musicians 13* (pp. 342–3). London: Macmillan.

Bohlman, P. (1999). Ontologies of music. In N. Cook & M. Everist (Eds.), *Rethinking music* (pp. 17–34). Oxford: Oxford University Press.

Ch'oe Pyŏngsam and Ch'oe Hŏn. (1992). *Samullori. Han'guk ŭmak 27/selections of Korean music 27*. Seoul: Kungnip kugagwŏn.

Ch'oe Pyŏngsam (2000). *Samullori paeugi: wŏllieŏ yŏnju kkaji*. Seoul: Hangminsa.

Ellingson, T. (1992). Notation. In Helen Myers (Ed.), *Ethnomusicology: An introduction* (pp. 115–47). London: Macmillan.

Hahn, M. (1993). SamulNori: Providing a musical release. *Koreana*, 7(4), 34–5.

Hesselink, N. (1998). *A tale of two drummers: Percussion band music in North Chŏlla Province, Korea*. Unpublished doctoral dissertation, University of London.

Hesselink, N. (2004). SamulNori as traditional: Preservation and innovation in a South Korean contemporary percussion genre. *Ethnomusicology*, 48(3), 405–39.

Hughes, D. W. (1989). ICTM/UK one day conference 1988 – Notation as a tool for ethnomusicology: extension of round table. *Bulletin of the International Council for Traditional Music (UK Chapter)*, 23, 3–12.

Hughes, D. W. (2004). When can we improvise? The place of creativity in academic world music performance. In T. Solís (Ed.), *Performing ethnomusicology: Teaching and representation in world music ensembles* (pp. 261–82). Berkeley and Los Angeles: University of California Press.

Kim D. (1999). *SamulNori textbook*. (Learning Korean Culture Series). Seoul: Overseas Koreans Foundation/Korean National University of Arts.

Kim S. (1998). About *mŏt*. *Koreana*, 12(3), 4.

Korean Conservatorium of Performing Arts/Han'guk chŏnt'ong yesul yŏnju pojonhoe. (1990). *SamulNori: Kim Tŏksu p'ae SamulNoriga yŏnju hanŭn changgo karak haksŭp p'yŏn 1*. Seoul: Samho ch'ulp'ansa. English version, (1992). *SamulNori. Korean Traditional Percussion SamulNori Rhythm Workbook 1: Basic Changgo*. Seoul: Sam-ho Music Publishing.

Korean Conservatorium of Performing Arts/Han'guk chŏnt'ong yesul yŏnju pojonhoe. (1992). *SamulNori: Korean Traditional Percussion SamulNori Rhythm Workbook 2: Samdo sul changgo karak/Kim Tŏksu p'ae SamulNoriga yŏnju hanŭn samdo sŏlchanggo karak haksŭp p'yŏn 2*. Seoul: Samho ch'ulp'ansa.

Korean Conservatorium of Performing Arts/Han'guk chŏnt'ong yesul yŏnju pojonhoe. (1995). *SamulNori: Korean Traditional Percussion SamulNori Rhythm Workbook 3: Samdo sul changgo karak/Kim Tŏksu p'ae SamulNoriga yŏnju hanŭn samdo sŏlchanggo karak yŏnju p'yŏn 3*. Seoul: Samho ch'ulp'ansa.

Ku, H. (1994). SamulNori. Taking Korean rhythms to the world. *Koreana*, 8(3), 24–7.

Merriam, A. C. (1964). *The anthropology of music*. Evanston: Northwestern University Press.

Park, S. (2000). *Negotiating identities in a performance genre: The case of p'ungmul and samulnori in contemporary Seoul*. Unpublished doctoral dissertation, University of Pittsburgh.

Provine, R. C. (1975). *Drum rhythms in Korean farmers' music*. Seoul: Private publication.

Provine, R. C. (1982). Die rhythmischen Strukturen in der koreanischen Folklore. *Korea Kulturmagazin, 1*, pp. 156–75.

Provine, R. C. (1985). Drumming in Korean farmers' music: A process of gradual evolution. In Dhu Shapiro (Ed.), *Music in context: Essays for John M. Ward* (pp. 441–52). Cambridge, MA: A. Harvard University Press.

Solís, T. (Ed.) (2004). *Performing ethnomusicology: Teaching and representation in world music ensembles.* Berkeley and Los Angeles: University of California Press.

Van Zile, J. (2001). *Perspectives on Korean dance.* Middletown, CT: Wesleyan University Press.

KEITH HOWARD is Reader in Music at SOAS, University of London, and Director of the AHRC Research Centre for Cross-Cultural Music and Dance Performance. A founding member of CDIME, he is author of more than 100 articles and author or editor of 14 books, including *Korean Musical Instruments: A Practical Guide* (Seoul: Se-kwang, 1988); *Bands, Songs and Shamanistic Rituals* (Seoul: Royal Asiatic Society, 1989); *Shamans and Cultures* (Budapest and Los Angeles, 1993); *Korean Musical Instruments* (Hong Kong: Oxford University Press, 1995); *True Stories of the Korean Comfort Women* (London: Cassell, 1995); *Korean Shamanism: Revivals, Survivals and Change* (Seoul: Seoul Press, 1998); and the forthcoming *Preserving Korean Music* (Aldershot: Ashgate, 2006), *Creating Korean Music* (Aldershot: Ashgate, 2006) and *Riding the Wave: Korean Pop Music.* In addition to teaching and performing music, he wrote the official book for Her Majesty Queen Elizabeth II's state visit to Korea (1999) and is active as a consultant and broadcaster on Korean affairs.

141

Indian Classical Music as Taught in the West: The Reshaping of Tradition?

Chad Hamill

During the tumultuous cultural reverberations of the late 60s and early 70s, north Indian classical music began to take root in the West, largely inspired by Beatle mania and dexterous hands of Ravi Shankar. Surviving the initial 'buzz' and faddishness of the 'East meets West', phenomenon, Indian classical music found its way into western academia, taking the shape of Indian classical schools and Indian classical departments at institutes and universities in Europe and the United States (US). Among the most celebrated of these were the Indian classical department at California Institute of the Arts, a program established by Ravi Shankar in 1970, and the Ali Akbar College in San Rafael, California, established in 1972 by Ali Akbar Khan. With hundreds of western students of Indian classical music having passed through their doors, they have contributed, as few others have, to a spreading of Indian classical music in the West, placing *sarods*, *sitars* and *tablas* in the hands of western converts, whose dedication and passion often defy the societal sensibilities that surround them. Has anything been lost in translation — in the *transplantation*?

What has been the process of transmission from the Indian musician to the western student? How have teaching practices and traditions been modified to accommodate western modes of learning? Have new methodologies developed through negotiations between teacher and student amounted to a reshaping of Indian classical tradition? I will approach these questions from two primary, first-hand perspectives: (a) by drawing from my own experience as a student and teacher of Indian classical vocal music, recounting different methods under which I learned and with which I subsequently taught, and (b) from excerpts of an interview I conducted with my primary teacher and *guru*, Rajeev Taranath, who has had extensive experience performing and teaching Indian classical music in both India and the US over his 50 year career.

Amiya Dasgupta and the 'Indian Room'

My initiation into the tradition of Indian classical music took place at California Institute of the Arts in 1990, where I was pursuing a BFA in western classical vocal music. While moving to and from class through the various hallways of the music building, I had often passed what was commonly referred to as 'the Indian room'. At any given time of day, a variety of muffled sounds associated with Indian music could be heard emanating from its walls and beneath its door. When the door was open, I could sometimes catch a glimpse of a slim and graceful Indian man with longish white hair holding a sitar that looked like it was woven into the flesh of his fingertips, a natural extension of his body. Often, he was surrounded by students holding a variety of instruments, both Indian and western, silver flute, violin, sitar, cello, *tabla*, and so on, playing pieces in various stages of development, sometimes sweet, other times raucous, always intriguing. He could also be seen facing one student in a process of mimesis, teaching in the manner of the guru-*shishya* tradition that binds a guru to a disciple in a continuum of the melodic, the rhythmic, the spiritual and the mundane. I was witnessing a centuries old tradition taking root in western soil, but as I would soon learn, not without compromise.

Amiya Dasgupta, in addition to teaching instrumental lessons and ensembles, also taught a vocal course called *Sargam*, a term referring to the Indian 'solfege' syllables *Sa, Re, Ga, Ma, Pa, Dha, Ni*. After two semesters of intermittent and 'muffled' contact with Indian classical music, I could resist no longer and decided to enrol in *Sargam*, a course that seemed well suited for someone with my vocal inclinations and experience. The first day, Amiya passed out sheets of paper containing a song, or *bandish*, written in a version of Indian notation developed and propagated in the early 20th century by musicologist and theorist Pandit V. N. Bhatkhande ('Pandit' is a term of reverence or respect). Bhatkhande set out to systematise Indian classical music, classifying ragas, documenting their individual characteristics and transcribing over two thousand *bandishes*, providing text as well as pitches (Bagchee, 1998). Dasgupta's system of notation, although Americanised, was very similar to Bhatkhande's in structure, with *sargam* syllables written in English instead of Hindi and words scripted in phonetic English equivalents (see Figure 1 for an example).

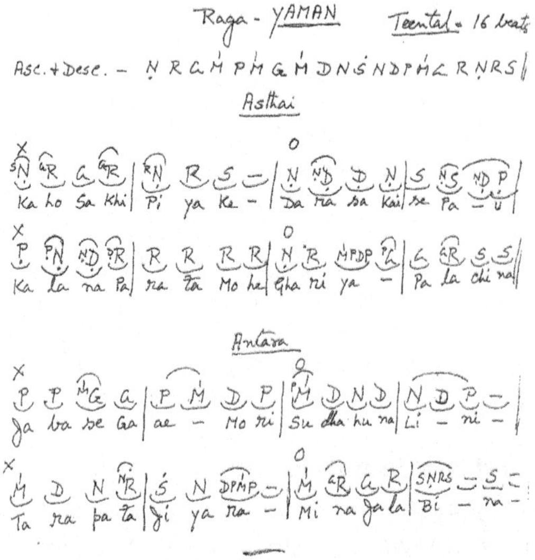

FIGURE 1

Example of a bandish in 'Raga- Yaman', transcribed by Amiya Dasgupta.

The process of transmission in Dasgupta's *Sargam* class was very consistent, with written *bandishes* handed out on a regular basis. Some classes would be an introduction to a new *bandish*, others would be a 'rehearsal' of one learned previously. The element of improvisation, essential in Indian classical performance, was absent. Instead, we read the notes off the page without variation in much the same manner as one reading a western score, a prescriptive approach that required the music to be rendered *as* written. Not recognising Dasgupta's pedagogical approach as a departure from Indian classical tradition at the time, I embraced the opportunity to delve into raga music and unlock some of its secrets. If I *had* known his approach was unconventional or untraditional, it probably would not have mattered, as it was serving as an introduction to a musical tradition I longed to understand and embrace. Dasgupta's approach allowed me to become conversant with the *sargam* syllables and provided an introduction to some basic raga movements, laying a foundation that would later prove useful when moving into the world of oral diffusion and improvisation occupied by my guru.

Dasgupta's methodological approach in the *Sargam* classes may, in part, be attributable to an overriding interest he had in western classical constructs. During his tenure at Cal Arts, which spanned over 20 years, he composed numerous choral and orchestral works built on raga forms infused with harmony and lush western instrumentation. His appropriation of a 'sheet-music' approach may have been a simple matter of adopting a method used throughout the music department at large, which had a strong emphasis on western classical music. Dasgupta rarely missed a performance given in the music department, whether it was Ewe music from Ghana, Stravinsky, a student recital or a faculty concert, he was there, taking it all in, and applying it to his craft. His approach in the vocal class may have also been a matter of conservation. Before I began learning from him, he underwent quadruple bypass surgery and although he continually played sitar, singing was difficult. Having music written helped him avoid endless repetition, one of the more taxing aspects of teaching in the traditional fashion. He passed away in 1994.

Ali Akbar College

Shortly after my BFA studies at Cal Arts, I relocated to the San Francisco Bay Area. I was anxious to deepen my study of Indian classical vocal music and signed up for introductory vocal classes at the Ali Akbar College of Music. Upon entering the college, I was immediately struck by a pervasive energy and ambiance. Ascending the stairs to the second story music room, I would soon discover the source of that energy — the great Ali Akbar Khan. Although he was seated quietly in the back of the room, he radiated with a quality that pulled your attention, like metal drawn to a magnet. As he approached the platform, surprisingly unassuming in movement and stature, people congregated onto the floor. I followed their lead and found a spot among the 40 or so students.

One of the first collective actions that preceded the utterance of musical sound was the pulling out of notebooks and pencils. Apparently I was unprepared, as all I had was my tape recorder and voice. Leaning down to the microphone, Ali Akbar Khan began to sing. As he finished the phrase, a chorus of voices responded and then stopped abruptly as almost in unison, heads turned down and a flurry of scribbling began. Khansahib continued with a new phrase, the chorus responded, heads bobbed, and the scribbling began again. It very quickly became clear that students were not simply transcribing the *bandish* for future reference, something easily

145

accomplished by the numerous tape recorders placed throughout the room. They were writing the notes for use *in the moment*, their eyes as critical to the learning process as their ears. What is interesting is that Ali Akbar Khan seemed detached from that process. He simply went on singing the *bandish* orally, in a traditional manner, seemingly unconcerned with how the students chose to receive the material. In a subsequent class, I observed a 'head-transcriber' standing at the front of the room next to a blackboard. Using a system of notation similar to Amiya's, he wrote out phrases with impressive rapidity and appeared to be enjoying himself while revelling in his ability to 'capture' the phrases. The question is: *was he capturing the phrase in its entirety or a just a remnant of it?*

Rajeev Taranath and Guru-Shishya Parampara

The oldest living disciple of Ali Akbar Khan, Rajeev Taranath, is a renowned master of the *sarod*. For the past 10 years he has been head of the Indian classical department at California Institute of the Arts, where he has taught *Sargam*, North Indian Theory, North Indian Ensemble, as well as private lessons in vocal and a variety of instruments, both Indian and western. In the following passage he gives his observations on the western students' propensity for reading music:

> Western classical music, you correct me if I'm wrong, requires a hundred percent mediation of the eye. You read music. The music is written. You read it, and from there you take it on to your fingers, your instrument, or for singing. There are other people teaching, great people teaching, who allow a lot more reading and writing than I did. You know that. I said, *now don't look at books. You just learn from listening to me; I sing, you listen; you sing, I listen*. And so that way we go on correcting it, polishing it, until it comes within the required range of acceptability. I found many students unable to hear because they're not used to mimesis, imitation as a mode of teaching/ learning (personal communication, May 7, 2005).

What Taranath seems to be suggesting when he states that 'many students were unable to hear', is that the act of reading music may act as a barrier to musical internalisation, with written music resting forever outside, rather than *inside*, the individual. The mediation of the eye requires a setting of the musical mould, a static representation of what should be in north Indian classical terms, fluid and dynamic, a pursuit of 'processes and transformations rather than permanent certainties' (Rowell, 1992). Even within the more set sections of an Indian classical performance, the *gat* (instrumental composition) or *bandish*, subtle changes are a constant. There are set overarching structures within which to operate, but no set script. Improvisation and spontaneity are at the very heart of Indian classical tradition.

Frustrated with the impersonal nature of the large classes at Ali Akbar College, in which one voice was usurped by the immensity of the vocal collective, I looked toward Cal Arts once again in the hope of finding a more personal, one-on-one approach to learning Indian classical vocal music. I was not disappointed. From the start, my lessons with Rajeev Taranath were arduous and intense. Nothing had prepared me for his furious approach to teaching (and I am sure nothing could) in which one was always being pushed well beyond their comfort zone. His methodology was uncompromising, and at times, exhausting. The approach was simple. He would sing a phrase and I was to repeat it. Miss it once and he was mildly annoyed; miss it again and I was sure to be shot with a look of disgust, loathing or ambivalence. Although the reprimands felt harsh, there was always the sense that I was being given the essence of the musical tradition, one phrase at a time. Looking

146

back, his reactions were understandable, as what he was giving was so precious. It must have been difficult for him to hear the exquisite phrases repeatedly battered beyond recognition! It was up to me to rise to the 'required range of acceptability'. He was not interested in making it easier through visual mediation. I was learning in the age-old fashion of oral diffusion practiced by generations of teachers and students in India, and as I would soon find, it did not end there.

Some time during my first year of study, Rajeevji asked me to 'come home' for additional lessons. This was about the time I began to forge a relationship with him that fell outside of the parameters of academia. It was a deepening of our relationship that became a sphere encompassing both musical and non-musical elements. I drove him to the store, did his dishes, helped him pack for sporadic trips back to India and carried his instrument wherever we went, all while continuing to be steeped in his aura and music. In the process he became my guru; I became his disciple. I do not know if I was aware of it at the time, but I was participating in the *guru-shishya parampara* (the master–disciple tradition) in much the same way it has been practiced for centuries, doing my 'disciple-duty' and spending much of my time with him. Daniel Neuman, in *The Life of Music in North India*, elaborates on the non-musical aspects of the *guru-shishya* tradition:

> Being devoted to one's guru also implies obedience to him and, as the musicians put it, giving "respect" (*izzat*). Being obedient refers not only to matters of music such as doing *riaz* [practice], and playing what one is told; the disciple must be obedient in his life style as well. In the ideal system, the disciple, whether he is related or not, lives with his guru as part of the household. As a member of the household, his position is like that of the guru's own son, although again there are differences in role-playing. The most important of these is that the disciple considers it his duty to provide services for his guru and make life generally as comfortable as possible for him (Neumann, 1990).

With the dissolution of the Mogul courts, and with it, a system of patronage for Indian classical musicians in India, living with one's guru became more problematic, as many musicians were forced to move to larger cities to find work. While living with Rajeevji may have been ideal in some respects, more important to my embodiment of the music was the process of steeping; taking my own lessons as well as being present for other lessons he was giving, imbibing the music whenever possible. In some ways I was making up for an other-cultural upbringing, in which I did not have the benefit of gradual exposure.

The Matrix and Relish

Taranath discusses the absence of a 'matrix' among western students, a resulting cultural disadvantage, and the importance of cultivating a sense of 'relish':

> These students [students in the U.S.] are *musically lonely* ... That is, they don't have a matrix from which the music can be taken. For example, when you talk, you're taking it out of a matrix of the language as it is used among you people. So you just handle it the way you like. All the structures that you are using are not learned, they are just absorbed because it is your language, whereas an Indian has to learn it. He doesn't have the context. Context and matrix, I'm using them interchangeably. In India, there is a lot more music available. If you're going on the road you're listening to music. Film music is blaring out at you. There are people humming. Servants hum, your mother hums. Here music is a performance. Otherwise you don't catch people humming. The Indian child has, from the beginning, been open, not only to an acquaintance, but also to a growing relish of that music. It is easy to pass on information about music. It is very difficult to pass on *relish*. Now yesterday, a very beautiful girl, she was talking about *eel*, eating an eel. Fine, I know what an eel is. I know the eel can be killed, cut, cooked, and eaten. But how does one pass on the

147

relish of eating an eel to a person who has not eaten it? Now that is where cultural matrix comes in. That girl is a Japanese girl. She has seen her parents, her friends when she was [a] kid, enjoying eel, and slowly she grows into that enjoyment. You absorb relish. Relish cannot be taught. If you only lived on what is pleasant, then today I promise you would be living on mother's milk and nothing else! [laughs] The fact that you enjoy whiskey shows that you are aware of the relish of a drink, which is not immediate. It is like *marwa* or *todi* [north Indian ragas]. *Acquired* relish. Now this is where a person native to that musical culture has a distinct advantage, provided he wants to use it, which I'm afraid many Indians don't. They would like to relish computers. Some students [American students] started relishing [early], like you. Now what is it due to? I can't quite place it. You came here and you very quickly became addicted. Now unless you become addicted, you don't go very far with anything. It could be opium, it could be music- one hopes it is music, that's all. That intensity and continuity, sustained intensity of an addiction is necessary for this music (personal communication, May 7, 2005).

Soon after completing my degree in north Indian classical vocal music, I was asked to join the department at Cal Arts where I taught alongside Taranath for four years. During that time, I taught North Indian Theory, North Indian Ensemble, private lessons in vocal music, and *Sargam*. In my time teaching there, I was inclined to utilise Taranath's approach and methodology, the 'traditional' way, as it were. Some students struggled with learning the music aurally; others excelled. Those with a 'good ear' came to it more quickly. In terms of 'relish', I have found, if the capacity is there, it shows up very quickly, as if it were triggered by an innate sensitivity to Indian classical phrases. It is a mystery that is difficult to quantify, but it seems as if some students have it, and others simply do not. One of my current Indian vocal students at Naropa University seems to possess a sense of relish but has struggled with conditioning. She came to our first lesson armed with a pen and notebook, prepared to sing, scribble and read. After a discussion about the importance of taking the 'eyes out of the equation' to more fully internalise the phrases, she put the notebook away for a few weeks and then stubbornly brought it out again, convinced it would give her a needed edge. I left it alone and much to my satisfaction, she has come to the conclusion that the act of writing and reading impairs her ability to quickly internalise phrases. She has since put the notebook away for good.

Conclusions

There is no doubt that the act of using prescriptive notations of Indian classical music is a departure from tradition. While learning from Dasgupta's transcriptions was not harmful and may have even been helpful in my case, I believe it was helpful primarily as an *introduction*. As a mnemonic device, due in large part to the efforts of Bhatkhande, Indian classical notation has been used for the best part of a century as a doorway to the world of infinite possibilities within a raga: a doorway that remains locked if one is relegated exclusively to reading notes off a page. What might be the long-term effects of deviations in teaching methodologies and performance practice? Do they amount to a reshaping of the tradition overall? I think it is too early to tell. Some students of the Ali Akbar College have been known to chart out entire performances, circumventing improvisation and therefore, the essence of the tradition. Having had the benefit of studying under both methods and working with students utilising a time-tested approach, I am left to conclude, after additional insights from a lifelong participant in the tradition, that Indian classical music has developed a specific and distinctive shape through the centuries with clear and conscious intention. The act of receiving music aurally leads more naturally to internalisation, essential to a tradition shaped around the improvisation and spontaneous creativity that emanates from a wellspring of embodied sound. Mimesis forms that wellspring, as musical tradition is gradually infused into a student or disciple, *one phrase at a time*.

References

Bagchee, Sandeep. (1998). *NAD: Understanding raga music*. Mumbai: Eshwar Publications.

Neuman, D. M. (1990). *The life of music in north India: The organization of an artistic tradition*. Chicago and London: University of Chicago Press.

Rowell, L. E. (1992). *Music and musical thought in early India*. Chicago and London: University of Chicago Press.

CHAD HAMILL has been singing the classical music of northern India for the past 15 years. Chad Hamill began comprehensive study under the direction of Rajeev Taranath, vocalist and renowned master of the *sarod*. In 1997, he was awarded a Master of Fine Arts degree in north Indian classical vocal music from California Institute of the Arts. Soon after receiving his degree, he was asked to join the north Indian classical department at Cal Arts, where he taught alongside his guru for four years. In 2003, he was awarded a graduate fellowship to attend the University of Colorado, Boulder, where he is currently pursuing a PhD in musicology/ethnomusicology. In addition to teaching Indian Classical Music for Western Instruments at Naropa University, Chad Hamill teaches a course on the music of Asia at CU while giving lectures and performing the classical music of northern India throughout the greater Denver area.

149

150

'I Sing My Home and Dance My Land': Crossing Music Boundaries in a Changing World

Dawn Joseph

I sing my home and dance my land aptly encapsulates my experience of teaching in formal educational settings both in South Africa (at both primary and secondary school levels) and in Australia (with teacher education students at Deakin University). This experience has convinced me that cultural diversity has now moved beyond mere exoticism and tokenism represented in education and the wider society up to the last decades of the 20th century. Rather, cultural diversity has now become an artistic, social and market-driven reality that is reflected in numerous activities in contemporary societies worldwide. The concept of studying music from a multicultural perspective is becoming an integral part of education at all levels.

After the first democratic elections in South Africa in 1994, the government of the day was faced with a challenge to transform education at all levels and be inclusive of its people, language and culture. According to President Nelson Mandela 'the imbalances created by apartheid education demanded urgent and immediate correction, not only in the provision of resources and infrastructure, but also by restoring the culture of learning and teaching' (Africa, Charles, Miller, & Sisulu, 1997, p. 5). He added that children should have access to quality education and quality skills, which would raise their living standards and allow them to participate in the global economy. President Mandela also declared that 'we need to inculcate the attitude that education has value: it means empowerment and hard work. In addition, education must be viewed as a lifelong activity, an ongoing process' (Africa, Charles, Miller, & Sisulu, 1997, p. 5).

Within the South African context, the notion of education as 'an ongoing lifelong experience' and the construct of music as an art form continue to be effective agents for transcending the ills of the past and for striving towards 'unity within diversity'. Therefore music — as both making and performing (process and product) — serves to be an important thread in the fabric of a changing society that is so culturally diverse. Similarly music as an art form within the Australian context allows students and teachers to experience what Thompson (2002) refers to as the Other, which is often represented by markedly different types of music and culture in a non-threatening and therefore highly approachable manner.

This article considers the dynamic interaction that music offers to pre-service teacher education students[1] and to practising music teachers in Melbourne[2] and

151

draws on the collective role of teacher change, attitude, belief and pedagogy as a vehicle to transmit the Other. It is proposed that, by engaging in meaningful dialogue with musics and cultures other than their own, both students and teachers have enhanced opportunities to experience music making and musical expression as well as to gain additional musical understandings within their own society as that society becomes culturally diverse as part of the worldwide phenomenon of globalisation. Embracing a 'new' and 'different' music like that of Africa can be viewed in terms of a 'music-as-culture approach' to teaching and learning. Hence music can then be used as a platform and/or a vehicle for understanding cultural difference in a pluralistic society.

The notion of music from other cultures representing an aspect of exoticism and/or tokenism when included in the school curriculum prevailed up until the last decades of the 20th century. A tokenistic approach may be well illustrated by the inclusion of an African song entitled *The Swazi Warrior* (with words in both English and an African language) in *Let's Have Music* for Grades 3 and 4 (Australian Broadcasting Commission, 1971). It was not specified where this song had come from, other than the word Swazi in the title, and there was no attempt to contextualise or otherwise locate the song in a social or cultural milieu. Numerous examples of exoticism exist in music — in David Fanshawe's *African Sanctus* (1972) for instance — which are designed to be an 'evocation of a place, people, or social milieu that is … profoundly different from the accepted local norms in its attitudes, customs and morals' (Grove Music Online, 2005). However, music included in the school curriculum for reasons of exoticism or tokenism does not allow for any meaningful and authentic engagement with the Other in terms of music, multiculturalism and lifelong learning. A prime example representing a move forward from exoticism and tokenism in music/art education is South Africa, where music making and performing now incorporates all cultures, peoples, language and other manifestations of ethnicity within the society as part of the post-apartheid reconciliation and development reform process. Australia, as a more Eurocentric society than South Africa, can build on this foundation of multicultural inclusivity and promote greater homogeneity, thereby strengthening both cultural unity and diversity through effective music programs at levels of education. Within the South African context, music has the single most effective means of realising the artistic, social and cultural reality of national reconstruction.

Theoretical Framework

For the purpose of this article, I consider some theoretical perspectives in relation to the notion of moving beyond exoticism and tokenism to engaging in meaningful dialogue in terms of perspectives on change, and notions of belief, cultural diversity and crosscultural transmission. The discussion that follows attempts to demonstrate how 'the global' can enhance 'the local' in terms of cultural enrichment of both teachers' experience and classroom practice.

152

Perspectives on Change

Embracing any new concept or tradition represents a change that can be either a 'dabbling' or 'deepening' experience. Guskey (2002) asserts that change is a multifaceted phenomenon and is a prerequisite to improvement. The topic of change in teachers and teaching is highly complex due to the very different approaches to the concept of change (Richardson & Placier, 2001). Richardson and Placier (2001) identified the various approaches to teacher change in terms of 'learning, development, socialisation, growth, improvement, implementation of something new or different, cognitive and affective change and self-study' (p. 905). They note that the underlying assumption is that teacher change leads to better teachers and teaching, although the relationship between this and better outcomes for students is often not established. This highlights the dichotomy of whether dabbling or deepening has occurred for both teacher and students.

A prolific writer on change, Fullan (1982) contends that:

> one of the most fundamental problems in education today is that people do not have a clear, coherent sense of meaning about what education change is for, what it is, and how it proceeds. … What we need is a more coherent picture that people who are involved in or affected by educational change can use to make sense of what they and others are doing (p. 4).

He proposes that teachers need to be considered in the role 'teacher as learner'. Such a view is enhanced by Clarke and Hollingsworth (2002) who proposed that the new perspectives of teacher change consider teachers as learners and schools as learning communities moving away from mere dabbling to a deeper experience of other cultures. It is through such pathways of educational change that the notion of the Other and multicultural music can be effectively realised.

The notion of 'change is progress' aptly describes my journey as an academic within the tertiary learning community. As a 'change agent' I not only have to pay attention to music content but use my teaching time and context for my students to be proactive in performing, creating, analysing and debating social issues hence making meaning in cross- and intercultural dialogue. Since learning and change are interconnected, the use of African music gave my students the opportunity to reflect on and discuss wider social issues than just what they aurally or visually experienced in terms of sound and movement. Such an innovation was a 'change in action', something different from what students normally experienced at university.

As there are many facets of teacher change and teachers' practice, accordingly it may be argued that teachers who want to change are teachers who want to grow and want to embrace diversity and challenge current practice. They are teachers who are reflective and who are continually trying to do what is best for their students within a global context. As Schubert and Ayers (1992) argue, it is only reflective teachers (not those who teach by recipe, technique or doctrine) who are able to grow continuously and alter and deepen their beliefs in the what, who, how and why they teach.

Notions of Belief

It is argued by several researchers that teachers' beliefs strongly influence classroom practices (Borko & Putnam, 1996; Calderhead, 1996; Guskey, 1986; Thompson, 1992). Cooney (1985) and Dossey (1992) both suggest that teachers' beliefs have a significant impact on the way they teach, while Calderhead (1996) argues that although teachers hold various beliefs in relation to their work, it is contestable whether or not such beliefs influence their classroom practice. Elmore (2002) contends that improving teachers' instructional practices requires a change in beliefs, norms and values about what teachers can achieve through their practice and what practices are possible.

153

One aspect of improving the quality of teaching is often unlearning the deeply seated beliefs and implicit practices that work against the development of new and more effective practices (Borko & Putnam, 1995; Clark & Peterson, 1986; Feiman-Nemser, 1983). Teachers' beliefs about teaching and learning are challenged when adopting new and innovative practices. In the case of teaching and learning African music, teachers either move from the unknown to the known or adapt their western training and understanding to teach and cross music boundaries of the Other. Such small changes can become the basis for broader, more 'fundamental transformations' (Borko, Davinroy, Bliem, & Cumbo, 2000). In essence, such deepening as opposed to dabbling in the area of teachers' willingness to change are an essential link between beliefs and practice becoming explicit for those involved, especially when teaching music-as-culture.

Cultural Diversity

As music educators the constant challenge we face in a changing world is preparing students and teacher graduates in a global village to be inclusive of a variety of musics and culture. Hence, by opening up the mind's eyes and ears to the many musical languages, we strive to explore and make connections to the broad diversity of people, their lives, musical heritage and culture. Music and culture have multidimensional characteristics that contribute to shaping one's identity.

It can be argued that music is used to express aspects of personal identity, national identity and youth identity. However, MacDonald, Hargreaves, and Miell (2002) argue that many individuals also construct identities *within* music, for instance as a performer or teacher. This was evident in both my African music student and teacher projects (see endnotes 1 and 2). I concur with Thorsén (2002) who believes that music is connected to identity and it is within such an understanding of one's own and other music that culture is then viewed as pluralistic. The word 'music' is commonly referred to in Africa as a verb rather than a noun supporting the notion of 'music as making and doing'. Nketia (1966) aptly describes this 'music making as part of the traditional way of life, and not as embellishments of it' (p. 15). It is necessary to the fullness of living as any other human need that has to be satisfied. Music making is, therefore, an index of a living community and a measure of the degree of social cohesion among its respective units. Nketia's student, Aduoum (1980), restates this view that 'African music is life, it permeates all daily activities' (p. 19). The notion of using music as an education tool to learn about and or get to know other musics is two pronged: it serves as an engaging hands-on activity and/or experience as well as a form of knowledge system of the music itself.

Incorporating music of another culture and/or finding oneself in someone else's music may assist in assimilating new elements and experiences into one's own background knowledge, thereby establishing new understandings of musical style and the broader culture (Nketia, 1988). The array of diverse cultures and musics that surround us has to find pathways in which musical cultures can compliment one another. This view is supported by Campbell (2004), who suggests that if a global approach to teaching music is to be successful, a broader perspective about music and culture is to become the norm rather than the exception across the board (from schools to higher educational settings). Such a perspective of making and learning music is commonly referred to as music-as-culture.

Nettl (2002) aptly captures the music-as-culture approach in his *Encounters in Ethnomusicology: A Memoir* by reiterating that music is not separated from culture: it

154

is culture. Therefore the notion of learning about the music thus enhances one's cultural understanding and meaning of the music. According to Nketia (1988), such:

> practical experiences of a simple aspect of the music process that we can manage, such as singing a simple song, clapping or stamping where this is part of the music or some simple movement, helps in our efforts to get to know and understand the music (p. 103).

He further contends what appears to be different crossculturally may operate in similar contexts, hence the discovery of common principles, usages and behavioural patterns (Nketia, 1988, p. 98). I agree with Nketia who argues that it is not just the music we hear, but a knowledge of the culture of music makers, their lives, what they do and the occasions when they make music that puts us in a frame of mind to explore their music (p. 101). A similar such view is shared by Gibson (2003) who claims the 'work of music' cannot be divorced from the social networks of people who make and promote it, and the sites they occupy in order to do so. It is within such realms of transmission that both music and culture carry equal credence and compliment each other just as music and dance are seen as inseparable art forms in African life.

Crosscultural Dialogue

Learning African music requires an understanding of the cultural system, the creative principles of the music and the method by which that music is transferred from one person to another. The aural–oral and practical approaches are essential aspects of African music that allows such crosscultural interchange. According to Flolu and Amuah (2003), by establishing this aural–oral and practical approach, they prepare students for musical literacy in later years. Within the Australian context, the learning of another music and culture different from western enables learners and teachers to embrace diversity and be inclusive of all types of music, culture and people, thereby educating learners in a changing world to experience culture and express music. Such an education, claims Wang (2002), seeks to prepare students to live in an increasingly globalised world and society, to be active, participating citizens in that society who can contribute to the shaping of a better future. A consequence of this is the movement of people beyond a local community — to look beyond the boundaries of the known to the unknown. Although music is being made and taught at all levels of education in Australia, there is a need to seek ways of fostering continuous growth and development of this unknown and/or the Other.

What and who is this Other and why should one cross music boundaries? Thompson (2002) raises the point that the Other is often constructed as a homogenised category, which she refers to as that which is 'static to geographical spaces'. In relation to this Other, the notion of music is understood as an aspect of the culture of which it is a part. This point is further highlighted by Nettl (1992) who contends 'understanding music in turn can help us to understand the world's cultures and their diversity' (p. 4). It is only when we move out of our own framework and into the Other that we begin to cross boundaries and make the crosscultural connections that are absent in the music of our own culture. When you 'find yourself in someone else's music' (Missingham, 1998, p. 426), you engage in crosscultural dialogue not only about musical discourse but also about the canopy that holds that group of people together. Within my own experience in South Africa and now in Australia, connecting the disconnected through the

155

notion of the Other in music is an effective way to transcend the past and find meaning in the present, whereby new pathways for the future can be built.

Music-as-Culture Approach

Miller (1989) affirms that understanding the differences between cultures not only opens the way to a deeper appreciation of the people who create and use that music, but it also brings a new perspective to the western musical world. A music-as-culture approach exposes students to other cultures and musics, thereby exploring what Oehrle (1991) calls 'crosscultural possibilities' more fully, richly and critically than previously. She further states that 'a growing awareness of other cultures is not only more possible but also necessary to achieve ...' (p. 26). This is especially the case within the Australian context, given the diverse society one lives and teaches in.

The use of African music in my own teaching at Deakin University[1] and the African music teacher research project[2] (see Joseph, 2002, 2003, 2004, 2005 for findings and discussions) reports that the teaching and learning of African music as the Other was seen as an effective way not only to cross music boundaries (hence the notion of music-as-culture approach) but was an effective way to transmit music knowledge, skills, confidence and competence and understandings of another music and culture. My students not only felt empowered in their ability to improvise and create, and their learning, understanding and skills improved and increased, but rather, they came to new and greater understandings and tolerance of African music, life and culture. The students in the Deakin University project realised that music is inseparable from life and even though there may be much poverty, AIDS and drought in Africa, music continues to play a central role in the life of the African — as 'singing is the essence of happiness' (Zulu saying — the Zulu tribe is one of the indigenous population groups in South Africa).

Findings from both my student and teacher projects indicate that, through the learning of African songs and drumming, students at both university and school levels came to know about the music — who performed it, why, where, when, how it was performed and what values were told through it. The use of 'storytelling' was another effective way to teach about African music and culture. Music teachers in the teacher project commented that the use of an artist-in-residence authenticated the learning experience even more so for their students. They claimed that the use of an artist-in-residence continues to be an effective way to 'bridge the gap' between schools and local communities. Such a nexus provides students with a global understanding of Music and/or the Other. I refer to Music here with a capital 'M' for, as Campbell (2004) rightly points out, few students know Music for its global and crosscultural manifestations. Such knowledge she claims can only come by discarding 'the west is best' perspective (p. xvi).

It can be argued that, by crossing musical boundaries and transmitting African music at both school and university level as something 'new', 'different' and 'interesting', changes occurred in pedagogy (from western notation to African traditional oral and aural ways of teaching and learning) and in attitudes and beliefs about embracing the Other. The findings from both projects indicate that music teachers and students moved away from the commonly held belief that *I am not an African*, therefore I cannot play, move or dance to I can play, move and dance as a global citizen. Such engagement represents a move from just mere dabbling locally with the Other to a more global and holistic understanding of the Other.

156

Crossing Boundaries and Making Connections

Music making (singing, moving/dancing, improvising and playing) is a wonderful arena to cross boundaries and make connections (musical as well as social) and is a fruitful meeting place for cultural discourse: a place for output, input and exchange. In my past experience in South Africa and my present one here in Melbourne, I come to the conclusion that the teaching and learning of music can be used as a platform for understanding cultural differences and for thinking about implementing changes to music programs and pedagogical practices.

In thinking 'for change' one moves beyond the notion of exoticism and tokenism to broader meanings. Both students and teachers in the African music project reported that they had to change their thinking about learning and experience a new music like African music, which changed their beliefs and expectations of African music and culture. By changing their expectation about the music and its people, they began to change their attitude about the Other. Having a low expectation of the Other can contribute towards a bad attitude about embracing this Other. Thus by changing one's attitude, one's behaviour is subsequently changed, hence one's attitude is receptive to receiving something new like African music. As such, the change in behaviour changes one's performance skills, knowledge and understanding, which in turn creates and fosters a lifelong change to engage and interact with all musics in a global and diverse world.

By crossing musical boundaries in a changing world, the principle underlying the inclusion of the Other is a multicultural one, although one's practices do not always demonstrate a real awareness of what this might be. As Volk (2004) points out 'the greater the knowledge one has about the culture, and the expectations or rules of its music, the greater the understanding, or perception of meaning, of that music will be' (p. 6). As music educators we need to find ways to encompass a broad range of musical genres in our teaching. There are many ways to do this but they all begin with the education of the self. Specifically in the area of teacher education in music, course content needs to be more inclusive of the world's musics and not only focus on the predominant western paradigm.

Currently, most universities in Melbourne do not offer music curriculum content and teaching methodologies that are representative of the wider society in which we live. In the main, there is a significant need for universities to reconceptualise their curriculum offerings to incorporate more of the Other in their music education programs. As part of change efforts within the university sector, one of the few instances of including the Other is currently taught in my Deakin University arts education elective study that focuses on African music. In line with the reality of a growing pluralist Australia, all universities should embrace the notion of 'internationalising the curriculum'. At Deakin University this policy actively promotes 'an understanding of international perspectives and competence in a global environment' (Deakin University, 2002, p. 1). Teacher education students at Deakin University are currently gaining global understandings through experiencing supervised teaching placements in Vanuatu, Canada, Ghana, India and Australia's Northern Territory. Such initiatives are a positive move for students to have a 'hands-on' global experience and impart this locally in their future teaching.

Another worthwhile initiative has been that some Melbourne schools and universities are now promoting the Other, including African music, through artist-in-residence programs. Teachers are gaining professional development in African music through short courses offered by universities and professional associations.

157

Universities need to establish collaborative learning communities that practice the Other in music and build stronger links and networks to actively engage with more authentic and culturally diverse practices.

As earlier stated, I agree with Campbell (2004) who contends that if a global approach to teaching is to be successful at schools it has to infiltrate courses in higher education so that broader perspectives about Music and Culture becomes the norm rather than the exception. This can be done during teacher training and in future professional development. Further, educational institutions now invite artists-in-residence and members of local communities to work with teachers and students to learn about 'other musics' in an authentic way — a positive move from monoculturalism towards crossculturalism.

Finally, I concur with Reimer (1993) who affirms because Australia has a 'multi-musical culture', care should be taken not to marginalise or patronise one ethnic group's music over another. Hence *The National Agenda for a Multicultural Australia* (Office of Multicultural Affairs, 1989) identifies a 'cultural identity' dimension (the right of all Australians to express and share their individual cultural heritage) and a 'social justice' dimension (their right to equality of treatment and opportunity and the removal of barriers associated with race, ethnicity, language, culture, religion, gender etc.) to overcome multicultural barriers and incorporate the Other. Such dimensions of inclusion creates the opportunities to cross music boundaries in a changing world where music-as-culture can be a vehicle to effectively teach and learn beyond exoticism and tokenism.

Endnotes

1   I undertook research at Deakin University with teacher education students (2002 and 2003) into the use of African music (students were in their fourth year of study of the Bachelor of Education Primary degree). The project reported on findings from questionnaire and interview data on attitudes, beliefs, competence and motivation, cultural and pedagogical understandings of generalist primary teacher education students in relation to a new genre (African music) through which music and culture were taught (see Joseph, 2002, 2003, 2004).

2   The African music teacher project took place in 2004 through an anonymous web-based survey; go to http://education.deakin.edu.au/music_ed/afr_mus-survey for primary and secondary music teachers in Melbourne (see Joseph, 2004, 2005). Currently, voluntary interviews are being held in 2005 with music teachers as an extension of that project. The focus of that project was to investigate the extent to which effective teaching and learning of African music takes place at both primary and secondary schools in Victoria (see Joseph, 2004, 2005).

References

Aduonum, K. (1980). *A compilation, analysis and adaptation of selected Ghanaian folk tale songs for use in the elementary general class.* Unpublished doctoral dissertation, University of Michigan, Ann Abor, Michigan.

Africa, H. P., Charles, H. J., Miller, A., & Sisulu, S. (Eds.). (1997). *Education African forum.* Pinegowrie, South Africa: Education Africa.

Australian Broadcasting Commission. (1971). *Let's have music* (for Grades 3 and 4). Perth, Australia: Australian Broadcasting Commission, Western Australia Branch.

Borko, H., Davinroy, K., Bliem, C., & Cumbo, K. (2000). Exploring and supporting teacher change: Two third-grade teachers' experiences in a mathematics and literacy staff development project. *The Elementary School Journal, 100*(4), 273–302.

Borko, H., & Putnam, R. (1995). Expanding a teacher's knowledge base: A cognitive psychological perspective on professional development. In M. Huberman (Ed.), *Professional development in education* (pp. 35–65). New York: Teachers College Press.

Borko, H., & Putnam, R. (1996). Learning to teach. In R. Calfee (Ed.), *Handbook of educational psychology* (pp. 673–708). New York: Macmillan.

Calderhead, J. (1996). Teachers: Beliefs and knowledge. In R. Calfee (Ed.), *Handbook of educational psychology* (pp. 709–725). New York: Macmillan.

Campbell, P. S. (2004). *Teaching music globally.* New York: Oxford University Press.

Clark, C., & Peterson, P. (1986). *Teachers' thought processes.* New York: Macmillan.

Clarke, D., & Hollingsworth, H. (2002). Elaborating a model of teacher professional growth. *Teaching and Teacher Education, 18,* 947–967.

Cooney, T. (1985). A beginning teacher's view of problem solving. *Journal for Research in Mathematics Education, 16*(5), 324–336.

Deakin University. (2002). *International and culturally inclusive curricula, principles and guidelines* [draft document, August 2, 2002].

Dossey, J. (1992). The nature of mathematics: Its role and its influence. In D. Grouws (Ed.), *Handbook of research on mathematics teaching and learning* (pp. 39–48). New York: Macmillan.

Elmore, R. (2002). *Bridging the gap between standards and achievement: The imperative for professional development in education.* Retrieved January 28, 2005, from http://www.shankerinstitute.org/Downloads/Bridging_Gap.pdf

Feiman-Nemser, S. (1983). Learning to teach. In G. Sykes (Ed.), *Handbook of teaching and policy.* New York: Longman Publishers.

Flolu, J., & Amuah, I. (2003). *An introduction to music education in Ghana for universities and colleges.* Accra: Black Mask.

Fullan, M. (1982). *The meaning of educational change.* New York: Teachers College Press.

Gibson, C. (2003). Cultures at work: Why 'culture' matters in research on the 'cultural' industries. *Social & Cultural Geography, 4*(2), 201–215.

Grove Music Online. (2005). Retrieved July 28, 2005, from http://www.grovemusic.com/

Guskey, T. (1986). Staff development and the process of teacher change. *Educational Researcher, 15,* 5–12.

Guskey, T. (2002). Professional development and teacher change. *Teachers and Teaching: Theory and Practice, 8*(3/4), 381–391.

Joseph, D. (2002). Umoja: Teaching African music to generalist teacher education students. In J. Rosevear & J. Callaghan (Eds.), *Research matters: Linking outcomes with practice. Proceedings of the XXIVth annual conference* (pp. 86–98). Melbourne: AARME.

Joseph, D. Y. (2003). An African music odyssey: Introducing a cross-cultural curriculum to Australian primary teacher education students. *Music Education International, 2,* 98–111.

Joseph, D. (2004). Smaller steps into longer journeys: Experiencing African music and expressing culture. In M. Chaseling (Ed.), *Proceedings of the XXVIth Annual Conference of the Australian Association for Research in Music Education* (pp. 216–225). Tweed Heads, New South Wales, Australia: AARME.

Joseph, D. (2005). Celebrating the use of African music: Change in motion. In D. Forrest (Ed.), *A celebration of voices. Proceedings of the XV National Conference of the Australian Society for Music Education* (pp. 128–133). Parkville, Victoria, Australia: ASME.

Kesler, R. J. (1985). *Teachers' instructional behaviour related to their conceptions of teaching and mathematics and their level of dogmatism: Four case studies.* Unpublished doctoral dissertation, University of Georgia, Athens.

MacDonald, R. A. R., Miell, D. E., & Hargreaves, D. J. (2002). *Musical identities.* Oxford: Oxford University Press.

Missingham, A. (1998). Working in the third world: Evangelist or rip-off artists? In C. van Neikerk (Ed.), *Ubuntu- music education for a humane society. Proceedings of the 23rd World Conference of the International Society for Music Education* (pp. 411–426). Pretoria, South Africa: ISME.

Miller, A. (1989). *Music making: Survival and celebration.* Retrieved December 10, 2003, from http://www.mcc.org?respub.occasional/26survival.html

159

Nettl, B. (1992). *Ethnomusicology and the teaching of world music.* Paper presented at the XXth World Conference of the International Society for Music Education, Seoul, Korea.

Nettl, B. (2002). *Encounters in ethnomusicology: A memoir.* MI: Harmonic Park Press.

Nketia, J. H. (1966). *Music education in African schools: A review of the position in Ghana International Seminar on Teacher Education in Music.* Ann Arbor, MI: University of Michigan.

Nketia, J. H. K. (1988). *Exploring intercultural dimensions of music education: A world view of music education.* Paper presented at the 18th World Conference of the International Society for Music Education, Canberra, Australia.

Oehrle, E. (1991). Emerging music education trends in Africa. *International Journal for Music Education, 18,* 23–29.

Office of Multicultural Affairs. (1989). *The national agenda for a multicultural Australia.* Canberra: AGPS.

Reimer, B. (1993). Music education in our multimusical culture. *Music Educators Journal, March,* 21–26.

Richardson, V., & Placier, P. (2001). Teacher change. In V. Richardson (Ed.), *Handbook of research on teaching* (4th ed., pp. 905–947). Washington, DC: American Educational Research Association.

Schubert, W. H., & Ayers, W. C. (1992). *Teacher lore: Learning from our own experience.* White Plains, NY: Macmillan.

Thompson, A. (1992). Teachers' beliefs and conceptions: A synthesis of the research. In D. Grouws (Ed.), *Handbook of research on mathematics teaching and learning* (pp. 127–146). New York: Macmillan.

Thompson, K. (2002). A critical discourse analysis of world music as the "Other" in education. *Research Studies in Music Education, 19*(June), 14–21.

Thorsén, S. (2002). Addressing cultural identity in music education. *Talking Drum, 84.*

Volk, T. M. (2004). *Music, education, and multiculturalism.* Oxford: Oxford University Press.

Wang, L. (2002). *Global perspectives: A statement on global education for Australian schools, Australia.* Australia: Curriculum Corporation.

DR DAWN JOSEPH is a lecturer in Music and Education Studies at Deakin University, Melbourne campus, Australia. Dawn is formerly from Johannesburg, South Africa, where she taught music at independent schools (primary and secondary). She holds a PhD degree from the University of Pretoria where her thesis focused on outcomes-based music education in Johannesburg, South Africa. Her current research interests include teacher education programs, African music, and cultural diversity and teacher change. She is currently the Chairperson of the Australian Society for Music Education (Victorian Chapter) and is the Pan African Society for Musical Arts Education MAT Cell coordinator for Melbourne.

Honouring and Deriving the Wealth of Knowledge Offered by Mother Music in Africa

Christopher Klopper

T he world has suffered and continues to suffer from a profound loss of indigenous peoples and rural groups and their knowledge about a natural world constructed from intimate ties to land and place. This loss has been accompanied by neglect and marginalisation of their practices and beliefs, often fig-ured as inferior forms of knowing to be replaced by universalised knowledge derived from the western scientific tradition. Due to the impact of globalisation and legacy of colonisation, many African countries and therefore societies find themselves having less and less cultural identity. Although the effects of globalisation have assisted with the world transforming into a global village, the negative impact is a lack of cultural identity and the emergence of a unified yet substance-less society. The legacy of colonisation is realised through many school curricula in Africa approaching music education from a western perspective. This results in educators being uncertain of their own cultural wealth and music education being presented from a foreign, detached perspective, destroying the natural innate 'music' that exists in Africa. Ntuli (2002, p. 53) strongly points out that:

> Africa is neither Europe nor America. African problems are not European or American problems. Africa's solution to her problems cannot be anybody's but Africa's. If we accept this truism, we then accept that Africa had to find her own indigenous ways to define, identify and address her challenges.

Vilakazi (2001, p. 14) argues further that:

> The correct history of African people shall be written by people who, through knowledge of African culture and languages, can use both oral sources and written sources. This means that such scholars shall need to be in close, broadly embracing contact and commu-nication with ordinary, un-certificated African men and woman in urban and rural areas. Serious methodological issues arise. This should be the great fruitful encounter between African culture and civilisation, stored in oral traditions, on the one hand, and evidence stored in written documents and archaeological finds on the other hand. Many questions arise here: the identification of sources, the reliability of sources, the critique of sources, oral tradition as a critique, corrective, supplement, or confirmation, of written ad archaeo-logical evidence; written and archaeological evidence as critique, corrective, supplement, or confirmation of oral tradition.

The above expression of anguish benchmarks challenges faced by critics of 'things not African' in the context of the existing programs and inputs (Masoga, 2005,

161

p. 4). Music and education are not immune to these challenges. It is not the intention of this article to pursue the history behind such a challenge, but to acknowledge the fact that every discipline finds itself challenged to rethink its African relevance — the contextualisation process of our disciplines in the face of challenges. It does not surprise one to notice the contestation that exists between scholars in favour of indigenous knowledge systems as opposed to those in support of endogenous knowledge systems (Crossman & Devisch, 2002). The former relegate endogenous knowledge systems to being inborn generic systems born out of need for survival, while indigenous knowledge systems refer to the complex set of knowledge and technologies existing and developed around specific conditions of populations and communities indigenous to a particular geographic area. The Centre for Indigenous African Instrumental Music and Dance (CIIMDA) creates the space for the systematic examination, within a holistic research and scholastic framework, of the sociocultural context of indigenous African instrumental music and dance, humanistic underpinnings and materials acquisition, development, innovation, transfer, composition, usage, design, and sustainable utilisation.

African Perspective

A number of black African languages do not have an equivalent for the English word 'music' (Keil, 1979, p. 27). There are words for song, sing, drum and play, but 'music' appears to be semantically diffuse (Agawu, 2003, p. 3). Agawu encourages students to recognise the many nuanced ways in which thinking African musicians talk about what they do. 'Music' in John Blacking's definition (1973, p. 25) is 'sound that is organised into socially accepted patterns'. Nzewi (2003, p. 13) reminds us that in African cultures the performance arts disciplines of music, dance, drama, poetry and costume art are seldom separated in creative thinking and performance practice, and the term 'musical arts' should be adopted when acquiring knowledge of the musical arts in traditional society.

In traditional Africa there were no subject area boundaries. The system of individual subjects within a curriculum currently in use in the majority of African countries was inherited from Africa's colonial education past. Even though different African countries have, at various stages, responded with attempts at educational reform that takes into consideration the cultural relevance of arts programs, very few have outlined the process by which educators can meet these goals (Flolu, 2000; Mans, 2000; Opondo, 2000).

Kwami, Akrofi, and Adams (2003, p. 262) point out that many African countries have to cope with cultural integration in various forms, including in the arts. Where music-making is concerned, integration embraces other significant 'world music' cultures to the extent that the African continent can be seen as being unique in its musical arts, while also representing a microcosm of the major musical traditions that exist throughout the world.

Addressing the issue of 'Africanised' education always meets with criticism. Byamungu (2002, p. 15) asks the following questions:

162

> When you were an African child and you go to school, what do you learn after the initial alphabet? When you have known to read and write, which books are you given to read? What is the final aim of the fascinating stories you are made to summarise for the exam? Put differently, what is the aim of the initial project of education? Is there any correlation between what is learnt at school and what life demands? As it were, is the thematic choice, thrust and goal of the African academy relevant to the conditions of the Africans?

Byamungu (2002, p. 16) concludes that the overall answer to the questions asked above is a big *No*. Undeniably this challenges music education researchers and teachers to revisit the issue and reorganise themselves. The challenge for music education is not to find clarity of viewpoint, but is aptly presented by Reimer (1992, p. 25) as follows:

> If research in music education is to be scientific in a meaningful sense, it should serve the purposes of more effective, useful, and relevant teaching and learning of music. But what would that consist of? Clearly that is a philosophical question at base: it is a question of values. Effective for what? Useful for what? What *do* we want music education to achieve, so that research might help in achieving it and thereby fulfil the function of being science?

African music is reinforced by African ways of thinking that inform African ways of being and functioning in the world (Primos, 2003, p. 302). However, musical arts can differ from region to region. Diversity is thus as typical in Africa as it is elsewhere in the world.

Method and Organisation

The CIIMDA is the brainchild of the Pan African Society for Musical Arts Education (PASMAE). The in-service training of teachers from SADC[1] countries is funded by NORAD through the Rikskonsertene (the Norwegian Concert Institute). CIIMDA aims to promote and advance indigenous African instrumental music and dance performances. Honouring and deriving from the wealth of knowledge offered by Mother Music, the CIIMDA draws on the indigenous knowledge philosophy, theory and practice to nurture musical arts education.

CIIMDA is based in Pretoria, South Africa, and offers intensive programs in the playing of the African classical drum, bow, mbira, xylophones and other African instruments. The performance practices offered are not only embedded in the indigenous social–cultural philosophical contexts of African music and dance, but also explored within the context of contemporary practices. African researchers indicate that in the African culture there are different ways music education takes place:

> African music education is firstly an informal process. The first principle in traditional African music education is the encouragement of mass musical cognition through active participation. Then participation enables the identification of special aptitudes and capabilities. The second principle is the production of specialized or specialist musicians who become the culture's music referents, with responsibility for maintaining as well as extending standards of repertory. Formal music education is found in African cultures in the form of apprenticeship systems, initiation schools, and music borrowing practices. The aim is to produce master musicians (Nzewi, 1999, p. 73).

The transmission of indigenous African music in a formalised educational context is a matter of interest for a number of reasons. Arguments that communal avenues offer more appropriate and conducive environments and other reasons can be rehearsed, but as the teaching of the music is recognised as a legitimate component of music education, it is important that methods, means and ways in which this is affected, need to be scrutinised to ascertain their quality and effectiveness (Kwami, 2005). In 1989 a Ghanaian, Robert Kwami, approached the learning of Ghanaian music with a western attitude, but found this to be unsuccessful. He concluded that the village musicians were the best teachers of African music and that 'the traditional context is the best environment for a student of African music' (Kwami, 1989, p. 24).

163

At CIIMDA master musicians that have been located in and around South Africa provide the 'teaching'. The participants, although having left their home environments, are accommodated in a temporary home environment, which provides an element of community in the program. All 'lessons' are conducted through a traditional African education manner that employs practical, aural–oral and informal approaches. Despite the introduction of the writing culture of the West, listening and observation interwoven by memory remain the key elements of acquiring the basic skills of social adjustment (Flolu, 2005). Indigenous and family history, rites and even complex constitutional matters of modern day politics continue to be transmitted orally. This practical approach to African civilisation is still vital and remains a key medium of adjusting to modern technology.

Context, Concepts and Intangibles

The context of CIIMDA has been established through the documentation of the method and organisation of the instruction offered. Prior to illustrating the relationship of context, concepts and intangibles, each term will be analysed initially. It is important to recognise that no musical performance would be possible without a stimulus. Documentation in this regard is outside of the scope of this article.

Context is explained as the circumstances of an event. Rudimentarily referred to as the *Why?* Key words in this identification would be historical, sociocultural, political, environmental, healing and pleasure. Within the category of sociocultural there are many examples: weddings, rituals, births, death, rite of passage, initiation, succession, correction of social ill, spiritual and worship.

Concepts are identified as the *How?* in the musical performance. The concepts of pulse, balance, symmetry/asymmetry, form, energy, mood, repetition and variation, choreography, rhythm, tension/relaxation, relationship, fusion, vision, timbre,

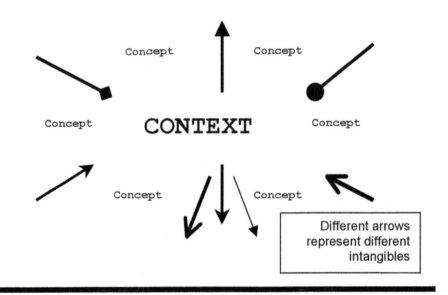

FIGURE 1

Relationship between context, concept and intangibles.

tempo, weight, locomotive, axial, direction, levels, contrast, symbols, time, mime, dress, costumes, props and texture.

Intangibles are the illusive, uncertain areas that for non-Africans are most difficult to comprehend. Intangibles account for taboos, magic, emotion, unknown, illusive, interface of mask/person, hypnotic and symbolic transition.

To illustrate my understanding of the relationship between context, concept and intangibles, Figure 1 graphically illustrates how the context is the underlying feature. Africa as a whole and the many cultures within Africa all possess a specific and recognisable environment and framework within which they exist. This environment in turn is full of ideas, notions, conceptions, theories and models. However, there is a certain element of elusive or indefinability (intangibles represented as differing arrows) emerging from within the context and from outside of the context. All three collectively represent the intricate nature of societal existence. Foregoing any one of these can result in misrepresentation of a society and the society's invaluable contribution to human endurance.

In order to facilitate an understanding of the context, concepts and intangibles of CIIMDA and the essence of Africa, extracts from the CIIMDA curriculum are elaborated here. The curriculum was designed by Professor Meki Nzewi and is currently in use for all training sessions at CIIMDA. The vision of realising African philosophy in all sessions is secured through the traditional approach that each component is administered. Extracts from the CIIMDA curriculum are:

Rudiments of African Musical Thoughts and Practices [RD]
- The social, environmental and humanistic derivations as well as rationalizations of rhythm, pitch, tone, melody, harmony, form, texture and scales and part relationships.
- Basic musical literacy; elements of musical sound for conventional practices: pitch/tone, rhythm, melody, harmony, scales, music writing and reading.

Theory & Practice of African Drum Music [TPDM]
- Learning theory and meaning of African indigenous creative & performance arts through practical experiences.
- Philosophical, Psychological, Social, Scientific and Health basis of African musical arts.
- Intentions, creations, and practice.
- Playing technique — oral and literary.
- Notation and rudiments of classical drumming.
- Pulse and metric sense — common and compound times.
- Thematic (Tonal/Melodic) principles.
- Part playing and part relationships.
- Formal principles and structures.
- African harmonic philosophy and principles of part-playing.
- Theory of duality and space consciousness.
- Creative drumming; Group and solo drumming.
- Development devices and Improvisation.

Performance Principle of African Xylophone Music [PPX]
- Playing techniques
- Single line and two-part playing including repeated notes.
- Principles of creativity on the xylophone as a melodic–harmonic instrument.
- Historical and contextual perspectives of the African xylophone traditions and types.

165

- Performance practice and polyphonic/harmonic principles on the xylophone, from the single xylophone style played by one or more performers to the complex *Chopi* xylophone orchestra.
- Thematic development devices and improvisation.

Performance Principles of bow Music/Mbira Music [PPB/ PPM]

- Playing technique.
- Construction technique.
- Tuning.
- Scale/Tone row.
- Melodic construction.
- Solo & group playing.
- Improvisation and accompaniment.
- Research motivation.

Ensemble Practice [EP]

- Principles of African orchestra and ensemble music instruments.
- Ensemble composition and arrangement — ensemble roles and structural relationships.
- Oral and literary ensemble music practice — classroom musical arts making.
- Musical arts theatre — combining music, dance and drama activities for concert repertory production.
- Principles of creativity and improvisation.
- Workshop orientations and techniques.
- Concert production.

Theory & Practice of African Dance [TPD]

- Social relevance; philosophy and social intentions of African dance.
- Sense of Pulse.
- Movement, space and body awareness exercises.
- Experiencing music and dance symbiosis — practical experience of dance as visual music/music as sonic dance.
- Dance creativity and improvisation.
- Principles of choreography — stylised formation dance creation.
- Dance characterization/dramatization — mime.
- Music and dance games.

Practical Presentations by Participants for Evaluation [PPE]

Participants are expected to prepare a lesson plan as a guide to a 45-minute individual presentation at the end of the second week of the Centre program. The assessment is forwarded to the relevant Ministries of Education and Head of School.

The curriculum of CIIMDA allows observers of Mother Music in Africa to approach their experience and observation of African music through the identification and acknowledgment of context, concepts and intangibles. CIIMDA ensures that a suitable context is created through the use of master musicians as instructors who make use of traditional teaching methods through the aural–oral tradition. Concepts are effectively identified through this practical involvement in the learning process that provides platforms from which the concept is discussed, experienced and taught within a given context. Where possible, intangibles are explored by careful facilitation between the participants where the intangible is acknowledged and discussed within context by a master in his/her own community.

166

Honouring and Appropriation

The PASMAE initiated the concept of Music Action Research Teams (MAT cells) at grassroots levels for the collaborative sharing and learning of educators throughout Africa (Klopper, 2004).

PASMAE is affiliated to the International Society for Music Education (ISME), and in turn to the International Music Council (IMC) and United Nations Educationally Scientific Cultural Organisation (UNESCO). The mission of PASMAE is to enhance and promote musical arts education throughout Africa. In delivering the mission PASMAE concentrates on actions and tasks such as:

- Identifying and pooling the expertise of resource persons all over Africa and creating links beyond the boundaries of the African continent;
- Assessing and disseminating available relevant literature and learning materials;
- Advancing the increased use as well as methodical learning of indigenous music instruments in practical music education;
- Resourcing and effectively using music materials available in a community for creativity and music theory;
- Assisting the teaching and research capability of local music teachers through local, regional and pan African seminars;
- Consultation and workshops;
- Dialoguing with ministries of education as well as curriculum planners on emphasizing African music, content in music education at all levels, in recognition of the centrality of music in building cultural–national identity in the global context (PASMAE, 2001).

With such actions and tasks to be delivered it was not possible to rely on a small group or a select few to deliver results. So from these noble intentions grew the concept of MAT cells.

167

FIGURE 2
The MAT cell structure.

TABLE 1

Waves of Induction of MAT Cells in Africa

Initial Wave 2002	Second Wave Prior 3rd Biennial Conference of PASMAE 2003	Third wave Post 3rd Biennial Conference of PASMAE 2003	Fourth Wave Post CIIMDA 2004
Botswana	Kenya + (1)	Ethiopia	Botswana + (5)
Kenya	Nigeria + (1)	Kenya + (2)	Namibia + (1)
Malawi	South Africa + (6)	Malawi + (1)	Malawi + (4)
Namibia		Mozambique	Mozambique + (5)
Nigeria		South Africa + (2)	Zambia + (5)
South Africa (2)			Zimbabwe + (5)
Ugabda			
Venda			
Zambia			
Zimbabwe			

Description of a Music Action Research Teams Cell

MAT cells are best described as a group consisting of the leader and four to six other persons solely for the identification and pooling of the expertise of resource persons all over Africa and beyond for the sharing of knowledge and experience relative to musical arts education in Africa and with the rest of the world.

To illustrate the very simple nature of the MAT cell structure, Figure 2 gives a graphical representation developed and suggested by myself as Director of MAT cells.

A cell in biological terms refers to a living 'thing' and, fed with the correct nutrients, it will grow bigger, eventually divide and start the growing process all over again. MAT cells are viewed in the same light; they are living and dynamic groups of people feeding from each other's experience and in so doing growing and enriching many other lives. This concept links human resources through collaborative networking. Through this collaborative networking I have been able to gain information at grassroots level about the delivery of music in South Africa and Africa. The MAT cells representation has grown from each of the PASMAE conference encounters and more recently due to the outreach work of CIIMDA. To date there have been four waves of induction (Table 1).

The ultimate concept of the MAT cells is to generate and capture a wealth of knowledge of human resources as the essence of musical arts education, signifying the integrated nature of music and dance and theatre in Africa and its people. Musical arts education is not learned or taught from books about theories and methodologies, but rather it is learned from people who have the experience and practice at grassroots level, and who are not reliant on academic theorising that has little linkage to the grassroots-level practitioners or children.

All participants of the CIIMDA training sessions are required to sign a commitment contract. This creates an opportunity for the MAT cell structure to empower individuals to share their knowledge gained at the CIIMDA and to promote the aims and objectives of the project. Through such structures the indigenous musical arts in Africa are being honoured, appropriated and preserved for future generations.

Conclusion

To non-African observers the wealth of knowledge offered by Mother Music in Africa can often be misinterpreted or misunderstood creating a skewed view of Mother Music. However, observers of Mother Music in Africa need to approach their experience and observation of African music through the identification and acknowledgment of context, concepts and intangibles. Yes, Mother Music sparks from a stimulus, but if this stimulus is not explored in terms of the intricate nature of societal existence, the exploration can result in misrepresentation of a society and the society's invaluable contribution to human endurance being lost. The collective representation of context, concept and intangible is crucial to honouring and deriving the wealth of knowledge offered by Mother Music in Africa.

Endnote

1   Fourteen countries in southern Africa comprise the Southern African Development Community.

References

Agawu, K. (2003). Defining and interpreting African music. In A. Herbst, M. Nzewi, & K. Agawu (Eds.), *Musical arts in Africa: Theory practice and education*. Pretoria: Unisa Press.

Blacking, J. (1973). *How musical is man?* Seattle: University of Seattle Press.

Byamungu, G. T. M. (2002). The polity of the syllabus: Pattern shifting the African postcolonial episteme. In L. Imunde (Ed.), *Reflections on education systems in Africa*. Rehburg-Loccum: Loccumer Protokolle.

Crossman, P., & Devisch R. (2002). Endogenous knowledge in anthropological perspective. In C. A. Odora Hoppers (Ed.), *Indigenous knowledge and the integration of knowledge systems: Towards a philosophy of articulation* (pp. 96–125). Claremont, South Africa: New Africa Books

Flolu, E. (2000). Re-thinking arts education in Ghana. *Arts Education Policy review, 101*(5), 25–29.

Flolu, E. (2005). An ethnic approach to music making as a strategy for teaching African music: The need for systematic research. In A. Herbst (Ed.), *Emerging solutions for musical arts education in Africa*. Cape Town: African Minds.

Keil, C. (1979). *Tiv song: The sociology of art in a classless society*. Chicago: University of Chicago Press.

Klopper, C. J. (2004). *Variables impacting on the delivery of music in the learning area arts and culture in South Africa*. Unpublished doctoral dissertation, University of Pretoria.

Kwami, R. M. (1989). *African music education and the school curriculum*. Unpublished doctoral dissertation, University of London.

Kwami, R. M., Akrofi, E. A., & Adams, S. (2003). Integrating musical arts cultures. In A. Herbst, M. Nzewi, & K.Agawu (Eds.), *Musical arts in Africa: Theory practice and education*. Pretoria: Unisa Press.

Kwami, R. M. (2005). Indigenous African music in a relocated context: A case study. In A. Herbst (Ed.), *Emerging solutions for musical arts education in Africa*. Cape Town: African Minds.

Mans, M. E. (2000). Creating a cultural policy for Namibia. *Arts Education Policy Review, 101*(5), 11–17.

Masoga, M. (2005). Establishing dialogue: Thoughts on music education in Africa. In A. Herbst (Ed.), *Emerging solutions for musical arts education in Africa*. Cape Town: African Minds.

169

Ntuli, P. P. (2002). Indigenous knowledge systems and the African renaissance. In C. A. Odora-Hoppers (Ed.), *Indigenous knowledge and the integration of knowledge systems: Towards a philosophy of articulation*. Claremont, South Africa: New Africa books.

Nzewi, M. (1999). Strategies for music education in Africa: Towards a meaningful progression from traditional to modern. *International Journal of Music Education*, 33, 72–87.

Nzewi, M. (2003). Acquiring knowledge of the musical arts in traditional society. In A. Herbst, M. Nzewi, & K. Agawu (Eds.), *Musical arts in Africa: Theory practice and education*. Pretoria: Unisa Press.

Opondo, P. A. (2000). Cultural practices in Kenya. *Arts Education Policy Review*, 101(5), 18–24.

Primos, K. (2003). Research-based musical arts education. In A. Herbst, M. Nzewi, & M. Agawu (Eds.), *Musical arts in Africa: Theory practice and education*. Pretoria: Unisa Press.

Reimer, B. (1992). Toward a philosophical foundation for music education research. In R. Colwell, (Ed.), *Handbook for research on music teaching and learning* (pp. 21–37). New York: Schirmer.

PASMAE. (2001). *What is PASMAE?* South Africa: Paperprint.

Vilakazi, H. (2001, September). *Indigenous knowledge systems and the African Renaissance*. Paper presented at the International Conference on Indigenous Knowledge Systems, University of Venda.

CHRISTOPHER JOHN KLOPPER obtained a Higher Diploma in Education in 1995 from Edgewood College of Education, Pinetown, South Africa. In 2000 he was awarded a Bachelor of Music (Hons) with distinction and in 2001 Master of Music with distinction — both from the University of Pretoria, South Africa. He gained extensive experience through teaching at both state and private schools nationally and internationally, from pre-primary right through to university level as well as undertaking curriculum development, design and delivery for the education department. In 2004 he received a Doctorate in Music from the University of Pretoria, South Africa. Currently he is the administrative manager for the Centre for Indigenous African Instrumental Music and Dance (CIIMDA) and a part-time lecturer of arts education at the University of South Africa.

Professional Development in the Diamond Fields of South Africa: Musical and Personal Transformations

Kathy Robinson

Diversifying the landscape of musics shared in American classrooms and rehearsal halls has been of great concern to the music education profession. Unfortunately, a great majority of music educators find themselves ill-equipped to broaden their music curricula, and are uncertain as to where to begin or how to move beyond surface level inclusion or how to connect with the various music traditions within their own school communities (Chin, 1996; Miralis, 2003; Montague, 1988; Robinson, 1996).

Most in-service teachers today went to school at a time when their teacher preparation programs did not address musics and music making beyond the western canon. Volk (2002) considers that 'many of the preservice teachers in colleges right now will not receive adequate information to feel confident teaching even one music other than the Western art tradition in the classroom' (p. 24).

If limited experiences with diverse musics and populations continue to be provided in music teacher education programs, how then will teachers develop the knowledge, skills and attitudes to be effective with our 21st century students?

Current curricular demands to include diverse musics have been repertoire driven and have been supported to some degree with a substantial body of audio, video and print publications and workshops, symposia and special courses (Campbell, 2002; Lundquist, 2002). There has, however, been little to no attention given to broadening our field of vision regarding music and music making or changing perspectives on concomitant issues including transmission of music, defining who is a 'musician' and what is good music, and 'how people make music meaningful and useful in their lives' (Wade, 2003, p. xi). Opportunities for teachers to be musically and culturally 'other'; to see and act upon the world using a different lens; and to ponder their values, beliefs and perspectives have been limited (Benham, 2003). Multicultural scholar and educator Sonia Nieto (1999) believes that without a perspective transformation, teachers' attempts at developing a multicultural curriculum will be 'shallow and superficial and of questionable effectiveness' (p. xviii). I believe this is where many music teachers are in terms of diversifying musical content and perspectives.

How can we change perspectives about music and teaching and learning? What does a changed perspective look like? 'Any process of "becoming" assumes willingness for self-change ... it demands a caliber of personal engagement foreign to most school experiences' asserts Boyle-Baise (1996, p. 5). Change does not depend on intelligence, motivation or skill; it requires more. 'Transformative learning shapes people. They are different afterwards in ways both they and others can recognise' declares Clark (1993, p. 47).

In his transformation theory for adult learners, Jack Mezirow (2000) states that our meaning perspectives are how we perceive, comprehend, remember and interpret information; they are acquired in childhood and solidified in adulthood. All information received is filtered through our frame of reference — our perspective. The process of changing one's perspective requires some sort of experience that causes new learning to contradict the old. This new learning is strong enough to cause a 'disorienting' dilemma and, through critical reflection, can result in the acceptance of the new knowledge and a change in perspective.

Experiences appropriate for perspective change require going beyond acquisition of knowledge and the cognitive level to the affective level where emotions and feelings lie. Emotions must be validated and worked through before critical reflection can begin (Coffman, 1989; Sveinunggard, 1993). The path between experience and perspective change is most often cyclical, fluid and individualistic. It is often unclear what warrants a 'transformation' and an individual may be unaware that a change has occurred. Perspective change, which is not inevitable, most often occurs over time in a cumulative process rather than as a result of a singular experience.

Clark (1991) identified three dimensions to a perspective transformation: psychological (changes in understanding of the self), convictional (revision of belief systems) and behavioural (changes in lifestyle). While perspective changes are individualistic and the types are often difficult to determine, researchers have identified some likely characteristics of a transformation: increase in personal power, spirituality, compassion for others, creativity, shift in discourse, courage of liberation and new connectedness with others (Taylor, 2000).

For music educators, one avenue for perspective changes relating to diverse musics and learners is cultural immersion. In undergraduate music education, cultural immersion programs most often consist of ongoing or short-term field experiences with coursework, such as Campbell's (2001) work among the Yakama in Washington state and Emmanuel's in the city of Detroit (2003), and long-term student teacher placements or summer programs such as Addo's in Ghana (2004). Immersion programs often include homestays with local families and independent interactions with individuals/groups often encompassing field research, service learning or internships that frame the experiences required for perspective change. Opportunities for critical reflection often take several forms including participation in discussion sessions, and writing essays, field reports and systematic entries in journals.

While some cultural immersion opportunities exist for pre-service teachers, few programs exist for the in-service music educator. This article explores one **172** such program, Umculo! Kimberley, a professional development program involving cultural immersion in South Africa, for the ability to transform its participants personally, pedagogically and musically.

Parameters and Goals of *Umculo!*

Umculo! Kimberley is a professional development program that offers experienced general and choral music educators a teaching and learning experience immersed in the South African communities of Kimberley and Galeshewe. Each year in July and August, *Umculo!* has been offered by my university in cooperation with South Africa's Northern Cape Department of Sport, Arts and Culture. The program began in 1998 in one school for Galeshewe's black South African children, which was located on the edges of Kimberley. As people's trust grew in the program and in me, as facilitator of the program, we moved deeper into the township of Galeshewe and *Umculo!* teachers currently work in two public primary schools and one private high school.

Umculo! experiences include:

- 10 days touring South Africa from Capetown to Kruger Park to Johannesburg and Soweto before arriving in Kimberley
- teaching general/choral music to grades 1 to 12 in a manner aligned with South Africa's Curriculum 2005 goals for music
- six weeks living in Galeshewe via homestays with families or teachers from participants' assigned schools
- leading or accompanying a school choir in both western and world musics
- attending concerts, choir festivals, community events, including weddings and funerals
- assisting South African musicians with preparation of western choral pieces and the reading of staff notation
- assisting South African educators with strategies to reach Curriculum 2005 goals for music
- learning South African traditional choral music by becoming a 'member' of Galeshewe's Salvation Army Church Choir
- daily opportunities to dialogue with fellow *Umculo!* teachers and facilitator.

Through the above experiences, *Umculo!* teachers work side by side with South African teachers, students in schools and community and church choir members and their leaders. They are daily in the role of musical and cultural 'other', and have first-hand opportunities to examine issues of equity and access which remain after the end of apartheid. All involved, South African and American, children and adults alike, act as cultural translators and countless opportunities for cultural dialogue are provided.

Structure of the Program

The time frame for *Umculo!* is six to eight weeks which coexists with the beginning of the third term (mid-July) in Northern Cape schools and the late August commencement of the school year in many American communities. *Umculo!* is offered as a graduate course and participants are required to register for one to three graduate credits through my university's summer session and thus pay tuition, their sightseeing expenses and air travel between their homes and Atlanta's Hartsfield airport. Through my university, additional air and car travel, and all teaching materials and supplies including keyboards, percussion instruments, recordings, sound systems and the like are provided.

Who Participates?

Umculo! is open to any experienced choral/general music teacher and participants have had from one year to more than 20 years of teaching experience. The typical

173

participant has been European-American, single and female, although one male, two mothers, one mother-to-be and two African-Americans have participated. Three or four teachers participate each year and this collective group now includes three university professors; one assistant director of a community multicultural choir; one choral director at a creative and performing arts high school in a major city; three middle school choral and general music teachers from the suburbs of two major cities; and six elementary school general music teachers working in urban, suburban and rural schools in five states and one Canadian province. For all participants the desire to learn first-hand of another culture and its music is strong; however, teachers enter into this learning experience at a variety of entry points depending on age, experience, and cultural and ethnic background.

The Goals of Umculo!

Participants of *Umculo!* were guided in their development of seven goals, including intellectual understanding, cultural sensitivity, musical skills and pedagogical knowledge:

- deeper understanding of the role of culture in learning and music making in black South Africa specifically, and unfamiliar cultures in general
- expanded frames of reference musically, socially and pedagogically
- skill in learning and making music (choral dance songs) with black South African choirs
- awareness of the lens through which they see the world
- empathy
- value for another way of being and doing — musically and/or culturally
- ability to share their teaching and learning experience with students and teachers in America in such a manner that honors and respects the tradition, the music makers and the aural transmission process.

Role of Facilitator

As facilitator of this program my responsibility is to plan the experiences and to act as a guide as participants make their way through them. This year, for example, *Umculo!* preparation began four months prior to departure with the provision of readings; Curriculum 2005 goals for music; previous year's lesson plans; and a resource listing of readings, books, video and audio materials that could inform teachers of the educational, social, political and historical issues in South Africa and in the Kimberley region. Teachers also received an audio tape of children's and choral dance songs I have learned throughout the years in South Africa and a video of Galeshewe community life including students at their assigned schools. Participants were asked to 'check in' with me via e-mail at the end of each month, reporting their preparation activities and communicating any concerns. It is a heuristic approach that operates within the program, as I have sought to set the stage for them and to be on the sidelines acting as coach, ally, authority figure, colleague, confidant, as the situation and the individual warrant. Wanting to encourage their sense of adventure while being responsible for their wellbeing, health and safety and for maintaining the goodwill, hospitality and tolerance of the Galeshewe community can be at times daunting.

In the classroom, I asked teachers to share musics that were personally meaningful to them and provide experiences that would aid children in attaining some of

174

the broad, goals for music found in Curriculum 2005. I asked teachers at the primary level to not engage children in reading melodic and rhythmic symbols, because they would not have opportunities for reinforcement after our stay. I did ask them, however, to use graphic notation and other means to deepen musical understanding; to address the function, role and power of music in the lives of the world's peoples; and to capitalise on the rich singing heritage of the children through the use of indigenous folk music and literature, and musics of many cultures, periods and styles.

I interviewed 13 of the 14 teachers who participated in *Umculo! Kimberley* between 1998 and 2002 via a 30- to 60-minute telephone interview during a one-month period in the spring of 2005. For many participants this interview came several years following the experience. Interview questions were open-ended and consisted of 'grand tour' questions and specific ones focusing on their teaching and learning experiences. Interviews were audio taped, transcribed and scanned to find common themes to get at the essence of the relationship between the immersion and expanded personal and musical frames of reference and transformation. All personal names used in this article are pseudonyms.

Personal Frames of Reference

All participants reported feeling different from the South Africans within the community they visited. However, the depth of that feeling was mediated by the warm acceptance and the generous spirit felt from the community. Paige shared: 'I loved being different. We were so accepted and so unique and so cherished that I loved that our difference was embraced'. With her whiteness, Jill, however, became painfully aware that she could not 'blend into the background', which she found quite tiresome.

The two African-American teachers were hoping to 'melt' into and feel 'one' with the African community. However, members of the South African community immediately pointed out that they were different: 'You are an American'. Both women, at times, felt discriminated against particularly when among Afrikaners who were slow to serve them or refused service altogether.

It was the 'privilege that comes with being American' that caused all the participants to feel most different. Teresa recalls vividly:

> when I left the Brothers' house on Friday mornings with that keyboard in my hand and all those people were out there waiting [for bread to be given to the poor]. That's when I felt different. That was not by ethnic — that was by socioeconomic.

Suzanne, too, felt that:

> it was awkward to be the "rich" American. It was a difficult conflict to resolve. What is rich when it comes to wealth and money or quality of life? I felt awkward being perceived as that. I mean I absolutely have more money than the students that we saw. But would I say I'm wealthier or richer or better? You know, I don't think so.

The stereotype of the 'rich American' disturbed everyone. While all teachers hoped to change this, many were unsure of how to do so.

175

Despite the wide gap in monetary wealth, connecting with people on more than a surface level required a concerted effort and taking a risk, which each teacher handled differently. Stephanie shared:

> I approached being different in that kind of setting as a challenge. I see that I'm different but I also feel like I want to figure out a way to find the common or to decrease what might have been an expectation that they had of being separate, so I started eating in the lunchroom with the rest of the teachers. That to me was a huge challenge. As soon as I

> told them that I wanted to eat what they were eating the doors to that relationship were opened in a different way.

No matter the depth of relationship with the community, being immersed in Galeshewe gave each teacher a broader view of the world. For Suzanne:

> it brought into my view the concept of culture and it made me realise how narrow they are here and how much we believed that our culture is the only culture. Personally it has opened my eyes to that bias. I think. It opens my heart a lot too, personally, and that kind of goes to emotionally — they're sort of tied together but my priority since I've been back has shifted as opposed to being subject centered to being more student centered.

While Suzanne became more humanistic because of the immersion experience, it caused Teresa to question her whole sense of rightness after touring the Kimberley diamond mine museum:

> I never saw anything like that in my life. It overwhelmed me, how it all came from a White man's point of view and it made me rethink my entire life learning of history. It's probably been tainted by the one telling the story. That was huge for me.

While Jill felt that the experience helped her understand herself better, Elisabeth, who found it 'hard to become intimate with people right away because of the difference — and being the one who was different', felt that it helped her to reach out to 'others' at home:

> I think it was a good feeling to feel different in that it made me aware of being in situations where there are people who might be feeling different — for example, high school. If there was an exchange student or somebody like that from another country, I'd usually feel kind of awkward and maybe not go out of my way to be friends with them: if it happened, it happened. Now I would say that I'm more likely to go out of my way to be friendly with somebody who might be feeling different in that situation because of the people who are [were] friendly to me.

While teachers noted many differences between themselves and the South Africans, they also searched for commonality. As they got to know the community better, they realised that in many ways 'people are not very different. We have much more in common'.

Musical Frames of Reference

The activities of teaching black South African students by day, and by night helping community and church choirs with their western choral pieces and learning traditional choral dance songs, greatly expanded teachers' views of music and music making. None of the teachers had ever been immersed in a culture where music was so much a part of everyday life. Stephanie's words captured the feeling of many:

> I was given a first hand glimpse into what an actively musical culture looks like. I don't think I realised how little we have of that in our country, so to experience the contrast was huge for me. To feel like I was able to participate in the full way — in that tradition — was inspiring as a teacher, to have something to hold in your mind that you can put forward in your teaching.

Music's ability to create community became apparent to several teachers. It was attendance at funerals that powerfully illustrated the bonds between music and community for several teachers. Stephanie believed that attending funerals provided:

> windows into what life really is for Kimberley and the township there. The funeral was powerful not only as a marker to see how much AIDS has impacted that community, but also musically. There was music happening that entire day, and there are all of these songs, songs, and songs, happening as just something that flows out of the people. It was just powerful — very, very powerful as a way to celebrate someone's life and mourn.

176

Teachers reported feeling themselves shifting into the role of musical 'other' as they were immersed in the world of the choral dance song. Words such as 'amazing', 'emotional', 'awesome', 'powerful', 'beautiful', 'invaluable' and 'embraced it' characterised these experiences. Barbara's comment was typical of many:

> It was challenging but it was great. It was great to be part of making that sound. Here was a time for us to be in this role reversal. You have to really be open and take the risks and try to do it.

The challenge of being open and letting go was met differently by each teacher according to age, musical upbringing and experience. This was Stephanie's experience:

> I think I felt a little inept at times to stand in the complexity of their music. I remember when they start with the feet patterns it's like this whole different way of thinking and feeling music that takes time to adjust your musical self to. To jump in there and let things activate in you so that you can do multiple things at one time — singing and the rhythmic stuff with the feet. It's kind of a rush to feel that complexity come together. It didn't feel like I was ever satiated with new material and for me I could have done African pieces with them for hours.

Isabelle and Teresa, both very active musicians with over 20 years of teaching experience, felt 'inferior' in the 'other' environment and were surprised that their considerable musical skills were not of much help. Teresa shared:

> It sounds so easy but it's so not part of my hearing. I felt slow physically in the moving and I felt slow only because I have a music degree. My expectation was I should be able to learn this quick, but that's not true — I'm not in their world of music. My skills only help me with what I know, what I bring. When you put me out of that area, then it's all brand new to me and based on what I'm bringing it might make it easier or more difficult. I think it's the same for them.

While transmission without notation was a great test for many, everyone found the experience left them with sharper aural skills. As a result Suzanne believes she came back as a stronger aural teacher: 'I have confidence in that as a way to learn something'.

The aural learning experience was perceived differently by those whose musical roots were embedded in folk and pop music or the Pentecostal or African-American church. Debbie offered:

> When I got into music school I was trained to read, read, read, read and analyze and theorise, breakdown and call chords and spell chords and everything was visual in terms of how you were processing. It was really refreshing for me because it took me back to what is most natural for me, which is the sound.

During the experience Michele discovered how much she had strayed from her aural roots: 'I'm so focused on having music in my hand. I didn't grow up that way. Notation is the score not the music'.

Each teacher noted that the Galeshewe community took great pride in sharing their music. Being 'immersed in a sea of experts' made the learning easier for Tom. Barbara found her teachers 'were so pleased that we were trying and just so helpful. They'd stand beside me and they'd try to help me along'. Teresa, too, felt lots of support for her efforts: 'the community rejoiced with you when you got it. So there is no finer positive reinforcement than that'. While most felt that they needed more repetition for retention, the pieces that they knew were solidly known and could be passed on to others with confidence.

177

Assisting choirs in the preparation of western choruses for their choir competitions helped Elizabeth see that 'there are much bigger cultural differences in the music' that she had never noticed before because she had 'grown up singing it':

> It makes you hear the music in a very different way when you heard them learning it ... it made me see it all on a more level playing field. I think it just made me view music in a different way.

The choirs' commitment to singing western music was unexpected by all of the teachers. Teresa shared:

> Their dedication and their loyalty — the commitment to getting it right just touched me. I don't know any American choir that would stand in an unheated church for 2 1/2 hours of practice 3 or 4 nights a week.

Barbara waxed enthusiastically of the beauty of the western and African music:

> surprised to see how much value and importance they put on preparing the western piece. For them the African stuff they did was always just right on target and so beautiful. The western was like this always striving, striving to get it.

Teachers heard first-hand that skills in the African tradition did not serve Galeshewe choirs well in singing western choral music. The dark, heavy, rich sound, short melodic phrases devoid of half steps, and narrow range used in tradition song caused difficulties in western pieces. Many teachers felt that the directors did not possess the knowledge and skills to help their choirs with the western tradition. Paige observed: 'during rehearsals they'd say that this didn't work, "now fix it", instead of giving real rehearsal techniques'. Isabelle's impression was that the vocal technique that they're so used to using 'prohibited chromatics to occur the ways that they should have'. The teachers were in agreement that addressing these issues cannot be accomplished in a short amount of time. Elizabeth offered:

> There were lots of things that were problems in the western pieces that weren't problems in the African pieces like tempos and singing together as an ensemble. It almost feels like trying to sing something that is completely foreign to you. It's not part of your aural vocabulary — your frame of reference. It's like speaking a different language.

While observing and helping choirs provided a powerful lens on the unique skills needed within each musical system, one skill that did transfer was that of solfege, which the choirs read as Tonic Solfa, to learn western pieces and composed South African pieces. Dianne, a professional singer, noted: 'their solfege is pretty tight and that to me was more advanced than any choral group I've ever been with here — even the professional groups I work with'. Paige, however, was quite disturbed with transmission via Tonic Solfa:

> I felt discouraged that they didn't know how to read western music even though the white South Africans did. I felt very upset by that disparity. They didn't have the opportunity and they should have. It was right at their fingertips. ... What did the missionaries think of these human beings that they weren't capable of reading five lines and 4 spaces?

The inordinate amount of attention focused on western music was disturbing to several teachers. They wanted to see more value placed on African music. While Jane thought the preoccupation curious, she believed it to be a natural intellectual pursuit:

178

> I was very surprised that they were paying so much attention to all of this western music and wondered how it really connects to them and their lives and why they are so interested in it, but of course intellectually, why wouldn't they?

The observation of choirs in a local church choir competition singing western pieces, followed by African pieces, made a huge impression on Tom:

When they shed the artificial facade of western music their entire visage changed. They became holistically musical — not forced into a box of what they thought western music was.

Umculo! Kimberley and Transformation

It is clear that participation in *Umculo! Kimberley* deeply affected these teachers. When asked if the *Umculo!* experience had transformed them in some way, 11 teachers were very sure that it had. Declarations ranged from Michele's 'Yes! I lived it' to Teresa's 'In every essence of who I am' to Suzanne's words: 'The human being that I was before I went to South Africa and the human being that I am when I came back were two very different people. It was transformative'. Elizabeth and Stephanie shared that they were definitely transformed; however, specifically how the experience had changed them was hard to quantify or 'put into words'. Jill and Barbara knew that the experience affected them but were unsure that they had been 'transformed', which aligns with the elusive nature of transformation or perspective change. Their statements, however, do reveal perspective change. Jill offered: 'I felt that the experience made me understand myself better' and Barbara shared how the immersion 'affected my teaching tremendously'.

Changes in understanding of the self, changes in lifestyle and revision of belief systems exemplify Clark's (1991) dimensions of perspective transformation and characterise the collective experience of *Umculo!* teachers as evidenced through their own words. Cultural immersion through *Umculo! Kimberley* transformed its participants. It caused the lenses through which they saw the world to be 'ground' anew, resulting in expanded personal and musical frames of reference.

References

Addo, A. (2004, November). *Transformational learning: Music and culture in situ.* Paper presented at the meeting of the American Orff Schulwerk Association, Long Beach, California.

Benham, S. (2003). Being the other: Adapting to life in a culturally diverse classroom. *Journal of Music Teacher Education, 13*(1), 21–32.

Boyle-Baise, M. (1996). *Finding the culture in multicultural education: A theoretical exploration.* Paper presented at the Annual Meeting of the American Educational Research Association, New York.

Campbell, P. S. (2002). Music education in a time of cultural transformation. *Music Educators Journal, 89*(1), 27–33.

Campbell, P. S. (2001). Lessons from Yakama. In L. Wing (Ed.), *The mountain lake reader: Conversations on the study and practice of music teaching* (p. 45). Cincinnati: University of Cincinnati Press.

Chin, L. (1996). Multicultural music in higher education: A description of course offerings. *UPDATE: Applications of Research in Music Education, 15*(1), 28–32.

Clark, C. M. (1991). *The restructuring of meaning: An analysis of the impact of context on transformational learning.* Unpublished doctoral dissertation, University of Georgia, Athens.

Clark, C. M. (1993). Transformation learning. In S.B. Merriam (Ed.), *An update on adult learning theory* (pp. 47–56). San Francisco: Jossey-Bass.

Coffman, P. M. (1989). *Inclusive language as a means of resisting hegemony in theological education: A phenomenology of transformation and empowerment of persons in adult higher education.* Unpublished doctoral dissertation, Northern Illinois University, DeKalb.

Emmanuel, D. T. (2003). An immersion field experience: An undergraduate music education course in intercultural competence. *Journal of Music Teacher Education, 13*(1), 33–41.

179

Lundquist, B. R. (2002). Music, culture, curriculum and instruction. In R. Colwell & C. Richardson (Eds.), *The new handbook of research on music teaching and learning* (pp. 626–647). New York: Oxford.

Mezirow, J. (2000). Learning to think like an adult: Core concepts of transformation theory. In J. Mezirow (Ed.), *Learning as transformation: Critical perspectives on a theory in progress* (pp. 3–33). San Francisco: Jossey-Bass.

Miralis, Y. C. (2003). Multicultural-world music education at the big ten schools: A description of course offerings. *UPDATE: Applications of Research in Music Education, 21*(1), 44–56.

Montague, M. J. (1988). *An investigation of teacher training in multicultural music education in selected universities and colleagues.* Unpublished doctoral dissertation, University of Michigan, Ann Arbor.

Nieto, S. (1999). *The light in their eyes: Creating multicultural learning communities.* New York: Teachers College Press.

Norman, K. N. (1999). Music faculty perceptions of multicultural music education. *Bulletin of the Council for Research in Music Education, 139,* 37–49.

Robinson, K. M. (in press). *Sing it! Strum it! Move it! Drum it!: School music – Make it real! Mary E. Hoffman Festschrift.* Annville: Lebanon Valley College Press.

Robinson, K. M. (1996). *Multicultural general music education: An investigation and analysis in Michigan's public elementary schools, K-6.* Unpublished doctoral dissertation, University of Michigan, Ann Arbor.

Sveinunggard, K. (1993). Transformative learning in adulthood: A socio-contextual perspective. In D. Flannery (Ed.), *35th Annual Adult Education Research Conference proceedings.* University Park: Pennsylvania State University.

Taylor, E. W. (2000). Analyzing research on transformative learning theory. In J. Mezirow (Ed.), *Learning as transformation: Critical perspectives on a theory in progress* (pp. 285–328). San Francisco: Jossey-Bass.

Wade, B. (2004). *Thinking musically.* New York: Oxford University Press.

Volk, T. (2002). Multiculturalism: Dynamic creativity for music education. In B. Reimer (Ed.), *World musics and music education: Facing the issues* (pp. 15–30). Reston, VA: MENC.

Zimbardo, P.G., & Leippe, M. R. (1991). *The psychology of attitude change and social influence.* Philadelphia: Temple University Press.

KATHY M. ROBINSON is co-director of *Umculo! Kimberley*, a professional development program featuring immersion in Kimberley and Galeshewe, South Africa. She has studied Ghanaian drumming and dance at the Institute for African Studies, University of Ghana, Legon, and has researched children's songs and choral music in Ghana and South Africa. She is a frequent presenter of workshops focusing on world musics in education.

180

Collision or Collusion?: The Meeting of Cultures in a Church Choir

Kay Hartwig

Collision (crash, smash, accident, impact) or collusion (agreement, knowledge, consent, approval)? What are some of the issues that arise when a conductor who has been trained in the western classical music tradition works with a Samoan church choir?

The establishment of sharing music and cultures through the church choir was previously reported in the paper *A Cultural Exchange in Music* (Hartwig, 2004). When invited to be a part of this project, my first thoughts were that I could not do this. I did not know the language or understand the music; the music was not available in print form. The beginning of the journey challenged me to rethink how I conduct a choir, what techniques I employ and what the important issues in such an activity could be. It also enabled a group of choristers to achieve their aim of being able to sing both Samoan and English hymns for church services. The project extends to the social/cultural context and is a part of their life and their worship. Through the project, I have become more aware of diverse ways of knowing across cultures and have grown both personally and professionally. I have been given the opportunity to learn to appreciate and understand some Samoan music, and to perform it with the members of a Samoan choir. On their part, the Samoan choir has been able to continue to sing Samoan hymns as well as to learn new repertoire and to sing a selection of hymns in English.

Reflective Practice

To continually monitor and record this project I engaged in a reflective practice model. This commenced at the beginning of the activity and still continues. This has involved keeping a weekly journal recording my reflections after rehearsals and performances. At random intervals, I conduct interviews with willing members of the choir in order to gain further data that support the researcher's personal reflections. Sometimes these interviews are held individually or in small groups. There is no set pattern to the timing of the interviews and this reflects aspects of informality in Samoan culture. These interviews can be held before or after rehearsals or performances — whenever an opportunity arises. The interviews are unstructured, with open-ended questions giving the participants the chance to raise points of interest that are important to them. The interviews are recorded and later transcribed.

Reflective practice presents an opportunity to look into one's own praxis, probing the boundaries of how one works and attempting to understand how one impacts upon the learning of others. Taylor (1996) reports that reflective practitioner research demands discovery of self, recognition of how one interacts with others and of how others read and are read by the interaction. This stance is at the heart of this project and its inquiry. Cochrane-Smith and Lytle (1993) acknowledge that positive aspects of inquiry conducted by teachers include ways to build knowledge both locally and more publicly for the individual teacher and for communities of teachers. This project seeks to build knowledge about cultures working together, collaborating and sharing each other's music.

Music Culture

> Music tells us something of the particular culture from which it comes ... and each musical culture also has its own way of being processed ... (Nettl, 1998, p. 27).

According to the International Society for Music Education's panel on musics of the world's cultures (International Society for Music Education, 1994), music can best be comprehended in the social and cultural context in which it is a part. Therefore, understanding a culture requires some knowledge of its music and its associated culture and society. The same panel also contends that an outsider to a culture can learn to appreciate and understand a culture's music, and even to perform it, but there may be limits to her or his ability to gain an insider's perception of it. When one is trained in a specific musical tradition there can be problems in knowing and understanding another tradition. Stock (1994) notes that we cannot necessarily apply our own, familiar definitions of music to foreign musical sounds and that basic, fundamental principles, which we take for granted in our own music, may not be reflected in other kinds of music. Therefore, for those working with music from cultures other than their own, there is new learning to take on board.

Music anthropologist, Merriam (1964), also wrote about this, noting that the cultural context in which learning takes place and the ways music is taught, are shaped by the particular culture's own ideals and values. He believed that the learning process in music is at the core of our understanding of the sounds we produce. Writing just over three decades later, Nettl (1998, p. 28) listed numerous perspectives that ethnomusicologists have learned to use to investigate the world's musics:

- as a group of musics to be looked at from a comparative stance

- as musics to be understood in their own terms

- as art closely tied in with the other domains of cultures

182
- as sound, behaviour, and ideas

- as something that has continuity but constantly undergoes change

- as a phenomenon separating cultures and one that facilitates culture contact

- as the result of particular kinds of transmission

- as the result of the guiding principles of individual cultures

- as something to be studied and analysed from the outside

- as something to be learned and performed under the guidance of the cultural insider.

Nettl's perspectives can become guiding principles when educators, or musicians, such as conductors, are concerned with the presentation of the world of music to and with others.

The Samoan Choir and the Western Conductor Interact

We sing because we must (Keri Kaa, 2002).

Kerri Kaa explains that one of her abiding childhood memories is drifting off to sleep to the droning and chanting of her father's singing. She reported that 'he would sing and we would imitate'. She was explaining how music is inextricably bound to the language, rituals and cultural practices of the Maori people. This view of music is similar for the Samoan community, as is evident when they tell me stories of their childhood and their desire to sing, especially in the church setting:

We love to sing (Arietta).

We always sing (Jimmy).

Singing is for the Lord (Junior).

I love to sing in the choir (Mary).

The mass must have singing (Pale).

We sing all the time so we sing in church (Leo).

We love to sing in church. We come as a family to sing (Antonio).

McGrath (2002, p. 315) reported in her interviews with Samoan people that everyone she had talked with mentioned the importance of church: 'All Samoans share the same goal, to serve God, to teach, to speak about the word of God'. Opetaia Fo'ai (2001) explained that in her culture, music is something to celebrate with and to enjoy. It is a natural part of life. These explanations of the role of music and singing in life represent a vast difference to those I had experienced in my own musical background.

Due to these different experiences in music traditions and music learning, I constructed a table of the diverse ways of knowing in music that were presented in this collaboration of different cultures and musics (Hartwig, 2004). These are presented in Table 1.

Due to further experiences and reflections, I wish to now add another layer in the table (see Table 2).

How does the information presented in the tables impact on the learning and strategies used in the choral rehearsal? How does a conductor prepare to cope with the diverse range of differences presented in this setting without compromising the integrity of each culture, music and tradition, and without allowing domination of the western environment to overtake? Nettl (1998) writes that knowledge of social and cultural context is necessary to understand and appreciate a music. How does one obtain this knowledge and understanding? Can an 'outsider' to a cultural community work effectively in this new setting? These were the many questions I posed, explored and reflected on at the

183

TABLE 1

Ways of Knowing in Music

	Conductor	Samoan singers
Training	Classical western art music (formal training)	Music skills passed from generation to generation (informal learning context — Merriam, 1964)
Music notation	Dependent	No music notation reading skills
Text reading skills	Fluent	Various levels
Music memory	Developed	After initial learning stage — advanced music memory skills
Choral learning style	Combination of aural/oral and written	Aural/oral
Language	English	Samoan plus some with knowledge of English, others fluent in English
Teaching/learning methods	Various modes	Rote learning

beginning of the activity. While some discoveries have been made, the struggle of this inquiry continues.

In all aspects of this collaboration there needs to be compromise and sharing as well as 'impregnation'. According to Corpataux (2002, p. 11) impregnation refers to learning that occurs through immersion in a local culture. The rigid structure I bring to the rehearsal, gleaned from my formal classical training in western music and singing and conducting of choirs, is sometimes put aside as the group break into stories of days past or discuss an upcoming event. The elders of the community may want to talk to the group, or the children may simply be running around and making lots of noise. The rehearsal may not start on time, or may not take place at all, as only a few members may come on time or arrive. The atmosphere at rehearsals is not formal. It is one of engagement with the music and a genuine part of life that is shared with family and friends. I have learned that to the Samoan people all these diversions from what I call 'formal structure' are considered a valued part of the rehearsal:

> (Vignette 1) I arrive for a rehearsal 10 minutes before the designated start time and I find I am alone. *Where is everyone? Don't they know we have a service on Sunday and we are not yet ready?!* Within the next 20 minutes only 5 singers have arrived. My stress levels are elevated. *Where are they?* Gradually others stroll in after playing football in the park. I am the only one concerned about the lack of practice for the next service. They assure me that all members will be present for the Sunday service and all will be well. And in fact it was.

My securities are enhanced when we work with English hymns and the printed notation, whereas my comfort zone is threatened when I need to work without a score or change a score to reflect what the choir is singing, and not what was

TABLE 2

Ways of Knowing in Music (Additional Layer Added)

	Conductor	Samoan singers
Training	Classical western art music (formal training)	Music skills passed from generation to generation (informal learning context — Merriam, 1964)
Music notation	Dependent	No music notation reading skills
Text reading skills	Fluent	Various levels
Music memory	Developed	After initial learning stage — advanced music memory skills
Choral learning style	Combination of aural/oral and written	Aural/oral
Language	English	Samoan plus some with knowledge of English, others fluent in English
Teaching/learning methods	Various modes	Rote learning
Focus of rehearsals	**Technical aspects**	**Expressive, emotional and sentimental value**

originally written. This has assisted in improving my own music skills, reflecting what Ellis (1985) found with her tertiary students in the ways that their music skills were enhanced when learning music from traditional Pitjantjatjara elders. Various ways of learning music knowledge such as rote learning, demonstration, imitation, memorisation, repetition and use of a written score are all implemented in varying degrees depending on the music to be learned, its origins and the purpose of the music. Barton (2003) and Campbell (1991) both highlight that the methods and strategies used in communicating music knowledge can be varied and complex and that the purpose of music in a culture can greatly affect the manner of acquisition, teaching and learning strategies:

> (Vignette 2) I was presented with a printed version of a setting of the *Kyrie* that they choir knew well. I was extremely pleased to see Western notation on a piece of paper. To my horror I discovered that the left hand side of the paper was torn and half of the music from the first three lines was missing. After listening to each section sing their parts I was able to reconstruct the music. However after hearing a complete performance of the piece, the sopranos were not singing the coda as written. We rehearsed over and over until I was sure the sopranos could sing what was on the score. On putting the piece together once again, the sopranos promptly went back to the version they felt comfortable singing. I realised I was the one who needed to change.

185

When preparing to teach a new hymn I endeavour to present the music and the text in a variety of methods, and to use many teaching strategies. The written musical score is presented when available to the members of the choir, as well as cassette tapes to assist with the learning process. Sometimes just the text is made available. The parts for the choir are modelled for copying and some sections are rote learned. At times the vocals are accompanied by organ and at other times sung *a capella*. None of the adult members of the choir can read western music notation. Some of the teenagers are acquiring this skill through participation in various school music programs. The repertoire for the choir is drawn from both English and Samoan church music. The English hymns are taken from hymns suitable for the Catholic Mass, and sacred Christian choral arrangements. Samoan hymn repertoire has been gathered from music members of the choir and from conductors of other Samoan church choirs. These conductors have all been Samoan and are always happy to share music and repertoire:

> (Vignette 3) We had finished a rehearsal one Friday and everything went silent. I was unsure of what was happening or about to happen as there were never many quiet or silent moments in the rehearsals especially with many children running around. I then realised everyone was quiet as the leader was about to speak. The leader then presented me with a beautifully bound Samoan hymn book. He explained that a member of the community had just returned from Samoa and had brought back this hymn book so that I could teach the choir many more Samoan hymns. It was their present to me. I was overwhelmed.

Sometimes, before attempting to teach a hymn in English, where music and text are provided, there needs to be an English lesson where pronunciation is rehearsed and the meaning of the text is explained. The choir are very patient with my attempts in pronouncing the text in the Samoan hymns. Although the strategy of teaching by rote when the aural/oral tradition is exclusively employed takes many rehearsals, once learned, advanced memory skills come to the fore and the hymn is committed to memory forever. The advantage here is that one is able to use a hymn at a service that was learned some time ago but may not have been practised recently. For the Samoans singing is part of life and they (men, women, girls and boys) sing with skill and enthusiasm. They find singing in harmony an easy task. For Samoan people, singing expresses and embodies their culture; there is no need for encouragement and motivation to sing at rehearsals as singing is widely practised and is perceived to have social and personal value.

Conclusion

This continuing journey is one of excitement, enjoyment and learning for the members of the choir and for the conductor. There are many challenges and issues now and for the future endeavours of this exchange in music and culture. As Bresler (1998, as cited in Russell, 2003) reports, the values, attitudes, expectations, assumptions and practices of at least three nested sociocultural contexts converge in the music classroom, in this case, in choir rehearsal and performance: the micro (classroom/personal), the meso (institutional/teacher) and the macro (larger community). Will there be collision or collusion? This collaboration has resulted in a group of choristers achieving their aim of being able to sing both Samoan and English hymns for church services. It has resulted in the conductor becoming more aware of diverse ways of knowing in music across cultures and has allowed for both personal and professional growth. There has been collusion — agreement, consent and approval as knowledge is shared and gained by participants in the project.

The activity in this project is a practical example of sharing music in a church setting across cultures using reflective practice as the framework to record the activity and allow investigation of one's actions and involvement. We have endeavoured to honour the traditions of each music tradition, and the relationships between each music tradition, and the ways they have been handed down have been respected. Music has been taught in a manner that has endeavoured to respect both traditions and not allow the traditions of the western environment to dominate, enabling the cultural identity of all participants to stand proudly.

Patricia Shehan Campbell (2002, p. 20) used a song from the Appalachian foothills to emphasise that as unique as we may all seem to be in our individual contexts, there is nothing like a song to help us determine how faint the shades of difference among us are:

> My life flows on in endless song above earth's lamentation.
>
> I hear the real though far-off song that hails a new creation.
>
> No storm can shake my inmost calm while to that rock I'm clinging.
>
> It sounds an echo in my soul. How can I keep from singing?

Embedded in that text is a meaningful message to us all.

References

Barton, G. (2003). *The influence of culture on instrumental music teaching: A participant-observation case study of Karnatic and Queensland instrumental music teachers in context.* Unpublished doctoral dissertation, Queensland University of Technology.

Campbell, P. S. (2002). Shades of difference: Meanings of diversity for those who teach music and children. In J. Drummond & D. Snell (Eds.), *Taonga of the Asia Pacific Rim* (pp. 13–20).

Campbell, P. S. (1991). *Lessons from the world: A cross-cultural guide to music teaching and learning.* United States: Schirmer Books.

Cochrane-Smith, M., & Lytle, S. L. (1993). *Inside/outside: Teacher research and knowledge.* New York: Teachers College Press.

Corpataux, F. (2002). Children's songs around the world: An interview with Francis Corpataux. *Journal of the International Society for Music Education, 40*(1), 3–14.

Ellis, C. J. (1985). *Aboriginal music education for living: Cross-cultural experiences from South Australia.* Brisbane: University of Queensland Press.

Hartwig, K. (2004). A cultural exchange in music sau e fai ma maiaoga — come and be our teacher. In J. Searle, C. McKavanagh, & D. Roebuck (Eds.), *Doing thinking activity learning* (Vol. 1, pp. 209–214). Brisbane, Queensland, Australia: Australian Academic Press.

International Society for Music Education. (1994). International Society for Music Education policy on musics of the world's cultures. Reprinted in B. Lundquist & C. K. Szego (Eds.). (1998), *Musics of the world's cultures* (pp. 17–19). Perth, Western Australia: Callaway International Resource Centre for Music Education.

Keri Kaa. (2002). We sing because we must. In J. Drummond & D. Snell (Eds.), *Taonga of the Asia Pacific Rim* (pp. 2–5).

McGrath, B. B. (2002). Seattle Fa'a Samoa. *The Contemporary Pacific, 14*(2), 307–340.

Merriam, A. P. (1964). *The anthropology of music.* United States: Northwestern University Press.

Nettl, B. (1998). An ethnomusiciological perspective. In B. Lundquist & C. K. Szego (Eds.), *Musics of the world's cultures* (pp. 23–28). Perth, Western Australia: Callaway International Resource Centre for Music Education.

Opetaia Fo'ai. (2002). The music of the Pacific: A personal journey. In J. Drummond & D. Snell (Eds.), *Taonga of the Asia Pacific Rim* (pp. 6–12).

Russell, J. (2003). Singing "practice" and the importance of community. *Canadian Music Educator, 45*(2), 15–19.

187

Stock, J. P. (1994). Concepts of world music and their integration within western secondary music education. *International Journal of Music Education, 23*, 3–16.

Taylor, P. (Ed.). (1996). *Researching drama and arts education: Paradigms and possibilities.* London: Falmer Press.

DR KAY HARTWIG has taught music in preschool, primary and secondary schools including conducting choirs at each of these levels. She is now the coordinator of music at the Mt Gravatt campus of Griffith University where she lectures in music and music education to primary and secondary music specialists, as well as primary pre-service generalists teachers. She is also co-convenor of the Master of Teaching program for international students at Griffith University. She has a particular interest in church choral music and works with a number of choirs ranging from children to adults.

'Without a Song You Are Nothing': Songwriters' Perspectives on Indigenising Tertiary Music and Sound Curriculum

Steve Dillon and Jim Chapman

'Without a song you are nothing'. Dr Liz Mackinlay, an ethnomusicologist, made this statement in a 2004 lecture about the relationships of song in indigenous spirituality. Mackinlay, a non-indigenous academic, recognises the importance that song plays in traditional Aboriginal custom and tradition. Speaking for and about country and spirituality for country are inherited and learned components of Aboriginal identity and relationships to land and kin, story and song.

As a songwriter, this triggered a wave of personal philosophical and phenomenological thought. The implications of this in relation to my understanding of the relationships between sound and society and the power of song to communicate, store and reference important cultural knowledge was profound. At Queensland University of Technology (QUT) where I work as an academic doing research and teaching music and music education, part of my role has been to 'indigenise' the music and sound curriculum. My colleague Jim Chapman has spent many years teaching and studying crosscultural musicianship in Australia, Africa and South America and is primarily a songwriter. In this article we provide two songwriters' perspectives, which appear in case study vignette form. These vignettes are personal journeys of understanding that have led us both to develop dynamic indigenous perspectives. We examine the processes and outcomes of 'indigenising' a tertiary music and sound curriculum and notions of Australian indigenous knowledge. We explore points of intersection and understanding and divergence and the role of music and sound as knowledge. This article combines these perspectives and proposes 'rules of thumb' for developing culturally inclusive tertiary music and sound curriculum.

Indigenising the Music and Sound Curriculum

> To teach Indigenous musics is also to teach the historical, social and political contexts, in which they exist, to raise debates over the efficacy of the pedagogic act, and to uncover the dialectic and musical tensions that surround it (Mackinlay & Dunbar-Hall, 2003).

Over the last two years I have been involved with a formal process of indigenising the curriculum at QUT in creative industries. This process involved both a formal audit of current approaches, initiatives and resources and a process of developing awareness, staff education and the implementation of new initiatives to enhance and develop indigenous perspectives and the understanding of indigenous knowledge.

These processes have occurred in partnership with the Oodgeroo unit and a committee of indigenous and creative industries staff. This vignette describes insights gathered from observations drawn from several music units (subjects).

Over the past few years the notion of musicianship that is appropriate to musical genres that are not based on western art music constructions of aural perception have been the subject of constant debate within our discipline. Indeed, what is western music?

As Edward Said (1995) has suggested in his work *Orientalism*: the West has defined itself by pretending to master the 'Other's' cultural manifestations and it has been through this concept of others as 'them' that we have created music, our arts and ourselves and yet this appropriation is mystified, made problematic and made unsurprising.

It is often felt that a musicianship that focuses on European constructions of how sound is organised and valued as expression missed the essence of meaning inherent within non-western music and also jazz and popular musics that have evolved from syncretic relationships between western music and African musical expression. Indigenous Australian constructions of how sound is organised and the connection of the purpose and indeed the relationship of context and function have relegated study of indigenous music to the realms of ethnomusicology or anthropological views of Aboriginal music.

Initial development of aural perception has come from extending traditional musical elements beyond the confines of melody, harmony, rhythm and form as with Pratt (1990), who expanded the elements of aural perception to 13. This included deeper notions of rhythm by including pulse and uniformity and the idea of the location and source of sound as represented in space. Interestingly, it was the incapacity of conventional common practice notation to represent or describe electronic music that has led to a change in the structure of aural perception criterion.

Recently at QUT we shifted the focus of our aural perception ontology to a 'time and space' model as articulated by Vella in *Musical Environments* (2000). This model asks simply what is happening with sound in time and space and what are the relationships to the context and culture that structures these sounds. The consequences of this shift in philosophy were felt most in the reconstruction musicianship classes. Most importantly, this shift in the way music is perceived and analysed potentially moved us towards a more culturally and chronologically inclusive model for music learning. This had interesting implications for the inclusion of indigenous cultures within music learning as a contemporary example of how human society expresses itself in sound in a unique response to culture and environmental context.

What this meant in curriculum terms was a shift in the central philosophy of how we perceive and make music. This approach has allowed us to include notions of 20th century art music, western popular music and non-western musics. This curriculum process began with core musicianship subjects and radiated out to music education for double degree students (Bachelor of Music/Bachelor of Education, music electives and specific genre musicianship units such as jazz and popular, crosscultural, sound musicianship and art music). The long-term effects of this have yet to be determined but the immediate effects have provided a basis for understanding of musics from a broad variety of cultures, times and contexts.

This is important because the strategies to create databases of Aboriginal and Torres Strait Islander cultural and human resources, which formed the basis of the university's indigenous perspective initiatives, became part of a genuine partnership

190

with the indigenous communities. Here, the shared focus was upon expressive music-making in a unique context and phenomenological interest in the power and importance of music within culture.

The three broad curriculum areas identified for indigenising were concerned with:

1. expressive making

2. understanding the interaction between sound and society

3. focusing the above for music education at the pre-tertiary level, for pre-service music teachers and for general primary teachers.

From an audit of subjects and their capacity to include indigenous content and knowledge frameworks was added an annotated multimedia resource database and a network of indigenous human resources. Strategies were then put in place for the subject/unit coordinators to access these resources in the planning of more inclusive learning and teaching experiences. While this process has become an auditable aspect of all subject development, further policy for indigenisation of curriculum has been developed through involving the Oodgeroo unit in the development of a new unit/subject that features indigenous perspectives as an integral part of the architecture of the unit rather than as a post-development addition.

The unit/subject Music and Spirituality was developed using a phenomenological framework in consultation with the Oodgeroo unit. The analogy that I use to describe the experience of this unit was drawn from a recent experience with indigenous foods. I remember leaving a restaurant that served exclusively indigenous Australian meats, fish, fruit and vegetables, remarking that this was the most exotic food I had ever tasted. I felt it strange that after 45 years in this country the flavours of Europe and Asia were more familiar to my palate. So too was the experience we planned for Music and Spirituality. For five weeks of lectures, the focus was upon indigenous construction of sound and its role in community, lore and knowledge and its function in organised society. The experience was delivered through the intensely spiritual improvised song of Delmae Barton, which evoked intense emotional response from participants, Dr Liz Mackinlay's discussion of the role of song for Yanyuwa women, Gordon Chalmers telling of Yanyuwa story and Victor Hart's notion of 'naming the gaps between stars'.

The ideas that emerged from the experience of the unit were both presented and responded to by students in song, story, dance and pictorial form and elicited an understanding that was unique in my experience as a teacher. It triggered an evolving dialogue about the power of song to reference knowledge, to store it and communicate precise meaning when it referred to relationships and context (Ellis, 1985; Will, 2000). This not only affected the creative practice of many of the participants who demonstrated their developed understanding through creating new creative works but also suggested that indigenous constructions of knowledge, which reference deeper knowledge and relationships in context, may have implications for creative practice research (Martin, 2001). For learning and teaching, the implications were that knowledge could be communicated through experience with creative practice, that is, performance or exhibition of multimedia content, and that responses could also be articulated in media form rather than text alone. These experiences became personalised for each student and fostered an environment of reconciliation through experience and understanding that was as profound for the participants as it was for the staff.

191

Jim Chapman's Vignette

In 1997 I began preparations to teach a unit entitled World Music that would be available to students from any faculty in the university as an elective and that would also be available to students enrolled in the Bachelor of Music. I worked together on the early development of the unit with the Head of school, Andy Arthurs, and one of the issues that was at the foreground of our thinking was that indigenous Australian music and culture had to be strongly featured in the unit. It was in this preparation phase that I made contact with Victor Hart from the Oodgeroo unit at QUT, whose advice and patient inspiration has been invaluable.

Previous experiences at other institutions were instructive because they showed that an ethnomusicological approach, which dealt specifically and analytically with the music, could meet justified resistance from the Koori or Murri communities who were the culture-bearers. McNeil (1996) warns that the discipline of ethnomusicology has yet to fully shake off its origins in the colonialist academy. Further to this issue is another raised by Ellis (1994) where the inaccurate recording of song, or inappropriate use may have serious repercussions in Native Title law cases. More recently Smith (2002) reports from considerable experience with Asian and Aboriginal informants who 'spoke frequently of what they regarded as inappropriately "Western" ways of learning and teaching in music'. Of concern to many educational theorists are the colonialist distortions of traditional culture that come into play when indigenous music is treated and taught in the same ways as western music (Smith, 2002; Thompson, 2002). Even well meaning programs can still reinforce a Eurocentric and chauvinistic attitude to the music of the exotic 'other' (McNeil, 1996).

As we reflected on these inputs and my own limited experience with Murri groups in south-eastern and northern Queensland we felt strongly that a unit on World Music was most meaningful if it made an opportunity for Australian students to experience some part of the reconciliation process between black and white Australians. Before real understanding of the music could occur, understanding of the people and culture and the historical and present relationships between the dominant white culture and the peripheral indigenous culture must occur.

The approach that we decided upon involved the following principles:

- placing the understanding of Murri and Koori music in a context of world issues and perspectives including colonialism, post-colonialism and postmodernism
- addressing the music from an indigenous worldview rather than/or at least as well as a western worldview — focusing on meaning rather than sound
- enrolling the students in the issues around the music and identity in the country but personalising their perspective
- having the indigenous music delivered by indigenous Australians.

These principles will be expanded upon here, including some discussion of the learnings from these experiences as we have the taught the unit in the ensuing years.

192

Placement in World Issues

We took the position from the beginning that the most meaningful experience for students to have would occur if they were given a pathway to connect with Aboriginal music and musicians. This would also mean engagement with the issues of identity and meaning about living in Australia. In effect, we wanted to personalise the meeting of white and black identity in Australia through music. Our reasoning will be expanded in the following paragraphs.

The structure of the unit became important in delivering a narrative that could provide entry into such different worldviews. The structure we chose was to move from the familiar to the unfamiliar, and simultaneously move from the distant to the close-up. In this way we could begin by examining sensitive issues such as colonialism and discrimination in third person. Critical understanding becomes available when viewing issues in Africa or Asia. The focus then moved closer and closer to home until the last two weeks of semester when we examined the world music of Australia and engaged with the colonial and identity issues of this country. In this way the meaning of music was used to invert the usual relationship of the western scientific examination of objectified 'other' culture, into an examination of western identity within the frame of an Aboriginal view of reality and its meaning in music.

Indigenous Worldview

Musicians with a European background locate the experience of music differently to indigenous Australians. To the westerners, including me, music is an expressive and aesthetic activity, and it can be objectified. This sense of objectivity or psychic distance is a concept I borrow from Merriam (1964) who gave it first priority among six characteristics that he used to decide if an art form was aesthetic. Objectification has been important to the western culture because it has allowed the analysis of music that led to great refinements and development of the codes of expression (Kivy, 2001). It also has the consequence of cutting westerners off from other ways of experiencing music.

My own studies of African and western crosscultural music have provided a model to view the way that different cultures place music in their world orientation. Western culture primarily values music as an aesthetic and expressive activity (Kivy, 2001). African cultures, broadly speaking, focus on the socially participative aspect and the embodied movement within the music (Tracey, 1994). Each of these approaches are codes and are learned explicitly and contextually in the culture. Australian Aboriginal philosophy places music in an extra-musical setting. Music is a way of knowing country. Europeans might regard astronomy in a similar way, a way of knowing a complex world. It might be counterintuitive to ask a westerner about the aesthetic meaning or the expressive dimension of the maps of galaxies.

The indigenous Australian worldview includes music as a part of a range of life activities but it does not necessarily set music aside as an object. I cannot claim any great knowledge of the rich and detailed range of uses of the music in Aboriginal societies, but I know that it plays a part in ritual, social and spiritual activity and it provides an approach to connecting to the land that is almost entirely foreign to western civilisation.

Victor Hart lectures in this class and he once recalled a time when he was in his homeland of Cape York and they were singing country and western songs, but in the same way the old people sang the traditional songs. The country music, he noted, was used to sing up country, and singing up country is a way of making one's identity in that land. The use of Aboriginal music in a western course of study, which objectifies the music, may well be tolerable, but irrational to an Aboriginal experience. By way of analogy, imagine that you offered a visitor from another planet a $50 note. The visitor ponders the note and then sets it alight and uses it to start a fire. They then ask for

193

more of the $50 notes because they do the job so well. Asking Aboriginal people for their music to be used for academic dissection might be similar.

The commodification of music as part of a contemporary and economic cultural capital that one either owns or does has contributed significantly to the ways in which music and 'music being' have been disenfranchised from human relationships. Even the notion of music as cultural capital disconnects the most fundamental relationship that we as human beings organise our lives every day, where we live, who we love, what we are passionate about. Within the West this is expressed in the long held belief that to be a musician is an aesthetic lifestyle choice.

There may be a time and place for the analytic thinking of the western academy to be applied to Aboriginal and Torres Strait Islander music, but it must be after some more important connections between cultures have been made first. We cannot simply rely on romantic and often racist or anthropological constructions of Aboriginality emanating from post-colonial studies but a more concerted engagement with musical textualities and contestations about our own identity and identities. This is Australia, this is Aboriginal land, and we need to understand that we are working with materials that come from this place in time and space.

Langton (1993) suggests three types of Aboriginality: that which is made by white people for their own purposes, that which is created between Aboriginal peoples, and that which is negotiated between whitefellas and blackfellas. The negotiated interface is the anthropological/ethnomusicological perspective. It is one way that we could have approached the teaching of Aboriginal music, with its emphasis on the sociological and cultural conditions surrounding the music and its use and production.

In fact, we did use this perspective when dealing with many of the other world musics in the unit. The study of African and African-American, Middle Eastern, northern Asian and South-East Asian music all required a fairly broad scale perspective. The benefits of this approach were that it placed the music in a social, historical and political context, and also made it accessible to non-musicians who made up about 60% to 70% of the classes. But it was not necessarily the best way to deal with indigenous Australian music because it still separates the music from the lived experience of the society, and makes the music into an objectified commodity. This is playing tourist in the curriculum.

The understanding that I have gleaned from the conversations with Victor Hart and other generous hearted indigenous Australians is that song is about place and land and a spiritual connection between people and the land. This phrase is in danger of being interpreted through popular myths of Aboriginal dreaming as some kind of unconscious state of being. Rather it is an 'everywhen', a deliberate act of *being* based on a clear understanding that the land knows you and who you are. (Not the other way around). This is a journey not a destination ... but it is.

From this perspective the actual sound of the music, its aesthetic surface, which obsesses western analysts, is far less important than the meaning and the myth and story that are behind it. Our aim then was to give students a sense of the meaning of the music, rather than its mere aural exterior.

194

Engaging Students

The conduct of the lectures on indigenous Australian music follows a path that is designed to draw students from the objectified study of the music of other cultures, into a personal and direct way of thinking about their interaction with Aboriginal and Torres Strait Islander culture, sense of land and music. I begin the lecture with a brief analysis of western ethnomusicologists understandings and some of the hang-overs of colonial misunderstandings of indigenous music. I also defend the musical integrity of the music by citing cases examined by Carl (Neunfeldt, 1996). Victor (Hart, 2004) then gives his address on the meaning of country in music and during this lecture he asks the mainly white Australian audience to explain their culture to him. This is an opportunity to view the world from indigenous eyes.

On some occasions some students have expressed a point of view that we are shaming them. I find it interesting that they have found shame in the message. I do not doubt that it might create dissonance, particularly when they are asked to explain 'white Australian' culture to a Murri, but I am saddened to hear of their shame, because the aim to try to build a bridge to extend the white perspective far enough to comprehend the black perspective.

Let us be frank about this. This is still very difficult territory for all parties. The hegemony of western (white Australian) imperialism still lingers very thoroughly in our thinking and feelings. Even, or perhaps especially, in the context of the Australian university, it is easier to be sympathetic and yet obscure the past and continuing reality of the impacts of the cultural collision. In his 1968 Boyer lectures W. E. H. Stanner described this silence as 'a cult of forgetfulness' or 'disremember-ing' that has been 'practiced on a national scale' (as cited in Attwood, 1996). Awakening Australians from this sleep is very difficult because it challenges the very things that white Australians believe that they are.

What I read into the 'shame' is a lack of comprehension of the relationship between white and black Australia, not one that should be full of blame, but one that has never come together. It is an end to the emotional apartheid that we seek. It works more profoundly for some than for others, but the opening of the discussion of black and white identity is a foundation point for further understanding. It is understanding that is necessary to comprehend that the music is more than just sound with labels attached.

Indigenous Delivery of Indigenous Music

Our aim originally was to have all the material on indigenous music delivered by indigenous Australians. Due to the resource constraints on our department and the demand that there is for the few indigenous staff at QUT to deliver material to many courses, we have had to share the work. In some ways though, this has proven to have a positive effect. Students see a black and a white Australian share the lecture space, tackling, interpreting and discussing the issues. This description brings strains of the McCartney and Wonder song *Ebony and Ivory Live Together in Perfect Harmony* (McCartney & Wonder, 1997).

Fortunately for the students the lectures are not like this. The interaction is not always smooth. The students get to see us grappling with the issues that are embed-ded so deeply into the dualism of the Australian black and white culture. The ebony and ivory couplet is a romanticisation of reconciliation. We are teaching the 'real time' of our cultures. The reality is that we are teaching and we are learning and even when it is bitter or rouses shame, confrontation and awkwardness, we are doing it because we are passionate about it.

We question each other, extend each other's analogies, spar on ideas and sometimes disagree.

195

My part in this process has been to consult with the indigenous lecturer and check on the suitability of materials, including audio recordings and examples, so that we achieve our mutual aims of extending the students' experience of indigenous frameworks of knowledge and the role and meaning that music has in the many and varied indigenous communities in Australia. Let me also say that I am not just speaking about Aboriginal life and culture as represented in popular culture and arts, but also about those components of cultural expression that came out of surviving colonialism and racism. These are not your usual spiritual smoothies.

The unit World Music has been running for eight years and we have seen approximately 700 students complete it. I strongly hope that the structure of the narrative, the focus on indigenous understanding and the means of presentation have given those students a practical access to ways of knowing that spring from indigenous experience, and a pathway to reconciliation. The steps we have taken so far are just small ones towards greater indigenisation in music units, and we hope our strategies will improve with each iteration of development.

Resonating With 'Indigenist' Theory

Both the vignette experiences presented here have taken similar pathways of consultation and experimentation that raised essential issues. These are useful both for others who may be constructing units/subjects that deal with indigenous perspectives and also have implications for our own progress in the development of experiences that are able to adequately and meaningfully provide music education for non-indigenous Australians and indigenous students. At this point it is worth briefly comparing our individual institutional and deep subject development experiences with theories of indigenous knowledge that are being developed in indigenist research to compare how our case study experiences might draw from these more complex theoretical frameworks. Martin (2001) provides a framework for indigenist research, which has a surprising resonance with our experiences in indigenising curriculum. The reader might recognise examples of these tenets within the vignettes and identify them as examples of how this theory might play out in practice:

> Indigenist research [or curriculum] then, arrives as part of cumulative research activities conducted in Aboriginal lands and on Aboriginal people since European colonisation. Its main features are identified as:
>
> - Recognition of our worldviews, our knowledges and our realities as distinctive and vital to our existence and survival and serve as a research framework;
>
> - Honouring Aboriginal social mores as an essential processes through which we live, learn and situate ourselves as Aboriginal people in our own lands and when in the lands of other Aboriginal people;
>
> - Emphasising the social, historical and political context which shapes our experiences, lives positions and futures;
>
> - Privileging the voice, experiences and lives of Aboriginal people and Aboriginal lands;
>
> - Identifying and redressing issues of importance for us (Martin, 2001).

196

Each of these tenets is apparent within both vignettes in varying degrees. We do not intend here to explore this further nor be self-congratulatory about the success of the connections. Rather, we seek to highlight that they indicate some transferable outcomes and also some areas where more work needs to be done. By way of a summary conclusion we would now like to suggest a list of replicable experiences that might be drawn from the case study experiences and the literature and conclude with a brief outline of where more attention is needed.

Summary Conclusion

From the experiences outlined above we can draw some important and potentially transferable implications for curriculum and policy in tertiary music study. By means of a summary conclusion we have created a checklist of important issues that we have found influential in the development of indigenising curriculum. A need:

- to examine the underlying value structures of how music is perceived and valued to determine impediments and supporting and enabling policies, that is, inclusive aural perception framework
- to include consultation with community mediated by local community representatives, that is, Oodgeroo unit or school ASPA committee
- for access to multimedia resources, that is, video, DVD, CD, web sites of indigenous musics rather than text based resources that silence the meaning and obscure the context of the music making
- for staff training facilitated by local indigenous bodies (ASPA, Oodgeroo)
- to implement policy for the inclusion and auditing of indigenous perspectives within all subject areas
- to use multimedia for communication of ideas and human resource networks
- to devise inclusive assessment that uses multimedia responses, that is, documentary, web site, audio recording, video/DVD, song writing and story telling.

We have also identified areas where further research needs to be undertaken:

- examine the use of indigenous perspectives as a framework for media/practice based research
- examine the long-term effect of time and space models of aural perception on musical development
- develop further teaching and learning strategies for personalising the experience of non-indigenous students
- develop social processes rather than institutional processes for monitoring the honesty and trustworthiness of the learning experiences.

In this article we have sought to simply recount stories about two songwriter educators' experiences of indigenising curriculum in a tertiary music course. We have, through engaging with the issues and seeking to consult those who have knowledge in these areas, been able to draw out some rules of thumb that may have transferable implications. There is of course much work to be done to build upon these preliminary steps. What is most clear though is that progress has been made by action. Several of our patient indigenous mentors have said to us 'don't not do something because you are afraid you might offend me. If you offend me or my people I will tell you'. The way forward is to engage with the process of personalising our experiences of indigenous knowledge through experience and embodied understanding. 'What is certain is that the intersections of different knowledges, systems concerns and priorities will converge to inform and develop new practices in this area' (Nakata, 2002).

197

References

Ellis, C. (1994). Introduction, powerful songs: Their placement in Aboriginal thought. *World of Music, 36*(1).

Ellis, C. J. (1985). *Aboriginal music.* St Lucia, Queensland, Australia: University of Queensland Press.

Hart, V. (2004). *The meaning of country.*

Kivy, P. (2001). *New essays on musical understandings.* Oxford: Clarendon Press.

Langton, M. (1993). *Well I heard it on the radio and I saw it on the television.* Australian Film Commission.

Mackinlay, E., & Dunbar-Hall, P. (2003). Historical and dialectical perspectives on the teaching of Aboriginal and Torres Strait Islander musics in the Australian education system. *The Australian Journal of Indigenous Education, 32,* 29–40.

Martin, K. M. Booran. (2001). *Ways of knowing, ways of being and ways of doing: Developing a theoretical framework and methods for Indigenous re-search and Indigenist research.* Paper presented at the AITSIS Conference: Power of Knowledge and resonance of tradition, Canberra.

McNeil, A. (1996). Caught between a rock and a hard place: Post colonialism and the dynamics of teaching ethnomusicology in Australia. In B. Broadstock, N. Cummings, D. E. Grocke, C. Falk, R. MacMillan, K. Murphy, et al. (Eds.), *Aflame with music: 100 years of music at the University of Melbourne.* Melbourne: Centre for the Studies in Australian Music.

Merriam, A. P. (1964). *The anthropology of music.* Evanston, IL: Northwestern University Press.

Nakata, M. (2002, August). *Indigenous knowledge and the cultural interface: Underlying issues at the intersection of knowledge and information systems.* Paper presented at the 68th IFLA Council and General Conference, Glasgow.

Neunfeldt, K. (1996). *The dijeridu: From Arnhem Land to Internet.* Sydney, New South Wales, Australia: John Libbey & Company.

Pratt, G. (1990). *Aural awareness: Principles and practice.* United Kingdom: Open University Press.

Said, E. W. (1995). *Orientalism.* London: Penguin.

Smith, R. G. (2002). Going over the top: The evolution of Indigenous music pedagogies and educational practices in post colonial Australasian contexts. *Research in Music Education, 19,* 65–72.

Stanner, W. (1979). *White man got no dreaming.* Australian National University Press.

Thompson, K. (2002). A critical discourse analysis of world music as the 'Other' in education. *Research in Music Education, 19,* 14–21.

Tracey, A. (1994). *African values in music.* International Library of African Music.

Vella, R. (2000). *Musical environments: A manual for listening, improvising and composing.* New South Wales, Australia: Currency Press.

Will, U. (2000). *Oral memory in Australian Aboriginal song performance and the Parry-Kirk debate: A cognitive ethnomusicological perspective.* Ohio State .

STEVE DILLON is a singer, composer and senior lecturer in music and music education at Queensland University of Technology in the faculty of Creative Industries: Music and Sound, Brisbane. His major research foci revolve around music and meaning, creative practice as research, eportfolio systems, philosophy of music education and the development of interactive music software for children. Steve is also a researcher with the Australasian CRC for Interaction Design (ACID).

JIM CHAPMAN lectures in crosscultural musicianship and world music at Queensland University of Technology in the faculty of Creative Industries: Music and Sound, Brisbane. He has spent many years teaching music in Africa and South America and is currently undertaking doctoral studies in composition that examine the syncretic nature of music. Jim regularly performs and composes for the crosscultural ensemble Kabombo Combo.

198

CPSIA information can be obtained
at www.ICGtesting.com
Printed in the USA
BVOW09s0822080118
504715BV00019B/1101/P